2020

Jim Mosquera

The Sentinel

2020

A novel introducing Chandler Scott

Mosquera, Jaime (Jim) Jr.

2020 / Jim Mosquera

ISBN: 0-9832966-3-4
ISBN-13: 978-0-9832966-3-8

The text type was set in Adobe Garamond Pro

DEDICATION

To Jaime Mosquera Sr. who taught the valuable lesson of hard work.

Jim Mosquera

A novel introducing

Chandler Scott

The financial crisis of 2008 precipitated intervention by governments and central banks the likes the world had never seen. World economies and stock markets recovered but the definition of "recovery" meant different things to different people. Income inequality surged as the chasm between Main Street and Wall Street widened. The recovery lasted until 2016.

- ➢ DOW JONES PLUNGES 4,000 POINTS!!!

- ➢ SHANGHAI COMPOSITE DROPS 10,000

- ➢ ILLINOIS STATE EMPLOYEES RIOT AFTER DEEP WAGE CUTS, NATIONAL GUARD DISPATCHED

- ➢ BIG THREE AUTOMAKERS LAY OFF THOUSANDS

- ➢ MUTUAL FUNDS STRUGGLING WITH REDEMPTIONS

- ➢ STATE PENSION FUNDS IN PERIL

- ➢ MILITIA GROUPS GROWING IN MEMBERSHIP

The markets and the economy staged a mild recovery, though insufficient to calm everyone's fears. An already polarized nation, the red and blue states, found new entrants to the political arena as two, third parties were born out of the distrust. The new parties gained political seats in state and national races in the 2018 elections. Exacerbating the political and economic chaos were a series of domestic and international terror attacks, both cyber and kinetic.

- ➢ NEW YORK CITY POWER GRID DISABLED BY HACKERS

- ➢ BOMB DETONATED ON WORLD'S LARGEST CRUISE SHIP

- ➢ MAJOR U.S. BANK SUFFERS DATA BREACH

- ➢ POPULAR SOCIAL NETWORKS DISABLED BY CYBER TERRORISTS

The public demanded and received more security. This led to a greater degree of authoritarianism on the part of government. Random email and phone surveillance became commonplace. The seeds were sown for the next crisis, a crisis that would shape the future of the United States of America and the world.

Part I

Chandler Scott

CHAPTER ONE
EL MUNDO

"Good morning ladies and gentlemen, this is your captain. We will land in Buenos Aires in two hours. Our breakfast service will begin shortly. *Buenos días damas y caballeros...*" American Airlines flight 953 from JFK to Buenos Aires flew smoothly throughout the night, but even business class did not make for a restful experience. The noise canceling headphones were wonderful as long as your head didn't tilt too far to one side. It didn't matter since his hunger made him look forward to the eggs and bacon he pre-ordered when he booked his ticket. Maybe it's because he flew so often, but he didn't mind airplane food. He tilted his nose towards his shoulder, inspecting the freshness of his shirt. It passed. The flight attendant came by with a fresh, hot towel. His first hot towel experience, a few years ago, confused him. He unwrapped it thinking there was something inside. Then he expected a razor and shaving cream. The woman sitting next to him got a towel, nullifying the razor idea. After spying on another passenger, he figured it out.

He cleaned his hands and face, getting the sleep out of the corner of his eyes. "Mr. Scott, your breakfast." He appreciated the attendant knowing his name. His stomach rumbled from emptiness. Instead of a full dinner before boarding, he opted for a light snack.

His first trip to Buenos Aires came fourteen years earlier, in 2005, with Gustavo Sáenz, his father, a native Argentinian.

This was his senior trip after graduating high school in Texas. Chandler Scott did not grow up around his father, who had enjoyed a brief love affair with his mom, Renee, while she attended the University of Missouri in Columbia. Gustavo fit the image of the classic Latin lover - tall, dark and handsome. His accent made the ladies swoon. As an assistant professor of banking and finance, he was a kid in a candy store. There were many coeds, and his own father cautioned him to keep his pants zipped.

Renee captured his attention. Taller than average with light brown hair, she had a svelte figure. Though she'd never make the cover of a fashion magazine, she was in every respect a pretty woman. Renee worked in an academic support office, mostly tutoring members of the men's athletic teams. Fending off advances from athletes, she was grateful when Gustavo showed up at a tense moment with a football player. Gustavo did not fit the mold of her suitors, being cultured and speaking a couple of languages. His looks didn't hurt him either.

Gustavo referred many freshman students to Renee, then in her senior year pursuing a degree in business administration. It started innocently enough with lunch and progressed to a brief, though intense love affair - intense for her. Renee grew up in a solid middle class family in Columbia, Missouri. She checked off every achievement in high school – straight-A student, head cheerleader, class president and prom queen. She was the most likely to succeed. When the opportunity arose to attend Mizzou, she jumped at the chance to stay close to home. Greek life beckoned her and eventually she took residence in the Kappa Kappa Gamma sorority house.

Three months after starting her relationship with Gustavo, her pregnancy came as a shock. She was never that sexually active and always took precautions. Hiding it from her sorority sisters worked for a couple of months, but the bump eventually became too big to hide. What a disappointment she would be to so many who looked up to her. She moved back home with her parents and dealt with the shame of being unmarried and pregnant. Shame drove her from school, dropping out close to graduation. Gustavo would never know since they stopped seeing each other shortly before she discovered her pregnancy. On October 19, 1987, infamously known as Black Monday in U.S. financial markets, she gave birth to eight pound, Chandler Michael Scott. She didn't comprehend the gravity of what had happened that day in the stock market. Her father gained a bundle of joy and lost a bundle of money.

The embarrassment of being a single mom overwhelmed Renee. She couldn't raise Chandler alone in Columbia, not with so many people she knew living there. A sorority sister to whom she was close secured employment for her in Dallas at Lone Star Semiconductor (LSS). The course of her life and Chandler's would be forever shaped when she bade a tearful goodbye to her family.

When Chandler reached the age of five, Renee could no longer control his curiosity. She sent Gustavo a letter along with a picture of her young son and from there, father and son exchanged phone conversations for a couple of years. When Chandler reached the age of eight, Gustavo finally met his son while on a business trip to Dallas. After that, they might see each other on holidays when Renee returned to Columbia. Early adolescence marked a time of greater bonding between father and son. By that time, Gustavo was married with children. Chandler inherited his dad's good looks and the girls loved his thick, dark hair.

Chandler Scott grew up to be a handsome man of 6'2" with an athletic build, wide shoulders and small hips. As a non-participant in athletics, his body never reached its full potential. He cut an impressive look that played well as a news personality working for the hugely successful Argentine TV news network, El Mundo. His show, Centinela, focused on economic, financial, and political matters. El Mundo had international bureaus in Buenos Aires, Panama City, Madrid, Moscow, Doha, Johannesburg, Mumbai, and Beijing. In the U.S. there were bureaus in San Francisco, Denver, Dallas, Miami, New York, and Washington D.C.

Centinela received critical acclaim for its well-researched and highly provocative reporting. The show didn't worry about throwing cold water on the banquet guests. Recently the show won an award for their coverage of the U.S. public pension crisis and their focus on the State of Illinois. After the show's airing, the state undertook massive pension reform the outcome of which created another news story when state employees rioted in the capital of Springfield.

Summer in the southern hemisphere was winding down, though it would still be close to 80 degrees today, a far cry from the 40 degree temperature of early spring in New York. He sniffed his shirt once again just to be sure. Still good. Good thing he took a trip to the lavatory before deplaning. The day's temperature in Buenos Aires didn't pose a threat to someone accustomed to Texas heat. Chandler interestingly combined Texan and Midwesterner, the latter from his time as a student at the University of Missouri where he furthered his relationship with Gustavo. Now a polished international traveler, he reverted to metaphors he heard growing up in Texas. His mom had more than one boyfriend that made liberal use of the Texas lingo, and it surfaced during emotion or stress. His colleagues found this an endearing trait.

El Mundo sent Mauricio to pick him up at Ezeiza. *"Buenos días, Chandler."*

"Buenos días, Mauricio." Chandler's accent had improved. "Not too hot here today. Better than last year when it was as hot as Hades."

Mauricio paused for a moment to ponder about Hades. "Yes, better this year."

Their trip took them twenty miles to El Mundo's headquarters in the Puerto Madero section of the city. He'd made this trip before, but the width of the Avenida 9 de Julio continued to amaze him. And well it should, since the widest avenue in the world received its name from Argentina's independence day in 1816. Looking north while traveling on the Avenida 25 de Mayo, he saw the Obelisco de Buenos Aires, the icon of the city. Gustavo once took a skyward picture of Chandler with the obelisk in the background.

Puerto Madero was a brilliantly renovated waterfront along the Rio de la Plata whose streets pay homage to women. A striking architectural feature of the waterfront was the Santiago Calatrava designed Puente de la Mujer, a pedestrian bridge connecting both sides of the waterfront development. The bridge had a single mast with steel cables supporting a portion of the bridge that swung to allow water traffic.

El Mundo strove to connect viewers to stories they covered, though they pulled back, just enough to allow them to reach their own conclusions. Chandler's boss, Rafael "Rafa" Mendoza, requested his presence in Buenos Aires to discuss current economic events affecting the world and to strategize on segments for his show, and he wanted to see him. World economies had been wobbly since the stock market crash of 2016. Argentina emerged better than other countries after they rejected the leftist leaning, Peronista leadership in 2015 and implemented a series of reforms. The reforms caused significant hardship for a couple of years, but private investment poured into the country with the more favorable business climate. It became easier for foreigners to own Argentinian businesses, tax rates were lowered, and the banking system was shored up. Latin America as a whole avoided the terror incidents plaguing other parts of the developed world, which helped its cause too.

Rafa greeted Chandler with a big man hug in the first floor conference room of El Mundo's world headquarters, Chandler's home when visiting HQ. Rafa, a short, slightly built man in his early fifties with jet black hair, had no shortage of energy. Chandler wondered when the shorter man slept. The more statuesque Chandler always felt as if he was hugging the little brother he never had. That little brother had a great hand in making El Mundo the success that it is today. Chandler owed him much.

"How was the flight, Chan?" Chandler's close friends, family and occasional love interests used this nickname.

"All things considered. Not bad. You know I can never sleep on those overnight flights." Chandler's face looked groggy.

"You just needed a nice glass of Malbec for dinner. Then you'd have slept like a baby." Rafael folded his hands together next to his head.

"I guess my boss forgot to send me a bottle," Chandler said with a smile.

Rafael chuckled. "OK, we have much to cover Chan, let's sit down and get to work. You can sleep tonight."

It was near midday and Chandler knew they'd work straight

through until 5 or 6pm. Rafael would keep him well fed and hydrated. There were no shortages of stories for development.

Unlike Chandler, Rafa eschewed technology. He pulled out his yellow paper pad and discussed China. China began its economic contraction in 2016 when its stock market crashed and their real estate bubble popped. The government stepped in and rescued the largest banks. It was a sad sight to see investors hanging out in brokerage houses watching the stock market fall day after day. Chandler spent a couple of days there in late 2016 dodging violent demonstrations.

"You know what happens Chan when you get a bunch of young, unemployed, unmarried single men together in one place?" Rafa asked rhetorically. China's one child law backfired and demographically, there were too many men relative to women, throwing the yin and yang out of balance. "Those young men, they just need to have more sex to settle themselves down." Rafa thrust his hips in a vulgar manner. "We'll need to do some work before you go to China again." Chandler was in no hurry to return. El Mundo ran into problems last year with the Chinese government for releasing a story about a dissident without their review, and that was with their local correspondent doing the story. Since then, there were problems acquiring visas.

Rafa quickly flipped a page on his pad and shifted to the European continent. "I do want you to go to Spain to cover the Catalonian secession movement. I cannot see that turning out favorably," Rafa said angrily.

"That secession talk has been going on for years. People are split on the issue." Chandler recalled his visit to Barcelona years ago.

"That country just needs someone to unify them. Secession

17

will bring more chaos and disorder. The world doesn't need any more of that with as bad as economies are right now." Rafa was no fan of chaos.

Growing up in the shantytown of Villa La Cava near Buenos Aires made Rafa long for order and structure. La Cava, a small town of some 54 acres, sat near the more upscale Beccar neighborhood of historic San Isidro. Flat tin roofs, dilapidated walls, poor drainage and undisposed trash characterized the shanty town. The walkways between people's "homes" were so narrow you could touch two homes by stretching out your arms. The walkways were no place for pedestrians since motorcycles used them as thoroughfares. Every meal had a side of exhaust fumes. La Cava's 1,000 families seldom saw a policeman. The place had its own rule of law. People were itinerant. Rafa had no lasting friendships since kids his age wouldn't stick around long. Chaos and disorder were constant themes. The ambitious Rafa made it his life's mission to escape and vowed to press for order and structure in his life.

"You have big elections in your country next year, 2020. What if we spent some time interviewing candidates and what their economic plans will be?" Rafa had a mind that could change subjects quickly.

"You beat me to it. I was going to suggest that. The polls show that President Jefferson will beat any opponent but I expect the GOP to mount a challenge and the new third parties will have their voices heard I'm sure."

"I know your country is excited about your third parties. But really, what do they do? They just take votes away from the other two, but not enough to make a difference."

"It's good though, Rafa, to have other ideas, don't you think?"

"Americans think they have a tough time with politicians in Washington. Wait until you get more of these other ideas you talk about."

"Come on man, where's the optimism?"

"Those third parties will mess up your election. You will see. And those *locos* in the Theocracy Party. Those people are scary. Seriously, I do want you to interview whoever is going to run from the Independent American Party and the Theocracy Party. They deserve to be heard even though my feelings are that I don't think they will make a difference."

The Theocracy Party (TP) and the Independent American Party (IAP) emerged during the 2016 and 2018 elections. The TP was born in the South. Several televangelists banded together to support defecting candidates from both the Republican and Democratic parties who primarily carried the evangelical vote. Their aim was to return God to America, figuratively speaking. In their eyes, America was a moral cesspool that bred economic insecurity, inequality and hatred abroad. The IAP grew from elements of independent voters who often swung between GOP and Democratic candidates. Theirs was a blend of libertarian and Jeffersonian politics, advocating limited federal government and the will of the people expressed through elections.

"I think Matt Geringer will be the man for the IAP. I'm not sure who will run for the TP," Chandler suggested.

Geringer mounted an unsuccessful campaign for president in 2016 when he could not secure the GOP nomination. No candidate arrived at the GOP convention with sufficient delegates, leading to a brokered decision. Disaffected voters in his party encouraged him to mount an independent campaign. While he lost general election, the IAP grew in strength and numbers, capturing seats in the 2018 mid-term elections and securing other elected positions in the states.

"The TP candidate will be someone who will predict the Second Coming." Rafael laughed hard after saying this. "OK another story I think you should cover is what happened when the stock exchanges in New York City shut down last month. There's all this talk about sabotage. Can you interview Will Duncan?"

"Yeah, I think so." Chandler had met Will Duncan before, the very influential and respected head of the New York Stock Exchange.

"Your Federal Reserve has taken a bunch of heat for all the Quantitative Easing this and that. I can't keep it all straight. But man, those guys went from, what's the word I want to use, *carajo?*" Rafael scratched his head and cursed.

"Wizards?"

"*Sí, magos.*" Rafael would break into Spanish at any moment. He did that more with Chandler than others primarily due to the familiarity and comfort he had with him. "I don't know if you will even get an audience with them."

"Let me see what I can do. I might have to get creative," Chandler offered with confidence.

The two men worked the rest of the afternoon developing questions and structure around the stories they discussed earlier. Chandler knew interviews with Presidential candidates could wait, so he prioritized discussions with Will Duncan and the Fed. As the clock approached 6pm, Chandler informed Rafael that he'd had his fill for the day. Their solid relationship allowed Chandler to declare the day's end.

Rafael gave Chandler his first job. After Chandler completed his Master's degree at the School of Advanced

International Studies (SAIS) at John Hopkins, he interviewed with Al Jazeera, BBC, and CNN. Everyone liked his journalism degree and, of course, his prestigious degree from SAIS, but none of those news organizations offered him the opportunity to collaborate on a special news show. They all wanted him to be a correspondent in a far-flung part of the world. Not that he minded being overseas, but he craved variety. The Centinela show progressed through various hosts, but none seemed to be the right fit. He worked behind the scenes on Centinela and eventually rose to be a special contributor. Rafael saw enough to give him the position of host. He felt a kinship towards Chandler, whose father hailed from Argentina.

Gustavo escaped the military government in Argentina in the late 1970s. Chandler's paternal grandfather, Armando, had a close association with the left wing Peronist party. Armando served as a finance minister during the last Perón reign from 1973 to 1976. When the military staged a coup, Armando feared limited opportunities for his son. Gustavo had recently graduated from Universidad Argentina de la Empresa with a degree in economics and finance. Armando sent Gustavo to America to live with exiled friends of the Sáenz family in Miami. Eventually Gustavo received his Ph.D. in Finance from the University of Miami at Coral Gables. The coeds at the "U" swooned over him. Freshly armed with his Ph.D., Gustavo had no appetite for returning home with the military still in power and embroiled in a war in the Falkland Islands or Islas Malvinas. A good option materialized with a family connection at the University of Missouri when a position opened up for an entry level professorship.

Chandler left El Mundo's HQ and began the much-awaited walk to the Hilton Buenos Aires. The temperature cooled into the high 60s so his shirt, no longer fresh, gave him good protection from the breeze. He'd stayed at this property on most of his trips here. The building had a unique atrium design that gave passersby a view directly into the property. He made his way to the suite with stunning vistas of Puerto Madero, cursorily greeting familiar hotel staff along the route - he felt too tired to engage in lengthy conversation.

He reminded himself that he needed to tip Mauricio when he saw his luggage stowed in the closet. Mauricio, one of the original employees of El Mundo, took good care of visitors. He managed check-in details and if you caught him at the right time, there could be an adult beverage waiting for you in the mini-frig. The shirt that he'd had on for twenty-four hours finally told him it was time for a change. After taking a long, tepid shower, his cell phone rang to the tune of Jimi Hendrix's Voodoo Child. Renee beckoned.

He had difficulty imagining his life without her sacrifices. Renee had to be a judicious saver by choice. During the late 1990s she invested in many of the dot com stocks and her own company, LSS. Feeling good about the state of her investments and a promotion at work, they moved to a larger home in Richardson. Unfortunately her portfolio, like those of many others, crashed in 2000. The boy born on Black Monday witnessed another crash, this time a slow one.

"Hi Mom."

"Chan, how was the trip?"

"Same as usual. I didn't sleep but I'm sure looking forward to it tonight."

"OK, I won't keep you long. I just wanted to check in. I really hope we can see each other soon. You know I worry about you being in that big city and all over the world. That sweet boy who sang at his school's Christmas program became the host of an international show."

"Oh Mom," Chandler said sheepishly.

"I really hope we can spend Christmas together this year. I don't care where it is, I just want to spend it with you, OK?" Renee longed for companionship. Sure, she had friends in the Dallas Metroplex, but being single for all these years made her realize that she didn't have anyone with whom to share her life. Boyfriends didn't last long during Chandler's early years. She didn't want to introduce a man into her life that wouldn't be around. She couldn't do that to Chandler again, not after bailing on Columbia. Chandler's connection with Gustavo made life easier for her. She rid herself of some guilt, some, but not all. After Chandler went away to college, dating proved more difficult than expected. She found it hard to open herself emotionally.

"Mom, I promise that if I'm not on assignment somewhere, we'll spend Christmas together either in New York or Dallas, deal?"

"Deal. Now you just need to find a nice young girl."

"Not many women want a relationship with someone who is always gone."

"You keep working on it. It can't happen if you don't try. OK, I know you're tired. I love you, Chan. Sleep well."

"Love you too, Mom."

Chandler ordered room service with a glass of Malbec to accompany his light meal. Just like Rafael said, the Malbec promoted a great night of sleep.

***

He met Rafael for breakfast the next morning in the Hilton's restaurant. Rafael lived in Puerto Madero in a high-rise condominium. The term high-rise meant something different in Buenos Aires than in New York City. He'd only been to his condo once and it was definitely a bachelor pad equipped with industrial shelving, several framed photographs of barely dressed women, and minimal gear in the kitchen. Rafael had no steady girlfriend and was not close to his family, as evidenced by the lack of family pictures. Rafael was all about work and hard play.

Trips to Argentina were very nostalgic for Chandler. The first time he visited as a high school senior, he met the Sáenz side of the family. His grandfather Armando enthralled him with tales about Juan Domingo Perón and what it was like in a country in the middle of a military coup when you're on the losing side.

Gustavo took him on a whirlwind tour going as far south as Patagonia and as far north as the spectacular falls at Iguazú. Iguazú overwhelmed Chandler. He traveled little as a child and had never seen a real waterfall. He'd seen Niagara Falls on TV, but these cataracts took it to another level. The Garganta del Diablo, a horseshoe-shaped waterfall 500 feet long by 250 high, depicted a path towards Lucifer's throat, and provided the highlight of his tour of the falls. The fall's deafening roar transmitted a concussive pulse in the teen's ear.

The first visit to the country of his father's birth would be a life changing experience for the young Texan. He knew there was more to the world than Dallas or Columbia, and he yearned to see as much as he could.

"¿Dormiste bien, Chan?" Rafael knew the answer to how he slept since he didn't reply to his text early last night.

"Like a rock. I had a glass of Malbec."

"Qué bueno. I told you." Rafa said assuredly.

"I talked to my mom, had a quick dinner and after that I

hardly remember anything."

"How is Renee?"

"She misses me. She's lonely. She needs a man in her life, honestly. And I think she sees her life moving on without one. I don't know how to help her."

"Bring her to Buenos Aires. I'm sure she would have many lovers." He shrugged and shook his head. Rafael never had a serious relationship, so his emphasis was always on carnal knowledge.

"I think she needs more than a lover." Chandler shook his head.

They continued their meeting from yesterday over a long breakfast. It was not the typical Argentinian breakfast of toast and coffee - it was a full American buffet. Their waiter commanded a large tip. He refreshed their coffee several times. There were many assignments on Chandler's El Mundo plate.

Both realized the economic turmoil and terrorism facing the world would worsen before it improved. Rafael saw the need for more international cooperation and stronger institutions. Chandler didn't really know what to believe. Part of him viewed the turmoil as part of a larger process of creative destruction. The other side of him struggled with the suffering the turmoil wrought. He didn't think more government was the answer either. The men agreed to disagree on this point. They knew there were no easy answers and both agreed they needed elected leadership to provide solutions.

Rafael planned to be in Washington to attend the White House Correspondents' Association dinner where he would see one of his own, Michelle Reyes, a native of Venezuela, receive an award.

While waiting for the check, Rafael needled Chan about his

personal life. He raised his eyebrows in rapid succession. "When are you going to settle down and meet a nice girl?"

"You sound just like my mom!"

"Seriously, you're at that age."

"This from the perpetual bachelor?"

"You need to think about it Chan."

"I guess I could if my boss stopped flying me around the world."

They both broke out in laughter.

CHAPTER TWO
ARIANNE

The White House Correspondents' Association Dinner was always a swanky affair, and 2019's would be an important one for El Mundo. It brought celebrities from government, business, sports, and Hollywood. Chandler and Rafael were there to support their colleague, Michelle Reyes, who would receive the Journalism Excellence award for her interview with the Venezuelan president. Last year Michelle scored an exclusive interview with the Venezuelan leader, leveraging her Venezuelan citizenship, after the historic visit to the nation's capital to meet with President Jefferson. It was no easy feat bringing him to Washington given his regime's long criticism of U.S. imperialism.

The U.S.'s economic problems made these accusations less frequent since Pentagon budgets were greatly scaled back due to exploding Federal deficits that led to a shrinking U.S. empire. Venezuela looked for economic cooperation with the U.S. after their own economy tanked.

Chandler never ceased to be amazed by the number of people that Rafael knew, well acquainted with many, though close to no one. Growing up in La Cava, he had to make acquaintances. He needed a ticket out of the shantytown. His parents fed the insatiable appetite for reading. His father brought home day-old copies of La Prensa and the Buenos Aires Herald, the latter an English-language daily he used to teach himself the language. He took every opportunity to spend time out of La Cava.

One day while helping his father, a mechanic's assistant, a couple of hoodlums demanded money from a customer. When the scene got violent, Rafael grabbed a tire iron and beat an assailant off the man. Blood splattered all over the garage, but the hoodlum survived. The customer did not realize his defender was the son of the mechanic's assistant. He was president of the University of Belgrano and offered Rafael a chance to attend on scholarship - his ticket out. Living in La Cava and going to university proved a challenge. The shanty town that never slept made studying difficult.

Upon graduation, he took a position in local TV sports production covering his favorite soccer club, Club Atlético Boca Juniors, one of the most successful soccer clubs in South America. While sports were never his passion, it gave him great exposure in a soccer-crazed country. Rafael eventually made it to the BBC and had many worldwide assignments, including stints in D.C. and New York City. When the Spanish language network El Mundo launched from his hometown of Buenos Aires, he proved a cinch to land a position. From there his career took off.

This dinner proved to be a great event for people watching. Starlet Jessica Walsh headlined the Hollywood list. Jessica became one of the youngest actresses to receive an Academy Award for her portrayal of a single mom raising a future president. NFL MVP Vernon Mayfield accompanied his date, the singer Champion. Supermodel Victoria Hill would appear in many photos. Victoria graced 2019's cover of the Sports Illustrated swimsuit edition shot on location in Carlisle Bay in Barbados. The issue sold more than any in history. Chandler contributed to that statistic every year. President Benjamin Jefferson accompanied his elegant wife, Carolyn.

Chandler had never attended this dinner so he would get a taste of mass produced fine cuisine. The meal began with jumbo lump crab meat followed by a mango salad. British comedian Ricky Summers served as the master of ceremonies. He did not disappoint, delivering strong one-liners.

"Tonight's event is being broadcast on C-SPAN, so to some viewers watching at home, hello, but to most viewers watching, wake up!"

"It is great to be here at the Washington Hilton. That's something a prostitute might say to a Congressman."

"The Washington Hilton, you guys. If these walls could talk. They'd probably say, 'clean me'."

"Tom Williams is retiring after serving 30 years in Congress. Now many people don't know this, but Williams was a boxer before he spent five terms as a punching bag."

In the middle of cutting into his smoked paprika rubbed filet, Chandler noticed someone at an adjacent table who looked like a celebrity, but he did not recognize her. He leaned over to Rafael and inquired as to the celebrity's identity. Rafael did not know but asked him, "¿Te la quieres cojer?" Rafael had a penchant for thinking with his sex organ. This woman defined spectacular. Her auburn colored hair, long and flowing, struck him. Her eyes appeared to be a deep blue. She wore a black sequin gown. The sequins were nice, but the long slit to mid-thigh proved better. He couldn't gauge her height but she appeared on the taller side. She had broad shoulders and a taut waist. If he had to guess, she was probably a C-cup. Then again, he'd never been on a show where he had to guess these things.

Later, during one of the awards, Rafael leaned over and whispered, "I know who that is."

"Yeah. OK. And?" Chandler tugged at his partner's shirt.

"Is it worth something to you?" Rafael grinned and leaned in the opposite direction.

Now Chandler needed to lean into his dinner companion. "Come on Rafa. Didn't you say I needed to meet someone?"

"What makes you think you will meet her?"

"*Rafa, por favor no te hagas el pelotudo.*" Chandler knew he could get his attention if he cursed at him with Argentinian words, albeit in a whispered tone. Hopefully, he called him a dumb ass.

"*Bueno Chan. Muy bueno.* Her name is Arianne Maxwell."

That name did not strike a chord with Chandler. She might be a celeb for all he knew. "Is she famous?"

"She is a lawyer at the State Department. That's all I know."

Serendipitously, an audio problem delayed the award presentation for Michelle. Chandler used the opportunity to introduce himself to Arianne. He was never shy and traveling as much as he did and interviewing people pretty much eliminated any conversational hesitation. The delay presented another opportunity. The person at his table sitting closest to her left suddenly so it opened up a chair. Chandler deftly took over the position. He'd experienced chemistry many times. This reaction proved different. When dinner ended, guests cleared tables all around them, yet they stayed engaged in conversation. It's as if the world around them stopped. Arianne was there alone. Her boss at the State Department injured his back earlier in the day and could not accompany her. Chandler was not there alone and got lost in her deep blue eyes, forgetting about Rafael.

When it became clear Chandler would not excuse himself,

Rafael interrupted their conversation to say he wanted to talk to Michelle before she left with her husband. Chandler apologized for his rudeness and quickly introduced Arianne. Michelle and her husband came by and Chandler gave her a big congratulatory hug. He didn't want to look away from Arianne for too long since he had more to say. After excusing himself, he returned to Arianne, who had ventured to the coat check. Chandler assisted her with her lightweight wool coat, noticing the curves of her body. They quickly exchanged contact information before she got in a cab. This spring evening ended much too early for Chandler.

Rafael met him outside and gave him a frown and then a big smile. The evening took an unexpected twist with this celebrity encounter.

***

The week after the correspondent's dinner seemed like it lasted a month. Chandler had asked Arianne out the day after the dinner. Fortunately, he didn't have to travel in the last week, but unfortunately, it just made time go slower. They met in a Georgetown area restaurant, Muay Thai, eponymously named by the owner after the combat sport, where he excelled as a champion. Chandler had eaten food from all over the world and had what his mom described as an iron stomach. He let Arianne decide where to eat and this place was a convenient stroll to her condo. While they chatted successfully at the correspondent's dinner, Chandler wondered how the evening would go. He arrived first and waited at the maître d' station. *Will she want to talk shop or politics? Is she into sports? Does she know much about El Mundo? I better turn off my cell. No sense in being distracted.* He turned it off and looked up. She was a vision of beauty as she entered.

"Good evening, Miss Maxwell."

"Miss Maxwell? So formal, Mr. Scott."

Chandler lowered his head. "Sorry, Arianne." He turned his gaze slowly towards the maître d' and said, "Reservations for Scott."

As they walked towards their table, he noticed her very pleasing figure. It was exactly as he remembered it, this time in a blue, knee-length cocktail dress. He tried to keep his thoughts pure. The restaurant had a light crowd which allowed the maître d' to give them a fairly private table. As she sat, he tried desperately not to stare at the plunging neckline of her dress. Just before contacting her seat, Arianne glanced at Chandler who quickly averted his eyes. She appreciated his attention. A girl never tired of being noticed.

The Maxwell family didn't escape notice. Her father, Lawrence, headed the company that bore his name, Maxwell Technologies that developed consumer and business software. Arianne, born the same year as Chandler, grew up in privileged surroundings in the Chicago suburb of Winnetka where she attended the very exclusive North Shore Country Day School. Later she attended Northwestern University, graduating with a degree in Political Science and followed with a Juris Doctor from Washington University in St. Louis. After law school she took a position as associate legal counsel at her father's firm, though her tenure there was short-lived. Her fortunes took her to Washington D.C. where she found work as a legal adviser for the State Department.

"Arianne, in case I forget to say so later, you look stunning" Chandler said with a big smile.

"I'll remind you later, just in case." They shared a brief laugh.

"So how long have you been at State?"

"About 5 years. After I graduated from law school I went to work for my dad's company. You may have heard of it, Maxwell Technologies?"

Chandler had not heard of it but wanted to sound intelligent. "Is it a biotech firm?"

"No, it's software. High-tech stuff. Honestly kinda boring for me." Arianne was skilled in her craft but not technologically savvy and had no interest in becoming so. Though her father's company enjoyed success in the industry, she never took offense when others were unfamiliar.

"Ahh. Good thing I'm not interviewing for a job there." Chandler's remark drew a quick smile from her.

"So you told me you've been with El Mundo for several years I think you said?"

"Yeah, I guess about 9 years now. I was fortunate to land with them."

"Well I guess so, having your own show. Impressive." Arianne had an air about her that seemed girly and sophisticated. She seemed like she could be hot college coed one moment and serious attorney the next. "Have you been to China? Our ambassador may have to move due to all the unrest in Beijing. I have a colleague who was there in 1989 as a ten-year-old and had to hole up in a hotel due to Tiananmen Square."

"It's funny you mention that. My boss and I were discussing the development of a story there. He says they could solve a lot of their problems if there were more women."

"You men always think it's about sex don't you?"

He couldn't tell if she was being serious. It was too early to read these cues. He treaded cautiously. "Well, the one child policy created this problem. With so many men relative to women, it just creates a large group of restless young men."

"I'm just teasing, silly," Arianne giggled. "Has anyone ever told you that you are rather serious?"

Chandler pivoted quickly. This girl must be more easygoing than he thought. "I try not to be, only if I'm around serious people."

"Then let's declare this a serious-free zone." Arianne's declaration afforded great relief for him.

The waiter came by to ask for their drink order. Arianne asked for a Pinot Grigio. Chandler opted for a Sauvignon Blanc. He was particular about his wine pairings and found this grape to be the best with Thai food. They made a little more small talk and he discovered her affinity for professional team sports. She knew players on the Nationals and Redskins and often attended games. He had a hard time being a dedicated fan due to his travel. He also had to split his loyalties between New York teams, where he had his main residence in Manhattan, and D.C. teams, where he shared an apartment with a colleague at El Mundo. Then, of course, he had his loyalty to the teams from his youth, the Cowboys and Rangers. If this were to develop into a relationship, Arianne would be the source of D.C. sports knowledge.

After returning with their drinks, the waiter prompted them for their entrée requests. She ordered Som Tam with mild spiciness. Chan opted for Pad Thai with Thai hot spiciness. He'd never ordered it like this but surmised he could handle anything that came his way. He got exposed to spicy chili con carne by his mom and the chili cook-offs he attended in his youth. He'd eaten spicy foods on his overseas travels.

"Chandler, have you ever been to Thailand?"

"No, that is one place I never made it to. I guess there was nothing there for me to cover."

"My family took a vacation to Phuket years ago. The beaches were divine." He eyes sparkled at the memory.

Chandler's eyes sparkled imagining what she looked like in a two piece. "I've heard that."

When the entrees arrived, he could tell his dish was hot - he smelled it. But hey, he'd been to the Terlingua chili contest and sampled their hottest, so how tough could this be? He found out with his first bite. He'd tasted hot, but this was altogether different. He imagined Lucifer feeding him liquid fire.

Arianne sensed his discomfort. "Chandler, are you OK?"

"Why do you ask?" By now it had to be apparent that his eyes looked like they'd been to a funeral. His forehead collected beads of sweat.

"That is the hottest thing they serve here and it's rare that anyone other than a native Thai asks for something that hot."

"Oh?" Great, now she told him. "Excuse me for a moment." He made a beeline towards the bathroom. By now he looked like someone in the early stages of the flu. His nose dripped.

He excused himself three times. Everything comes in threes, he told himself. He convinced himself it would get better soon.

"You know Chandler, we can leave if you need to." Arianne bordered between sorrow and laughter.

"Arianne, my mouth is hotter than hell's brass hinges!"

Arianne chuckled. "Who knew they had brass hinges in hell?"

She asked for the check when he excused himself for the fourth time. Events did not come in threes after all. The waiter suggested visiting the ice cream parlor next door and made a flavor suggestion - sweet cream. Apparently, Chandler wasn't the first guest to experience Thai hot. When he returned from the restroom, Arianne grabbed his hand and escorted him to the parlor where she ordered him a double scoop sweet cream cone. He first laid the cone against his tongue and then wrapped his mouth around it holding it steady for a few seconds - finally, some relief.

Chandler had two thoughts running through his brain. The first was the obvious discomfort of the Thai food. The second was the embarrassment of being a total flop on his first date. *What does this beautiful woman think of me now?* To his surprise, she showed no signs of annoyance.

"Arianne, you really didn't need to pay. I would've-"

"In your condition?" She smiled.

"Well, thank you. Seriously."

"Too bad you didn't get to finish your Pad Thai."

Chandler, still in the midst of mouth pain, appreciated the humor. "Actually, I enjoyed the first tenth of a second of flavor."

Arianne laughed. "You sure it was even that long?"

The ice cream calmed his mouth. Despite it being a cool spring evening, Chandler wanted to rip off his shirt. He remained on fire. Maybe a bucket of ice water over his head would do the trick. As they walked outside the ice cream parlor, he surveyed other restaurant patrons entering Muay Thai. He thought he should warn them.

"Chandler, it has certainly been an interesting evening. I need to go now. Please don't lean over to kiss me goodnight. I'm afraid you might burn my mouth."

That pretty much settled it. He blew it. At least he couldn't fault himself for standing on the sidelines. He got in the game, but regrettably fumbled the ball.

"Arianne, I-"

She gently placed her hand on his shoulder and kissed him on the cheek. "Good night Chandler." She walked away into the night, presumably toward her condo. The spicy food did not affect his eyesight. The extra water in his eyeballs sharpened his vision, he could see her pleasing figure fade away into the night. Fortunately for Chandler, the evening was not a flop, and would mark the first of many dates.

CHAPTER THREE
INTERVIEWS

El Mundo occupied an office and studio complex on West 55th St. near Broadway in the heart of Manhattan. On nice days, such as this one in late spring, news staff migrated to Central Park to enjoy the oasis of the city. The complex sat on the top three floors of a forty story tower. Chandler would interview the legendary head of the New York Stock Exchange (NYSE), Will Duncan, a man destined for Wall Street. After getting a finance degree at Cornell and an MBA at Wharton, he progressed to managing director for the large investment bank Stark & Wells. He made his name there by keeping the firm out of the 2008 crisis with a decidedly conservative investment posture. The bank made a huge bet shorting oil when it fell from $140 per barrel to $50. The bonus checks were good that year.

In 2009, a group of influential bankers and fund managers asked Duncan to lead the NYSE - he declined. During the crash of 2016, the heads of many investment banks and the NYSE board reached out to him again. He still would not bite. When the outgoing president called, he accepted. During his leadership, he brought reforms in electronic trading, particularly high frequency trading. The recent disruption of trading on the NYSE and other exchanges made his job even harder.

This would be a good interview for Mr. Scott. Duncan was a straight shooter who, to date, had not provided a one-on-one interview on the trading disruption incident with any journalist. Duncan apologized to Chandler that he had less time than originally planned due to a call with President Jefferson. Duncan ran in important circles. Chandler realized they would have even less time now because of a lighting problem in the studio. Any amount of time with Duncan was a major score for Chandler and El Mundo.

"Centinela welcomes the head of the New York Stock Exchange today, Mr. Will Duncan. Mr. Duncan, it's a great pleasure having you on our show."

"The pleasure is mine, Mr. Scott."

Duncan, a middle-aged man, below average in height with a medium build, dressed like an investment banker. For the interview, he wore a charcoal, fitted suit, a light blue shirt with cuff links, and a red tie. His shoes were freshly polished, black loafers. Chandler attempted to match his guest's attire, out of respect, but fell short of the mark. His suit did not fit like a glove, the shirt bore no cuff links, and his tie hung loosely around his neck. The two men faced each other while sitting in leather club chairs.

"Investors and traders felt the pain a couple of months ago when the exchanges abruptly shut down. What can you tell our viewers about the incident?"

"First, I'd like to personally apologize for the disruption of the NYSE. My office received numerous calls from brokerage houses, investment banks and mom and pop investors. Had this event occurred, say, prior to 2016 or even 2008, the response probably would have been different. But in the aftermath of the 2016 crash, people are understandably more nervous. We know there is blame directed at high frequency traders, terrorists or even some glitch in our trading systems. Let me say categorically, there were no glitches in our systems. Since I arrived three years ago, we have made our trading systems even more redundant. For those that think it was the high frequency traders that overwhelmed our servers, I can tell you that was not the cause either. Our processing capacity trebled from when I first got here. So this places the spotlight on terrorist activity." Duncan delivered his message in a calm, unemotional manner.

"To be fair, there were many Internet disruptions in Manhattan that day, which made everyone even more nervous. I know I was." Chandler struggled that day conducting a video chat with colleagues from the D.C. bureau.

"Yes, the communication carriers were slow to acknowledge the problem. They determined that something happened in a data center and the physical communication links in the city."

"Data centers are vulnerable to kinetic terror threats unless they're isolated or underground," Chandler added.

"Keep in mind that physical security, by itself, cannot defeat a terrorist. This is where the human intelligence gathering comes into play. But regarding data centers, the carrier I spoke with indicated it was not a kinetic or physical attack. It was cyber all the way."

"Mr. Duncan, that is troubling." Chandler lifted a worried eyebrow.

"Investors should know that the New York Stock Exchange, and other exchanges, work closely with Office of the Director of National Intelligence, or the ODNI, and various agencies under its direction to identify these threats." Chandler elected not to interrupt Duncan despite not understanding what the ODNI actually did. The ODNI provided direction to all 17 agencies comprising the nation's intelligence community. Included in this list was the CIA and even a quasi internal CIA for the Treasury Department.

"I met with the president and the National Security

Director to talk about this disruptive event. I told them, and this is no great national security secret, that we have always been concerned about Internet vulnerabilities with undersea cables coming into the city. These cables traverse oceans and come into major financial centers all over the world, say like London or New York. No matter how good of a job we do on the exchanges or how secure a carrier data center is, we have those cables. So even though the most recent attack was cyber, we also have the physical concern with these cables. The president, however, related to me plans for safeguarding these cables."

"Such as?"

"Sorry, I am not at liberty to discuss," Duncan retorted, the corners of his mouth creased slightly.

"But you feel good about the plans?" Chandler hoped to get something out of Duncan.

"It is a step in the right direction. I feel confident in our collaboration with the ODNI and I get the sense that everyone is on the same page." Duncan looked down at his watch and adjusted his tie, which did not need attention. "Mr. Scott, I'm going to have to depart now. I am behind schedule."

"Mr. Duncan. Thanks for your time today."

Duncan got up from his chair, buttoned his suit and brushed the sleeves. This had to be a habit. As Chandler walked him out of the studio he said, "I hope you have a productive call with the president."

"Yes, I hope so too. We have much work to do to keep us all safe."

***

The brief interview with Duncan proved a ratings success, no doubt aided by his infrequent interactions with the press. Chandler needed to discuss economic safety to continue the progression of stories laid out with Rafael in Buenos Aires. The unemployment rate hit a post-crash high in May 2019. This frequently proved to be the most debated government statistic. If you were unemployed and had been out of work for some time, the rate always seemed too low. Critics always pointed to the measuring criteria.

The Bureau of Labor Statistics made seasonal and other adjustments that were easy targets of criticism. The other hotly debated stat was the gross domestic product. It seemed like it always got revised. After the Commerce Department said the economy grew at 0.5% in the first quarter of 2019, they revised it and said it contracted by 1.5%. Quite a miss. Even the normally reliable Treasury auctions required the Fed to step in as a buyer of a bunch of government debt. Traditional creditors like banks and pension funds were wary of budget deficits that had no boundary. Depressed conditions characterized the U.S. economy.

The Fed occupied the role of an institution that would somehow always come to the rescue of the economy and help unemployment. They were supposed to help with growing the economy. They did QE. After a few years, their economic tinkering did not have the desired effect. Traders no longer waited with bated breath for the pronouncements of the Chairman. The Fed, however, was still relevant and not going away. Chandler knew that getting an interview with current Fed chair Anna Walker would be impossible. Rafael told him as much and suggested he not even waste his time talking to this mysterious institution. The Fed defined people's perceptions about how things were going. The Fed chair still had the aura of being an oracle. The public and even some in government were now challenging that aura.

Chandler hit on an idea. Mark Lansing recently retired as Fed president from Kansas City. Interviewing a sitting member of the Fed would be impossible, but perhaps a retired member would be a willing participant. He called Lansing and to his surprise, agreed to speak with him off-camera and only if he was not quoted. It seemed like a good compromise. Lansing, or the unnamed source at the Fed, would be part of his segment for Centinela. When he told Rafael that he was heading to Kansas City, his boss seemed annoyed, thinking the interview a waste of time.

Chandler agreed to meet Fed President Lansing at a restaurant in Country Club Plaza called The Big Pig. The restaurant sat in a two story building with an exterior of washed brick and stone. Once inside, you got the impression you were in a fine steak place with generous use of wood on the walls and ceiling. Unlike many restaurants, this one had no TVs. Only serious appetites should walk through the door. Lansing arrived first and occupied half of a richly appointed leather booth. The restaurant bustled especially for an early dinner crowd on a Thursday. Lansing selected this establishment. Who was Chandler to argue with someone versed in the fine art of barbeque?

"Good evening, Mr. Lansing. Thanks so much for meeting me. How are you?" Chandler was unsure how to address the former Fed president.

"I am well, thanks. Please call me Mark. They've called me Mr. Lansing for too long, frankly. I've been treated like royalty and trust me there is nothing regal about me."

Lansing's candor disarmed Chandler. Mark Lansing had the resume one might expect from a Fed official. He had two degrees in Economics from Princeton University and began his career as an academic economist and monetary policy scholar. After a brief career in academia, he moved to a research position at the Fed in Kansas City where he eventually rose to the position of president. Mark appeared to be in his early sixties, average height, a round pale face with thick white hair and a slight paunch. For this dinner interview, he dressed nothing like the suit and tie he no doubt wore for years at his Fed post. He dressed in jeans and a long sleeve, button down, cotton oxford.

The waiter approached. "Good evening gentlemen. My name is Stuart and I'll be taking care of you today. What are we drinking?"

"Bring us a couple of drafts, Boulevard unfiltered wheats," Lansing said confidently. "It's a local beer. You'll like it Chandler. It goes well with the barbeque."

"Sounds like a winner, Mr. Lansing, um Mark," Chandler corrected himself as the waiter departed. After a couple of minutes of staring at his menu, Chandler must have projected some degree of bovine indifference.

"Let me suggest the ribs and burnt ends." Lansing pointed at the menu selection.

"You know the place better than I do," Chandler replied. Stuart returned with the unfiltered wheats in frosted pint glasses, placing one in front of each man.

"Have you gentlemen decided on what you're ordering?" Stuart inquired.

"Let's get the full rack, dry rub only and the dinner-sized portion of burnt ends." Lansing may not have thought himself regal but he gave the order in a stentorian tone.

"Yes sir," Stuart answered obligingly.

Lansing had no immediate interest in talking about Fed policy. No doubt when he had dinners like these, it was to chat about esoteric topics and analysis. Chandler instead got a heavy dose of KC Royals baseball. Kansas City fans were understandably proud of their team. They won the Series in 2015 and had a very good team since. It just so happened the Yankees were in town and Lansing wanted to trash talk a bit. Many people outside the Big Apple presumed the standard New Yorker supported the Bronx Bombers. Chandler didn't reveal his allegiance to the Mets and allowed him to carry on. Fortunately for Chandler, this only lasted about 5 minutes. Chandler's lack of engagement on baseball was no doubt a cue for Lansing, who suddenly morphed into a former Federal Reserve Bank president.

"OK, I'll stop rambling about the Royals. You want to talk about serious stuff. Probably the biggest misconception people have about the Fed is that somehow there is something federal about it. We tried using the central bank moniker in the 18th and 19th century, but that didn't work out. But we're not a federal agency. Excuse me for a moment." Lansing peeked at an incoming text. "Sorry, the wife. Gotta stop by the store. All right, you want to hear something else that most don't know? The Fed is always bashing gold as some obsolete money relic, but guess who holds one of the largest gold stashes in the world?"

"I think you're going to say the Fed."

"Yeah, we might have a bigger stash at the New York Fed than they have in Fort Knox or West Point." Lansing used the pronoun "we" though he no longer worked for the bank.

"I had no idea." Chandler wrote notes on his tablet. The average American knew about Fort Knox, heck the gold was even the subject of a James Bond movie once. The New York Fed or West Point were not locations typically associated with gold.

The meal arrived quicker than expected. "Gentlemen, I'll put the full rack and burnt ends in the middle here since it appears you're sharing." Stuart moved the beer glasses aside to place the feast between Chandler and Lansing. "I brought some wipes also. Anything else I can get you?"

Both men shook their head. Lansing split the rack in half with his knife and continued.

"Here's another one for you. All that QE stuff we did starting after 2008. People would be floored if they heard the screaming matches we had. I remember one time I got so mad at Fran Schwartz that I had to leave the room for fear that I was going to cuss her out." Lansing related an unfortunate exchange with the former Federal Reserve President of San Francisco. "But the real problem are the politicians who want us to solve all of *their* problems. We don't have the tools to do all that. The Fed is just a bunch of academics." He should know being one of them.

"Econometrics," Chandler said, trying to inject something intelligent.

"Yes, but at the end of the day, all the QE and the tinkering is a massive experiment. We don't have a master plan with some known outcome. We'll try something and see if it works and maybe if it does, we'll do more," Lansing said, doing damage to a rib.

"And if it doesn't work?"

"Someone takes the blame. Sometimes it's government and sometimes it's the Fed. Lately it's the Fed. The president is popular. The reality is we've created these financial bubbles misdirecting people towards riskier investments since interest rates were so low. We really put the pension funds at risk. They had to make their 8% or 9% and no way could they do that with their usual investments. Honestly, we don't really know what we are doing." Lansing took a large swig of his beer, the glass now stained with barbeque residue.

He stunned Chandler with the admission. Public servants like teachers, policemen, firefighters as well as private company employees were unsuspecting victims in a grand monetary experiment. A former Federal Reserve president confessed his sins to a journalist. Lansing felt secure confessing since he knew Chandler wouldn't quote him. He had nothing to lose.

"What sort of powers could the Fed use if the market were to crash again?"

"Powers? We're not magicians, son. Damn, we've tried just about everything. I mean, in theory, we could go into the market and buy stock directly. There has been discussion about having the Fed just credit commercial bank accounts." Lansing got more frustrated, as if he'd answered this question before, chewing forcefully on his meat.

"Like free money?" Chandler covered his mouth with a napkin, concealing momentary shock at the words leaving his mouth.

"Sometimes people call it helicopter money," Lansing snickered at the metaphor.

Chandler remembered what a former Fed chair said about dropping money from helicopters.

Lansing had a reputation for being outspoken but never this candid. His candor distracted Chandler so much he forgot to savor the barbeque feast. Chandler chewed, swallowed, listened, wiped his hands and took notes on his tablet. The interview proved a success. Chandler thanked Lansing for his time and thanked him again when he picked up the tab. Lansing reminded him not to attribute any quotes to him. It was a fair deal. Chandler rushed out to his car to hurry to his flight at Kansas City International and immediately called Rafael.

"Hey Rafa. You won't believe how my conversation went with Lansing."

"A waste of time?"

"Quite the contrary." Chandler gave him the Cliff Notes version of the conversation and ended it with, "he even said they don't know what they are doing."

"*No me bolacees!*"

"Rafa, I am not bullshitting you. I never expected this sort of a stunning admission on his part. I can't wait to incorporate that into a story."

"No. We are not putting that into a story. Lansing is a disgruntled former Fed president. How can he call out his colleagues like that? That is a betrayal." Rafael had editorial control, but to Chandler's recollection he'd never been so adamant about censoring content.

"Rafa, I wouldn't have come all the way out here just to not put something like that on the show. That doesn't make sense. Besides, I'm not attributing any of the quotes to him."

"Chan, we can't have an institution like the Fed made to look like fools. I know they've had their issues but this is too much. No!"

"When did you get so gun shy?" Chandler struggled to understand the motivations of the person on the other end of the phone.

"*¡Anda a cagar!*" Chandler did not need to be told to empty his bowel.

"Rafa, come on, are you serious?" He did not answer. "Rafa, you still there?" He hung up. This was very unlike him.

They'd argued before, but this bordered on internal censorship. *Where was this anger coming from?* The argument bothered him all the way to the airport. He concluded that Rafael was probably just having a bad day or maybe something went awry with a lady friend.

He couldn't worry about this exchange for too long since he'd need his thinking cap soon. Before returning to New York, Chandler would spend part of the weekend with his friend and mentor, Axel Schultz, a resident of Chicago. Other than Rafael, Axel had been the most influential male role model in his life.

CHAPTER FOUR
MENTOR

Axel Schultz fit the modern definition of a renaissance man. While independently wealthy, he'd never make a Forbes list. Not even close. He had enough to do what he wanted - when he wanted. Born in Albuquerque in the late 1950s, his family settled in Alamogordo shortly after his birth. His father, an Austrian immigrant, ran his own auto repair shop. His mom also hailed from Austria. Her father was a respected economist from Salzburg and a protégé of another famous economist, Eugen Böhm von Bawerk, who made important contributions to the development of the Austrian school of economics. Ana grew up in a house immersed in the Austrian school. She passed whatever she knew about economics to her young son.

The energetic Axel proved to be quite an athlete. He played football, wrestled and threw the shot put. By the time he graduated high school, he could have attended several schools on athletic scholarship. Instead, he used money scraped together working in his father's garage and set out for a European expedition that took him to several countries, including the country of his parent's birth. When he returned to New Mexico, he realized that traveling and exploring were passions. To fulfill these passions, he had to be his own boss. After taking classes in community college, he hired onto IBM selling fifty pound desktop computers in southern California.

While at IBM he encountered the work of Polish mathematician Benoit Mandelbrot, who discovered that irregular shapes had similar structure at different scales - they looked the same no matter how big or small. Mandelbrot called them fractals. Many people were unwittingly familiar with fractals if they wore Grateful Dead t-shirts or hung the band's posters on their walls. Fractals would later be influential in Axel's future investment tactics, tactics that would make him a great deal of money in the markets and provide him freedom to pursue his passions. IBM had a generous college reimbursement program of which he availed himself and completed an electrical engineering degree at the University of Southern California.

The fifty pound computer proved to be a problem requiring innovation. When he heard that a small northern California company named after a fruit developed a revolutionary computer, he took notice and invested heavily. That spawned a series of stock investments in technology companies that would net him considerable profits. Another northern California company whose name was an abbreviation of the city of San Francisco made him another small fortune. After leaving IBM, he started and sold various companies in computer and networking technology.

His fortune made, Axel began a deeper study of financial markets and trading systems. He delved into Austrian economics, which he had a small taste of as a youth. In the last dozen years Axel shared his wisdom in economics and financial markets in a monthly newsletter with a small, but dedicated international following paying handsomely for his thoughts. His passion was now research and writing.

Chandler met Axel because of the former's graduate level project at SAIS. One of his professors subscribed to Axel's letter and suggested Chandler work with him. The professor facilitated the introduction. Axel took an immediate liking to Chandler. He saw Chandler as a willing student with a mind like a sponge, someone who asked thoughtful questions. In Axel's opinion, Americans had gone soft intellectually and were not willing to put forth effort to learn. A young Chandler provided a breath of fresh air. For the unmarried Axel who had no offspring, Chandler would become his surrogate son.

The ninety minute Southwest Airlines flight on the 737 from Kansas City to Midway went without incident, at least while airborne. The short runways at Midway were always an experience for even the most seasoned traveler. His stomach, still full from the barbeque feast with Lansing, made the abrupt landing bothersome for his mouth as he relived the taste of burnt ends, this time with a little acid. The thirteen mile cab ride to Axel's condo at Great Lakes Tower went smoothly. There were no accidents or construction delays on I-55 or Lake Shore Drive. The cabbie engaged him with conversation about the Cubs who finally won the World Series.

"It only took 110 years! It had to happen sooner or later don't you think?" said the long-suffering fan of the baby bears. 'We can only take so much of the Cardinals, you know."

"Yeah, it was great for baseball no doubt. Watch out for my Mets this year, though."

Great Lakes Tower was a seventy story building jutting out into Lake Michigan. Axel's condo on the 55th floor overlooked Navy Pier and on a clear day, it was said that you could see the states of Michigan, Wisconsin, and Indiana. The condo reflected the essence of Axel Schultz. There were no signs of any connected family save but a small picture of his mom and dad. Axel had no siblings. He covered the living room walls with fine art, much of it purchased in Europe. Furnishings in the main living area included a fine Italian sofa, two chairs and a marble top coffee table.

There were two bedrooms with the second one serving as his office. The office had a picture of Austrian economist Ludwig von Mises and Axel's favorite, one of himself with Benoit Mandelbrot. There were also many charts on wall-mounted cork board. The charts illustrated some of the most memorable days in the stock market's history. Axel's condo suggested a juxtaposition of a literal view of the world while looking out towards Chicago and the figurative one with his writings and research.

Some would call Axel a health and fitness guru, though he showed no passion to write on these topics. For someone in his sixties, he sported the physique of someone half his age with a face bereft of wrinkles. Much of his hair left him in his forties and now he wore it like a recruit at boot camp. He stood six feet in height and weighed more than most guessed. His physical fitness routine produced a sculpted body. He tried to eat according to his regimen whenever he could, though he realized traveling to far-flung corners of the world required adaptation.

Chandler arrived at 11pm in an enervated state. The time with Axel would be a continuous skull session, so he needed to get to bed soon. Chandler asked for this session to create stories Rafael asked him to produce. The Schultz office served as his sleeping quarters for the next couple of nights. To his surprise, the sofa in the office had a pull out bed.

The thing about living in a 70 story tower with great views of Lake Michigan was what happened during an early summer sunrise in an eastern facing unit. Sun reflected off the lake and bored in like a laser into Axel's makeshift bedroom, a room without curtains. If Chandler wanted to sleep longer, it proved impossible with photons bombarding his eyelids. Axel, an early riser, occupied himself in the kitchen whipping up eggs and toast for Chandler and a protein shake with fruit for himself. His commercial grade blender homogenized ingredients so much the shake looked appealing to Chandler, though he would decline if offered.

"Ax, up early as expected I see.   Thanks for making breakfast. Man, I gotta tell you, I'm still really bothered about my boss' reaction to my interview with Lansing." Chandler needed a catharsis of the still lingering argument.

"And Lansing really admitted that they didn't know what they're doing?   I have been saying that in my letter for a few years now."

"Yeah, but then Rafa went cuckoo on me when I told him that."

"Well who knows Chan, he was probably having a bad day. You may have caught him at a bad time. There are people who still view the Fed as saviors. He may be one of them."

"He was none too keen about me quoting an 'unnamed Fed official' as a source for my story. That was the deal I had with Lansing all along."

"Let's talk about the Fed later. Sit down." Axel motioned Chandler towards the dining area. "When you get done eating, we can take a walk on Lake Front Trail. I think you'll be interested in the scenery if you know what I mean."

That message came through loud and clear. At least the scenery could take his mind off the argument with Rafael and prime it for the discussion with his mentor.

The liveliness of the lake shore in the summer always impressed Chandler. The trail filled with people riding their bikes, blading, running or just walking. Volleyball games were being played in the sand. This was the modus operandi that

Axel liked to follow - relaxed at first to ease into the conversation and then increasing in intensity. The post breakfast walk relaxed his mind and benefited his digestion. Heck, for all Chandler knew, Axel just wanted to check out the girls on the beach. He never talked about girls much nor did he address his love life, but when someone of the opposite sex attracted him, he made every effort to stare. By the time they reached Oak St. Beach, Axel turned back towards the condo. The time to start discussion had arrived.

"Chan, you know I'm a critic of the Fed, but it's not personal. They're good people trying to do the right things. I just think their models are inadequate. They think risk is like the old bell curve. It turns out risk is anything but. We've had extreme events like Black Monday in 1987 when you were born, the crashes of 2008 and most recently 2016. If it was a bell curve, those crashes would happen once in earth's history. I exaggerate, but really they might happen once in a lifetime." Once Axel started, he dove straight in.

"But aren't these the same models they use to make predictions about the economy?" Chandler knew the answer, but it would slow the pace and get Axel agitated.

"Why would anyone listen to their forecasts? Their record is bad. It's like having 500-year floods every ten years. Are you kidding me?" Whenever Axel got animated, he always punctuated or started his thoughts with "are you kidding me?" The agitation made him walk faster.

"Yeah but at the end of the day isn't that their job? They're supposed to give guidance." Chandler had to pick up his own pace.

"Guidance. Sheesh. You know they do things also because they have this mandate to keep the economy humming, but that's not originally their charter. After the dot-com bubble, they lowered rates. Then they did the same thing after 2008. When they do these things, they create these cones of speculation. Whether it's housing, stocks, bonds, car loans, high-yield debt, emerging market debt, they cone up the world! This new money flows somewhere and next we have these bubbles. They pop, people get mad, and we have Congress hauling people in to find out who's responsible. Then we get laws that supposedly make everything better. It's a vicious cycle."

"Lansing pretty much admitted to what you said. He was also upset about all the financial reporting going on too in the name of terror."

"I have no doubt. Go try to buy something at the electronics store and pay with cash. See how nervous the clerk gets." Axel quivered his hands.

"But we at least still have cash. It's not like it's going away," Chandler hoped.

"Well, keep in mind that we used to have paper money bigger than the $100 Benjamin. Before 1969 I could've bought a car with a $5,000 bill. I think that note had Madison's picture on it. Why did they get rid of those large notes?" Axel abruptly stopped and extended his arm to halt Chandler's advance, who stumbled for half a step.

"I give up Ax, why?"

"Are you kidding me? I just told you." Axel dropped his arm and turned towards Chandler. "Quit looking at the girls playing volleyball! I thought you had a girlfriend now. It's harder to make large purchases with small bills. It forces people into credit, which leaves a trail."

"I guess I should have picked up on that. Try me again, Ax.

Even a blind hog can find an acorn once in a while."

Axel laughed and resumed walking. "You and your crazy metaphors. We have plenty of time to talk." Truthfully, it would be Axel speaking, Chandler listening.

After arriving back at the condo, Axel poured two tall glasses of green tea and sweetened them with turbinado sugar. Refined white sugar had no home here. Chandler remembered the lecture he got about the white stuff. They sat down in the living room and took in the spectacular lake view. For a landlocked Texan, Lake Michigan might as well have been an ocean. Axel continued with his thoughts about the Fed.

"You know this whole idea about a national bank goes all the way back to Sir Isaac Newton. The one and only who had the apple hit his head. I know it's hard to believe but he was a director of the British Mint. Yeah, that Isaac Newton was a money man! Newton practiced alchemy, you know when they turn a base metal into gold." Axel pointed to the gold candle holder on his coffee table. "Imagine what someone could do with that skill! Are you kidding me?"

"I'd take that skill and put it on my resume," Chandler lifted his index finger in sarcasm.

"Later he formed the Royal Society, which eventually founded the Bank of England and with that founding a monopoly over money. That same idea spread to the early days of our nation when they created the First Bank of the United States.

"Oh, yeah, Lansing mentioned the first central bank."

Axel continued. "The alchemy, so to speak, was when the Bank of England bought the country's debt by creating lawful fiat money. Fiat meaning government said it was money. It's not as if the money really existed."

"That's the part that still blows me away. A central bank creates money out of thin air and then buys debt. I could dominate in Monopoly if I could make my own money and then buy Boardwalk and Park Place," Chandler ruminated.

"Except this is the real world." Axel paused briefly to sip his tea and frowned. "Though the First Bank of the US died in 1811, it came back as the Second Bank a few years later. The Second Bank died in the 1840s until it came back in 1913 as what you know as the Federal Reserve." Axel got up abruptly, walked to his bookshelf and grabbed "The Secrets of the Federal Reserve". "Remember this book?" After sitting down, he placed the book on the table in front of them. Axel had loaned him the book last year.

"Ahh yes, the famous creation on Jekyll Island." Chandler referenced the island off the Georgia coast.

"Do you really think it's better for a central bank to coordinate money? Wouldn't it be better if the market did that on its own? These types of debates aren't won on television or in the press. The Fed and government try to pick winners and they're not always successful." Axel shook his head.

"But the Fed and all these central banks seem so powerful. They've been around for so long, they're so dug in. I mean, it's not like they are going away."

"They may not go away entirely but they may take on a different form. Nothing lasts forever. There is always entropy or lack of predictability."

"Please Ax, no physics. I'm a journalist!"

"Since you think the Fed will be around forever, it's time to chat about cycles. Things move in cycles." Axel traced a circle in front of his face. "We all move to the rhythm of the day and night. You woke up this morning based on some cycle, though hopefully not too much earlier than you wanted."

"The laser beam coming into your condo did the trick." Chandler looked out towards Lake Michigan.

Axel smiled. "We pay attention to the tides. Child-bearing women are cognizant of cycles. Why should it be any different with human behavior? Human behavior influences trends we see in financial markets. Nothing moves in a straight line. People get fooled into linear thinking. Hell, the president of the New York Stock Exchange in September 1929, the month before the crash, suggested the world was done with economic cycles. Talk about a bad call."

"He was probably one of those guys who thought the sun came up just to hear him crow. He no doubt broke his arm patting himself on the back when he said it. Lansing didn't think the Fed was going away though."

"Nothing lasts forever Chandler, even the Fed. We'll probably go through some major bumps along the way, but the cycle will turn. Everyone can see how ineffective they are. Even government leaders don't have faith in them like they once did. But then, maybe, just maybe, there will be something to replace them. You know the power elite does not go quietly."

"Well, I guess if the Fed goes away, you could say that Father Time is undefeated."

"Undefeated and ready to take on new challengers."

"Like who?"

"Great question. I have no answer. If the Fed goes away or if they play a smaller role, government will no doubt have a Congressional hearing or a commission or something and sell everyone on a new idea. Maybe the new idea is not any different but it gets presented that way or maybe it becomes about national security with the way things are today. They'll say something is temporary and it won't be. Like I said, the power elite will not just walk away. Those that have fought them in the past did so at their own peril."

"Sounds ominous. So you won't get fooled again, huh?" Chandler made an oblique reference to a famous song by a British rock-and-roll band.

"I'm impressed, Mr. Scott. A 'Who' reference. Did not figure you for a rock-and-roll historian."

"Don't give me too much credit. I picked that up doin a story in a London pub a couple of years ago. You're basically saying history will repeat, but not exactly the same way."

"Precisely. Which is why we need to be prepared. Let's take a break and have some lunch." Axel motioned Chandler towards the kitchen where they would have their midday meal.

After a simple lunch of sandwiches and green tea, they continued their skull session in the living room. The early afternoon sun laid the tower's shadow on Lake Michigan.

"Ax, some people, I know you do, blame the Fed for all these financial bubbles. I heard that these bubbles created other hidden bubbles that are as big as hell and half of Texas."

"So let me tell you, this is a house of cards. The pyramid of debt, and what we call hypothecation and rehypothecation of financial assets, is the hidden bubble. That's what people don't focus on enough."

"Hypothe what?" Chandler asked with a blank look on his face, so blank he couldn't come up with one of his expressions.

"Hypothecation. Geez, do I need to spell it? It's when someone pledges collateral against debt. Like a house being collateral against the mortgage. Didn't you learn anything at SAIS?" Axel expressed fake outrage at Chandler's graduate school.

"Come on Ax, give me a break!" Chandler shrugged his shoulders while smiling.

"Banks and brokers do this all the time. They'll take something pledged as collateral by their clients and use it in their own transactions as collateral. How can you keep using the same collateral over and over? That is a dangerous practice based on extreme confidence." Axel became more animated and raised his voice.

"So what will that mean?"

"If that house of cards falls, you'll get big time deflation, the Fed's worst nightmare. Everyone will head for the exits. You'll end up with hot markets."

"Hotter than a billy goat in a pepper patch."

"Yeah that billy goat will be on fire. But you know what will happen next?" Axel sat up before delivering his next line.

"Ahh. I have a feeling you want to lay it out for me, maestro," Chandler exclaimed with artistic flair and waved his arms as if conducting the Schultz orchestra.

"You get a crisis, people get hurt in their pocketbooks and the system will wobble. There will be calls for government to do something. There will be scapegoats or maybe billy goats. Then investigations and special committees to study the whole thing. Then a new plan that will fix everything. The new plan will mean more regulation." Axel's face contorted with anger.

"But what about the cycles you talked about?

"This is just my opinion, but I think government will grow even larger before it gets smaller. Everyone always complains about government's size, but I have not detected a sea change in the public's attitude. I suppose the Presidential elections will tell us something about where the country wants to head. President Jefferson is popular right now so I think you'll see more government before you'll see less."

"I know. I have some interviews to do." Chandler pondered his busy schedule.

"It could be a hell of a field," Axel suggested.

Chandler advised they take a short break so he might check email. Axel agreed, wanting to do the same and ducked into his office. Chandler remained in the living room. After about an hour of staring at their screens, they resumed their conversation in Axel's office, aka Chandler's sleeping quarters. Axel wanted to use reference material for the rest of their discussion. He sat in an executive chair behind his well-organized desk and Chandler sat across from him.

"OK, I get the stuff about the Fed. But if I'm a company, say a publicly traded one, how is all this bubble stuff changing our behavior?" Chandler wanted to swing the discussion to something that might directly concern an investor. His mother remained heavily invested.

"Well, one thing they've done is borrowed a bunch of money cheaply and then bought their stock back." Axel pulled out one of his newsletters where he wrote about this very topic. "I don't know if you remember this letter from a couple of years ago." He flung the letter in Chandler's direction.

Chandler scanned the newsletter quickly, reading the headline. "But why would they do that? Most buying seems to happen near highs in the markets so it's like they're paying more for their stock," Chandler concluded.

"Well for one, their earnings per share go up since there are fewer shares in circulation. The analysts then say that a particular company's EPS was unexpectedly higher, so maybe they change the rating of the stock. Look at this." Axel directed Chandler's attention to a stock chart on his oversized monitor.

"Here is where the company started buying their own stock." Axel used his index finger to point to a particular place on the chart. "See and they kept buying their own stock as it got higher and higher, then it crashed like other stocks did in 2016." He traced the stock's fall down to a point lower than where it started. "And what's funny is that this company's top execs triggered bonuses as the stock kept rising."

"So you're saying then that cosmetically, the company looks better but shareholders are not really better off in the long run?"

"I think it was a former VP candidate that said something about putting lipstick on a pig. But seriously, instead of the company using debt to invest back in their business, they are throwing it out to make their stock look better. The purpose for companies taking on debt is to improve the productive capacity of their business. That's not what they did the last few years and that is one reason our economy sucks. These companies that borrowed so much now have to pay it back at higher rates."

"So the Fed inadvertently created these bubbles but it really takes individual companies and investors to bring the bubble to its full glory."

"That's right, Chan. The Fed led all the horses to an endless supply of water, but it was up to the horses to drink. Like those over there on the wall." Axel pointed to his painting of Moors on horseback near the city of Granada in Spain. "Once they started drinking, they got real bloated. Now they have to pee it all out."

"Ax, you sound almost Texan there."

"Man, I hope not!" Both men laughed.

After a day-long skull session, Axel declared its end. A couple of hours of daylight remained before the sun set on the opposite side of the tower. The two walked out of the office towards the main living area. He directed Chandler to retrieve a bottle of wine from his cooler, preferably a white, to pair with the pasta con broccoli he would prepare. Chandler then made himself comfortable in the living room while Axel played chef. Chandler turned on Axel's massive television screen.

The 2020 elections will be unique in the recent history of American politics. Pundits feel the two third parties should mount a reasonable challenge to the GOP and Democratic Party. Reaching and persuading the electorate is no longer a daunting task for these third parties. Popular Senator Matt Geringer, who split from the GOP in 2016 after a brokered convention, is the heir apparent to represent the Independent American Party or IAP. The IAP has struck a chord with voters disenchanted with the growth of government and its inability to address economic problems plaguing the nation. The Theocracy Party should be considerably stronger after their showing in 2018. We expect they will pull votes from the Democrats and GOP from evangelicals who are disenchanted with the country's moral compass and economic inequality.

"Hey Ax. I'm going to interview both of their candidates."

"Geringer seems like a good man. I have a great deal of respect for him. I don't know who will represent the Theocracy guys, but they'll appeal to many voters too. I've heard some people concerned that they'll create some sort of Christian caliphate." Axel said from the kitchen.

"Yeah, I don't know. I'll have to ask them some real hard questions." Given the nation's economic state and the cult of surveillance, he was sure voters would have many questions of their own.

"No matter what happens with these third parties, and by

the way I don't think either has a snowball's chance in hell of winning, the country is well overdue for some new ideas, some fresh voices. I'm sure there are people out there who think the IAP or Theocracy guys are wacky, but so what. At least it gives people more to think about and we need that." Axel put out some deft thoughts amid whipping up pasta.

After a very nice pasta meal and a little too much Sauvignon Blanc, Chandler called it a day. He bid Axel good night and looked forward to a night of restful sleep. Better to get to bed early since he knew the solar system would interrupt his sleep by 5:30am.

"Guess I won't need to set an alarm. The sun will wake me up just fine," Chandler said.

"I suspect it will. No doubt you'll want to get the hell out of here so you can see your girlfriend," Axel replied.

Chandler grinned. Tomorrow he would take a late morning flight to D.C. and have time to see Arianne. He missed her. The relationship had come a long way since burning his mouth on their first date.

CHAPTER FIVE
ROMANCE

Chandler Scott's romantic history was broad but shallow. High school romances were short-lived with an ever vigilant mother serving the dual parent role screening his female interests. He blossomed in college. The freedom to roam on a campus with a high percentage of women and another all girl college in the same town, developed his interactions with the opposite sex. He met many women, though he really never got to *know* any of them except in the biblical sense. This pattern continued in his professional life. There were opportunities to develop more meaningful relationships, yet his peripatetic lifestyle made it almost impossible. And he was comfortable with that to this point in his life.

Arianne presented him with something he'd never faced. She might be the person that slowed him down. She had beauty, smarts and there was a clear mental connection, prerequisites he told himself were important. He'd encountered plenty of women with some of those traits, though never all of them in one person.

There was a girlfriend in college with beauty and brains, but they had little in common other than great sex. There were plenty of smart girls at El Mundo, though he found no attraction to any of them, never mind the concern about dating someone at work. There were a few dalliances while serving as an international reporter, but those had little chance of blossoming. Arianne's personality flowed easily. She didn't take herself too seriously and was self-effacing. She checked the beautiful and smart boxes and their mental connection grew daily.

He anticipated the flight from Midway to Reagan National (DCA). Chandler braced himself for another short runway landing - short at least for a 737. If it worked out, they might land on the longer runway. Landing at DCA had added complications of restricted airspace and noise regulations. Veteran travelers understood the stair step landing pattern. Every twenty miles, the aircraft would abruptly drop the next 1,000 foot increment. The maneuver awakened sleepy travelers. Chandler's anticipation produced no sleep, so the landing pattern would be inconsequential.

Arianne texted him before he left Axel's that she'd pick him up, a nice treat. It was always good to be welcomed home, even to an infrequent home. When Chandler exited the secure area, he saw a uniformed driver holding a card saying "Chandler Scott". Miss Maxwell apparently ordered the car service because of a work commitment. The driver offered no other explanation. A disbelieving Chandler texted her and received a very prompt reply.

Yeah sorry meet at my place. Sent driver for U. C U soon.

Something must have come up, but to send a limo driver? He could have easily taken a cab or the Metro and bus combination. *Maybe this is her way to impress me. I'm impressed.* Dutifully, he proceeded to the limo arranged by Miss Maxwell. It was a warm night in D.C. Fortunately he didn't have to worry about a stale smelling shirt from a long flight, though a shower beckoned. A shower for two would be even nicer. He wasn't sure if their relationship had reached the communal shower stage.

No matter how many times he flew into D.C. he remained in awe of the city. D.C. was a living history lesson with monuments, museums, and seats of legislative, executive and judicial power. *What a great country. How many have fought to make and keep it great?* The last few years have made so many question the country's direction. The existence of third political parties provided great evidence of this. Government surveillance in the name of protecting its citizens against kinetic and cyber terror threats offered a topic of hot debate. He wondered about the extent of government reach.

Arianne's small condo in Georgetown featured one bedroom and one bathroom in a boutique building built in the 1960s. One could only detect the building's vintage on the outside. Modernity characterized the inside. He noticed her car on the street in its usual parking spot, after the limo pulled beside it. He quickly tipped the driver and grabbed his bags.

As he walked up the brick-lined path to her building, his heart beat strongly as if he were on Kilimanjaro again. His mouth watered slightly. He followed the red brick road to the main door. The yellow iris flowers in the planter box gave a musky fragrance. He took a deep breath to calm himself. She buzzed him in. It would be but a short walk to her first-floor unit.

She greeted him dressed in a gray silk robe about mid-thigh length, perfect for revealing her gams. Her long auburn hair rested gently on her shoulders. Her face showed no traces of makeup. *Wait a second. How is it that she was at work and now she's looking like she's been lounging around all day?* That thought lingered but a millisecond until he moved towards her to give her a kiss. She smiled and put her hand over his mouth just before the moment of contact. She paused for a moment, allowing him time to gaze into her eyes. He could stare at this woman for hours and get lost in time. The richness of her eye color allured him. She grabbed his right index finger and then slowly the rest of his hand. She still said nothing. His male parts were now at full attention.

The luggage fell near the entryway as he kicked the door closed. She led him to the bedroom, illuminated with many candles and the smell of lavender in the air. Just off to the right he saw a bathtub drawn with rose petals skimming the surface. He wanted to play along in this skit but was unsure of his next move. *OK, I'll take off my shoes.* Good thing they slipped off easily. She released his hand and turned around to face him.

"Ari, what-" She placed her hand once again over his mouth. She still said nothing. *How long has it been since I arrived? Why am I thinking about that?* His shirt came off easily. The pants were more challenging. Arianne helped now. She worked on his boxer briefs, though she had to pull the waistband well away from his body. He was convinced that most of the blood in his body must have been between his legs.

Her fingers traced small circles on his chest. She moved behind him and continued, though now she pressed close to his back, her chin on his shoulder and hands on his chest. He felt skin and not silk. *When did she lose her robe?* She gently nudged him into the bath and he settled in. *She lost her robe.* Her legs were long but not skinny. The shoulders were broad and her mid-section defined with just enough roundness on her hips. He'd fantasized once about licking chocolate syrup from her navel. Chandler's night would only get better.

***

He awoke first, oblivious to time. He knew a gorgeous woman lay on his chest. Her auburn hair, whose smell he loved, grazed his chin. He could get used to this. Not long after, she awoke to his gentle caress of her hair.

They strolled hand in hand to a small cafe for breakfast. During the meal, they couldn't take their eyes off each other. They were giddy, reliving last night in their own minds without verbalizing it.

"Chan do you really have to leave?" She directed wistful eyes at her plate.

"Yeah, Rafa has me going to Spain, I think I mentioned it. Gotta go cover the unrest in Catalonia. I won't be gone that long." He planned this trip during his meeting with Rafael in Buenos Aires.

"Define long."

"Long enough to cover the story," Chandler said ruefully.

"Why does it seem we're always running out of time?" Arianne had said this to him more than once. Their relationship had been but a few short months and since he officially lived in Manhattan and traveled for his job, they were always on the clock.

"Because we are. Life is too short, so let's not waste any more precious time." Chandler stood up, grabbed her hand and led her out of the cafe.

Their walk led them to the Georgetown Visitor Center, marking their entry for a stroll on the C&O Canal Towpath, a historic path along the Potomac. Georgetown began as a tobacco port until its importance changed in the mid-19th century. The 184 mile canal with a terminus in Cumberland, Maryland was built to avoid natural obstructions on the Potomac and for 100 years served as an economic lifeline carrying coal, lumber, and agricultural products.

Today it's a national park covering D.C., Maryland, and

West Virginia. The two talked about obstructions on their romantic journey and hoped to find a path suitable for both. They would face other obstacles as well that had nothing to do with romance. Neither had said it yet, though after a couple of months of dating, they were falling in love. Goodbyes were more difficult. She understood the dedication to his career and suspected that would only increase. She would compete for his time alongside his journalistic adventures, although hoped to win a few battles and eventually the war. Arianne represented everything he ever wanted, and it was almost as if she arrived a little too soon in his life.

CHAPTER SIX
CATALONIA

His work at El Mundo offered many adventures. Economic turmoil provided a steady stream of new material for the network. It didn't make saying good bye any easier. She dropped him off at Reagan National and stared longingly in his direction as he entered the terminal. He focused his attention ahead, knowing that she might be staring. Usually it was him staring at her beautiful blue eyes. If he looked back, it would only distract him, better to focus on his trip.

The shuttle from took off from Runway 1, which meant a very sharp left turn, towards the west, as soon as the wheels came up to avoid restricted airspace over the White House. Another sharp turn to the right followed, towards the east, to realign for the flight to JFK. The economy also lurched from left to right and from up to down, making people wonder where it would head. This trip offered him the opportunity to see economic and political turmoil somewhere else.

Living in two cities, Chandler was never sure where he had clothes. He had a third location to consider now with Arianne's condo. Packing for trips required some degree of advanced planning and good fortune. Since he hadn't been back to New York in a couple of weeks, he hoped that between his shared D.C. apartment and her place, there would be an adequate clothing supply for his late June trip to Spain. Luckily, between the two he had a fresh shirt for the trip from JFK to Barajas in Madrid.

Chandler had little experience in Spain, not like Argentina.

His only visit came in 2011 after the government slashed public spending. Sky high unemployment characterized life for those under twenty-five. Scenes of young men hanging out or involved in active protests proved memorable. As a twenty-something himself, he wondered what he'd do in similar circumstances. Madrid's Metro provided his way around the city. Just seven years earlier, in 2004, terrorists attacked the Atocha station, killing nearly 200 and injuring multiples of that. Known in Spain as 11-M for when the attack occurred on March 11th, Spaniards were caught completely off guard by this Al Qaeda inspired terrorist attack.

His assignment in 2011 covered the anti-austerity movement known as Movimiento 15-M. The El Mundo bureau in Madrid actively tracked social media and suspected mass demonstrations were in the offing. Chandler also followed Twitter updates from Democracia Real YA, the grassroots organization critical of banks and big businesses, to direct his reporting coverage. He loved the energy of the protests and messages of fairness and equality. They offered great experiences for a young reporter. In parallel to these demonstrations, severe recession spurred the Catalonian region to pursue a referendum to secede from Spain. Eight years after his only visit to the country, calls for secession brewed again.

After landing at Barajas, he traveled by taxi via the M-11 to the El Mundo studio and offices. As luck would have it, an accident delayed his travel. The cabbie uttered something in Spanish that Chandler didn't understand. Castilian Spanish differed from the Spanish he heard in New York City or D.C. and other parts of Latin America. Fortunately, his meetings were in English. El Mundo had its Madrid Bureau in the Torre de Cristal tower in the appropriately named Cuatro Torres business area. These four towers, the tallest buildings in the country, were completed between 2007 and 2009 at the height of the skyscraper building boom. The Spanish real estate bust followed shortly thereafter. The buildings were on the Paseo de Castellana, one of the longest and widest avenues in Madrid. El Mundo moved their operation here in 2010 to elevate their profile befitting an up-and-coming network. It also didn't hurt that lease rates were favorable following the bust.

He took the elevator to the 42nd floor of the 52 floor building. In Spain, a building of this height stood out more than Great Lakes Tower in Chicago. These buildings were sources of national pride. The first person to greet him with a firm handshake was Joaquín Olivares, the Madrid bureau chief, and a pro's pro. Like Rafael, he was a high energy guy, serious about work, and not one to kid around. Both the network and journalistic community held him in high regard. Rafael followed a few steps behind and threw his arms around Chandler with a man hug. While they'd spoken on the phone since the Mark Lansing interview blowup, they'd not met in person. Chandler realized nothing in Rafa's demeanor suggested any lingering anger. *Good.*

The three men made themselves comfortable in a conference room with a lunch of tapas and wine. Chandler never got used to having wine for lunch, especially one of a working variety. But when in Rome, or in this case Madrid, he adopted the custom of his host, Joaquín, who unlike many Spaniards, did not go out for the midday meal. Chandler welcomed this lunch since dinner time fell at 9pm. Joaquín, ever the taskmaster, got down to business. He poured wine for his guests and gave each a plate to serve from the assortment of tapas that included fried black pudding, ceviche, empanadas, and bread with olive oil.

Chandler barely took his first bite before Joaquín started. "Chandler this is a big story for us in Spain." Joaquín dipped his bread in oil and took a small portion. "The Catalonian region has always had talk of secession but with everything going on economically not just in Spain but all over Europe, the separatists see this as a great opportunity to revive the feeling."

"I did a little research on my flight over. I understand there will be a secession vote in a couple of weeks?" Chandler asked.

"Yes. That's right. I suggest you focus your attention on the human chain announcement made on Twitter recently. It's called Vía Catalana," Joaquín replied.

"Do you really think Catalonia will secede this time?" Chandler inquired. It's hard for him to imagine a big chunk of any country deciding they would just go off on their own. While he recalled hearing secession talk in the Lone Star State, it didn't compare to Catalonia where there were actual votes.

"I don't know." Joaquín sipped his wine. "This thing has gone both ways. There was a poll recently that said the majority did not want secession."

"*¡Ni en pedo!* Why?" Rafael interrupted with a flake of empanada leaving his mouth. "Why mess up the country? It sounds good, but then they'll actually have to run a country. Come up with money, a government budget. Then they'll see how hard it is!" Rafael, no fan of disorder, came down on the side of national unity. He raised valid discussion.

"*No es tan simple Rafael,*" Joaquín suggested the decision was not quite that simple. "You need to consider the history of the language and the region too."

Catalan emerged as a Romance language named for its origins in Catalonia or an area of northeastern Spain extending into France. The Principality of Andorra, a speck of a country the size of Albuquerque, New Mexico, also claimed the language. The language evolved from Vulgar Latin and if you were fluent in Spanish, you could negotiate your way around the Catalan tongue.

To get a glimpse of the issues in the Catalonian region, one had to visit Barcelona. When you arrived at the Aeroport de Barcelona-El Prat, the directional signs were in Catalan, English and finally Spanish. Much of the street signage in the city was in Catalan only. A visitor likely saw the Catalonian flag more than the Spanish flag. In 1977, the Spanish government granted the region more autonomy, giving rise to strong nationalistic feelings. The million person marches on 9/11/12 and 9/11/13 demonstrated just how strong secession desires truly were, via peaceful or violent means.

"Joaquín, don't be so foolish. There is no need for this secession. Madrid just needs to strike a balance with them. The Catalan region just needs to feel that they're not a milk cow." Rafael seemed presumptuous telling Joaquín how his own country should function, though Catalonians frequently used the milk cow metaphor.

"Rafa, please don't lecture me about my country." Joaquín put down his fork that had speared a piece of ceviche and pointed at Rafael. "We could talk the rest of the day about Argentina. Talk to me about your Peronistas and your military government with their misadventure in the Malvinas taking on the British," Joaquín retorted sternly. That seemed to silence Rafael.

"Chandler, let me suggest what I think you should cover." Joaquín turned away from Rafael and steered the conversation back to the business at hand. "I would appear at the parliament building in Parc de la Cuitadella." Ciutadella Park was named after the citadel constructed there in the 18th century. "I can also suggest which diputat to speak to from the Junts Pel Si coalition." Junts Pel Si or Together for Yes emerged as a pro independence party from a coalition comprising several left-of-center groups. Joaquín suggested he target a specific member of parliament to get a political take on the secession vote. "Cover the human chain, Vía Catalana. If it is as long as the last time, there will be many places where you can interview people." He finished the piece of ceviche.

"That sounds good." Chandler noticed how much he was enjoying the black pudding, which was a spicy piece of sausage. It paired well with his red wine, no doubt a Tempranillo.

"Now Chandler, let me tell you something else," Joaquín added. "Some say that much of the problem comes from changes the Catalonians want in taxing and spending policies. So yes, Rafa, Catalonians do feel like a milk cow."

"If Catalonia broke off, I bet they would have a real hard time outside the EU," Rafael claimed.

"Maybe, but who knows, maybe they receive admission to the EU," Joaquín reasoned.

"*Es posible*," Rafael agreed.

"Let me continue. Chandler something else you should know is that many people living in Catalonia are not Catalonian, they are immigrants. Many of them don't care to secede," Joaquín explained.

Chandler never considered this aspect of the secession movement. He figured secession opposition resided outside of Catalonia when in fact much of it lay within. He couldn't view Catalonia through a narrow filter.

"So Joaquín, really, this issue is more complex than I thought. You have some people who are very passionate about leaving and probably others that are just as passionate about staying. Being an outsider, it seems both sides have valid reasons," Chandler concluded, taking in Rafael's comments too.

"*Sí Chandler.* You may face the same thing in your country. There is so much surveillance there now and there are strong and different opinions about how to handle your economy. I'm sure some in America feel like milk cows too. The trick is figuring out how to satisfy the opinions while keeping the whole together." Joaquín added sage words. It had been over 150 years since the U.S. had to face a similar situation during the Civil War when part of the country seceded.

"How has all this secession talk affected stock trading at the Bolsa? Have there been any terrorism concerns? I interviewed the head of the New York Stock Exchange recently and he focused on cyber terrorism." Chandler wiped his hands from the olive oil as he prepared to note Joaquín's response.

"There was a disruption in trading a few weeks ago. They tried to keep it quiet. The Bolsa closed for a couple of hours, but they never told us why. But when the Bolsa came back online, the IBEX dropped 3% in a few minutes. I can also tell you that investors are getting real nervous about holding Spanish debt. You know the markets don't like uncertainty," Joaquín stated. "Catalonia is making everyone very uncertain."

"That's for sure," Chandler answered.

"I've arranged for you to speak to the head of the Bolsa tomorrow. You can ask him the same questions you asked Mr. Duncan," Joaquín said.

"Thanks. That will be good." Chandler didn't expect this interview, though he felt more comfortable after interviewing Duncan.

The three men worked on Chandler's schedule and

interview questions. After interviewing the head of the Bolsa the following day, he would board the AVE high-speed train to Barcelona. A cameraman from the Madrid bureau would accompany him.

As the sun got lower on this summer day, Chandler wondered when they would finish. The tapas meal was now a distant and pleasant memory. Normally he might give Rafael a signal, but since he was in Madrid, he'd defer to Joaquín. Not long after, as if reading his mind, Rafael signaled the end of the day and announced he'd made dinner reservations for three at El Botín. Joaquín could not go and excused himself to attend a dinner with his wife and her relatives. Chandler would be hungrier than a moth on a nylon sweater by the time they ate. The reservations were for 9:30pm.

El Botín staked its claim as the oldest, continuously operating restaurant in the world. The establishment, on Calle Cuchilleros, featured suckling pig and roasted lamb. When the two arrived, the host directed them to the basement level dining room. The descent to the dining room proved an adventure for the more statuesque Chandler. They negotiated their way down a steep, winding, and narrow stairway with old stone walls. Fortunately, the proprietors fashioned a wooden handrail on the right side for those with a challenged sense of balance. When they finished their meandering descent, they encountered a musty, very narrow, arched dining room with brick and mortar walls. Sound had nowhere to escape in this room, making for a noisy conversation.

"*Buenas noches, caballeros.*" The waiter greeted them in Spanish, Castilian style.

"Good evening." Rafael replied in English, establishing the proper language of communication. El Botín received so many tourists that having bilingual waiters became a necessity.

"Can I interest you in a bottle of wine?" the waiter asked.

Rafael ordered a bottle of Rueda Verdejo that paired well with the suckling pig and asado cordero, or roasted lamb as it's called in the States. The waiter complimented him on his selection.

Rafael dove right into businesses by recapping their earlier meeting. "You can tell I did not hide my feeling about the secession movement."

"Do you really think secession would be such a bad idea for them?" Chandler remained torn, at least conceptually, on secession. He sensed passion for it and wondered if the country could hold together.

"Look. They are going to have to come up with a constitution or some form of government. They then will have to build armed forces or make one up from whatever they get from Spain. And they will need their own central bank."

The central bank supposition surprised Chandler.

"You don't think they could survive without a central bank? When I interviewed Mark Lansing, he sounded almost apologetic about being a central banker." Chandler had not raised this issue since their argument. Maybe the wine would soften things.

"Gentlemen, your wine." The waiter poured it for Rafael, who lightly swirled his glass and took a vigorous whiff of the aromatic wine. After a slurp, he gave the waiter his approval who then promptly served Chandler.

Unfazed by the momentary interruption, Rafael continued. "The central bank will give them policy and help them control their money and matters of foreign exchange. Who are you going to leave that to? A government? Politicians? Shit, they'll fuck it up." He took a large drink, held it in his mouth for a moment and swallowed.

"My friend and mentor, Axel Schultz, I've mentioned him to you, talked about central banks recently and was highly critical of their usefulness."

"Oh, you mean the newsletter writer? I don't want to offend you Chandler, but I have heard he has radical ideas about government."

"Let's just say he wishes for more individual freedom. He is not anti-government. He just wants less of it."

"Be careful about how much wisdom you get from him, Mr. Scott." Chandler sensed that calling Axel a mentor offended Rafael. He felt fortunate to have both men as mentors. "You know something like this could drive Spain into a civil war. They had one of those and there was a lot of outside interference. The Nazis. The Italian fascists. The Soviets. Who knows what will happen if there is another war, especially with Europe the way it is and things in the Middle East. That's the last thing they need here."

The waiter returned to get their order.

"You good with the specialty of the house?" Rafael asked his dinner guest. After Chandler nodded in approval, they ordered the suckling pig and roasted lamb.

"Yeah, you make a good point about the potential for civil war. There are definitely other risks I hadn't thought of," Chandler conceded.

"Consider my country and, of course, your father's. We had all this political instability, default and currency devaluation. What did this get Argentina? Nothing. The country is better off now. We got rid of the Peronistas and have a business-friendly government in place." His remarks struck a chord since

Chandler's paternal grandfather, Armando, was a Peronista himself. Gustavo didn't share his father's politics, and would definitely side with Rafael on this point.

"My father's given me a good primer on the tales of the Argentinian economy," Chandler commented.

"The only thing better now for Argentina would be to sponsor some sort of political and economic union for all of South America like the EU."

"Wow, I didn't know you wanted a larger political entity like that," Chandler remarked. "When you have that much power concentrated in the hands of a few, that can lead to other problems you know. Look at all the resentment in the European Union."

"They don't know how good they have it. I hope we have even larger economic, monetary and political unions. It will be good for the world economy with everything as fucked up as it is." Rafael's comments expressed a strong internationalism, a feeling he recently articulated.

"Man, I don't know about that."

"You have much to learn Chandler."

Chandler would, in fact, learn a lot on his trip to Catalonia. He saw the passion engendered by many sides in a debate about the right course of action for an entire nation. The aftermath of the Catalonian secession vote, and how people related to one another, might be more important than the vote itself. He wondered if his own country would ever be at such a crossroads.

CHAPTER SEVEN
FAMILY

Chandler's hectic schedule last month slowed down to allow a visit to his mother, regrettably, in the middle of an August heat wave. His trip to Spain took a little longer than expected. There were times he had to stop being a journalist so he wouldn't become part of the story.

Twice, he and his cameraman escaped to the safety of their hotel due to riot conditions in Barcelona. The human chain he saw could no doubt have made the Guinness Book of World Records. It appeared a secession vote was in the cards for Catalonia. The world would not doubt be watching that development.

He took a mid-afternoon American Airlines flight from Newark to DFW. Flying out of Newark's Liberty offered more convenience, especially on domestic flights. A quick hop from Penn Station on a NJ Transit train to AirTrain made his journey to Liberty efficient. It took longer than a cab, but was much less expensive and had a component of adventure.

His mom greeted him outside DFW's Terminal A, where Chandler skillfully timed his exit to meet her as she departed the cell phone lot. No sense in spending any more time baking in the Texas heat.

He threw his bag into her back seat. "Great timing, Mom."

"Oh Chan. It's great to see you!" She leaned over for a quick hug. "You look a little thin. Are you eating enough?" Renee's observation while she grabbed his arm made him wonder if his lack of working out deflated his arms.

"I think so. You know how much I eat out."

"Not today. You're having a home-cooked meal."

Could it be chili con carne?

Renee lived in the Richardson home she bought near the 2000 stock market top when she felt good about her dot-com and LSS stocks. Though it's been years since he lived there, about fifteen to be exact, his room remained unchanged.

His mom prepared one of his favorite Tex-Mex dishes, chili con carne. Chandler always liked it spicy. Nothing compared after the beating his palate took at Muay Thai with Arianne. It had been difficult for him to find good Tex-Mex food in Manhattan or D.C. so this trip broke the drought.

The smell wafted through the house and hit Chandler when he walked in. "Are we eating soon?"

"Why don't you go to your room first and unpack. Freshen up a bit and we'll eat in about thirty minutes."

He followed orders and headed to the room of his adolescent years. The 2001 Dallas Cowboys team picture still hung above his queen-size bed. America's Team wasn't good that year, finishing in last place in the NFC East. He remembered attending a game at Texas Stadium, a thrilling victory over the 49ers. Renee's boyfriend at the time worked in PR for the team and this was his Christmas gift to the Scott's, a football game the day before New Year's Eve.

His chest of drawers still had his old clothes, though none would fit now. With a quick change of clothes and a splash of water on his face, he declared himself fit for eating and scurried back into the kitchen.

"Could you set the table?" She commanded from the kitchen.

He followed those orders too. *When are we eating?*

This reminded him of a Thanksgiving dinner when he was thirteen. They'd just moved into the home and Chandler's grandparents were visiting from Columbia. He purposely didn't eat a big breakfast so, he'd have more room for turkey and sweet potato pie. When it was 1pm and Renee's boyfriend had not arrived, Chandler pleaded with Renee for stuffing. Renee admonished him for asking. An hour later and two hours after they were to dine, her boyfriend showed. He couldn't recall the excuse and this boyfriend eventually got tossed into the dustbin of history.

There would be no such delay this time. All guests were present and accounted for. The gastronomic moment had arrived.

Chandler stuck his spoon squarely in the middle of the bowl and took a healthy scoop. "Mom, this is delicious. Man, have I missed this!"

"My boy comes home for Momma's cooking. It's good to have you around." She beamed with delight.

"If I would've come next month, we could've gone to the state fair. I used to have so much fun on all the rides, eating all the great food," he said as he took a swig of iced tea.

"Yeah remember that time you got sick cuz you ate so much?" Renee, who watched her son eat, had to bring up that unfortunate moment.

"Don't remind me. I haven't thrown up since. It was so traumatic. Seriously." Chandler lost track of all the corn dogs and cotton candy he ate that afternoon.

"I also seem to recall you liking the Red River Showdown. It's a shame you never really had an interest in playing football. I remember how strange I felt telling your coach that a red-blooded Texas boy had no interest in the state's pastime. You had a lot of natural speed."

"Nah, I'd rather watch Alfonso Chancellor throw TD passes," Chandler commented, hoisting his arm next to his ear.

"I hear great things about him down here. There's talk that he might be Geringer's VP on the ticket next year. What have you heard?" Renee finally took her first bite of dinner.

"Nothing yet. You know the candidates said they won't start campaigning until after the New Year. Could you pass the cornbread?" Chandler pointed to the cornbread squares.

"We have to do something about this economy. LSS is struggling. Our overseas sales took a big hit. My boss keeps saying the dollar is too high. No one wants to buy our stuff."

"Currency wars," Chandler said matter-of-factly. "One country wants to make their money cheaper so they can export more. These countries have been fighting the dollar for a while now to make it more expensive to buy American-made things. Could I get some more ice tea?" Chandler raised his nearly empty glass.

Renee grabbed it and walked towards the kitchen. "Well, that figures. What do you think about the stock market? I'm pretty invested right now. My advisor says to stick with it. It's been nerve-wracking what with 2008 and then the crash in 2016. And my advisor keeps saying to stay patient. You know I don't have a pension. My 401(k) is all over the place. I want to retire at some point, but right now I can't see it. I know not to be dumb enough to think about having a big social security check." She returned to the dining table and handed him the refilled glass. "Here you go." She sat in her chair and bowed her head. "Oh, I'm sorry, I know you don't want to hear all this."

"It's OK. Really." Chandler took a sip. "Other people are saying the same thing. It's tough out there investing. My portfolio, glad I don't look at it very often. It's like one of those rides at the fair - up and down with plenty of twists and turns."

Renee had no one to talk to about these things, at least no one she trusted. She remained saddled with guilt about moving to Texas and away from her family. "I think almost every day about moving you away from my family in Columbia. I cried every night for the first 6 months after you were born. A young mother questioning her every decision. Dropping out of school. Walking away. So embarrassed. I didn't talk about your father. I didn't know how to explain that to you. Heck, your father didn't even know he was a father. That was unfair to him too - not that he would've married me. But I really didn't want to marry him either." She got teary-eyed recalling the experience.

"Mom. Seriously, it's fine." He reached out and rubbed her arm. "Everything turned out fine. Me and Gustavo, we're good. We get along great. It's not like father and son. It's more like he's my much older brother. That's not a bad relationship for an only child," Chandler offered consolingly.

"I know you get tired of hearing this but I am so proud of what you became. You really did this on your own. I didn't help much."

"You did a lot more than you think," Chandler reassured her.

"Thank you, Chan. That means so much to hear you say that." Renee broke a smile.

They finished their meal and per house rules, Chandler helped Renee with the dishes. After dinner, they migrated to the family room. They sat next to each other on the sofa, the TV on at a low volume.

Renee, though she shied away from the topic earlier, remained concerned about her financial well-being. "Tell me. What do you think is gonna happen to the markets and the economy? You're closer to this thing living in New York and D.C."

"I have no idea. I don't think anyone does. I interviewed someone a couple of months ago who said he didn't know what he was doing and this is someone who creates the impression that he's a wizard. Talk about scary." Chandler reflected on his conversation with former Fed President Lansing.

"So what's the answer? Is government going to fix the economy again?" Texans would be divided on this topic.

"Could be. I guess we'll see what the Presidential candidates have in store for us. I get the sense that the 2020 elections will be like nothing we've ever seen in our history. I don't know why. It's just a feeling."

Chandler didn't make a habit of spewing prophecy. This sentiment also emanated from his mentor Axel. After spending time in Spain, he got a great sense of what happened when a country gets pulled hard in several directions, to the point of a breakup. Spending time with his mom made him view things as more than just a journalist.

***

Whenever he visited Renee, he reflected on making an effort to spend more time with her. She made many sacrifices, even if she thought she did a bad job of raising him. Before leaving for the airport, Chandler verified his departure time. The American Airlines app indicated his flight was on time. During the electronic check-in process, however, the app quit abruptly. He ruled out the phone's operating system since his other apps worked fine. A phone reboot didn't do the trick either. *No big deal, I can just check in at the airport kiosk.* He could do that after his mom whisked him the twenty miles to the airport.

"Chan, have a safe flight. I'm so glad you visited your dear old mother," Renee added theatrics to the departure. This was never a good time for her, returning to an empty house.

"Thanks, Mom. Talk to you soon." He reached over and gave her a kiss on the cheek. After grabbing his luggage from her trunk, he rushed into Terminal A - no sense spending more time in the August heat, a heat more concentrated with vehicular traffic. By chance, one kiosk had no travelers.

He entered his record locator and poof; the kiosk froze. He noticed others faced a similar predicament. Agents at the ticket counter were no help either, they were having the same problem. One agent called tech support and they blamed it on a server malfunction. Ugh. Chandler didn't need this. He had to be in New York City for an important meeting the next day. He'd been through something like this before, and assumed the delay would be brief. After about thirty minutes, a large line spilled outside of Terminal A.

He texted Arianne to let her know of his circumstance since they planned a video chat after he got back to his Manhattan apartment. New update. An agent popped out from behind a door at the counter.

"Folks, at the present time we have no update on when the system will be back online." Questions about manual check-in were rebuffed.

The flight board showed departing flights delayed or canceled. After twenty minutes of texting Arianne, they got another update.

"I'm sorry, y'all. I just spoke to my supervisor and she said they don't have any information. They're still working on it."

He popped into a cafe outside the security perimeter. Larger restaurants weren't a choice since they were all within the secure area, which he couldn't get to since he had no boarding pass! Surely by the time he finished a snack, there should be an update. Moments after finishing his bag of chips he got up and glanced towards the kiosks and noticed that nothing was happening.

The delay offered him a good opportunity to catch up with his father, Gustavo.

"Gustavo, it's Chandler." Chandler never called him "Dad" or "Father".

"*Ah Chandler, todo bien?*"

"Yeah, it's good. How's the semester shaping up?" The PA system came alive.

Attention all passengers. American Airlines continues to work on the system malfunction. We are sorry for the inconvenience. Please check the flight board to see if your flight will be delayed or canceled.

"Where are you? An airport?"

"Yeah DFW, my home for probably the next few hours." Chandler paced.

"Oh, sorry to hear that. Over here, you know, things have gotten more restless on campus. We've had so many student protests and leadership changes that parents aren't sending their kids here like they used to. Our enrollment is way down. I'm not sure how much longer I'm going to stay here. If it weren't for my research paper about the Fed, it would be a grim semester."

"Yeah, I saw confrontations with the National Guard on TV. That place has changed a lot since I left. Oh, and speaking of the Fed, I interviewed someone who used to be at the Fed and I was shocked by what he told me. I guess I better not give you a spoiler here. That show should air sometime next week."

"All right, I won't ask. I'll just point during the Centinela show and tell everyone that's my son," Gustavo said proudly. Chandler appreciated the compliment.

"Nice, Gustavo, thank you. This sucks here. American Airlines systems are down. Maybe Omni hacked these guys."

Omni was the infamous hacker group responsible for cyber-attacks on businesses and governments. Frustratingly, the authorities could not figure out who they were or where they came from. This proved more amazing given how much the NSA and other agencies sampled and collected all manner of digital data.

Five years earlier, in 2014, the NSA completed a massive data center in Utah warehousing user activity from Internet searches to health records. To the chagrin of civil liberty supporters, the NSA justified the center based on top secret interpretations of the Patriot Act and the Fourth Amendment. They stored encrypted data with the hope their computing power might permit future decryption. The center's motto read, *"If you have nothing to hide, you have nothing to fear."*

Omni could be a benevolent group. They could come to the rescue of organizations held hostage by cyber crooks placing ransomware on their devices. Ransomware was malware preventing users from accessing their system. They also knocked down web sites of Middle Eastern terror organizations. Omni operated by its own set of rules and had truly become an enigma, friend to some and foe to others.

Gustavo laughed. "Yeah, Omni. Those are some nasty people. Did you see your mother? How is she?"

"She fed me well. She's worried about stuff just like everyone else."

"She is right to worry. The market is up and down, I sometimes think I should just put my money in a bunch of T-bills and forget about it, but frankly I worry about our government too."

"Like default? Like Argentina?" Chandler recalled his grandfather, Armando's, stories about that difficult time.

"Probably not like Argentina but maybe they change the terms, like instead of ninety days it is one year or one year becomes five years, you know pushing it back. Maybe they freeze trading on government securities. There are many things they can do if it gets bad enough."

"Never thought it would go to those extremes."

"Some of my friends in the banking industry are saying they can't push as many home loans over to government. The GOP and IAP sponsored that legislation a couple of years ago after the 2017 banking crisis. Those new regulations put a tighter noose around banks."

"It impressed me how President Jefferson calmed everything down so quickly. He'd been in office just a few months and showed great leadership working across the political aisle," Chandler said. His network covered bank runs in a few states.

"I'm afraid the next time will be more difficult. Then people will ask for more rules and for government to step in and do something. And they'll get exactly that and probably a whole lot more authority than they wanted." Gustavo sounded like Axel.

"Gustavo, that sounds as welcome as an outhouse breeze."

Gustavo laughed hard. "As many places as you have been around the world and you can't get rid of Texas!"

"I guess not. You can take the boy out of Texas, but you can't take Texas out of the boy!"

American Airlines announces all departing flights are now ready for check in at the kiosks. Please see the ticket agent if your flight's been canceled.

"Hey, Gustavo. I guess I can finally check in." A mass of people descended on the kiosks. Chandler surveyed the flight board, verifying his departure.

"What else about your mom?"

Chandler walked towards the queue. "She's lonely. I wish she'd married that professor. You know the guy from SMU? It would make her life easier if she had someone. I just cannot be around for her. My schedule can get so crazy. I'm not trying to make you feel guilty, but this is how it is for her. I appreciate you asking. And now my love life has taken a new twist."

"*La bella, Ariana.*" Gustavo had only seen pictures of her.

"She is beautiful, but it's Arianne." Chandler moved one step closer to the kiosk.

"Ariana in Spanish. Is it serious?"

"It might be. She's smart and we connect really well. It's not easy though with us living in two different cities."

"Hopefully, I will meet her. Go get on your flight. *Hasta luego, Chan.*"

"Yeah, I hope this kiosk gives me my boarding pass. *Hasta luego, Gustavo.*"

Chandler would finally get to seat 3A about four hours later than expected. Fortunately, his flight wasn't canceled. When he landed in Newark, he opened his El Mundo app. His network reported that the American Airlines reservation system failed as a result of a cyber-attack on their servers in Dallas. No group claimed responsibility.

Part II

The Crisis

CHAPTER EIGHT
THE CRASH

Chandler had three weeks of vacation each year, though he seldom took his full allotment. Many times he extended business trips by appending a couple of days for personal time. In September, he made the conscious decision to take a few days off, otherwise he'd end up losing vacation at year's end. His plan was to hang and enjoy Manhattan with Arianne. Tonight, he'd see her after her meeting at the UN. During the day, he hoped to don his virtual reality headset to take a tour of St. Peter's Basilica.

Chandler lived near the corner of West Street and Battery Place. The typical Manhattan apartment contained one bedroom, maybe 800 square feet and a price tag to match. In just a couple of minutes he could be in Battery Park or as the locals called it, The Battery. The park got its name after the artillery batteries positioned there in the city's early years. The location served as a great place for Chandler to reflect, particularly when he passed the Sphere, the large metallic sculpture damaged in the 9/11 attacks. Somehow the sculpture, located between the two towers, survived in the rubble. Ironically, the sculptor, Fritz Koenig, conceived the Sphere as a symbol of world peace. Whenever he passed the Sphere, he drew strength from it.

For months he reminded himself he needed to save more. He gave little thought to his own investments. His conversation with Renee last month brought money to the forefront again. He received guidance from Axel, though his financial advisor was often at odds with his mentor's advice. The job at El Mundo had elements of glamor, although pay was not one of those. He traveled for work in style, but could not do so on salary alone. Small CDs, a brokerage account that his financial advisor controlled, and his checking account comprised his financial universe. Student debt, while manageable, lingered.

He had the expense of living in two cities, though sharing his apartment in D.C. helped. He owned no real estate or a car. He didn't need one with addresses in Manhattan and D.C. and living out of a suitcase. For a thirty-something, he felt like he'd done an adequate job of preparing for the future, "adequate" being the operative word. Axel cautioned him about adequate preparation and saving for a rainy day.

His personal digital assistant, the cylindrically shaped Venus, would let him sleep in this morning. Last night, he told Venus to stay silent. With his extensive travel schedule, sometimes when he returned to New York and woke up in the morning, he forgot where he was or what time it might be. He'd programmed Venus to announce the time and location. Venus had a built-in GPS. When he finally woke up, he recognized his surroundings though the exact time eluded him. There was no clock in the room and his phone was in the kitchen.

"Venus, what time is it?" He yelled from the bedroom.

"The time is 11am. Would you like an important news brief, Mr. Scott?" Venus answered from the kitchen/living area.

The only thing on his mind was baseball. "No. What was the score in the Mets game last night?" The Mets had a late game in San Diego and he retired well before its end.

"The Mets won 4 to 3. Would you like a box score?" Venus anticipated his next request.

"No. Play a selection from Wynton Marsalis, random," he

commanded.

The sweet sounds of jazz filled his apartment. Venus emitted surprisingly good sound given her small tweeter and woofer. Among his friends, Chandler owned one of the few CD players. Most of his contemporaries streamed their music, played their lists from their phone to small speakers, or engaged personal digital assistants. He enjoyed the purity of CD sound and often lectured his friends on the poor sampling rates of their MP3-derived music. Though not the quintessential audiophile, Chandler Scott cared about his music. His laziness this morning caused him to outsource music playing to Venus.

As he made his breakfast of toast, eggs, and juice, he noticed orange juice stocks were low.

"Venus, add orange juice to shopping list."

"Frozen or fresh squeezed?" Venus understood his voice over the jazz.

"Fresh."

These were rare moments for him and today, a vacation day, he enjoyed his breakfast with music and solitude. When he stuffed dishes in the dishwasher, the clock, or Venus, struck high noon. His personal email awaited. Venus performed many tasks including interaction with his laptop.

"Turn on laptop and run email."

The cell phone rang and Hendrix's Voodoo Child mixed with the ambient sound of Marsalis' Cherokee. He noticed several unread text messages. Renee beckoned. "Pause music," Chandler commanded. He answered on his cell's speaker phone.

"Hi Mom."

"Chan, oh my God."

"Mom. What!"

"Chan seriously. Oh, my sweet Jesus." Renee seldom invoked deity, so he surmised something was wrong, but what?

"Do you have the TV on? Have you been online?" Renee's questions were rapid and demanding.

"I just started my laptop and was about to open email when you called. And, no, I don't have the TV on. It's been good just to unplug."

"Son, today is not one of those days," Renee said conclusively.

"Mom, you're as jumpy as spit on a hot skillet." Renee's nervousness made him jittery. "Let me see what's going on."

"Venus, close music, open web page, El Mundo." He'd never seen El Mundo's home page with a headline in as large a font as this.

"Chan, what am I gonna do?"

He listened to his mom while trying to process what he read. He read it again just to make sure. *This headline can't be right, can it?* Maybe El Mundo got hacked with this fake headline. He turned to another news website.

"Venus, open new tab, open web page, WNBC." Same headline as El Mundo's. It did not appear to be a hack, unless they attacked several news sites.

"Chan, are you listening to me? Stop talking to that damn machine!" Renee said desperately.

"Show Inbox." His inbox was flooded. His senders forwarded stories to him. He looked to his phone. Various alerts confirmed what he saw everywhere else. It must have been true. During the time he scanned his email and texts, he ignored his mother. The distraction proved overwhelming.

"Chandler!!!" Renee's voice boomed so loud she became unintelligible through the phone's speakers.

"What the mothershit happened here?" Chandler finally acknowledged the headline. There was no mistake now. The El Mundo headline said it all.

STOCK MARKETS IN FREE FALL!

"Mom, there's a big ole yellow jacket in the outhouse."

Renee felt momentary relief at her son's acknowledgment. "I can't get a hold of my broker!" Renee's voice conveyed sheer panic. "He told me it wasn't gonna be like 08 or 16. My retirement, my 401(k). I'm screwed."

"Let me turn on the TV. Maybe there is more to this story." Chandler's attempt to assuage her panic fell short of the mark. "Venus, TV on. Tune El Mundo." El Mundo's Wall Street correspondent reported the situation.

"This is Derek Thomas reporting from Wall Street. September 10th of the year 2019 will go down in the history books! The Dow and S&P are down 30%. The Nasdaq is down 35%. Trading was halted on all exchanges. We have just received word that President Jefferson will have a press conference later tonight discussing the day's historic events."

Behind Derek Thomas were several traders on the floor of the New York Stock Exchange who look like they'd run a marathon in work clothes - they were whipped.

"I can't live through another time like 2000. My LSS stock dropped 80% that time. Remember when you were here and I told you my fears. I don't know what to do." Renee cried, echoing the sentiments of many.

He did not know what to say. The look on his mom's face

in 2000 when she canceled their summer vacation flashed in his brain. For many nights, he heard his mom crying and praying that she had enough to pay the mortgage on their new house. When the 2008 crash occurred, he was in college so he didn't witness her emotions, but he heard her silent cries on the phone. During the 2016 crash, her advisor told her to remain invested and to consider buying the dips. She had little strength left.

"Mom, let me see if I can get into my brokerage site."

"Venus, open new tab, open web page, Lindbergh and Sons."

The screen showed the URL in the browser address bar and a blank screen. "I can't get in. I'll try to call my broker and see what he says. Let me let you go for now. Maybe we can chat later. Try to stay as calm as possible." He said that knowing she'd be nothing but a bundle of nerves. This was a bad day for Chandler, but for someone closer to retirement, this was a disaster.

"I'll try to stay calm. But this is hard."

"I know. Bye, Mom."

"OK, bye."

Calls to his broker were unsuccessful. The Lindbergh and Sons website remained down. The rest of the afternoon proceeded like a blur. His phone displayed a barrage of alerts and texts. Markets shut down early as mandated by rules enacted after 2016. Back on TV, Derek Thomas appeared visibly worn from the reporting. Derek watched his own nest egg vanish while he reported it. He probably aged ten years in the two hours of air time. There were more reports of broker web sites crashing as investors scrambled to place sell orders. Many brokerages were no longer equipped to handle voice orders, leaving investors more panicked.

The bond market proved no better as corporate bonds of all stripes fell in heavy trading. Futures markets experienced record volume. Even the Treasury markets were no longer reliable safe havens. Mutual funds sold heavily to raise cash for redemptions. Market makers no longer wanted to participate. Everyone was in a selling mood and heading for the narrowing exit doors.

Banks reported high amounts of withdrawals while some branches had to shut down when they ran out of cash notes. Police in bulletproof vests stood by disabled ATMs. Retail outlets also saw a run on cash as shoppers used their debit cards to get cash back on purchases. The public demanded liquidity in any form imaginable. With social media, news spread quickly while some individuals dispensed advice on how to deal with the coming apocalypse. This market crash produced more anxiety than the one in 2016.

Arianne was in town attending a meeting at the United Nations at the request of the U.S. Ambassador. She arrived at Chandler's late in the afternoon, well aware of what transpired in the markets.

"Chan. What a day, huh?" Arianne proved the master of understatement as she kissed him. "They interrupted our meeting several times with updates and finally the ambassador said we should just stop for the day. When this happened in 2016, everybody seemed calmer."

"I know. My mom's a wreck. I felt so bad for her." He related the conversation with Renee.

"I'm so sorry, Chan. It had to be stressful, I know. Are you hungry? I brought some Thai food from that place around the block." Arianne felt largely insulated from the gyrations of the stock market. Her father's wealth management firm handled her money. She paid little attention to her investments. As far as she knew, that firm managed her savings conservatively.

"Yeah, I've only had breakfast. I guess I could eat a little," he added.

"Mild spice on the food too. Just how you like it." Arianne did not want to relive the experience at Muay Thai. She wanted to be kissed again tonight.

"Funny, Ari. Very funny. After this crazy day … Let me get out some plates." Chandler set the dishes on the kitchen counter, retrieved the day-old bottle of wine, a Pinot Grigio, and poured two glasses.

During their meal, they managed a conversation that did not involve the stock market. Arianne had peripheral awareness of the markets through conversations with Chandler. She couldn't tell you the balance in her account or how it was invested. She never reviewed her monthly statements. She liked it that way. Out of sight, out of mind, and on a day like today, that was comforting. Arianne wasn't unusual. Many Americans adopted that approach. They seldom reviewed their balances and during previous stock market drops, ignored their statements for fear of creating greater worry. Those fortunate enough to have a pension, whether public or private, seldom gave consideration to how these gyrations affected their retirement.

After dinner, they moved to the living room to watch the news. Voodoo Child alerted him of an incoming call.

"Chandler. I know you have been watching everything so there is no need to rehash it," Rafael said in his usual direct way. "I want you in DC soon to cover this. We need to see how government is going to handle this. This could be good for your show."

"Sounds good. I agree today's events could be weaved into

the other stuff I've been working on. Poor Derek. He had to be in the middle of all that today." Chandler commented on the aging of Derek Thomas on live TV.

"Yeah. I can only imagine what it must have been like watching this develop right in front of him," Rafael added.

"Is there anything else you want me to do?" Chandler wanted to get back to the TV and Arianne's company.

"No, that's it. Just plan on being in DC soon. I think the president's address tonight won't be anything more than to calm everyone. Have a good evening."

"See you later."

"Was that Rafael?" Arianne asked.

"Yeah, he wants me in D.C. soon. I guess I won't have a problem with that since my girlfriend lives there."

"I'm sure your girlfriend will appreciate it. I think she will appreciate your attention tonight too." Just after she uttered that sentence, El Mundo's anchor announced the president's address to the nation from the Oval Office. As noted earlier in the day, President Jefferson would address the wild day in financial markets. He looked very composed, confident and assured. During stressful times as these, he looked very presidential, a trait Americans desperately sought.

"My fellow Americans. Today will no doubt be the beginning of a crucible for the nation. We've had other challenging days in 1987 and in 2016. In 2008, we had a prolonged crisis lasting months. I know this about the fiber of our country. This will not break us. We will emerge stronger and we will learn from today. America is more than just a country. It is an idea, an idea that will not diminish regardless of the challenges posed.

"In order to see us through this crisis, I am ordering the stock markets closed for the remainder of the week. I have asked the Fed for a commitment to provide as much liquidity as needed to financial institutions. Moreover, you have my solemn promise that this administration will do everything in its power, and I mean everything, to see us through this time. Very soon I hope to provide you with more steps on how the Jefferson Presidency will address the crisis. Thank you. Good night and may God bless the United States of America."

"It's just about how Rafa said it would go. Brief and to the point," Chandler affirmed.

"Like he said, we've been through this before so everyone should just remain calm," Arianne said reassuringly.

"I was too young when the markets crashed in 2000. In 2008, I was too distracted with college coeds." For a moment he forgot he spoke to someone who might not appreciate that comment. "And in 2016, it felt different from this time. This one seems more serious. People are going to want some answers and soon."

"I have an answer for you. I'll be waiting for you in the bedroom. Give me a few minutes to take a quick bath." She eased herself off the couch and walked to the bedroom. His eyes tracked her all the way. It was amazing how this woman, amid financial chaos, distracted Chandler enough to make him forget how much money he may have lost.

"Venus turn off all lights and TV." Those were Chandler's last words to Venus. He had other words for Arianne.

***

He enjoyed a sound night of sleep. The intimacy with Arianne no doubt helped. He always slept more comfortably with her nearby. Being on assignment provided excitement and rewards until it was time to go to bed. He missed her terribly now. He slid out of bed carefully to not wake her and headed to the kitchen.

"Venus, turn on kitchen lights, open web page El Mundo." Those were his first words of the day. He hoped he had loaded the coffee maker before issuing the next command. "Brew coffee regular setting." Thankfully, the coffee started.

El Mundo's website opened sharing more bad news.

CHINESE AND JAPANESE STOCKS CRASH
EUROPEAN BOURSES SHOWING HEAVY LOSSES

He heard Voodoo Child. Axel called.

"Ax, I'm actually kinda surprised you didn't call last night." He remembered the excitement in Axel's voice after the 2016 crash.

"Honestly, I didn't have more to add. You know I've been warning about this in my letter for months. How are you doing?"

"OK. I was told to be in D.C. soon. The president's going to make another address in the next couple of days."

"I bet he won't mention the hacking that occurred." Axel knew how to drop a bomb. That skill came across in his newsletter too.

"What!" Chandler yelled. "Hacking?" He dropped a coffee cup on the counter. *Crap, I hope I didn't wake Ari.*

"One of my contacts said Russian and Chinese hackers exacerbated the market's collapse by submitting fake sell orders into trading systems. They didn't start the crash, but they made it worse."

"You sure you want to talk about this on the phone?" Chandler asked quizzically, fearing heightened phone surveillance.

"I don't care. I'm sure *they* will figure out the Russians and Chinese had their hands in it." Chandler presumed "they" were the authorities.

"I bet I can guess where you may have gotten the tip," Chandler asserted.

"Now that is something I'm definitely not talking about on the phone. But your instinct is probably right."

Chandler's instinct led him to Omni, the same group suspected of delaying his departure from DFW last month. No one knew how the reviled hacker group started, at least as an official organization. Their calling card was a series of three concentric circles on hacked sites. They first gained notoriety in 2013 for a series of Denial of Service attacks on oil company web sites. Repeated oil spills in the Gulf probably had something to do with that.

Then they attacked Asian governments involved in a free trade agreement in 2015. After a series of terror incidents in France in 2015, they knocked out several militant Islamic web sites. They saw themselves as modern day, digital vigilantes. Others saw them as cyber bullies or thugs.

The U.S. and Israeli governments blamed them for a cyber-attack on the electrical grid in Tel Aviv during a cold spell in 2016. This galvanized public opinion against the group. An Islamic militant group ultimately claimed responsibility. Omni got their revenge by hacking servers, exposing embarrassing information about elected officials and celebrities who called them out over the Israeli incident. They won over public opinion in 2017 when they revealed that banks were sharing private account information with the government under the guise of fighting terrorism. In response, politicians from the TP and IAP used Omni's revelations to propose legislation attempting to combat governmental reach. Axel mentioned his contact's name once. Chandler thought it was something like "Phish". Maybe it was "Mish" or "Gish".

"I think I can connect dots," Chandler assured.

"Whatever you do, don't start talking about hacking around your network. My guess is that you know who is going to be blamed and that won't be the truth. I need to keep them friendly with me." Axel faithfully protected his sources, since he cited their information in his letter. Axel's response led Chandler to conclude that Omni would receive blame but they were, in fact, the informant passing along intelligence about the Russians and Chinese.

"I understand," Chandler replied. A call came in from Rafael. He let it go to voice mail.

"Let me do more digging on this. If my instincts are correct, there's a lot more to this. I'll talk to you later, Chandler."

"Sounds good."

"Coffee ready," Venus announced.

He heard stirring in the bedroom. At least the coffee was ready. Time had gotten away from him with his web browsing and Axel's call. He reminded himself about the voice mail from Rafa. Arianne entered the kitchen.

"Good morning, sleepyhead. Sorry if I woke you," Chandler said apologetically while hugging her. He found it remarkable how good she looked first thing in the morning, messy hair and all. He liked it that way.

"It was time for me to get up, anyway. I need to check my

messages to see if the ambassador still wants to have the meeting today."

"Coffee's ready. Sorry I haven't fixed anything." Truthfully, Chandler lacked breakfast foods, especially orange juice. It was time to have Venus send the shopping list to his phone.

"That's OK. I'm not hungry. Why don't you turn on the TV?" Normally, Chandler would already have it on.

"TV on. Tune El Mundo," Chandler commanded. He poured two cups of coffee.

"Let's go to Senior White House correspondent Michelle Reyes. Michelle? Yes, Tom. El Mundo has obtained information that the president will hold a press conference tomorrow at the White House addressing the market's crash. No advance details about his address have been released. In other developments, El Mundo expects the Secretary of Treasury and the head of the Federal Reserve to address bank runs and ATM closures occurring in some large cities. Back to you."

"Huh, I wonder if that's happening here?" Arianne asked.

"Good question. Here, take your coffee. Why don't you check your messages and I'll head outside to check things out? I could use some air, anyway." Chandler gulped his coffee, leaving half in the cup. His tongue let him know he disregarded the temperature.

He walked a couple of blocks east from his building and encountered a bank run. The line wrapped around the block from the branch. Some people pitched tents. NYPD tried to maintain order. The unmistakable pitch of a drone rang overhead. Bank patrons were actively involved in shouting matches with New York's finest who were simply trying to keep streets clear. Yelling directed at the branch fell on deaf ears since the branch appeared empty inside. Private security stood guard. Chandler filmed the happenings on his phone. No doubt the overhead drone was filming him and everyone else.

Something in a nearby coffee house caught his eye. The proprietor fashioned an outward facing cardboard sign that said "cash only." Nothing in the news reported businesses only accepting cash, so he put on his journalist hat to find out. The lack of customers allowed him to go to the front of the line.

"Why are you only accepting cash?" Chandler inquired.

"Oh, I guess you haven't heard. The credit card networks are down. Nobody knows why. We had to turn away most of our customers who didn't have $6 in their pocket for a latte," the clerk explained, looking as if he'd already had a rough day.

Axel warned him many times about the importance of cash in times of financial panic. He did not mean just cash in the bank but physical notes, bucks, dough, moola or whatever you wanted to call it. Feeling obligated to buy something and given that he only had half a cup earlier, Chandler placed an order.

"Let me have a small chai latte."

"Just a moment, sir, I have to check out this other gentleman," the clerk quickly replied.

Chandler hadn't noticed the middle-aged man with coarse salt and pepper hair, a closely cropped beard, and cinnamon skin standing about five feet away flanking the other side of the register. He moved behind this man and studied him while the bearded one pulled money directly out of his pocket. He appeared to have no wallet. The man dressed in a black shirt, khaki pants, athletic shoes and displayed a calm, serene demeanor. *How could someone be this calm with the chaos just outside the door? Maybe he just woke up from a multi-day slumber?*

"We live in troubled times it seems," the stranger said as he turned towards Chandler while simultaneously paying the clerk.

"Oh, ahh, yeah. I ahh, um, think you're right, sir." *Of course he's right. He's just being understated. Maybe he's British.* Chandler beat himself up for not thinking of something more intelligent to say to Mr. Calm.

"I get the strong sense that this country is going to face major events in its history soon," the stranger added prophetically while moving away from the register.

"You say that with some conviction." Chandler didn't stammer this time, taking out his credit card to pay for the latte.

"Sir, remember please no credit cards," the clerk reminded, pointing at Chandler's plastic.

"Yes, of course. Sorry." Chandler pulled out a five dollar note. He looked foolish yet again in front of this stranger. He should not have cared. Hoping to redeem himself, he said, "Keep the change."

Wow, a whole thirteen cents. That's impressive. The clerk showed his disdain for the token gesture by rolling his eyes.

"I say that with some conviction because I believe it to be true. *Hasta la próxima, amigo.*" With those Spanish words, the stranger bid farewell and walked out. Chandler stood there with his mouth agape.

"Is there anything else, sir," the clerk asked, hands on hips.

Chandler was dumbfounded. "Ahh, no. Not really. No, thank you. Thank you." He stood there a few more seconds staring at the exiting stranger before deciding to pursue him to engage him in further conversation. He broke for the door and headed outside. He turned his head right, left and then right again as if he was crossing a street, but to his surprise he didn't see the stranger. *Weird.* The stranger should have been in sight. It's not as if the man sprinted out. Chandler headed back inside.

"Excuse me, sir. Do you know who the person was who paid just before me? You know the man with the salt and pepper hair and the close beard?" Chandler said excitedly to the clerk.

"No, I'm afraid I don't. I've worked here for seven years and I've never seen the guy. Sorry." *Mr. Big Tipper.*

The stranger had a calm aura similar to the Dalai Lama. His Holiness once told him,

"Our prime purpose in this life is to help others. And if you can't help them, at least don't hurt them."

He took the words to heart, dedicating his professional life to helping others by uncovering truth through reporting and providing insight. In the digital age of web and social media, being a journalist got more complicated. While there were many citizen journalists providing editorial material for dissemination through various channels, investigative journalism required a different level of immersion. Chandler prided himself on providing his viewers a substantial level of immersion.

This stranger's aura didn't have the profundity of the Dalai Lama's, though he emitted similar feelings of calm and peace. He wore no religious vestments. His origin appeared Middle Eastern, or maybe Latin American. Chandler thought about the encounter for a few more seconds and decided he'd dedicated enough time to the distraction. Back to his apartment he headed where he found Arianne engrossed in TV viewing.

"Hey, I've had the TV on though I've struggled with your

assistant. I don't think she likes my voice. No matter what network I put on, the news is the same." She seemed energized by the TV's reports. "They said that financial asset prices are collapsing since there are going to be a bunch of, I think, margin calls, when the markets reopen. Oh, and also, some banks are calling in credit lines."

"Really? Holy shit. You should see the lines outside the bank a couple of blocks away. Oh, and I went to this coffee shop where they were only accepting cash. And there was this stranger that-" Chandler seemed equally energized when Jimi Hendrix interrupted him. He forgot to call Rafael and he would forget to tell Arianne about the stranger.

"Rafa, I'm sorry. I was-"

"Chandler. Listen to me. I need for you to be in D.C. tomorrow for the president's presser. Michelle will be there too, but I think there is good material there for your show."

"OK, but I wanted-"

"And another thing, make sure you leave today! Who knows what the hell will happen with flights or trains. Have a good trip." Dead silence. Rafael wasted no air in the exchange. Chandler thought he'd be mad for not returning his call, but Rafael had his game day attitude, all business.

"Ari, honey. What's going on with your meeting?"

"Sorry I meant to tell you, there is no meeting. The ambassador's been recalled to Washington for a conference with the Secretary of State."

"OK, I have to leave for D.C. like ASAP. You ready to head back?" Chandler asked rhetorically.

"You have to ask? I can be ready in an hour."

"I'm thinking Acela," he suggested.

"Yep, let's do the train. Get online and see when the next

departure is."

"Venus, find next Acela departure to Washington, D.C." Venus had no problem understanding this command from her master. She found two business class seats leaving Penn Station in a couple of hours. Tomorrow would be an important day in the presidency of Benjamin Jefferson.

***

What we know as the White House Briefing Room was a product of the expanding press corps during the Nixon administration. Originally, the room served as a therapeutic swimming pool for FDR. The room received its name from former Reagan Press Secretary James Brady, paralyzed during the attempt on the president's life. There were 49 chairs in the room arranged in a 7x7 pattern with your privilege assigned by the White House Correspondents. Fortunately, Michelle Reyes, recent recipient of an award, figuratively had her name on a chair. Her seat for this show would be a good one, unlike Chandler who had no room privileges. A phalanx of camera operators surrounded the seated press corps. Though his advisers suggested another White House location for this address, the president wanted to be out front, hiding nothing.

President Benjamin Jefferson entered the room from a door on the left, followed by Treasury Secretary Sheldon Kiefer and Fed Chair Anna Walker. Only the president stepped up to the podium, the one with the Presidential Seal. The other two stood off to his right. The president paused to allow residual noise of waning conversations and camera clicking to die down.

"My fellow Americans. Two nights ago I reminded you how resilient our nation has been to the financial setbacks of 1987, 2008, and 2016. Let's not forget how our nation rallied around our flag after the heinous attacks of 9/11. Ladies and gentlemen, what happened two days ago will test our resolve but it will not break us. We have the proper institutions to deal with this or any other financial crisis. Secretary Kiefer and Fed Chair Walker have assured me that we have the tools in place to initiate corrective action. I have been in contact with key leaders of the world's most important economies and I can assure you the spirit of cooperation is as good as any time in history. We have a common enemy so we will work together to address this matter.

"I would like to announce the creation of a special commission of leaders from the fields of government, finance, and economics who will make recommendations to my administration 30 days after convening. These recommendations will then be adopted by the United States and potentially other nations. It is anticipated that their recommendations can begin to be implemented shortly after their announcement. I would ask everyone to be patient during this thirty-day period. Let us never forget what makes this nation exceptional. Our resourcefulness and ingenuity will get us through this. I will now field a couple of questions."

"Yes, in the front here." He pointed to a reporter in the first row on the far right.

"Mr. President. Will markets reopen on Monday as planned?"

"Yes, Fed Chair Walker has assured me that there is plenty of liquidity in the system and more will be made available as required. I've also spoken to the heads of the various exchanges and they plan on an orderly open on Monday. "

"All the way in the back. No, the lady dressed in blue. Yes, Michelle." Jefferson pointed to Michelle Reyes. Maybe he recognized her from the dinner.

"Mr. President is the country more vulnerable to terror attacks now that attention is diverted to financial matters?"

"We reject that notion. Our military and internal security agencies have not been affected by the events of the last couple of days. They will continue to protect our nation. Our intelligence agencies will monitor terrorist chatter and take appropriate action. Our posture remains strong."

"OK, one more question. Yes, Tom." The president pointed to Tom Moore of the Washington Post.

"Mr. President, can you tell us who will be on the commission? Is it only domestic leaders or will there be some international component? The International Relations Council and Global Settlement Bank have been quite vocal in recent months about the markets and banking. Are they involved?"

"At this time, not all members of the commission have been notified so I will refrain from any further commentary. Thank you all for attending."

"Mr. President. Mr. President!!! Should Americans feel secure about the markets reopening Monday in light of suspected hacking activity?" Tom Moore tried to sneak in a followup question and was summarily ignored. The president took solemn steps towards the door on the left, followed by Kiefer and Walker. "Mr. President!" The cacophony of reporters drowned out anything intelligible. After the president's exit, reporters typed on their phones, chatted with each other, or headed for the exit.

Chandler, who watched the address on a monitor outside the Briefing Room, met with Michelle Reyes to compare notes.

He said nothing about the hacking suspicion, or more accurately Axel's suspicion. The hacking story must have had some legs if someone from the Washington Post brought it up. Chandler mulled how to integrate this press conference with some of his recent work.

***

If the International Relations Council was to have representation on the president's special commission, the occupant of a mansion in San Ramon, California, would have great interest. It was an elegant mansion, all 12,000 square feet of it with Las Trampas Regional Park providing a superb backdrop. Visitors traversed a long winding driveway from another long winding access road. The place had a secluded feel. Above the front door hung a green and white coat of arms. Green meant hope and white signified peace. Oak leaves on the coat represented antiquity and strength. The wolf demonstrated the rewards of perseverance. Judging from the large paved area in front of the mansion, the place hosted many parties. The owner wanted you to understand that he yearned for hope and peace, though he'd have no compunction unleashing the wolf to achieve those goals.

Emmet Seamus Callaghan, a self-made billionaire, owned this property. His middle name, never to be used, was a term of endearment reserved for his mom's scolding. The wealthy man served the role of philanthropist and power broker in the International Relations Council or IRC. His physical appearance was unremarkable. What was once a substantial mane of dark, reddish hair had turned mostly white. The creases on his forehead revealed his age. His teeth were mildly stained from years of smoking and coffee drinking. His fingers were thick and his hands perpetually chapped.

Born in the late 1950s, he spent his early life in Hell's Kitchen, the son of an Irish mobster by the name of Padraig or Paddy. Paddy served in the Westies gang and eventually became one of Mickey Patton's right-hand men. Emmet's mom, Siobhan, shielded him from gang activity, but Paddy's influence proved too great. As a young lad, Emmet helped his parents run the tavern. The typical Irish establishment concealed a parlor behind the bathroom where bookies took bets for illegal lotteries called numbers games. There were also popular card games in that parlor. Hell's Kitchen, in Manhattan's west side, proved to be a profitable area for the Westies. The cops stayed out of it except for those who were on the take. The powerful gang roamed the area in the 1960s and 1970s, providing young Emmet lessons in the art of thuggery. More than once, Emmet saw a rival gang member, often from the Italian Mafia, lying dead on the street.

Paddy met a similar fate in a retaliation by the Italians. One of their lieutenants, Francesco, had his throat slit one night after leaving a club by someone waiting in his car. The Italians presumed the Westies were to blame, but it was Francesco's brother-in-law who caught him with a whore. A family matter erupted into unnecessary gang violence.

Emmet found his father's body in the alley behind the tavern. The image of Paddy's corpse stayed with him and fueled a rage that continued to drive him. Siobhan moved Emmet far away from New York to escape his father's legacy and to get a fresh start in life. They settled in San Leandro, California, just south of Oakland. With very few Irish-Americans in the area, the Callaghans could live in the shadows.

He attended community college and received a certification in aviation maintenance. Later he completed a business degree at San Jose State. He quickly rose through the ranks at Pacific Airlines and became its CEO in 1999. All the while Emmet used leverage and partnerships to build a real estate portfolio in the Silicon Valley area with property in Cupertino, Sunnyvale, and Santa Clara. He invested heavily in dot-coms getting in early investments with a variety of companies. Fortunately, he had the foresight to unload most of his shares early in 2000. By the time we entered the new millennium, Emmet Callaghan, formerly of Hell's Kitchen, joined the billionaire's club.

When 9/11 occurred, it affected Pacific Airlines like all other carriers. Whatever order existed in the world unraveled. He felt a personal affront since the terrorists attacked Manhattan, his birthplace. He reviled the terrorists and felt anger towards his own government for not protecting the country from this attack. After 2001, Emmet threw his considerable wealth to various organizations and political parties that, in his estimation, could restore order. He retired from Pacific Airlines in 2014. He spent the five years since his retirement as an activist investor and running the IRC. His stated goals were to restore world order through strong international organizations. If government couldn't do this on their own, then he would do everything in his power to make it happen.

The Callaghans hosted a gathering that coincided with the president's news conference announcing the formation of a special commission. Among the invitees were members of the IRC including Nial McPherson, the Scottish-born former UK Prime Minister from Glasgow, Malcolm Holloway, the former Secretary of the Treasury and now a director at the Global Settlement Bank, and Francine Schwartz, the former Fed president from San Francisco. Emmet assembled a powerful array of leaders at the IRC. Emmet had no loyalty to a political party - just the one who met his goals. When the press asked him whom he voted for, he always said he voted for the best candidate. The best candidate was the one sympathetic to the views of the IRC. That meant greater international ties and more powerful federal institutions.

The public face of IRC promoted international trade, cooperation, and student exchange programs. They had a strong lobbying arm in D.C. They didn't allow reporters in their meetings, which was where they developed monetary and economic policy subsequently channeled through their lobbying arm. But even these policies were well-publicized via their position papers on their website. Their members didn't hide with well-known individuals from business, banking, government, and academia comprising their core.

Emmet had clear goals for the IRC. He abhorred the disorder and chaos he saw as a youth. No institution represented authority other than lawless gangs. Police stayed away and those that came wanted a piece of the action. Economic and financial disorder present in the world created that perfect vacuum for the IRC to fill.

Emmet coaxed Nial and Fran out to the expansive patio after the president's news conference.

"Emmet, that commission's going to be a great opportunity for us," Nial said while twirling his drink comfortably in his hands.

"That's a fact. We need to be all over it. I've been waiting a long time for something like this. Don't get me wrong, our lobbyists have done great things in Washington. We've made good inroads. I just have a feeling this will allow us to get even deeper," Emmet declared passionately.

"Any ideas on who we should push?" Fran asked. Fran had a distinguished career at the Fed where she served as president of the San Francisco bank and in leadership positions at various academic institutions.

"For sure we have to have Jean-Claude and Holloway," Emmet replied. Jean-Claude Bienfait served as a managing member of the Global Settlement Bank or GSB and was widely considered a foremost expert on international banking and trade. After leaving his post as Treasury Secretary, Malcolm Holloway went to work at the GSB as Chairman of the Financial Stability Institute.

Established at the end of World War II, the GSB helped central banks in their pursuit of monetary and financial stability and international cooperation. In their eyes, stability and cooperation were preconditions for sustained economic growth and prosperity. Central banks and world leaders turned to them during financial crisis for guidance and tactical responses. They were never in the news and few knew who they were or what they did. They were easily the most powerful international organization that no one had ever heard of.

"It's not going to be that easy for us though, Emmet. The commission requires some sort of Congressional approval. And it's not as if the IAP or TP boys are gonna let something like that just fly through," Fran challenged.

"I have it on good authority that the president will do this mostly on his own. We should be good. Frankly, these maggots from the third parties are starting to wear on me. One group sounds like a bunch of libertarians and the other harps about inequality and the Bible." Clearly, Emmet had no affinity for the IAP or TP. They were inimical to his plans.

"What would the old Hell's Kitchen gang do about that?"

Nial joked.

"Tread very lightly there, Nial. Very lightly." Emmet never discussed the Westies. He seldom acknowledged that life and took offense when someone brought it up.

***

Chandler stole more time with his girlfriend since Rafael wanted him in D.C. for a few days. They were in Arianne's living room watching TV. Chandler tuned the El Mundo evening news broadcast. He did this the old-fashioned way, with a remote controller. Venus stayed in Manhattan. Arianne made the mistake of grabbing the controller and changing it to the Nats game and was quickly rebuffed.

"Ari! Come on." *Doesn't she understand that it's a man's job to hold the remote?*

"Don't you want to watch something more fun? Besides, the season's almost over and I won't get to see them until next spring." The Nats were fading in September and appeared unlikely to make the playoffs.

He grabbed the remote and quickly changed it back. On the glass table in front of them sat a partially filled glass, a bottle of Riesling, and a tray of assorted cheeses and sausage. Neither felt like fixing dinner, so they fashioned some finger food. Arianne, sporting a Washington Nationals tee shirt and bottom-hugging red shorts, draped herself across his lap. In his left hand Chandler held the Riesling while he placed the right affectionately on her leg.

"Honey, do you think you'll be here next week?" She asked longingly.

"Don't know. Guess it depends on what's gonna happen with this commission thing. If it were up to me-"

123

We have breaking news. The White House has issued a press release indicating that all members of the president's special commission have been named. The president has given the commission 30 days from today to make recommendations and sweeping reforms that will bring stability to the markets and the economy. In the spirit of international cooperation, the president has included a contingent including Jean-Claude Bienfait, currently a managing member at the GSB, Malcolm Holloway, the former Treasury Secretary and now at the GSB, and well-known leaders such as Will Duncan of the New York Stock Exchange, and Francine Schwartz, former Fed president from San Francisco. The twelve member commission is expected to arrive in Washington in the next couple of days for a series of meetings with the administration.

"Does this mean you'll stay around for a while?" She turned her head to look up at him, hopeful he'd answer in the affirmative.

"Could be. It's weird that the press release didn't say that these guys were part of the IRC. I don't even know that much about the GSB. I should really read up on that organization. I wonder why they didn't mention the IRC? It's not like El Mundo to leave out details like that. Maybe Ax knows something about the GSB." Chandler spewed a stream of thoughts.

"You and Ax. Where would you be without him?" Arianne said sarcastically as she rolled over on his lap, her head now facing up.

"Hey, Ax is one smart dude," he said with a frown on his brow looking down at her.

"I was just teasing you, silly," she replied. "You get so serious sometimes. I know you're close with him. He's good for you. Relax. I'm sure Ax will help you understand more about the GSB and everything else. Quit being so intense. If you want to be intense, why don't you come get intensely naked with me?"

With that, she rose from his lap and sauntered into the bedroom. Chandler tracked her movements like a lion tracked his prey. He hesitated for a moment and realized there were no pressing matters left to resolve. Even if there were, they could wait until tomorrow.

"Venus turn off-" Chandler stopped himself and turned off the TV and flipped all the light switches. *Ari really needs an assistant.*

CHAPTER NINE
WORKING IN THE SHADOWS

The presidential commission held court in Washington the first two weeks of October; nothing leaked out of their meetings. Even the location of their meeting was unknown. They were on a three-day break coinciding with an IRC meeting at the Presidio in San Francisco. Or maybe the elected spokesperson of the commission, Malcolm Holloway, structured it that way.

The Presidio had an interesting history extending back to the time of the Spanish in 1776. The Mexicans later established a stronghold in the 1820s before the U.S. Army settled it in 1846. The name Presidio derives from the Latin praesidium indicating a garrison or fortress. Appropriately, Emmet pushed for the IRC headquarters to be located here. For him, the fortress represented authority, strength, and perseverance, exactly the symbolism he looked for when he chose the site. Getting the IRC headquarters built in the Presidio proved another matter. Emmet used his considerable influence to get the National Park Service and the Presidio Trust to allow construction of a low rise building on the location of the former Crissy Field, site of the first non-stop flight to Hawaii in 1927. The building's proposed location upset park preservationists. The Trust had a great incentive to gain rent from another tenant. Considerable volunteering by Pacific Airlines employees and generous donations to the Golden Gate National Parks Conservancy paved the way for the LEED-certified building's completion in 2014.

Emmet's office on the building's top floor overlooked the

Farallone Marine Sanctuary. The adjacent conference room served as home for IRC board strategy sessions during the presidential commission's break. IRC support staff, comprising twenty and thirty-year-olds, congregated on lower floors. Many of them would have preferred a virtual reality meeting instead, but Emmet would have no part of that. Industry titans, former government officials, and GSB members would surround the large wood oval table in the conference room with Emmet and Nial on each end.

Jose Torres ran Petromex, a large vertically integrated Mexican oil company. Leopoldo Sabatini manned the helm of Luz, a media conglomerate. Li Zhang was the CEO of Intercommerce, an international shipping company well connected to the Communist Party. Vasily Mozgov, a former Russian Foreign Minister, headed TransGaz, one of the largest oil and gas companies in the world. Sheik Fawwaz Hakim was the scion of a family controlling oil and construction companies based out of Dubai. Byung Park served as Chief Economic Adviser at GSB. Agnes Bomutu was the former UN Ambassador from South Africa. Sanjay Prakesh formerly served as board member of the Reserve Bank of India. And, of course, attending the meeting were Fran Schwartz and Jean-Claude Bienfait. Malcolm remained in Washington, where he met with key members of Congress.

Nial served as board president the last two years, yet Emmet drove the agenda. Emmet liked it that way, operating behind the scenes. Nial was charming, well-spoken and highly regarded internationally, after brokering a peace agreement with rebels fighting the government in Egypt. This agreement positioned Nial as a contender for the Nobel Peace Prize. He was also known for his impromptu sense of humor. He thanked everyone for attending and commended the appointment of Jean-Claude, Holloway, and Fran to the commission while singling out Holloway for being instrumental in furthering the IRC's policies and for being elected spokesperson.

"This is a unique time for us to influence policy amid economic uncertainty. The President of the United States has given us a mandate, and we have a unique set of assets to carry out his wishes," Nial beamed with the accompanying applause. "Thank you, thank you. Jean-Claude, can you give us an update on the commission's progress?" Nial took his seat.

"*Merci, monsieur McPherson.* As the board knows, the GSB has been working for some time on a framework for new economic guidelines that we've gotten into the hands of central bank officials. That has had limited success. Central bankers are not the most welcome people at cocktail parties these days." The group, save for Fran Schwartz, the former Fed president, shared a brief laugh.

"*Da,* those assholes screwed me when they stopped supporting the Swiss Franc. I lost a few million that day," Vasily snarled and pounded the table. He referred to the Swiss National Bank's removal of the Euro peg in 2015. Investors who thought Swiss central bankers had their back found out quickly what it felt like to get stabbed in the back.

Jean-Claude folded his hands and interlaced his fingers. "*Monsieur Mozgov,* I was referring to all the failed attempts by central banks to fix economies with government bond purchases and interest rate manipulation. We need to push our policies more directly through government." He countered in a polite, but commanding voice. Besides, he felt no sorrow for the Russian billionaire, especially when the GSB warned that such action by the Swiss was imminent.

"Yes, we called it QE for quantitative easing," Fran added, leaning in towards the table.

The Fed started buying mortgage-backed securities and Treasuries in 2008 to stabilize the economy. The European Central Bank and the Bank of Japan executed similar strategies. Then they tried negative interest rates. All central bankers were under fire given destabilized financial markets and weak economies.

"Correct. The GSB advised central banks to stop doing this, but politics wins sometimes." Jean-Claude pivoted towards Fran, giving her a wry smile. "The moment is right for us and now we have a vehicle to express this with the American Presidential commission. Some members of the commission were frankly surprised by their selection. This was good for us since we already knew what to do and how to do it. Holloway has been a brilliant tactician, injecting our ideas into the heads of commission members. We are supremely confident our platform will be fully recommended to President Jefferson. Mr. Park will hand each of you a printed report now that outlines the structure of the proposed monetary and financial union that will be presented to the American president." Jean-Claude poured his sparkling water into a glass while Byung Park distributed the report as he walked around the oval table.

"Please take the rest of the day to read the recommendations thoroughly and come prepared with questions tomorrow. We are due back in Washington in a couple of days," Jean-Claude added.

Emmet, quiet until now, stood up on his end of the conference table. "I for one would like to thank you, Mr. Bienfait and you Mr. Park, for your outstanding work. Aye, this will fix our banjaxed system." Emmet offered congratulatory words for both men, but puzzled the entire board with his Irish slang.

"The key to making this happen is to get the Americans on board first. That should lead to European adoption, which hopefully will then bring the Russians and Chinese on board. Once this occurs, we will have other major economies support this, I'm certain," Jean-Claude concluded.

Nial popped up like a jack-in-the-box. "If nobody has questions, it's time for a drink!"

***

The Oval Office was thirty-six feet on its longest axis and twenty-nine feet on its shortest one. It was little changed since the FDR administration except for the furnishings. The floor was an alternating light and dark wood chevron pattern whose crests intersected in the middle of the room. Each president designed an oval-shaped carpet to rest on this floor. The president's desk sat at the end of the oval with the U.S. and presidential flags flanking it and the Presidential coat of arms on the carpet immediately in front. Flanking the lower edge of the coat of arms were two sofas facing each other.

President Jefferson requested large, deep colored leather sofas since it reminded him of home. Smaller staff members felt like children sitting in them due to their extended depth. End tables were next to the sofas with two smaller wooden leather chairs completing the horseshoe in front of the presidential desk. If you were to look straight up, you'd see a ceiling medallion of the Seal of the United States. Portraits of former presidents lined the walls. Jefferson also had mementos of his state of California on display, with several pictures of Yosemite National Park and scenes from the Pacific Coast Highway. Behind the large, ornate desk sat an equally ornate table with picture frames of the president's family.

The president called commission spokesperson, Malcolm Holloway, to provide an update for his team. The president invited Trent Carter, National Security Advisor, Sheldon Kiefer, Secretary of the Treasury, Will Duncan, Head of the NYSE and Anna Walker, Chair of the Federal Reserve Bank. Duncan occupied a unique place in this meeting as both a member of the commission and a member of President Jefferson's circle of trust. Holloway and the president sat side by side in leather chairs and the rest were on the sofas. Holloway distributed a packet of information to each person, walking around the perimeter of the seating area and delivering it over their shoulders.

The president began the meeting looking relaxed with his legs crossed. "Thank you all for being here today. Just as a housekeeping detail, I would like each of you to turn your phones off. I really need your attention." They all complied.

"I know you are familiar with Mr. Holloway's work and his record of government service as Secretary of the Treasury. Mr. Holloway is the spokesperson of the commission I appointed to study the financial crisis. They are to come up with a set of recommendations and policies. This is a world-class team with the best and brightest from business, academia, and government. Mr. Holloway, I have been looking forward to this meeting since the time I addressed the American public. Please knock our socks off!"

Holloway leaned forward in his chair, his forearms resting on his thighs. "Thank you, Mr. President. And let me say it is an honor to serve on the commission and serve our country. I did not take this appointment lightly."

"Malcolm, with the job you did as Secretary before me, I

know this will be good," Kiefer said assuredly. Malcolm Holloway was often the smartest person in the room. He was a policy wonk and could easily slide into a distinguished professorship at the finest university in the country.

"Thanks, Sheldon. You've done well yourself." This was a perfunctory response from Holloway who did not hold Secretary Kiefer in the highest regard.

"OK, guys, enough glad-handing," the president added impatiently while snapping his fingers.

"Yes, sir. One of the first things we need to do is create stability, particularly in the banking system. We know people are spooked right now and cash has been leaving the system." Holloway straightened up from his earlier position and motioned toward Anna Walker. "Anna, thanks to you and the Fed for keeping liquidity flowing. The commission suggests a limit on daily cash withdrawals. We don't have the exact figure yet, but we need a limit."

"Won't that create more panic? We all remember Greece five years ago," Carter suggested, who was thinking in terms of security.

"Trent, we are not Greece, please!" The president uncrossed his legs, leaned forward and shook his head, offended with the suggestion.

"Mr. Carter, I understand the concern but it will be up to the administration to create patriotic themes around this. You know, like it is good for the country and so on." Holloway hoped that future interruptions would be more reasoned.

"Appealing to patriotism always seems to work. Continue Mr. Holloway," the president directed.

"We also know, and this should greatly interest to you Mr. Carter, that we have a bunch of these SuperNote, $100 bills in circulation. We think that is causing panic. I don't think there is any question that these fake notes are coming from North Korea. The trouble we are having is they're appearing all around the world, and especially in the Middle East. The commission has come up with new counterfeiting measures that we are prepared to present to the Bureau of Printing and Engraving. These measures should stop the SuperNotes cold. But Mr. President, we need to encourage the return of existing $100 bills to make this work. Hopefully, as we implement our entire plan, the whole SuperNote issue will go away."

The president placed his right hand under his chin. "I see. Some new technique?" He asked about the counterfeiting measure and overlooked Holloway's comment about the SuperNote issue going away with implementing the entire plan. No one else inquired, either. There was more to the plan than anyone realized.

"Yes sir, it will blow your mind and is easy for the naked eye to see."

"Excellent," the president responded with a thumbs up. He was happy this guy spoke for the commission.

"This next proposal will no doubt create controversy and some burdens on businesses but-"

"Mr. Holloway I think we are way past the point about being concerned about controversy, would you not agree Mr. President?" Kiefer addressed Holloway while looking at the president.

"Sheldon, Mr. Secretary, I do have a reelection campaign soon, so let's be sensitive about that, please. I presume you like your job?" said the president tilting his head down while looking up. Kiefer definitely liked this job much better than when he served as the Director of the Office of Management and Budget.

"To keep an eye, so to speak, on transactions we need to limit how cash is used. For example, we should set an upper limit on amounts used to say, buy furniture, clothes, etc. You know, just regular purchases." Holloway anticipated the next question.

"What would that limit be?" the president asked.

"The commission thought $500 would work. But sir, there is one more thing. The commission also suggests placing a reporting requirement on any cash payment over $200. That reporting would be made to the Department of the Treasury."

"What the hell! Mr. President, I gotta say something here." Kiefer blew his stack and a little saliva.

"Let him finish, Sheldon! Continue Mr. Holloway," the president asserted.

"Well, I basically was finished with that point. This was the part about being controversial and burdensome. Businesses aren't going to like it and sorry Secretary Kiefer but it places more burden on Treasury." Holloway felt no sorrow at all and, in fact, he didn't mind annoying Kiefer. Kiefer rubbed him the wrong way.

"But the reality is we're trying to get people away from cash?" the president asked rhetorically.

"Spot on sir. The quicker we can get people out of cash, the more we can see and the more we can control," Holloway replied.

"Madam Chairman. Any thoughts?" The president directed his attention to Fed Chair, Anna Walker.

Ana Walker was a petite, slightly built woman who spoke softly. "He's right, sir. The Fed can have more control over monetary policy if we can track economic activity through the banking system. Cash makes tracking impossible."

"Mr. Holloway you have all this cash restriction and then you'll end up pushing more people into DigiNote." National Security Advisor Carter had heard enough of DigiNote. DigiNote was an open source software project that quickly evolved into a widely used digital currency, after the failure of other similar currencies. Since it operated outside the traditional banking system, it proved useful in the underground economy and with terror organizations. Businesses and consumers accepted the digital payment scheme and it gained popularity in legitimate enterprise. Though it represented a tiny fraction of all payments, the authorities were concerned about its growing use.

"Yes, there is a danger these provisions will move the economy underground with the likes of DigiNote. I trust Mr. Carter has his own plans, however, for dealing with DigiNote. If not, we were studying this phenomenon at the GSB and can provide you some thoughts." Holloway answered Carter while addressing the entire group.

"We're working on the DigiNote issue but we would more than welcome your research," the National Security Advisor said in a relieved tone.

"Will do. The next thing we should do Mr. President is to stabilize the debt market. Debt prices, as you all know, have suffered, making our interest costs higher. With the national debt as it is, we can't afford higher rates. For this we propose that Treasury debt with a term of ten years and longer cannot be traded and needs to be held until maturity. Those holding the debt will still get their money back and the interest. The goal is to eliminate speculation in longer term debt."

"It's always the speculators, Mr. President," Will Duncan said, shaking his head. In his mind, speculators were often synonymous with hackers.

"Mr. Duncan, this goes beyond speculation. Now the Fed can continue to do what it needs to with this debt," Holloway answered.

"Whew, you had me worried there for a moment," Madam Chairman Walker added.

"Worry not, Madam Chairman, the Fed will continue to buy debt as needed. Continuing, we need to control the flow of gold in and out of the country. We suggest the same for other countries." Holloway continued.

"Why do we care about gold? It's not even money and it doesn't back our money. Who cares about this?" Duncan turned into a chatterbox.

"Mr. Duncan, that is a long discussion for another day. Maybe over a couple of beers. Gold has and will always be important but we can't have the public believe it is otherwise it would be difficult to issue money. In fact, Mr. President, we should encourage that people pay debt owed to any level of government in the form of gold but make gold valued at say, three times more than its market price or some other fixed price. So if the market price were $1,000 per ounce we can value it at $3,000 or more, but only for payment of government debt. This would help get gold, at least some, out of circulation." Holloway understood the sensitivity of a gold discussion.

"Should we ban the public buying gold?" the president asked.

Holloway shook his head forcefully. "No, sir, that would just create hoarding and other things we don't want. We'll encourage people to get rid of it voluntarily by using it to pay their taxes and other government fees. If someone questions why government would do this, I suggest Mr. Carter that you develop some national security story for it with patriotic themes, of course."

"Yes, we'll think of something," Carter indicated with an approving nod.

"Lady and gentlemen, I have saved the best for last. Maybe some of you won't think it's the best. We recommend a cabinet level department for management of these policies and others that you will find in your packets. This department should have broad powers, at the approval of the president, of course, to implement new policies for stabilization of the economy and financial markets. Our recommended name is the Financial Stability Board."

"Hang on a second! What will this position do that can't be done by Treasury?" Kiefer, the most vocal challenger, was about to get his lunch handed to him.

"Mr. Secretary, our concern is that you will have elements within Treasury that may not be on board with these new policies. This could lead to delays and sir, we can't afford delays." By "elements" he meant the Secretary himself.

"But what about the Fed? What about our independence in dictating monetary policy or our open market operations?" Now, Anna Walker feared her own disintermediation.

"I understand your concern, Madam Chairman. Our intent is to let the Fed continue to be the Fed with policy coming from this new board. So, in essence, the Fed would take direction from the board. I suspect some in the Fed hierarchy will want to join this board," Holloway clarified.

"Mr. President, I don't know if I like this." Walker looked at Kiefer for approval while directing this concern to the president.

"What about financial markets? What do you have planned

for them?" Now Duncan added to the challenges.

"Please review the packet, Will. Then ask me further questions. We do have new guidelines for the exchanges. Again, our intent is to provide policy and monitor its effects. The execution would remain with your respective organizations."

"This is all well and good Mr. Holloway but how the hell do you think we are gonna get this through Congress and get someone appointed czar or secretary or whatever title?" the president asked pragmatically, leaning back in his chair and once again crossing his legs, clasping his hands behind his neck.

"Glad you asked, Mr. President. The way this whole thing materializes is through an executive order, sir."

"Oh Christ, are you out of your mind?" Kiefer blurted this unaware of the short history lesson to follow.

"Mr. Secretary, there is precedent for this. Let's all recall the New Deal and everything FDR set up with all those agencies. The size of this department, however, does not depend on hiring millions of unemployed people or creating a large organization," Holloway explained.

"How are we going to fund this thing?" the president asked.

Holloway reached for a folder next to his chair and selected one of the tabbed pages. "Sir, we don't anticipate a big initial funding. Your packets will show our year one through five estimates." He turned the report towards his audience, showing a series of bars across a five-year chart. "As you can see, it is not high. Once we start, our charter will be on setting policy but letting other departments execute. Over time, as Congress sees our success, they will be amenable to providing more funding where the board takes on more execution responsibilities. If they decide they don't want to expand our funding, we can continue to have other departments execute. In time, more will be required of the other departments and Congress can fund those extra needs there." Holloway appeared to gain the president's approval with that explanation.

"Fine, but what about naming the secretary position itself? Getting someone appointed and approved will be a nightmare." The president had fought these battles before and would rather avoid them. He had an election to consider.

"Yes, it will sir, but once again I urge you to invoke a separate Executive Order to name this person," Holloway suggested.

"And who would you have me name?" The president thought he knew the answer but wanted to flush it out for everyone.

"Mr. President, that is your discretion. The commission urges the appointment of someone who understands economic stabilization and has experience in the matter."

"I think everyone from the FDR administration is dead." Everyone laughed politely at the president's comment except for Kiefer, still trying to recover from Holloway's response to his challenges.

"The packet I gave each of you includes a list of worthy candidates," Holloway said.

"I see you on this list, Mr. Holloway," Walker observed.

"Yes, Madam Chairman."

The president leaned forward in his chair from his formerly relaxed posture. "We can review the list. I need to share this information with my chief of staff and vice president. Does anyone have questions for Mr. Holloway?" His tone suggested he was ready to finish. No one said anything, as if they understood his question was perfunctory.

"Mr. Holloway, I should have asked if you were done."

"I am, sir. If anyone has questions, my email and cell phone number are on the last page. Please call me any time and I mean any time."

"Fine job, Mr. Holloway." The president shook his hand firmly as both men stood, the others remained seated. "I can see why the commission appointed you their spokesperson. This is a well-conceived plan. It won't be easy and I'm sure my Attorney General is gonna have some heartburn but hey, we have to start somewhere. The American people want solutions from me and frankly this is the best I have seen. Thank you once again."

Holloway acknowledged the audience with a slight nod. He took confident steps out of the Oval Office.

"Before anyone says anything, I know some or maybe all of you don't like what you heard. Mr. Holloway understands money and markets, which if I need to remind everyone are the center of our problems. When I speak to my counterparts in Europe, Russia, China and elsewhere, his name always seems to come up. The Global Settlement Bank, where he works, has been advising nations about their problems too. Since he is head of the Stability Institute or something like that, he's had to engage with world leaders now for the last what, three years. Let's everyone read our packets and we can meet in a couple of days." President Jefferson had confidence in Holloway, a person providing clarity in a universe otherwise devoid of solutions.

"I don't really have a problem with what he said, sir. I think you will run into problems here at home since even though he's an American, people will see him as part of an international organization," Carter opined.

"And he has strong ties to the International Relations

Council." It was difficult to tell whether Duncan thought this was good or bad.

"Yes, but think about everything the IRC has done to promote international trade, and exchange groups. And they contributed generously to my 2016 campaign and hopefully the 2020 one as well," the president countered.

"Let's not forget though how influential an American is on the IRC, Emmet Callaghan. Everyone knows he's at the controls," Walker added.

"OK, everyone stop thinking about this in strictly American terms. We have to think outside that box." The president traced a box outline with his index fingers. "It's 2019 people. We're twenty years into the millennium. When this is all said and done, this will be an international solution. And frankly, I don't care what Congress says and I'll say that to members of my own party. They haven't given me any damn solutions and can't get anything done. We gotta think ahead."

"Agreed. We are partnering with many foreign countries now on matters of national security. Terrorism is taking advantage of the world's economic weakness. We need to sell this to not just Congress but the American people as a matter of national security, which, in fact, it is." Carter stood in agreement with his president.

"Let's get back together in a couple of days. My chief will notify you of our meeting time." He dismissed everyone.

***

Two days after meeting in the Oval Office, the president's team achieved consensus on Holloway's plan. This plan was going forward since Jefferson wanted it. This set up the president for his presser announcing proposals in the Briefing Room. He entered the room alone this time. After he walked to the podium, he surveyed the crowd of reporters and took a deep breath before starting. These were long days and the president's visage showed it.

"My fellow Americans. Last month I asked a group of 12 respected and talented individuals to come up with a set of recommendations to right our economic and financial ship. They have met for the last three weeks and produced strong recommendations that will maintain economic stability and restore public confidence. I will now list the policies my administration will enact.

"First, I will issue an Executive Order limiting daily cash withdrawals. This includes cash withdrawals on purchases. Second, any cash payment over $200 will need to be reported and any cash payment over $500 will be illegal. This will also be an Executive Order. There will be cash notes issued that will have new counterfeiting measures. All Americans are encouraged to replace existing notes.

"By Executive Order, all Treasury obligations ten years or longer must be held to maturity and whoever holds them can value them at par. Foreign transfers of these Treasuries will be prohibited, except for central bank transactions. All holders will receive principal and interest payments. By Executive Order, all gold exports and transfers will be prohibited.

"These and other yet created financial regulations will be under the direction of a new department called the Financial Stability Board or FSB. The FSB will be a cabinet level entity. The secretary of this board is yet to be named.

"The following will be temporary measures until the end of the calendar year. In the event there are insufficient National Guard forces available, I am authorizing the use of the military to act as law enforcement in those cities where the local government has exhausted their funds to pay for these positions. This will involve a temporary suspension of the Posse Comitatus Act.

"Finally, we will initiate a temporary immigration freeze with the military supplementing Immigration and Customs Enforcement as necessary. I want to thank the commission once again for their service to the United States."

He cleared his throat and sipped from a water glass on the podium. "I will now take a couple of questions. I believe a couple of you were pre-selected. Go ahead, whoever is first."

The first of the three selected reporters stood from their chair in the first row.

"Mr. President, regarding SuperNotes do you suspect these have been introduced by regimes trying to further destabilize our economy especially with cash usage on the increase? Which regime or regimes do you suspect?"

"We have gathered credible intelligence that these notes are circulating here and abroad, but I would rather not divulge any more information. Next question."

Almost in unison, as the first reporter sat, the next stood, also from the first row.

"Mr. President, you mention a limit on daily cash withdrawals. What will that limit be?"

"This is to be determined and we hope to have an announcement on that soon. We're in consultation with the

Federal Reserve on this matter. Next question."

The last question came from a reporter in one of the back rows.

"Mr. President, these restrictions on cash payments are sure to ruffle feathers. What do you say to a small business that might be used to dealing in cash now with these reporting requirements?

He looked down briefly, pausing another moment before answering. "We'll make that process as seamless as possible. Our economic studies show that cash transactions between $200 and $500 are not that numerous, so we don't expect a large impact. Thank you, everyone and good night." The president directed his gaze towards the floor and began his walk off the stage.

Someone in the back of the room jumped up and yelled an uninvited question. "Mr. President, is it true that more significant international action or partnerships lie ahead? Mr. President? Mr. President?"

The president ignored the reporter and walked out of the Briefing Room, his head still down.

***

President Jefferson's chief of staff, a former senator from California, was well acquainted with Emmet Callaghan and arranged a private meeting with the president. Ostensibly the purpose of the meeting, held in the Oval Office, was to present the IRC's economic research and how it might help the special commission. Jefferson dressed casually, or at least casually by his standards. He ditched the tie and jacket and rolled up his shirtsleeves. His attire reflected someone getting down to business. For the last couple of weeks, his position evolved as less ceremonial and more tactical.

Jefferson's chief led Emmet into the Oval Office and then excused himself.

"Mr. President, I want to thank you for taking the time to meet with me." Emmet dressed in his best Sunday clothes. He extended his hand across the president's desk.

"It's my pleasure, Mr. Callaghan. Please have a seat." Jefferson reached across the desk to shake his hand. "How are things in the Bay Area these days?"

"Fine, sir. It's a good Indian summer now." The term Indian summer referred to a period of fall warmth preceded by a spell of cold weather seen in the months of October or November.

"Do you miss being at Pacific Airlines? I admire how you guys did after 9/11. I know it wasn't easy." He referenced difficulty faced by the airline industry in the wake of 9/11.

"Sir, perhaps it might be different when you leave this office, hopefully in January 2025, but once you get the sense that your work is done and that there are other doors to walk through, you are at peace with the decision," Emmet explained.

"I hope you're right about when they kick me out of this office," Jefferson replied, his eyes glancing around the office, hoping for reelection next year.

"Me too, sir. One door I'm walking through now is hopefully one where the IRC can make a contribution to the nation's recovery," Emmet said.

"Your help is much appreciated. I also want to thank you for your continuing support of our party. I appreciate your donations to our candidates in 2018. Hopefully, you will be as generous in the upcoming campaign." Jefferson faced the reality of third parties nipping at the Democrats' heels. He took this opportunity to coax a campaign donation.

"It's my pleasure. And yes, I plan on continuing the support. I gather from your press conference that the commission has done an admirable job and by extension Mr. Holloway?"

The president beamed. "They sure have. Malcolm Holloway is one sharp individual. I can tell you his name always comes up when I talk to other leaders around the world." The president expressed his man-love for Holloway to most everyone he met.

"Well, Mr. President, we are happy to have him as a member of the IRC. I gave a copy of our economic research report to your chief. I hope you find the content helpful. Mr. Byung Park of the GSB and Mr. Holloway contributed to this research."

"Oh, I haven't heard of Mr. Park. But I'm sure he's talented. Seems like all those people at the GSB are. We need talented people nowadays to solve these problems."

"Along that line, sir, is Mr. Holloway under consideration for the secretary position of the FSB?"

"Now, Mr. Callaghan, you know I can't get into those details." The president smiled showing tacit approval for Holloway's candidacy. "I think we both agree he's a talented man who would make a great cabinet leader. I can tell you that whoever gets named has to pass a detailed security investigation that will take a considerable amount of time. You know with our terrorism protocol. We don't have much time here. Those who are in cabinet level positions or who were recently have a significantly pared review. It also helps to have proper security clearance, which I presume he had at one time. Time will tell."

Few people avoided giving Emmet Callaghan direct answers. This was, however, the President of the United States. The president didn't guarantee Holloway's nomination, though he declared it by default. If Emmet still smoked, he'd light a victory cigar.

CHAPTER TEN
DEVELOPING A STORY

El Mundo's D.C. bureau, near the corner of F Street and 18th Street, occupied three floors of a low rise building. Chandler enjoyed extra time in the nation's capital, which allowed him to be closer to Arianne. He'd been in New York only once in the last month. He sat in a conference room with D.C. producer Jared Clarke while they waited for a call from Rafael.

"Dude, I am so excited about the Skins signing Mayfield last spring. He's tearing it up! Back-to-back MVP, baby!" Jared owned Redskins season tickets for many years. Chandler recalled seeing Mayfield at the Correspondents Dinner.

"Yeah, but what about their defense? Their 'O' was pretty good already," Chandler said.

"Hey, I'm just thinkin about my Skins beating your Cowboys next week. We took you guys down last month in Dallas and I can't wait for them to get their ass beat here next weekend." Jared trash talked about the Boys' November visit to the nation's capital and pointed his finger in Chandler's direction.

"Sounds like someone is pretty confident. Just how confident?" Chandler issued the challenge by pulling out his wallet.

"Maybe fifty dollars," Jared countered.

"You're on." Chandler extended his hand and the two shook. "And I'll make sure and take the Dallas defense for my fantasy team next week. We're gonna stuff Mayfield. Can't wait." Chandler pointed at Jared's face.

The phone interrupted their bravado and Jared fumbled with the instrument before pressing the speaker button.

"Sure hope Mayfield handles the ball better than you handle a phone," Chandler said mockingly.

"*¿Qué?* You talking to me?" Rafael got confused by the football talk.

"Rafa. Hey sorry man, I was just explaining to Jared how I was going to take his money," Chandler answered, his attention now focused on the conference phone.

"*Buenos días.* So Jared's in the room?"

"Yeah, Rafa. Present and accounted for," Jared answered.

"Sorry I'm a little late. Michelle said she would join but then texted me that she has a sick child she has to take to the doctor," Rafael added.

"No worries," Jared said.

"What's been the mood around D.C. to the president's stability measures?" Rafael inquired.

"Strip clubs are hurting since guys can't hide all those lap dances." Rafael and Chandler laughed at Jared's observation.

"I've talked to small businesses that don't like reporting requirements or cash payment prohibitions. But then they tell me that since it's impossible to withdraw too much cash at one time, it's forcing everyone to credit payments." Chandler recently interviewed a few small business owners. "And something else. These businesses were all suspicious about the whole SuperNote thing. They think it was overblown and were not real trusting about the new notes."

"These fucking small businesses. I knew they'd be the ones to complain. They just need to go along with the president. He had very smart people on the commission recommend this plan," Rafael complained.

"To be fair though, small businesses always bear most of the pain complying with government regs," Chandler asserted.

"Hmm. I don't know about that. What have you guys been hearing about DigiNote?" Rafael asked.

"I talked to a couple of people who contribute to DigiNote, and they were of the strong opinion that its use will increase cuz of all the reporting," Chandler replied.

"Just wait, government will make DigiNote usage illegal. No way that can continue," Rafael challenged.

"Well, you can't blame people. Nobody wants to mess with reporting and besides these cyber currencies are a good challenge to Fed issued money." Chandler felt proud of himself for espousing what he learned from his mentor, Axel.

"Oh, Chan. Come on. You know DigiNote probably made this mess worse," Rafael countered.

"How's that?" Jared asked.

Rafael ignored the question and moved on to the next topic. "I heard from a friend of mine in Buenos Aires who was trying to do business in New Jersey about payment problems in some states."

"Oh, yeah. Apparently, Illinois, California, and New Jersey. There may be others. Contractors have told those states that they won't do anything on credit. Those states owe some companies a bunch of money. You better warn your friend. And then with their pension crises; it's a freakin disaster," Jared contributed, shaking his head.

"So what are they doing?" Chandler asked.

"Word has it that they are only accepting cashier checks, cash notes or even DigiNote for new work," Jared replied. "And I guess civil litigation is on the way if contractors don't get paid soon. Lawyers are gonna love that! Cha-ching!" Jared pumped his fist as if ringing up a cash register.

"Federal government just needs to step in," Rafael suggested.

"I don't know. What would they do?" Chandler inquired, raising his eyebrows. The divide between Rafael and Chandler became more clear as their call progressed.

"I guess the FSB can figure it out," Rafael answered. "Holloway is a smart man." Malcolm Holloway was named Secretary of the FSB by the president a few days after his meeting with Emmet.

"Hard to believe Jefferson rammed that through the way he did and Congress didn't say 'boo'," Jared added.

"Hell, if they let Congress talk about it, they'd still be debating it or someone would do a filibuster," Rafael added, openly disgusted. "Can you imagine Congress debating this and meanwhile the economy gets worse? The voters would surely kick 'em out in 2020. Congress has other things to worry about."

"I know they're debating the situation with bank lending right now. Banks are being so tight they'd raise a blister," Chandler added metaphorically.

"Where do you get these crazy sayings?" Jared shook his head while he looked at Chandler.

"Hey, it's just where I grew up, man. But seriously, with so little lending going on you're getting all these new digital currencies and barter networks. I mean people have to run their business, right?" Chandler concluded.

"OK, gentlemen. Let's figure out how we want to cover these stories for Centinela. But let's make sure we support the president and the FSB." Rafael would normally not attach these sorts of recommendations. It raised concern with Chandler.

"That's fine, but we still have to investigate and let our viewers decide," Chandler remarked, narrowing his eyes while staring at the phone.

"Just be careful, Chan. Let's lay out how we want to do this." Rafael's comments seemed odd though par for the course lately.

After the call with Rafael, Jared drifted to another meeting while Chandler returned to his desk and worked on expense reports before meeting Axel. Axel was in town interviewing a government "source" for his letter. He told Chandler he had important news and wanted to see him as soon as possible. He met Axel in the lobby, checked him in, and they moved to the same conference room where he had the call with Rafael.

"You want some water or something?" Chandler asked, pointing to the bottled water on an adjacent table.

"No, thanks. I just finished a tall glass of tea so just tell me how close the bathroom is," Axel replied after sitting down.

"Not too far. We just passed it." Chandler pointed to a door across the hall from the conference room. "How was your meeting?"

"Good. In fact, I'm going to quote this source's intelligence in the letter next month. But you'll just have to wait to read about it. It has to do with the private pension crisis. It's even worse than you might imagine."

"There aren't many of those left, you know."

"Let's get down to business." Axel leaned forward placing both arms on the conference table. "I have a contact at Omni, as I told you. His call name is Phish."

"Funny name," Chandler said. "How do you spell that?" He feigned like he was about to write something.

"What does it matter? You're not writing a story about

him," Axel added derisively. He could be a patient listener, but once he got going, he did not care for interruptions. "Phish said Russian hackers were involved in the market crash. They didn't start it but made it worse once they saw what was going on. When the market tanked, Chinese hackers jumped in and caused more panic. Phish also said there was unusual hacking activity coming from Western Europe as well, including Germany, Austria, and Switzerland. This is not where you usually find hackers."

"Most of the time, there is some hacker group that just comes out and takes credit. But it's weird since it didn't happen this time. And hacking from Western Europe? Is there any chance Omni's playing you?" Chandler questioned.

"Phish has passed along stuff I've put in my letter before and it was legit. I can tell you that the person who introduced me to Phish is also someone I trust," Axel affirmed. "I guess 'introduced' is not the right word. This isn't a person you meet for coffee. I can't even tell you if Phish is male or female, singular or plural."

"All right. I won't even ask how you linked up with the genderless Phish."

"Good, because that's not up for discussion. The bottom line is that Omni is a great source of intelligence."

"So you gotta wonder who's behind all this. Seems like there was some coordination involved," Chandler speculated.

"Yeah, this was not just a bunch of random hackers. I know someone consulting at the GSB. Maybe this person can give me some thoughts on this," Axel replied.

"You know, Congress has been as quiet as a church mouse and even though some members are furious about executive orders, they've stayed on the sidelines for fear of being branded unpatriotic. Senator Geringer is supposed to have a hearing early next week where he'll bring in Holloway. Geringer's been the most vocal until now," Chandler said, referring to the senator from Colorado who unsuccessfully ran for president under the Independent American Party (IAP) banner in 2016 after a brokered GOP convention.

"It makes sense the IAP would be all over this. You knew the main parties would have nothing to say."

"Oh, and I forgot to mention the most important thing! My father is testifying in front of Geringer and company," Chandler beamed proudly.

"Chandler, that is fantastic. You have to be so proud of him. Rubbing elbows with the big boys." Axel smiled.

"Yep, I already told my boss I want to be at the hearing even if I'm just there as plain old Chandler Scott and not an El Mundo employee."

"So what's the hearing about?"

"I don't know all the details, but Gustavo said some research he did about the Fed."

"So maybe it will be a battle of Sáenz versus Holloway." Axel, who seldom injected levity into casual conversation, brought his hand to his mouth as if holding a microphone. "In this corner weighing in at 175 pounds, the challenger Gustavo Sáenz."

"Ax, keep your day job."

CHAPTER ELEVEN
THE CANDIDATE

Gustavo had never visited the nation's capital and traveled little for professional reasons. Budget cuts at his university further curtailed travel, but this was no ordinary engagement. This was a specific request to testify in front of a Senate subcommittee. He penned research on the Federal Reserve Bank, which caught the attention of subcommittee chairman, Colorado Senator Matt Geringer. Newly appointed FSB Secretary Malcolm Holloway would also appear, presenting an opposing viewpoint discussing measures his department recently enacted in the name of financial stability. The November hearing entitled, "Financial Crisis Intervention" was held in the Dirksen Senate Office Building.

The tall, lanky Matt Geringer sported cowboy-rugged, chiseled looks and a considerable mustache. He could have been the Marlboro man, except he didn't smoke. He could have done voice-overs for beef commercials. If he were a singer, he'd definitely be a bass. An avid outdoorsman, he felt as comfortable on a horse herding cattle as he did negotiating a double black diamond in Steamboat Springs.

Born in the early 1960s, the Renaissance Man label could apply. In high school he played a leading figure in stage productions, played rhythm guitar in a teenage band covering songs from Boston, Styx and Kansas, and worked as a hiking and skiing guide. After high school, a young Geringer tried his luck on a ranch as a cowhand. This proved satisfactory for about three years until he decided it was time to return to academic pursuits. With money saved and student loans, he enrolled in Pike's Peak Community College and later the University of Colorado in Colorado Springs, where he completed a degree in Criminal Justice. The state university in Boulder later called where he earned a law degree.

He served as a criminal defense lawyer in Denver for many years, a member of the city council and eventually state Attorney General. His arrival in Washington as Senator coincided with the great financial crisis of 2008. In 2016, he mounted a Presidential run on the Republican ticket. By the time of the GOP convention in the city of Cleveland, no candidate had enough delegates to secure the nomination. After a contentious battle in the convention, Geringer did not receive the nomination. Influential party leaders suggested a run as an independent. Geringer thought it a good idea but wanted something deeper and long-lasting. He wasn't looking for a one and done. That year marked the birth of the Independent American Party or IAP, a party focused on becoming a legitimate challenger to the established GOP and Democrats in future races. Though Geringer lost in the general election, his strong performance solidified the party's standing and helped them win seats in 2018 House and Senate races when more voters from the GOP and Democratic parties defected. He was the presumed IAP candidate in 2020.

This subcommittee on Economic Policy comprised ten members who sat elevated around a large oak, horseshoe-shaped podium, inside of a room with very high ceilings. Wood panels spanned the room's height. Gustavo and Holloway sat behind a ten foot plain wood table covered with green cloth. They lifted their gaze towards the senators, no doubt intimidating for some witnesses. These two witnesses, however, felt no intimidation.

Inside the horseshoe facing the witnesses were people authorized to photograph or film. Guests and visitors, including Chandler, sat behind witnesses in neatly arranged chairs. The heat ran warm on this November day, making the bottled water provided essential to combat dryness.

The two men shook hands and sat, the phalanx of cameras but a few feet from them clicking madly. Geringer ordered the session to begin, scattering the cameras to their position low inside the horseshoe. Guest chatter ended gradually.

"I would like to thank our guests today, Professor Gustavo Sáenz of the University of Missouri and Mr. Malcolm Holloway, Secretary of the Financial Stability Board. The recent stock market crash and Executive Orders enacted by President Jefferson make us keenly aware of the financial straits in which our nation finds itself. When I arrived in Washington in 2009, the country faced another important crucible and with it a barrage of programs to rescue the economy. I remember being overwhelmed when I heard about TARP, HARP, HARM, Maiden Lane, and these other acronyms. Then the Fed and other central banks decided we needed QE to infinity, ZIRP and NIRP. Now there are new proposals that allow for greater government control over the economy. Our guests today will present their opinions on the efficacy of such intervention. Professor Sáenz, you have the floor."

"Thank you, Senator Geringer. My name is Gustavo Sáenz and I am Professor of Finance at the University of Missouri. Recently I published research outlining Federal Reserve action beginning in 2008 and its actual effects in restoring economic prosperity. I hope to show you today that the Fed's record of success in these matters was spotty." Gustavo had a great deal of experience talking about financial topics in front of students.

The senators offered a new challenge, one he eagerly embraced. This testimony was important for him and the university, besieged by unfavorable publicity after years of student unrest and their clashes with local police and National Guard.

Gustavo began his review by giving a good primer on money and currencies. "Senators, it's important we first understand why we need money." He took a dollar bill out of his jacket pocket placed there earlier for easy extraction. "Without money, it would reduce us to barter. The issue then becomes how we define money. This is a definition that has changed. For many years money had an intrinsic link to something else. History has shown money existed as cacao beans, seashells, and even feathers." The last reference elicited a few laughs in the audience. Chandler imagined himself chasing turkeys.

"In fact, at one time people used salt. Incidentally, the word 'salary' derives from the Latin for salt, which is 'sal'." That comment got everyone to think.

"Clearly, some of those things were hardly practical. It's hard to divide a seashell or a bean and how long can feathers last? In the early part of the colonization of the Americas, there was an abundant usage of gold and silver coinage introduced by European settlers. This system worked well until our nation's early government came up with a Continental - bad money. The Colonial government created this money at will. Since government created so much of it, the Continental lost its value and nobody wanted it. If you owned this money, you wanted to get rid of it quickly!"

Senators on the panel were unaware of basic money precepts detailed by Gustavo. Geringer tried to disguise his satisfaction by rubbing his mustache and covering his smile.

"I want to add that there is nothing supernatural about gold, it's just well-suited to be money much like titanium is useful for aircraft and oxygen is useful for breathing. We want our money to be durable, divisible, consistent, convenient, and perhaps have intrinsic value. If we can create money from thin air, it does not have intrinsic value."

Chandler reflected on some of his conversations with Axel who told him the public never really stopped to think about how something becomes money.

Gustavo continued with a monetary history of the United States. "We were on a classical gold standard from 1870 to 1914 and what happened during this time? Our living standards improved, we had little inflation and it was the first age of globalization. In fact, the St. Louis Fed said the country performed better during that time than it has with money created out of thin air like we have today."

Holloway rubbed his forehead briskly with this comment. Senators leaned forward. Geringer remained satisfied. His party, the IAP, had been critical of the Fed since they joined the political stage in 2016.

"The Fed itself came about when some banks tried to corner the copper market. There were bank runs and depositors lost confidence. Then there was a stock market crash. Ironically, the bankers arranged for a private rescue but decided they needed to have a central bank - a bank for banks if you will." At this point Gustavo paused for a few seconds, perhaps for effect but also to quench his thirst in the dry heat of the Dirksen hearing room.

"The Fed has been so deeply involved in financial markets that they created severe distortions leading to speculation and financial bubbles. Then, we got derivatives and other synthetic financial products in the banking system. We had too big to fail. We now have too big to rescue. Who will rescue the Fed?" If Gustavo accomplished anything, he brought attention to this last point. Few had stopped to think who would help the organization that was supposed to rescue the economy.

At the conclusion of his testimony, there were a couple of questions which he answered thoroughly. The questions were polite, but it was clear the senators wanted to hear more about what was being done now instead of a history lesson on U.S. monetary and financial policy.

"Thank you, Professor Sáenz for a most enlightening presentation. And now I would like to introduce FSB Secretary Malcolm Holloway." Geringer's stentorian contralto made Chandler's pulse leap.

"Thank you, Senator Geringer and the rest of the committee members. My name is Malcolm Holloway and I am Secretary of the Financial Stability Board and former Chairman of the Financial Stability Institute at the Global Settlement Bank. Prior to that I was Secretary of the Treasury under the previous administration." Holloway established his credentials in a smooth, authoritarian tone. Given his appointment by the president without Senate approval, he wanted to leave no doubt about his qualifications.

"The Federal Reserve Bank and other central banks were instrumental in saving the financial system in 1987, 2000, 2008 and 2016. Without their intervention, we would have experienced something orders of magnitude worse than the Great Depression. Federal Reserve modeling brought financial order to a much diversified economy. We are no longer dealing with the economy of the first age of globalization, circa 1870." He glanced quickly over his shoulder in Gustavo's direction, in opposition to the professor's history lesson. He then took a drink to let this point settle in with the committee. After a couple of seconds scanning the Senate panel, he continued.

"The Fed uses a variety of tools in dealing with the complexities of intermingled financial systems. Monetary policy is but one tool. The challenge now is how to expand their tool box. The Financial Stability Board intends to provide a supervisory layer over the Federal Reserve and Treasury Department as well as monitoring and guidance to these fine institutions."

While he revealed his supervisory function behind closed doors to the president, he opened the kimono during this hearing. Holloway proved to be the master of the choreography. By reading the various senators' body language, he provided just enough information to get them more interested in the document he delivered to them before the hearing. That document provided more detail than Holloway wanted to reveal in such a public forum.

"We would like to get past the point of these currency wars where one country tries to fix its economy by altering their currency's exchange rate. If there is criticism to be leveled at the Fed and other central banks, this would be one area. Such action has not been productive and really amounts to an ongoing world war."

Holloway delivered his decisive blow. Using the term "world war" caught senators off guard as much as currency wars. They did not understand their use as instruments of economic warfare. The mention of war also ignited murmurs in the audience who imagined a digital battlefield where Dollars fired bullets at Chinese Yuan or Euros.

"Could we have some quiet in the audience, please?" Senator Geringer ordered.

Holloway finished his presentation and entertained several questions, far more than Gustavo, and made continual reference to a document delivered to the Senators prior to the hearing. The committee seemed satisfied with this answer and reserved the right to call him back.

"I would like to thank both guests today for what was a very informative session," Geringer concluded.

After the hearing, Holloway approached the committee table and spoke with a couple of senators. Senator Geringer came out from behind the table to speak with Gustavo about his research.

"Nice job, professor." Geringer extended his hand. "I wish I could have had you for some of my classes in Colorado."

Gustavo smiled proudly, satisfied with his effort. "Thank you, senator. You can come listen to my lectures any time. Look me up if you're ever in Columbia."

"I know it has been a rough go on your campus over the years with all the student protests and budget cuts," Geringer noted.

At that moment Chandler walked up to chat with his father and to introduce himself to the senator.

"Chandler, *què bueno*. Good to see you, son." Gustavo gave him a brief man hug.

"Son?" A quizzical wash covered the senator's face.

"Senator, hello, I'm Chandler Scott and yes Professor Sáenz is my father," he announced proudly while extending his hand.

"Nice to meet you, Mr. Scott." The senator's grip, crushed his fingers. "I was just telling your father what a nice job he did."

Chandler wiggled his recovering digits. "Yeah, he did OK." He winked at his father.

Geringer's height was imposing but not threatening. He

had a quiet confidence about him, like someone who'd had many experiences and knew how to react, calm under pressure. Though he had no formal party affiliation, Chandler could envision voting for the senator since the libertarian-leaning Axel Schultz influenced his political fiber. Since he figured Geringer to be the presumptive IAP candidate, he asked him for an interview.

"Senator, I work for the El Mundo TV network, and it would make my day and probably my boss' day if I could interview you regarding the 2020 election." Chandler did not presume Geringer knew who he was.

"I suppose that would be fine. Just call my chief, Molly Sanders, and she can set it up for you."

"Thank you, senator, will do," Chandler acknowledged.

"Gentlemen, I must head to another meeting. Thank you once again Professor Sáenz and it was nice meeting you Mr. Scott." Geringer shook both of their hands in departure, this time with greater care.

Geringer's departure allowed a few moments for father and son to chat, though they would have more of an opportunity over lunch. Feeling good about his father's performance and scoring an interview with Geringer, Chandler excused himself and moved aside to call Rafael.

"Hey, Rafa."

"Chandler, *cómo estás?*"

"Hey, I wanted to let you know the hearing is over and-"

"And Gustavo? How did it go for him?" Rafael felt great pride for his fellow Argentinian, having an audience in front of the committee.

"You know what I'm gonna say. I thought he did a fine job. Some of the stuff he laid on the committee, I could tell, left them stunned. Some of these guys leaned forward in their chairs and at least appeared interested."

"Your father was presenting his anti-Fed research wasn't he?" Rafael had no love for Fed bashing as Chandler found out after his interview with Mark Lansing.

"His research was solid and frankly irrefutable. No one argued with him about it and there were just like two questions at the end."

"Did your father go first or second?"

"First, why?"

"They were probably anxious to hear from Holloway. He's the one that would tell them what is happening right now. You know what I mean?"

"Yeah, Holloway acquitted himself well too. Sharp guy, very polished."

"He's the right man for the job!"

"Oh, and the other reason I was calling, I scored an interview with Geringer!"

"*Bueno.* When will you do it?"

"Next few days, I hope. I have to set it up with his chief."

"Sounds great. Let me say bye now since I have to go. *Hasta luego.*"

"Bye Rafa."

***

He figured he'd interview Geringer at some point, though not so soon. Geringer took a liking to Gustavo's presentation and through guilt by association, Chandler scored this interview not long after. Geringer's chief, Molly Sanders, arranged for the meeting to be in the Hart Senate Office Building, one of three locations that house U.S. Senators. The Hart facility, the newest of the three, contained a modern sculpture called Mountains &

Clouds. The Mountains stood as a separate component weighing a mere thirty-nine tons. The Clouds, a mobile structure, appropriately hung from the ceiling where each one weighed as much as a ton. The sculpture was a fitting reminder for the senator from the Rocky Mountain State. A central atrium bathed the sculpture and Senate offices with an abundance of natural light. In these troubled times, the Senate could use all the illumination it could get.

Senator Geringer's office conveyed the feeling of the West. The sixteen foot ceiling provided spaciousness, a feeling quite familiar to a resident of the wide open country of Colorado. A richness of wood permeated the surroundings. The massively wide and tall desk nicely accommodated the senator's 6'4" frame.

Two leather club chairs faced his desk. Behind the desk sat a credenza with a TV monitor and a few family pictures. Above the credenza hung a picture of the IAP logo, an aggressive looking eagle over a light blue background, wings fully deployed carrying an American flag. An outer blue ring surrounded the eagle with the words "Independent American Party" in gold lettering. Flanking his desk were the flags of the United States and Colorado.

On the right side wall hung a large painting of a cowboy herding cattle, no doubt in recognition of the senator's time as a cowhand. On the opposite wall were college diplomas and pictures of the Rockies and Pike's Peak. Right under the Peak was a picture of the senator with Sammy Hagar, the Red Rocker, taken in Cabo San Lucas.

"Good morning, senator. This is my cameraman, Trey. He will set up." Trey and the senator acknowledged each other. "Thanks for taking the time for this interview. Your office has that strong masculine look I expected, but the Red Rocker picture surprised me." Chandler walked over to the picture for a closer look. He was joined by the senator who moved from behind his desk.

"Sammy was kind enough to let me get on stage and play a little bit. I was in a teenage band way back in the day and covered some rock-and-roll. I took my wife to Cabo for our anniversary. She's a bigger Sammy fan than I am, if truth be told. She's got her *own* picture with him."

"That's cool, senator. Very cool."

"What sort of music are you into?"

"Wow, I'm all over the place. Rock, jazz, hip hop, R&B, classical, reggae. Not much country. My ring tone is Hendrix, Voodoo Child."

"That's good, really. That you have so many interests. I would imagine you've probably heard more music just traveling so much." Geringer didn't know too much about Chandler and had his staff do a little research to prepare him.

"Yep. And some strange instruments I've seen, too."

"I bet. Tell me, Mr. Scott, what are we going to talk about today?" Geringer said assertively as he walked to his desk. Chandler motioned to his cameraman and sat on the other side of the desk. The interview would now begin.

"I would imagine you are ready to announce your candidacy soon?"

"Yeah. I'm just glad that all parties agreed to wait until the first of the year to campaign. So I guess we've got another few weeks before the fun starts. The electorate I think gets overwhelmed starting campaigns eighteen months before the election. They finish one mid-term election and go right into a presidential campaign. It's too much. Yeah, I was planning on announcing soon, but I guess it's no real secret that I'm running."

"What do you think will be the dominant issue of concern to voters?"

"The economy. I know many are still troubled by surveillance and monitoring, but then you have probably an equal number that are happy as long as they feel safe. These Executive Orders though, they definitely have escaped scrutiny by Congress." Geringer's expression drifted toward sober.

"I guess it's hard to know what the FSB will have in store for us or what the president may do with the ongoing terror threats."

"George Washington warned about entangling alliances and public debt. He said debt would go up during unavoidable wars and be pared during peacetime. Now we fight a war against the unseen armies of terrorism so our debt goes up but it never gets pared since it seems there is never any peace. And who knows what sort of entangling alliances we'll get with the FSB." Senator Geringer's reference to one of the Founding Father's warnings seemed appropriate given the perpetual war on terror.

The discussion continued with Geringer's role in the formation of the IAP and how so many people look up to him now, even from the other parties, for doing something few thought possible just a few years ago - create a viable and lasting third party.

"Senator, I must say that if things don't go as you hope in 2020, at a minimum, you've made your mark on political history. I mean, look at how you started after the wild GOP convention in 2016. You have a strong, viable, third party. You've given voters a choice. A choice that's gonna be around." Chandler wasn't just going on script. He felt strongly about his words.

"The head of our party, Alex Carpenter, is always reminding me of that. He's a young gun, so he'll see more of this party's development than I will. He's been there from the start."

The interview swung to the recent Senate hearing. Geringer revealed how much he enjoyed Gustavo's presentation and that he agreed with everything in his research. Chandler and the senator found common ground on a variety of topics including the Fed and economy. They diverged with the recent stock market crash. Chandler told his cameraman, Trey, to take a break. He didn't want the ensuing discussion recorded, at least not yet.

Chandler's eyes circled the room before commenting, "Senator, I heard rumors that there was malicious hacking going on during the recent stock market crash."

Geringer paused and interlaced his fingers behind his neck. "Oh, I don't know. I think they're just looking to blame someone. The market just failed, plain and simple. There's just so much speculation now. It's a fake market."

"I was of the same mind, but my friend and mentor, Axel Schultz has sources that told him otherwise."

Senator Geringer leaned forward, placing his arms on his desk. "No disrespect to you, Mr. Scott, but who the hell is Axel Schultz and why would I pay attention to his sources?"

Axel had a small but loyal following. A web search on the name "Axel Schultz" referred mostly to his newsletter.

"He publishes an internationally read newsletter and he's a self-made multimillionaire." It's not often Chandler had to defend Axel, but he didn't talk much about him either.

"I lost big money in 2008 and 2016. I finally told my advisor that I was done after 2016. Much safer stuff now for this cowboy. If this Mr. Schultz is as good as you say, I guess I should look more into his letter. You seem like an honest man, Chandler, so I will trust you on this one. But you better be right or I'll steer wrestle you!" Senator Geringer winked on the last comment.

Chandler related more of Axel's comments about the hacking and how there were other culprits beyond the Russians and Chinese, including Western Europe.

"Senator, the interesting thing about the alleged hacks is that Axel's sources told him there was activity coming from Europe too. From usually 'friendly' countries."

Geringer expressed surprise at the Western Europe theory, but it piqued further interest. "OK, go on."

"Mr. Schultz, er, Axel thinks the hacks were coordinated, suggesting a single source."

"A single source like who?" Geringer furrowed his brow.

"Senator, what we've been talking about the last few minutes about the hacking and Axel is not part of the interview obviously since we're not filming. What I'm about to say now cannot leave this room, OK?" Chandler's nervous eagerness revealed his own stress about making such an audacious request of a senator and presidential candidate who he'd just met.

"If it's something about national security or something illegal, I suggest we end our discussion now."

Chandler scanned the room again as if looking for spies. He lowered his voice. "No. Nothing like that. He's not sure who the source is, but he has a contact at the GSB that he's gonna tap for more info. He thinks that these Executive Orders are the brainchild of the GSB and International Relations Council."

"Interesting theory on the single source. It did seem to happen all at once. Yeah and on the Executive Orders, I can tell you, off the record, that there are a bunch of senators in all parties that are not real comfortable with this FSB and how quickly it all came about. No votes. No vetting. Nothing. But the president is showing great leadership now and is dominating public opinion. For that reason you haven't heard anyone speak out. They don't want to be branded as obstructionist or unpatriotic." The president's popularity had gone up and Geringer voiced no protest either.

"So you think the IAP missed a chance to get in front of this issue?" Chandler challenged Geringer on his silence.

"Oh, yeah, and I'm as responsible as anyone else with my silence. But you know what, this FSB will be something the country will regret. It won't end well. I'll tell you what. I'll start looking into the things we discussed here today. Though we're not filming, keep this out of your notes." Geringer's voice deepened another octave while making the request.

Chandler received a text message indicating a long preview of his segment on DigiNote was about to air with a news broadcast. He asked the senator if he wanted to watch. Chandler's cameraman returned. The senator slowly rotated his chair towards the monitor and tuned the El Mundo channel. At the conclusion of the preview, Chandler realized key portions of his story appeared missing. *Was Jared Clarke responsible for this additional editing?*

"Looks good, Mr. Scott."

"Ahh senator, actually I'm not sure what happened but that preview was misleading. My boss and I had a difference of opinion on the content and I guess he did something to the story."

"Why would he do that?"

"Not sure."

After spending most of the last few weeks in D.C., Chandler set himself up to remain in New York for December. He was happy not to have any major trips planned over the holidays, his first with Arianne. As part of his series of presidential candidate interviews, John King, Theocracy Party (TP) candidate, agreed to come to El Mundo's New York studio. John King was elected to Congress from the state of Arkansas in 2016 and built a small, but powerful coalition of TP candidates who won a few more congressional seats in 2018. The TP understood they wouldn't win the election in 2020, though they hoped for greater exposure with a White House run. Mr. King graduated from Southwest Baptist University in Bolivar, Missouri, and subsequently from Midwestern Baptist Theological Seminary in Kansas City, Missouri. After graduation from the seminary, he became a staffer for televangelist Elmer Hawthorn who ran the popular "Rise and Shine" Sunday morning show out of Little Rock, Arkansas. He rose to become Hawthorn's protégé and helped create ministries in the U.S. and abroad. After failed attempts at public office, including governor and Congress, he broke through in 2016.

Chandler thanked King for coming to the studio and the two made small talk while technicians finalized preparations. The TP's base included disaffected Republicans and Democrats who felt the country's moral compass needed recalibration and for whom financial inequality was an ever-present concern. They understood free publicity and a having a platform for their ideas. King made himself available for as many interviews as his schedule could handle. Many media outlets either did not take them seriously or chafed at their religiously based messages. El Mundo did not share these reservations. The two men sat in club chairs with two bottles of water on a small table between them.

The 5' 9" King dressed like a minister. He wore a three-button, double-breasted, black suit, one appropriate for "marryin and buryin." The shirt was white with a tie, adorned in navy and gold British regimental stripes, arranged with a double Windsor knot. The shoes were classic oxfords, shiny black.

"Mr. King, it's a pleasure to have you on Centinela. Welcome."

"My pleasure, sir."

"The 2020 race is shaping up to be rather fascinating. Your party is more established. So is the IAP. President Jefferson's popularity has surged recently after his strong response to our economic and financial chaos. The GOP is more unified now after the chaos of the 2016 convention. What gives you hope that you can win this election?" Chandler opened with a question every viewer had for a third-party candidate.

"Our nation's decline goes back much further than 2016 or even 2008. And there are other components besides economic and financial ones. The signs of social and moral breakdown have been clear for decades. The fact that we have more than two political parties is a sign of that."

"So why do you think you can win?"

"I think the nation wants a government where God is recognized as ultimate ruler with his laws as statute. What we have instead is this edifice called the State, which inherently is evil and intrinsically destructive. We pay homage and high taxes to this State, with a capital 'S'. They've taught everyone to love and respect the State. But the State is merely a creation of man. Notice, I said man and not God. The State is so big now and getting bigger with the recent presidential Executive Orders. The State is controlling the political and economic essence of the country. And what parties are responsible for the expansion of this state? Primarily the GOP and the Democrats. America desperately wants to get away from this structure and the Theocracy Party can provide the path for it."

"So you keep talking about the State. Who or what is the State?"

"Look at the agencies created by government that are looking for terrorists like the FBI, CIA, NSA, or Homeland Security, the whole national intelligence apparatus, and now we have this Financial Stability Board that is pretty much going to be looking at all financial transactions. They're supervising the supervisors. What about the Fed? And let's not leave top businesses out of this. Without their help, it would be difficult for the State to operate. Oh, and you have organizations like the International Relations Council. That is the ultimate partnership of business interests and State interests. This is looking more like a corporatocracy all the time. Pretty soon we are going to have someone managing how we brush our teeth in the morning and what kind of toothpaste we use. This seems excessive. Consider these groups the State or their enablers."

"Well, there is no doubt the State, with a capital 'S', is extensive but frankly I'm not sure how the TP will dismantle it, which is what, I believe, you advocate?"

"That's our goal, but we have to show the American public that many of their ills, ah many of their ills result from the State. I know individual workers feel this pain. They can't get ahead and see the elite being enriched. Give us time and America will see the light."

"On to a more immediate concern. Since you are critical of

the FSB, give me one remedy for addressing our financial and economic concerns."

"So glad you asked that. Our problems are a product of debt. But much of our debt is fraudulent." King's tone had been mellow and now acquired a passion reserved for a preacher delivering the gospel.

"Fraudulent?" Chandler asked incredulously. "Fraud" and "debt" were two words he'd never heard used together, even from Axel.

"Yes sir. Just look at our government debt. This is irresponsible, fraudulent debt. Why should the American people be saddled by debt they did not request? There is a legal principle that says people should not have to pay for this debt. Look at how we bailed out Wall Street and the big banks. Look at all our military aggressions overseas. Look how much we spent fighting terrorism here and abroad. Do we feel more secure? No sir, these are odious debts that are only personal debts of the tyrants who incurred them." King shook his fist as he sat even more erect.

Chandler had never heard the word "odious" in the context of King's response and emotion. He figured it connoted a foul smell. He also knew there were other types of debt. "Well, but most of our government debt is about entitlements, people like their government payments. And at least at some point, Americans were OK with military action overseas in the name of national security."

"Entitlements are part of the problem. People don't realize we're just feeding the beast called the State. Also, this talk about national security needs refocusing. We are under constant terror threat because of our aggression overseas. We commit hostile acts against foreigners and then it blows back on us. Even international law says that debt incurred through wars of aggression is not enforceable."

"Could you give our viewers an example?"

"Certainly. When the U.S. seized Cuba from the Spanish, Spain insisted on the repayment of debt by Cuba. The U.S. said no, arguing that the debt was imposed on Cuba through Spanish aggression. Spain did not vanish because of non-payment. I think they're still around today." King added the sarcasm along with a historical point of which most El Mundo viewers were unaware. He gave the impression he wanted to stand up and go behind a pulpit.

"So what would the TP do with this fraudulent debt?"

"Let me tell you about the Jubilee. The Jubilee is the end of seven cycles of Sabbatical years or seven times seven years. Leviticus 25:8-13 says that in the Jubilee, debts are forgiven. The TP considers the start of our fraudulent debt to be 1971 when the world went off the gold exchange standard. Seven times seven years after 1971 would roughly be the year 2020. Since we have been dealing with counterfeit money, and by definition counterfeit assets amounting to trillions of dollars, we advocate erasing the debt associated with it." This was a bold pronouncement by King, who rubbed his hands and pulled them apart as if washing his hands of debt. It evoked an image of Pontius Pilate.

Chandler wondered about everyone who held government bonds. Would those certificates turn into toilet paper? What about people's retirement plans that depended on income from government debt? "Your debt forgiveness plan would be as difficult to implement as trying to put socks on a rooster."

King emitted a brief laugh and momentarily withdrew his passion. "Yeah, I think I heard that expression once. But debt forgiveness helps in two ways. First, we divert the large portion of people's productive enterprise away from unproductive obligations. Second, we clear a path for new creativity and invention. Does any sane person watching your show think this debt will ever be paid off? All we are doing is just piling new debt to service old debt. Debt models assume unlimited growth, which we all know doesn't happen. The American worker is bearing the burden of all these debts. We must stop this insanity!"

"What about those that say, that people or countries or as you say, States, just need to bite the bullet? They took on the debt and now it is their responsibility to pay it back?"

King showed a slight grin. "Oh, you mean austerity? These are fraudulent banksters and government types who will do anything possible to maintain the status quo and grow debt slavery. This is a web of parasitic theft. Who do you think benefits from this? I can tell you it's not Main Street." King displayed a knowledge of economics and history that Chandler did not expect. Political opponents who sized up King as an unsophisticated lout would do so at their own peril. This candidate knew how to make an impact and demonstrated absolutely no fear.

"Mr. King, this has been a very informative discussion. I don't know what will happen in the election, but I'm sure you will make it more colorful. You raise many interesting issues. Thanks for being here today."

"You're welcome, Mr. Scott."

The producer signaled the end of filming.

"Thanks again for coming, Mr. King. I will admit that the idea of Jubilee is bold although it seems like you're charging hell with a bucket of ice water."

"That's funny. I think I heard my grandpa say that once. Our party may not win, but they'll hear us.

***

Chandler met Senator Geringer and Axel at the IAP office in New York. The senator did some digging around the work of Mr. Schultz and emerged interested in his research and ideas. Geringer cloaked this meeting by informing IAP staffers about a follow up interview with Chandler and another El Mundo employee. It's unlikely anyone recognized Axel, since he didn't post a picture in his newsletter. Geringer sought to minimize attention to this meeting, given the sensitive material Chandler revealed during their earlier interview. The senator had both men escorted to a conference room on the 15th floor. IAP office security was moderate by current standards.

The office, nice but not posh, was located in mid-town Manhattan on the corner of West 56th Street. The office served as campaign headquarters and an organizing place for fund raising, strategy, and publication of position papers. Local staff also managed the heavily visited IAP website. The three met in a conference room with views of Central Park. Geringer greeted them in the room.

"Chandler good to see you again." Geringer extended his hand and gave a firm squeeze. Chandler's hand buckled.

"Good to see you too. Senator, I would like to introduce to you my good friend and mentor, Mr. Axel Schultz."

"Mr. Schultz, it is a pleasure." The force of their handshake could have cracked a walnut. "Please, everyone sit down. I took the liberty of reading some of your letters and I must say, I came away overwhelmed with your knowledge and your contacts. I think our intelligence services should consult with you," Geringer chided.

"Please senator, call me Axel. Thank you for your kind words. I dig deep for information and even though my readers don't agree with what I say all the time, I try to stay true to my beliefs. My gravestone will say that I believed in liberty." Though no fan of politicians, Axel appreciated the compliment.

"I trust that gravestone won't need manufacturing anytime soon," Geringer commented.

"Oh, senator, you have no idea how healthy this guy is," Chandler added.

"I studied health, exercise and nutrition many years ago and I just do what works for me. I could have written a couple of books on the subject, but honestly it's not a passion," Axel replied confidently.

"Mr. Schultz, ah Axel, growing up I skied in the winter and hiked all over Colorado in the summer so I was in good shape once. Then I took a few bumps and bruises working as a cowhand." One of those bumps contributed to a nagging hip problem for Geringer, which he rubbed for effect.

"Sir, the years have apparently been kind to you," Axel commented.

"Thanks. I have a feeling we might be on the same side on some of these issues," Geringer suggested. "Can I get you two anything to drink?" Both men declined.

"Senator, I wanted to let you know that you'll see my interview with John King air within a couple of weeks," Chandler advised.

"I respect them on some of their economic positions but they may be too far out there for most Americans," Geringer said.

"I'd be in jail for not going to church on Sundays if King was president," Axel retorted.

"Those jail cells would be quite full," Geringer added. "Chandler, did you ever figure out what happened to your DigiNote story?"

"Whenever I brought it up with a couple of people, they changed the subject. My boss Rafael must have had a hand in it."

"Troubling. I wanted to let both of you know that the GOP, Democrats, and even some in the IAP are content to stand aside and let this FSB thing expand without challenge. It's not some big conspiracy thing, so get that out of your heads. Honestly, no one is stepping up to challenge this and like I told you before Chandler, they're afraid to be ridiculed since the president's popularity is high right now."

It was never easy confronting a popular president if you're a newly formed third party.

"Part of the problem too is that when we had the 2008 and 2016 crashes, everyone just stood aside waiting for the Fed and then things didn't improve. Washington's decided the Fed is no longer effective, so they turned to the IRC and by extension the GSB. Then they layered this FSB on top of everything. Jefferson looks like he's leading and people like that." Geringer's delivery was methodical, tremulous, and deeper in tone.

"Senator, that is a good summary," Axel remarked.

"You know what, guys, just call me Matt from this point forward, OK?" Axel and Chandler nodded their heads in approval. "Axel, Chandler indicated you had a contact at the GSB who might tell you what lies ahead?"

"Yes. He's actually a consultant who saw position papers by the IRC and GSB floating around his part of cyberspace that seemed to suggest a greater level of international influence," Axel explained.

"So what was in these position papers?" Geringer asked.

"My contact didn't read them in detail but suggested that more substantive policies were forthcoming. He was looking at sensitive documents that were not for his eyes, so it limited his investigation. I told him not to press it since I don't want to lose him as a source," Axel continued.

"This is good info to know but not earth shattering either. But I understand," Geringer conceded.

"Also, this contact and another one confirmed that there was malicious trading activity during the September crash from the usual culprits but also from what you consider friendly regions. Chandler, did you tell the Senator, er Matt, about this information or the contact?"

Chandler concealed his defeated expression by looking down since he never mentioned Omni to Geringer. Axel interpreted Chandler's expression and realized the information vacuum.

"Matt, I want you to know this information comes from a contact I have at Omni." Chandler offered, conveying a nervous vibration of apology.

"Omni! What? The hacker group?" Geringer's voice rose an octave. "I might ordinarily end this thread but out of respect for you I will let you continue. Trusting a group like Omni for someone like me would be ah, political suicide you know, but hey, let's see what you have." Geringer glared at Axel with one eye half closed, the other open, but tense.

Axel explained how malicious trading didn't cause the market to fall initially but made the drop far more severe. After the U.S. market tanked there were similar moves in European, Russian and Asian markets. The attacks seemed to originate from various countries, as if coordinated.

"What you are saying, Axel, is disturbing on so many levels but I still go back to the fact this is coming from a reviled hacker group," Geringer remarked. Omni had no friends in Congress.

"I realize that, but keep in mind my GSB source also confirmed this. I have used Omni for years as sources for research and they have never let me down. I don't agree with some of what they do, but I'm not their keeper either, you know. They've upset the working order but some in your party benefited from information they released."

Axel referred to a state election where voters were made aware of illegal bribes taken by an IAP opponent. The information, released by Omni to a local journalist, revealed bank transfers from a convicted felon.

"Senator, I mean Matt, I realize this is a lot to digest especially given your pending campaign. I don't blame you for being skeptical, but what Ax says makes sense. You can kind of connect the dots here," Chandler asserted.

"Chandler, I can't just *kind of* connect the dots. They have to connect seamlessly. And candidly, even if they did, I'm not even sure how the American people or heck even my party would digest this. This is some heavy-ass shit, pardon my French," Geringer exclaimed.

He swiveled his chair and stared out the window towards Central Park. "You're suggesting some coordinated action that made the stock market fall, but you're unsure who. You talk about how the GSB and the IRC might influence our policy. I will say that there are too many unconnected dots and all of them are troubling. But I can't just ignore them either." He pivoted back. "No offense guys, I'm gonna have to check some of this out myself or at least try to makes sense of it. Everything's happening too damn fast. Axel, please keep this out of your letter for now, if you don't mind. Chandler, it goes without saying that I can't have you talking about this on Centinela."

"Matt, you saw what happened with my DigiNote segment. I'm not even sure my boss would run this, so mum's the word."

"Gentlemen, I have much to think about over the holidays. I was thinking I'd spend a nice restful time with my family before starting my campaign. Thanks for ruining it for the Geringer family." He fashioned a smile behind the thick stache. "I know both of you are just trying to do the right thing. I need to get to a meeting, so enjoy your holidays and we'll be in touch soon."

Senator Geringer bid the two goodbye with firm handshakes. Chandler's hand remained sore from the earlier grip of death. This meeting marked the beginning of a developing partnership between the three.

CHAPTER TWELVE
HOLIDAYS AND HABAKK

Christmas season in Manhattan looked like a winter wonderland filled with trees, holiday window displays, and millions of twinkling lights. Even most tourist-averse New Yorkers admitted to enjoying the spectacular sight. Manhattan's bright and brilliant nexus, the Rock Center Christmas Tree, a ten ton Norway spruce illuminated with 45,000 LED lights, stood a towering seventy-eight feet. If you were lucky enough to be in the Big Apple in early December, you'd get the chance to see the lighting ceremony along with the Rockettes and other theater acts. If skating was your pleasure, the Rink at Rockefeller Center beckoned you to join 150 of your closest friends.

Renee Scott had experience skating outdoors growing up in Columbia. Chandler, raised in Dallas, only got the chance through infrequent visits to her parents. She wanted him to know her parents, yet the shame of her pregnancy made it very difficult to return home. That meant visits by Renee's parents to Dallas. When Chandler was fourteen, she took him to Columbia for the Christmas holidays where he got to spend time with Gustavo. They took in a college basketball game and spent the entire day together. That trip launched the relationship that evolved into their brother-brother bond.

As promised, Chandler invited his mom to spend the holidays with him. This trip marked Renee's first visit to New York during the holiday season and she felt both excitement and trepidation meeting Arianne for the first time. When Renee arrived in Chandler's apartment, she noticed that it was devoid of holiday spirit. No tree or decorations adorned the premises. She expected as much from someone always on the go and with homes in two cities. Motherly instincts took over and she purchased a small, artificial tree with a few ornaments that she placed on his coffee table. At least they'd have something by the time Arianne arrived, who celebrated early with her parents in Chicago.

Traveling on Christmas Eve proved the only way for her to spend time with her family and the Scotts. Chandler hoped she'd arrive in time for dinner. Fortunately for him, Renee prepared their meal and he took time to relax. Arianne insisted that he stay in his apartment with his mom so he would not have to come to LaGuardia, yet another woman who looked out for his relaxation time. Christmas officially started for him when she walked through the door where he raced to meet her.

"Hey, you finally made it!" Chandler embraced her and gave her a big smooch. The lip lock lasted a few seconds until she pulled away.

"Chan, your mom." She pointed towards the kitchen where she saw a person she presumed was Renee. "The lipstick." She wiped the residue from above his lip.

"Oh yeah," he said sheepishly. "I'll get your bag. I guess I should let you come all the way in." After they took a few steps into the apartment, Renee emerged from the kitchen to meet them. "Mom, this is Arianne Maxwell." This was the first time he introduced a woman to his mom during his time as a journalist. The two women enjoyed a warm handshake.

"So nice to meet you, Miss Maxwell. Chan talks about you so much. You're even more beautiful than he described." Renee had seen pictures of Arianne, though she cut a more striking figure in person.

"Oh, Mom. Come on."

"Thank you so much. I know I must look tired right now. It's very nice to meet you too, Miss Scott, and please call me Ari."

"Very well then. Please call me Renee. Let me go back into the kitchen to finish. I hope you're hungry. Chan, I'll need you to set the table in a few minutes." Renee excused herself to let the two of them have some alone time. Chandler walked Arianne back to his room where she took off her coat and engaged him in a very passionate and long kiss, her right leg wrapping around his left, his hands squeezing her derrière. After a long round of lip pressing, Chandler had enough.

"If we don't stop now, we'll miss dinner."

"You think she'll come looking for us?"

"If she did, she'd get more than she bargained for!" The two smiled with the understanding they'd reacquaint later.

Their dinner could not have gone any better. The two women got along well and Renee showed great interest in Arianne's work. After ignoring Chandler for most of the meal, understandable since she wanted to know Arianne, Renee turned to her son.

"So, what's new at El Mundo?"

"Ahh." Chandler had to tread carefully here. The thing most on his mind outside of his girlfriend was the conversation with Axel and Geringer, which was not in the public domain. "Um, you know the usual. I interviewed the third party candidates and I don't think I'm scheduled for any out of the country trips, so that's good."

"Yes. You travel too much anyway. Come visit me in Texas more," Renee said longingly.

Renee directed her son to clear the table and told Arianne she should sit on the couch to relax from her trip. After cleanup, the Scotts joined Arianne, the small tree on the coffee table in front of them, to exchange gifts. Renee gave them tickets to a Broadway remake of Evita. She thought he could at least experience some part of Argentinian culture through this musical. Though Renee kept secret the identity of Chandler's father for the early part of his life, she tried since to make sure her son knew that part of his heritage.

Chandler and Arianne gave Renee several articles of clothing and an electronic tablet. Chandler gave Arianne a personal digital assistant - she'd have to assign a name. Arianne gave Chandler a full day at the posh Olympic Spa as part of her master plan to slow him down. The evening went so well that any trepidation Chandler had about the women in his life getting along melted away.

After a long conversation in front of the little tree, Renee excused herself for the evening and wished them a Merry Christmas. The two listened to Christmas music, this time from Chandler's CD player and not Venus.

"Ari, I can't help but think that the year ahead is going to be explosive. There seems to be so much going on. Tonight is a nice oasis, though."

"All right, then. Stay in the oasis. You have a fair maiden at your disposal."

"Yeah, it's hard not to think about what our government's doing even more than they have been already with the surveillance and you know, the FSB. Remember how the Third Reich-"

"Chandler, seriously do we have to talk about that tonight?" She got up, headed towards the kitchen and poured herself a little more wine, figuring Chandler would ramble for a while.

In the meantime, Chandler spoke to Venus. "TV on, tune El Mundo."

Retailers are reporting a sharp drop in Christmas sales. Analysts are attributing this to the wobbly economy and lower limits by credit card companies due to an increasing number of defaults. There is also speculation that more merchants are accepting DigiNote and keeping those sales off the books and official sales statistics.

She returned to the sofa. "Back to Christmas or are you still gonna talk about government?"

"I wanted to but-" Chandler halted for her expression.

She gave him a sultry look and walked to the bedroom. About halfway there, she removed her blouse and dropped it on the floor. Chandler hoped his mom didn't come out of her area, a nook near the apartment's entrance. When she got to the bedroom entryway, she turned away from him and removed her bra, dropping it at her feet. He focused on her back and her nicely contoured derrière. Then she disappeared from view, the bedroom door still opened. He popped up in more ways than one and stumbled towards the bedroom, hitting his toe on the coffee table in his haste.

He killed the CD music and had one more thing to say before he made it to the room. "TV off, lights off."

***

On Christmas Day, Chandler awoke early and reflected on his wise decision to stop watching the news and follow Arianne. She slept peacefully and so did his mom. There was nary a sound in the apartment. The nook where his mom slept functioned as a home office. He moved furniture aside and set up Renee in a small bed borrowed from a neighbor. Not wanting to disturb anyone, he decided it might be nice to take a walk at The Battery since it was an unseasonably warm day in New York.

"Outside temperature?"

"The temperature is 45 degrees Fahrenheit, 7 degrees Celsius, wind speed is 6 miles per hour, barometric pressure-"

"Stop." Chandler gave the universal command to halt Venus.

At 7:30am, the sun had been up only fifteen minutes and rose brightly this Christmas morning. He didn't need Venus to tell him about the sunrise.

At the empty park, he stared out at Lady Liberty, reflecting on what she represented and imagining the desires of immigrants who came to Ellis Island. In his mind, America enjoyed less liberty, though its people, at least tacitly, did not seem to mind. Everyone adjusted to how they spoke on the phone, what they wrote in emails, typed in text messages, or searched on the web. Now there were unprecedented Executive Orders with a silent Congress.

His mind drifted to Arianne. This time it felt different. Though neither admitted their love for each other, this would occur soon. *But what happens after they say this? Will she expect something else? Is he even ready for something else? They are both in their early 30s and maybe she wants a family. And what about Renee? Will she continue to live in Texas or move back to Columbia?*

Her own parents were getting older and had asked her to come home. *Surely she's past the embarrassment.* As these thoughts ripped through his mind, a stranger approached.

The man had a closely cropped beard with skin the color of

cinnamon. He had a warm, appealing face and a calm aura about him. His height and build were average. He dressed in a black sweater, no jacket, khaki pants and athletic shoes. He had a careful and light gait, gliding in half moon paces.

"Merry Christmas. So how do you think the Jets will do this weekend?" the stranger asked. The Jets had a game at the Meadowlands, on the other side of the Hudson in New Jersey.

"Merry Christmas to you. Well, I grew up a Cowboys fan but now living in New York, I do follow the local teams, but not a lot. I spend time in D.C. too so I guess I follow the Skins. I think there was a song in Texas that said something about mothers not letting their little boys grow up to be Redskins." Both men laughed. "I guess I really didn't answer your question."

"Aren't you the young man on the El Mundo channel? You have that show Centinela, right?" Chandler was not always recognized. For all its success, El Mundo had not reached the status of other major networks. Chandler took notice of the stranger's perfect Spanish accent. He didn't elongate the vowel sounds like most Americans did.

"Yes, that's right. I guess somebody's watching."

"Let me tell you, that show is good. You should be proud of your work."

"Thank you. I'll consider that my Christmas gift."

"What brings you out so early on Christmas morning? You seem troubled on such a joyous day." Was it so obvious to the stranger that Chandler was engaged in tortured reflection?

"Oh, why do you say that?"

"You know on a day like today you need to have faith. People forget what they're celebrating today. Have faith in yourself too. You're in the business of investigating and uncovering things others miss. It takes work to do this. Society doesn't want to open their eyes to what's in front of them. If it's difficult to see, people won't look for it."

Why is this man spewing this wisdom? He felt very uneasy since the stranger seemed to have an innate sense of what troubled him.

"Today, Mr. Scott, powerful men bend nations. The State is deeply embedded in everyone's lives." The stranger knew his name, too.

"Funny you mention the word 'State.' I recently interviewed a presidential candidate and all he wanted to talk about was the State. I never really thought about the State the way he put it. But the State is here and I don't see it going away either."

"The authority of the State is appealing since it provides freedom *from* something. In the twentieth and twenty-first centuries, it meant protection *from* poverty, or terror, or sickness. But when we give individuals freedom *of* something, we get independence and liberty." The stranger gestured towards Lady Liberty. "That places more responsibility on the individual and people get uncomfortable with that. But that was the premise of liberty in the eighteenth and nineteenth centuries." The stranger rotated clockwise and pointed towards Ellis Island. "People immigrated here to seek freedom *of* speech and religion. That's what liberty meant. Think about the Bill of Rights in the Constitution. The word liberty today means something entirely different than in the eighteenth and nineteenth centuries. Now people want freedom from hardship and there is only one organization that can promise that. But that organization can only do that by taking away other freedoms."

"You know, you sound just like a good friend of mine."

"Think about the founding of the United States. The colonists sought various types *of* freedoms and those are written in the Constitution. But when individuals look for freedom *from* something, they want the State to supply that protection. What do you think freedom is?" A long pause followed.

"Oh, that was not a rhetorical question. Sorry. I think freedom is the ability to speak or act without hindrance. Well, I guess there are some acts that should be hindered, especially if I am going to inflict harm on someone. I also think there also needs to be some freedom from domination by a foreign government or some sort of attack."

"What else?"

"Financial independence. If I don't owe money to anyone, that is a very liberating thought."

"Good. So why do you think the public accepts a larger State?"

"People are so concerned with living a risk-free life that they look for government to take away the risk. I don't think life works that way though. You gotta get out of the shadow of your mother's apron."

"I suppose you mean people can't be timid about life. Yes, Chandler, life has its risks. That is one thing that made America exceptional. Risk takers settled new lands, built new industries, and built great cities." The stranger turned away from the Hudson, spreading his arms wide as he faced Manhattan. "They created magnificent national parks and when they wanted a new frontier, they looked towards the cosmos. What if those people wanted freedom *from* the risks that came with all that? What would America look like?"

"Um, I guess America would be knee high to a

grasshopper."

"Indeed, it would. I wonder how Americans would feel about living in that kind of place. I dare say that America would not be America."

"OK, sir, you seem to have all this wisdom, and I appreciate what you are saying, but it's not as if the world will change overnight. And look at the current economic chaos. People are asking for help, and our president just gave it to them. Shouldn't government help people?"

"Societies change slowly and then suddenly. The question comes to how you manage change and whether you can identify the way a society changes. When you are in the middle of something, it is hard to see where the thing is headed. And yes, government should help its people, but it's how they administer that help that slowly changes society. Then one day, everyone wakes up and they don't recognize their country any longer."

"Yeah, I remember a history class in college talking about societies collapsing - the Greeks, the Romans, the Mayans."

"They were all great societies at one point. History will say that these societies collapsed due to some external event like drought or some natural disaster or maybe a war. I think the seeds of their collapse are sown over time and then when a significant event occurs, society cannot respond adequately to the challenge. Or their seeds led to unnecessary challenges. Like I suggested earlier, they woke up one day and did not recognize their country."

"Whoa. Are you saying we are about to collapse?"

"Not at all. No one knows when or if this might happen. But America, and other nations, have sown seeds that are growing and will continue to flourish in the great challenges ahead. That I can tell you with great certainty. Some challenges faced are entirely of society's own doing and unnecessary. Instead of trying to simplify society, the public is getting and accepting far more complexity. I don't mean technology, but organization and governance."

"Uh huh, I see what you mean." Chandler looked down at his phone for an alert with a headline about the FSB.

"There are people or organizations that are well intended but they may be more foe than friend. Be mindful of that."

"Now, you're going all Shakespearean on me."

"This above all: to thine own self be true." The stranger paused and raised his chin for effect.

"Oh that was, ahh, ahh, dang it I know this one. It was Hamlet!"

"That's right. Heed that famous quote. Be true to yourself and you won't go wrong, young man."

The stranger suggested they walk. They strolled leisurely, arriving at the statue of John Ericsson. Chandler finally got the nerve to ask the stranger his name.

"Sir. Can you tell me your name? I don't seem to know much about you."

"My name is Habakk."

"Interesting name. Can't say I've ever heard it."

"Chandler, I hope you have a Merry Christmas. *Hasta luego.*" The stranger bid farewell in a perfect Spanish accent.

Chandler, afflicted with temporary apoplexy, wanted to say something but his mouth would not move. He really enjoyed the conversation and wanted it to continue. *I should get back and see if anyone's awake.* After a few seconds he pursued Habakk to ask when they might meet again. Though he did not appear to be moving quickly, he moved twice as fast as Chandler, like he was on a moving walkway. Just when

Chandler started running, Habakk vanished from sight.

Chandler gave up the chase and then it hit him. The stranger was the man from the coffee shop the day of the stock market crash, three months earlier. A text from Arianne would snap him back to the present.

CHAN WHERE ARE U? IT'S XMAS!!!

He'd have quite a tale for Arianne when he returned to the apartment.

***

It was a festive time at the Callaghan mansion on New Year's Eve. Arriving guests had no reason to knock on the door or ring the bell. The open door welcomed them. With temperatures in the sixties, northern California enjoyed warm weather bathing much of the country. The Callaghans hosted a catered party with old friends and former business associates. Fran Schwartz and Nial McPherson were also on hand. Emmet walked around the mansion inspecting it as if he were responsible for its sale. Emmet hired a cleaning crew since Irish tradition suggested that a clean house brought good luck in the coming year. Emmet enjoyed good fortune in his adult life and this coming year of 2020 could present a great political victory for him.

Brenda, his wife, ushered guests into the dining room fit for a king. The table held 20 with the Callaghans at both ends. This year, there was an empty place set, an old Irish tradition, for Emmet's mom Siobhan, who passed away in January. Nial made dinner conversation lively as usual. Emmet told his guests he did not look forward to his next birthday, when Nial threw out a zinger.

"Emmet, quit talking about how you are feeling your age. Twain said that age is an issue of mind over matter. If you don't mind, it doesn't matter!" The guests got a good laugh.

He then told Emmet, "Where there's a will, there's a relative." Everyone enjoyed that one.

Guests ate a traditional Irish meal of corned beef and cabbage, potatoes, carrots and onions. For dessert, everyone had Christmas bread. Various forms of adult beverages circled the table. After a good hour of Nial's dinner entertainment, Emmet coaxed both Fran and Nial to his office for private conversation. The richly appointed office housed pictures of Emmet posing with important and influential people. He wanted visitors to know who he knew. They sat in leather chairs next to a fireplace.

"I hope both of you are enjoying the evening. This year could be the realization of my dream, our dreams. I know both of you grew up differently than I did. I can't tell you how many times I went to bed as a young lad worried about my dad. After mom shut down the tavern, my dad Paddy would head over to Mr. Patton's and come home who knows when. I know he was taking over the day's proceeds from the numbers games and drinking whiskey." Emmet drank very little and only during social occasions, vowing to differ from Paddy. After a little wine with dinner, he now had club soda in his glass. "He came home knackered every other night it seemed. Eventually that shite got him killed. That's what the world probably looks like to many people these days, wondering what can go wrong. I think we fix that this year."

"I know it must have been hard, Emmet. I don't have any basis of comparison. The biggest worry I had about my dad was that he would bring me something else to read," Fran added, whose father was a university professor.

"In my case, I was raised an only child which annoyed my sister," Nial joked. Fran and Emmet laughed as the Nial comedy hour continued.

"I spoke with Bienfait a couple of days ago. He told me he met with the German Prime Minister who is scared there won't be anything left of the Euro. There are so many problems in the EU that no one thinks this thing has a solution," Emmet said.

"So glad my blokes stayed with the Pound," Nial added.

"I would not exactly brag about that Nial," Fran retorted.

"We just need to restore order. Let's bring the monarchy to the whole bloody world!" Nial, who took a sip of his whiskey, clearly had a few too many since he never espoused love for the British monarchy.

"Nial, I'm thinking you are ossified right now. Easy on that whiskey, lad," Emmet suggested. How could he not be tipsy? Whiskey flowed for several hours. There was only so much the corned beef and cabbage could absorb.

"Tell your fucking help to quit serving me!" Nial blasted. Emmet and Fran bent over with laughter.

"Yeah Nial, we'll do that." Emmet wanted to talk about something else. "I think Holloway is getting the administration on board. His time at the GSB has really helped. Sanjay met with the Indian Prime Minister last week. I don't have to worry about Mozgov and the Russians. Talk about a partnership between government and business. Nobody is gonna fuck with those Russians! Our plans are slowly coming together. Good thing we don't have to rely on central bankers any more, huh Nial?" Emmet teased Fran with a wink.

"I know everyone always wants to take shots but what the hell did they want us to do. We had the president in our ass, the

Speaker of the House, and an untold number of business groups. They said do something, so we did, and then they didn't like it. Then we get blamed for all these so-called bubbles. I'll defend my record against any other chairman," Fran argued, banging a fist into her palm.

"Calm down Fran, I still love you like you were my own wifie." Nial blew a kiss at her. "You think Jefferson will make the big announcement before our Euro friends?" Nial asked Emmet.

"I don't know. These IAP fuckers may cause a problem." Emmet threw a scornful look at his floor. "And oh shite, those guys in the TP, who knows what they'll say. This is an election year, you know. But the public's docile and the president's popular. He needs to strike while the fire is still hot!"

"Without leadership, the people will perish," Fran raised her index finger to punctuate her statement.

"Here's to the right leadership." Emmet lifted his glass.

The three walked out of Emmet's office to join their significant others in one of the family rooms. They settled in for a night of Nial's incessant jokes. At midnight, Emmet looked at Brenda and told her he loved her. He rang in the 2020 New Year with, "To family, friends, and new beginnings."

When the party ended, guests, per Irish custom for good luck, left the house anywhere but the front door.

CHAPTER THIRTEEN
WITHDRAWAL

It had been a few short weeks since Geringer met with Chandler and Axel. This proved to be a trying time given his run for president while simultaneously digesting what Axel laid on him. Throughout the holiday season, he did his own investigation and had his staff read the IRC's and GSB's research papers. His own staff questioned this considering his pending announcement. After intense research and consultation with some of his well-placed internal contacts, he concluded that the country was falling under the influence of power brokers who were taking it in a direction he'd just as soon not see. He feared an even more authoritarian federal government. If he wanted to be true to himself, he needed to do something.

He remained convinced the new executive orders, and others no doubt to come, would make America worse, and not better as many thought. He also knew his old party, the GOP, or his new party, IAP, were unwilling to meet this head on. The TP was too inconsequential to mount a serious challenge, though he believed they would not be muzzled. The Democrats would not challenge their sitting president facing reelection. He hadn't connected the dots, but the dots themselves were troublesome. What could an old cowhand do? The answer became clear over the last weeks.

The senator invited IAP national chair Alex Carpenter and his chief of staff, Molly Sanders, to meet in his Senate office in the Hart Building the first Monday of the New Year. Carpenter and Sanders assumed the meeting's content to be about campaign strategy and location of the senator's announcement. Usually that detail might already be worked out, but Geringer abided by the new unwritten policy to defer campaigning until after the New Year.

"Molly, Alex, I hope you guys had a good vacation and are ready to get back to work." Molly and Alex sat across from Geringer's massive desk in two leather club chairs.

"You know it, Senator." Molly joined Geringer during his 2016 Presidential campaign providing support in his Denver headquarters. That year's GOP convention left many bruised feelings, hers among them. Geringer energized Millennials like herself, who felt an utter void after the GOP's machinations selecting the party's nominee. When Geringer pivoted to form a new party, she eagerly joined.

"Of course, Matt." Alex, the son of former Wisconsin GOP Senator Mike Carpenter, grew up around politics all his life and lived in D.C. for part of his youth. While attending the University of Wisconsin, he participated in student government, so naturally he would transition to a governance role later in life. Now he led the machinery of a still new political party at a very young age. Alex was instrumental in the recruitment of Gen Xers and Millennials, the future of the party.

"I don't quite know how to say this, which is unusual for me since I usually get to the point, but I've been doing a lot of soul searching. These holidays were a difficult time for me. I took time to reflect on my career in Colorado, the Senate, forming a new political party. And um, I have a great family who's supported me every step of the way -"

"Oh my God, Matt. Are you sick?" Molly shrieked, bringing her hands to her cheeks.

"No. I'm sorry. I don't mean to put that thought in your

head. Ah, I just wanted to say that I've given this a great deal of thought. This did not come easily for me, you know." He fidgeted in his chair, uncomfortable with what he had to say.

"Matt, what is it for heaven's sake?" Alex grew frustrated by the slow delivery and with the incessant barrage of texts vibrating his pocket.

"Ah, ah, I've decided not to run, for president." Geringer's voice trailed off into the low end of human hearing while he leaned back in his chair, locking his hands behind his head looking skyward.

"No fucking way, Matt! No! Fuck no! Tell me this is a joke, please." Alex boiled at the blasphemy pounding the desk in front of him. It was tough enough to run a fledgling new party without its de facto leader bailing out.

"Matt. No." Molly succumbed to her emotions. "You really are ill." She walked towards the door, tears streaming down her cheeks.

"Molly, please come back. I am not sick and this is not a joke." Geringer tilted forward in his chair and placed his hands on the desk. This was not going well. "I made a decision that was in the best interests of the family. 2016 was hard on us. We were a novelty in the last election. They're gonna come after us much harder."

"The Matt Geringer I know would not back out of a fight. Is someone blackmailing you with something? We can work it out. Is this about you smoking pot in college?" Alex folded his arms and bit his lower lip. The senator admitted cannabis use in college during the 2016 election. That hardly resonated in his home state who'd already legalized it and it would barely make a din now that it was legal in most of the country.

"No, Alex. There is no blackmail here. It's a, it's a family decision," Geringer repeated as he rubbed his mustache with his right hand. The thumb and index finger made a spreading pattern from the center of the stache out towards its edges.

"Then it must be an affair then, Matt. Come on, seriously, with everything you have going for you?" Molly returned to the conversation with bloodshot eyes. Geringer handed her a tissue.

"There is no affair. Louise has supported me all through my career and now it's time for me to honor her wishes. She just doesn't want to do it," Geringer emphasized.

This was not the way Alex and Molly wanted to usher in the New Year. They rehashed what Geringer told them. They were still in shock and asked him to consider the future of the party and the country. After much discussion, Alex challenged Geringer for a recommendation to replace him. Fortunately, Geringer had already thought this out before he invited them.

"The most logical person to replace me is Alfonso," Geringer concluded. Alfonso was Mr. Chancellor, a two-time All-American quarterback from the University of Texas and a second term senator from that state. Chancellor presented a unique profile with a Hispanic mother, a black father and fluency in Spanish.

Chancellor, originally elected as a member of the GOP in 2012, defected in 2016 to the IAP. He won reelection in 2018 with an astonishing 67% of the vote and was widely considered to be Geringer's running mate.

"As much as I am in shock, and you owe me a few drinks tonight, let's call Alfonso right away." Alex tapped his fingers rhythmically on the senator's desk. "No sense waiting."

"Agreed. Is he in Texas still? I think I have his number here," Geringer said while scrolling through his cell phone contact list. Alex nodded in agreement and the senator dialed placed the call on speaker. The phone rang but one time.

"Senator? Alfonso? Hey, I have Alex Carpenter and my chief Molly Sanders here with me. It's Matt."

"Matt. How are you, sir? Did you see the Cotton Bowl? Hook 'em horns, baby!" Alfonso responded enthusiastically. It remained to be seen if he would be as enthusiastic about the question he was about to face.

"It was a great season for them. Congratulations. Are you alone? We need to discuss something with you," Geringer asked.

"Yeah, I'm just in the kitchen getting something to eat. What's up?"

"Alfonso, you might want to grab a seat," Alex suggested.

Alex did most of the talking and explained Geringer's decision. Naturally, Chancellor was stunned. Then Alex posed the operative question."

"Alfonso, here's the deal. Matt's out, but I'd like you to replace him," Alex commanded. There was an unusually long silence. Geringer, Alex, and Molly stared at the phone. "Alfonso, you there? Alfonso? Did we lose him?"

"No, I'm here. Now I'm stunned again. You want me to replace Matt? He's the father of our party. How do you expect me to fill his shoes?"

"You can do this. Is this gonna be any harder than when you had to face Alabama in the Cotton Bowl with most of your offensive line suspended? No one gave you guys a chance." Alex remembered watching that game.

"OK, but this is no game. This is real. This is the presidency, of the United States. I'm flattered Alex but-" Chancellor replied.

"Look Alfonso. You know, the party needs you. I'm sure I

can calm our major donors who might freak out about Matt. I know the rest of the party caucuses will support you. I may have to do a little work on them, but I'm supremely confident I can get it done. Matt will be there for you. But we gotta get you in front of people ASAP. I guess one thing I haven't heard from you is if you'll accept the challenge?" Alex demanded.

Alex was an organizer and a marketer. He knew how to put a plan together and what was required to sell it. Since Chancellor was presumed to be the VP nominee, he felt no hesitation in selling this plan to his party.

For a young party like the IAP, there were no formal conventions or primaries. The party decided in 2017 that each state caucus would nominate a candidate to run for state or federal seats. Regarding the presidency, a state leader or Alex could serve as nominating agent. The presidential nominee would need a simple majority in the caucuses. Everyone presumed Geringer would receive 100% of the caucus vote. Alex figured Chancellor wouldn't achieve that percentage, though certainly an overwhelming majority. While the party had alternatives to Chancellor, they assumed he was next in line to succeed Geringer in 2024 or later.

"I mean I'm honored and very stunned, but yes, I accept." Chancellor's acceptance led to clapping from Geringer, Molly, and Alex.

"All right. I need to get on the phone and start calling state party leaders to get their consensus. Like I said, I don't see any trouble there. Get on the first flight to D.C. tomorrow and we'll meet at the IAP office and figure this thing out. Sorry to hit you with this Alfonso, but this is what we have to do. You know what I mean?" Alex asked.

"Understood," Alfonso answered.

"Matt, you better be ready to field a bunch of calls right after I talk to the party faithful. It's going to be a long night for you, cowboy. Hope you weren't planning on being anywhere," Alex commented.

With that short phone call, and over the course of about four hours, the election landscape of 2020 changed. Nobody understood the real reason Geringer decided to withdraw. He knew that fighting the power broker's plans would be a terrible distraction for him during a presidential run. He could be more useful working in the shadows. He made the ultimate sacrifice for his country and his party.

CHAPTER FOURTEEN
UNCOVERING THE PLAN

The holidays were not traditional for Axel Schultz. He spent a great deal of time unsuccessfully contacting Phish, to see if he had uncovered anything new. Apparently, Phish celebrated the holidays too.

Axel's contact at the GSB enjoyed the holidays as well, so he used the time to get caught up on writing and answering email from subscribers. Axel did all the writing and editing for his letter and sent it to a publisher for electronic or paper dissemination. The publisher handled marketing, billing and other back office functions. Some of his subscribers refused to use email, meaning the U.S. Postal Service saved the day.

Once New Year hit, things percolated. It took a few weeks in January for Phish to agree to a most unusual meeting. Phish changed normal communication, via the dark Internet, though he gave no reason. Perhaps it added mystery or intrigue, or perhaps there were security reasons. Maybe it was due to Chandler's presence. Axel would never know. Those were Omni's rules, you did it their way or no way.

Axel met Chandler at his New York apartment on a cold February morning and the two took a cab to an abandoned warehouse on 141st Street. Phish instructed both men to arrive without cell phones, timekeeping devices or anything electronic.

The day was windy and gray, conditions someone might expect for such a covert meeting. Before entering the dilapidated warehouse, Chandler ditched his coffee in a large waste container. He got the feeling there had not been trash service in some time by virtue of a folded newspaper covering results of the 2018 mid-term elections.

Chandler was none too excited to be there since it took him into parts of town he rarely visited. Not having a cell phone felt disconcerting too. *What if they needed help?* The men stared at metal bay doors with scarcely any white paint. *Should they go through those or the regular door at the end?*

Axel had no details other than to be at the warehouse. The warehouse's entry door only opened halfway since a loose hinge made it hang at an angle. The door ceased to be a problem after one of Axel's front kicks. Chandler had no inkling of his kicking dexterity. They walked in a few steps before assessing their situation.

"This place is as dark as a pocket Ax." *I'd rather be in a pocket right now.*

A glimmer of light emerged from a slit in the wall above one of the bay doors. Light filtering through small, closely aligned holes a few feet above ground made a dim light. The significance of the holes became clear when they saw torn three inch crime scene tape. They took cautious steps into the darkness. Were it not for these small amounts of light, it would have been almost impossible to see. Neither knew what to do next.

"I'm as nervous as a whore in church," Chandler whispered. *Even a whore could get out of a church quicker than they could get out of this building.*

After a couple of excruciatingly long minutes, the warehouse brightened. A burly man in a ski mask approached them, walking from a black van with no markings probably one hundred feet away. He dressed in jeans and a dark pea coat. He said nothing and approached with a scanning wand, passing it from head to toe on both men. "They're clean," he said into a cell phone.

Burly man slid behind them, clamping their arms and guiding them towards the van's cargo area. The rear door was already open. The cargo hold contained a single bench seat without seat belts, with no windows or view of the driver.

"And you still think this is a good idea, Ax?" Chandler muttered.

Axel had not said a word. Chandler, feeling more like a kidnap victim, surmised that Axel had been through this before.

Their speed felt normal. The starts and stops were smooth. At first they seemed to take lots of turns. Then a period of steady speed without stops followed. Sunday morning ensured a lighter amount of traffic. After about thirty minutes, they came to a stop, cold but alive. They heard the low frequency sound of a garage door. The van lurched forward and came to a stop. They heard the garage door once again, probably closing. It sounded like a residential door.

Burly man opened the door and escorted them, with a firm hold on their arms, to chairs behind a folding picnic table. The dimly lit garage looked like that of a suburban house, maybe 20x20 but stripped of everything except for a shelf with a few cans of oil, a gas can and a lawn mower in the corner, no bag attached. An interior door presumably led to a residence. They dared not take a step in that direction for fear of upsetting burly man.

Chandler watched his nervous breath escape his mouth. The garage door trembled like a leaf shaken by the wind. The bare picnic table had a laptop, two notepads and pens. The laptop connected via a CAT-6 cable to an RJ-45 jack in the nearest wall. After they sat, burly man powered on the laptop and walked towards the driver side door where he stood vigilant.

He remained silent and his mask never revealed his identity. The power cycle completed, an application auto loaded and opened a chat window, no doubt an encrypted session. Without a device for voice communication, the meeting would be about typing and watching a computer screen. A message at the screen's bottom indicated what occurred at the remote end.

REMOTE SIDE TYPING

The main text appeared at the screen's top.

PLEASE ENTER CODE

Axel typed "Vladimir". Maybe Phish was Russian after all, Chandler speculated. Axel never told him since he didn't know himself.

HELLO AXEL AND MR. SCOTT. I HOPE FOR
GOOD SESSION.

Chandler assumed Phish to be on the other end, but they did not identify themselves. Either Phish lacked English fluency or was intentionally curt. The laptop did not have a camera, at least not a visible one.

PROVIDE SUMMARY NOW AND ENCRYPTED FILE
LATER. STAND BY.

At this point in the transmission, Phish remained genderless or perhaps represented a group of people. What followed included more than either man expected.

THE GSB WILL BECOME DE FACTO CENTRAL BANK OF THE WORLD WITH UNPRECEDENTED CONTROL.

A NEW ELECTRONIC CURRENCY FOR INTERNATIONAL EXCHANGES WILL BE DEVELOPED AND CALLED THE "MUNDI".

ALL PAPER NOTES AND COINS WILL BE ABOLISHED. ONLY ELECTRONIC MONEY LEGAL.

GOLD WORLDWIDE STORED AND PROTECTED IN MILITARY INSTALLATIONS UNDER THE SUPERVISION OF GSB.

PRIVATELY OWNED GOLD USED TO PAY DEBT OWED TO GOVERNMENT AT A RATE OF THREE TIMES ITS MARKET VALUE. NO GOLD COLLECTION.

GSB WILL HAVE AUTHORITY TO DIRECT CENTRAL BANKS TO TRANSFER MONEY ELECTRONICALLY TO PRIVATE BANK ACCOUNTS.

THIS ALL FOR NOW. QUESTIONS?

The summary appeared pasted from another document since it came all at once. It flowed nothing like the rest of the interaction. Both men were writing furiously on provided notepads. Axel knew Phish would not understand the impact of these details so he kept the question direct. He asked if there was a timetable for all this.

NO TIMETABLE. ANNOUNCEMENT MAYBE AFTER
USA PREZ ELECTION. QUESTIONS?

Axel indicated that he had no further questions and thanked Phish for the information. He never asked Chandler if he had any. There was a notification at the bottom of the screen.

REMOTE CONNECTION TERMINATED

The laptop screen flashed twice then another application executed that appeared to engage the hard drive. Burly man walked towards them, closed the laptop, grabbed them by their arms and walked them back to the van. They got in and evidently backed out of the garage. After what seemed to be a little longer drive than before, the man stopped the windowless van and opened the door. Burly man waved them out of the vehicle, closed the door and sped away.

A few joggers stared with curiosity wondering if they should call the police. Axel and Chandler realized they were in Central Park on the 85th Street Traverse. They walked a short distance before hailing a cab for the return to Chandler's apartment. The two said nothing during the ride back. There was no need to reveal their morning to a New York City cabbie.

At his place, Chandler brewed coffee to warm up from their chilly experience. The absence of heat in the van and garage on a serious New York winter morning chilled their bones. After serving Axel, they debriefed in the living room.

"Well, you got a little taste of what it's like to gather information, huh Chandler?"

"A little?"

"Yeah, that was different than my interactions with Omni.

210

Phish wasn't real keen on having a journalist around, so consider yourself fortunate. But as far as what we learned today, I don't see how this will fly. Can't be constitutional."

"And you're still sure all this info is legit?"

"Yes. There's no reason for Omni to make all this up. Think about it. What would they gain?"

After a second's hesitation, Chandler replied, "Yeah, OK."

"Now another twist would be if this was fake information that government allowed to be hacked. But I don't know why the GSB would do that either. Let's just assume that all of this is legit for now. We can then validate this assumption and improve our understanding as we get more information." He'd encountered bad intelligence before, so there was always the need to verify and build. "I've mentioned this technique to you before, Bayes' theorem."

"Ahh, yeah. I seem to recall something from a statistics class, back in the day. I'll let you run with that one." Chandler's strengths were not in math.

Chandler knew he couldn't do anything with what he learned for a variety of reasons. He made an inviolable promise to Geringer. He committed to Axel not to reveal these details to the public, save for Arianne. Even without these commitments, he couldn't stake his journalistic reputation solely on information received in an encrypted chat session with a reviled hacker group.

There was no reason for him to talk about this until Axel learned more. He connected what they learned from Phish to the stranger's comments on Christmas Day. The State was definitely looking to expand. He never shared with Axel the encounter with Habakk. He did not feel compelled to share. In Chandler's mind, at least for a small nugget of knowledge, the student could become the master.

The information revealed in that garage pointed to an evolving crisis. Would Congress pass new laws? Would President Jefferson circumvent the legislative process with Executive Orders? How would Americans, struggling with economic turmoil and constant threat of cyber terror, respond to a loss of financial sovereignty? Would the hope of freedom *from* economic hardship make people overlook giving up their specific freedoms, their freedoms *of* something?

***

Chandler manufactured an excuse to be in D.C. to see his girlfriend and tell her about his secret meeting. That was no conversation for the phone. She picked him up at Reagan after his late afternoon flight and met him by door number three in the baggage claim level - destination Maxwell condo.

Chandler threw his bags in the already open trunk and scurried to the passenger side door. "Hi honey!" He stretched over to the driver's side to kiss his girlfriend.

"Chandler, you look so tired."

"Nice to see you too," Chandler said sarcastically. He didn't think he looked any different from usual.

"No, really. Did you get any sleep last night? Were you at the strip club again?" Arianne teased.

"Yeah, the girls were incredible last night. I kept it to a couple of lap dances." Chandler paused and sighed considering how to begin. "I told you I needed to see you and I didn't want to talk on the phone obviously."

"Must be something big. And here I was hoping you just wanted to see me!" She already had something on her mind for later.

"Well, yeah, but this thing is so much bigger than I

thought," Chandler's excitement was palpable.

"I can tell by your voice," Arianne acknowledged while steering her car north on the George Washington Memorial Parkway.

Chandler began with the warehouse. "You know, this warehouse Ari was scary. Hardly any light and we just stood there waiting, but I wasn't sure what we were waiting for. It's not like Ax got a bunch of details, you know it was just to go to this abandoned warehouse. And then there was this burly dude who-"

"You know, I don't think it was a smart idea to go to some warehouse. That could've been dangerous."

"Yeah, you know what journalists will do sometimes to get a story. Hey, not to derail this line of thought but are you hungry?" Chandler realized it had been several hours since he last ate.

"Absolutely. Chinese?"

"Yep."

There was a small Chinese place close to her condo. It was a popular take out joint since it had little seating. Chandler called in the order. "The usual for you?" he asked Arianne.

"Yes."

Chandler placed his order for chicken lo mein, Kung Pao chicken and hot and sour soup.

"Ten minutes? OK," Chandler acknowledged. "No matter what you order from a Chinese place it's always ready in ten minutes."

"Efficiency, Chan. Efficiency."

Chandler related the drive to the unknown destination. "Yeah, so burly dude puts us in the back of the van. Then, I don't know exactly how long we were moving. Maybe thirty minutes. You could just hear regular city traffic, regular for a Sunday. Then we got out in this residential garage. So I knew weren't in Manhattan. We might have been in Yonkers. I thought we got on a highway. Maybe. It was colder than hell in that garage after the ride."

They approached the takeout place and Chandler popped out of the car. Arianne circled the block a few times. No chance of finding parking after the place's glowing review in D.C. Cuisine magazine.

Chandler visited a barbeque place in Austin once where he waited for two hours just to get in. This Chinese place wasn't *that* popular but you had to be patient if you wanted to dine in. After fifteen minutes of Arianne's circling, he emerged with food. In a few minutes they'd be at her place.

After arriving at her condo, Arianne had one thing in mind and it evoked no images of food or his story. She knew she'd have to wait for her satisfaction. Chandler continued the tale while they ate at the kitchen counter.

"All the while burly dude keeps an eye on us." Chandler slurped on his hot and sour soup.

"Seriously, Chan. This sounds a little too spy versus spy, like something you'd see in a movie." She dug into her Kung Pao chicken.

"It was all legit. I was scared shitless about getting into a van with no windows and a masked burly dude that looked like he could break me in half."

"I know. I can't believe you got in that van. You must really trust Axel considering how dangerous this could have been."

"For sure. I mean this ride to who knows where. My stomach was in knots. But Ax? He looked as cool as a cucumber. So anyway..." He explained the encrypted chat session along with details Phish provided. "So when Phish transmitted all the big news in the message, we're writing like mad men trying to get it all. No telling how long it would be on the screen."

"But you said there was another file coming with detail, right?"

"Yeah, but Phish didn't say how it was gonna get to us or I should say, Ax. Can you pass the soy sauce?"

She handed him a packet. "I can't say I fully appreciate what all those things mean, the Mundi, the gold and such, but I'm sure some people are going to scream bloody murder. I mean, I don't know how this is constitutional."

"Spoken like a lawyer. That's what Ax said. There's going to be a fight over this and it could get ugly, real ugly - like a battle for control of government ugly."

"Since I work at State, I wonder if there is something going on there that I could dig up? I mean they have to know something you gotta think."

"No. No. Please." Chandler put down his chopsticks and shook his head. "Don't get involved in this. There's no need. We have a good stream of information and I told Geringer I would keep it quiet, which technically I guess I didn't by telling you. I think he'd be OK with that. He probably told his wife." Chandler realized at that moment he equated Arianne with a spouse, at least for this secret.

She smiled at the comparison. "I get it. Hey, what does your fortune cookie say?" She had finished her meal.

"Huh, I guess I've been doing all the talking so I'm behind." He cracked his open. "It says, 'If you have something good in your life, don't let it go.'"

"Hmm interesting. Mine says, 'Fortune favors the brave.'"

"Keep all this stuff we talked about to yourself, please. I don't want you to get involved in all this, OK?" He gestured with pleading hands.

"Sure. Sure," She repeated. A devilish grin spread across her face. "But my silence will be expensive."

He considered the cost as she walked him to her bedroom after dinner.

CHAPTER FIFTEEN
ARI'S ADVENTURE

The State Department building resided in the Foggy Bottom section of D.C. just north of the west end of the mall and Lincoln Memorial. The old building underwent a complete renovation. Arianne felt fortunate to have an office with a window, though she stood a fine chance with 4,000 windows in the place. Old-timers still referred to it as Foggy Bottom, though its official name was the Harry S. Truman Building. The term Foggy Bottom referenced fog and smoke that accumulated near the Potomac when the State Department settled there in 1947. Thankfully, for employees, they breathed cleaner air now.

Arianne had wrestled with the idea of helping Chandler despite her assurances to the contrary. He trusted her with this secret, a secret he promised a U.S. senator he'd keep. This mattered to her. She didn't doubt his feelings, though neither had used the "L" word yet. Still, her job at State might provide *something* that could help him. It wouldn't hurt just to poke around, and besides, her cookie told her that fortune favored the brave.

She had to be careful with her snooping. She couldn't go around asking about a world currency called a Mundi. Someone would be sure to ask her where she heard about it. More generically, she could ask about the GSB and FSB. It might take longer, but at least she could come at it without attracting as much suspicion. After a couple of weeks of frustration, she caught a break. Her snooping led her to a mid-level staffer by the name of Alyce Hampton. She didn't know Alyce, yet someone she knew did. Through this contact she learned that

Alyce was being considered for a position at the FSB. She closed the door to her office and called Alyce.

"Alyce Hampton."

"Hello, Alyce, my name is Arianne Maxwell. I'm an attorney here at State and I'm doing a little research. A friend of mine suggested I call you. I hear you may be up for a job at the FSB?"

"Oh, hello Arianne. Yes, you know that department is growing and it seems the place to be these days. What can I do for you?"

"I'm helping my boss, who is meeting with Swiss diplomats. The Swiss are concerned about new reporting requirements for their financial institutions. They still have heartburn about all the regs that came down after 2008. I don't know if you remember but there were all these accounts the formerly 'secret' Swiss banking system had to reveal and then it turned out there were a bunch of U.S. citizens with accounts there." Arianne skillfully crafted a viable story around her inquiry.

"I remember reading about it but that's about all. I know I didn't have any money in Switzerland and barely had any money here," Alyce declared.

"Yes, I know what you mean," Arianne giggled. Truth be told, she would be more likely to have an overseas account, at least one her dad may have set up for her. "So my boss wants me to figure out if there will be new requirements for foreign banks. He's afraid he'll get the runaround from the FSB. Would you know someone I could talk to? The FSB is tight-lipped these days."

"There is a guy who I was told to talk to who could help me. Sharp guy. He's a consultant who apparently is doing or will do work for the FSB and even knew about the workings of the

GSB."

"Sounds like a good resource."

"Let me give you his information." Alyce passed along the name, Levi Saltzman, and his contact information. "I hope it works out for you."

"Thank you so much and good luck with your hopeful move to the FSB."

"Thanks."

Something in the contact details caught Arianne's attention. The phone number did not appear to be a D.C. number. It looked like a New York City number with the 212 area code. For all she knew, FSB employees, however many there were, worked in D.C. Then again, it could be someone's cell number from New York. Arianne opened her door and peeked out, making sure no one stood nearby. Satisfied, she closed it again and called Mr. Saltzman. After an inordinately large number of rings, voice mail never kicked in, he answered.

"This is Levi Saltzman."

"Hello, Mr. Saltzman, my name is Arianne Maxwell and I'm an attorney over at the State Department. Your name was given to me as someone who could help with a meeting my boss is having."

"And someone gave you *my* name for that? For something with the State Department?"

"Yes, we're meeting Swiss diplomats who are questioning new bank reporting requirements by the FSB. The State Department thought we should handle this on a diplomatic level first and not get anyone from FSB involved." She stuck with the diplomatic smoothing ruse. "I got your name as someone who consulted with the Swiss during the 2008 crisis." Alyce never told her that Levi consulted with the Swiss. It was a chance she had to take.

"I'm not saying another word until you tell me who referred you."

"Alyce Hampton. Do you know her?"

"No. Where does she work?"

"She's a staffer here at State. Honestly, I don't work with her. Someone I know referred her. She's trying to get a job at the FSB and said you'd be a good resource for the Swiss banking issue."

"I don't know Miss Maxwell. I usually don't-"

"I just need your advice on how you handled them in 2008 or any regulation the FSB might propose and how the Swiss might react. Maybe what you know about the FSB would be of benefit too."

"How I handled them in 2008? I don't talk on the phone much, especially government phones. Too much snooping going on for me."

"Yes, I understand so how can we do this?"

"Next time you'll be in town, let me know and I'll carve out some time for you." Levi went from obstructionist to accommodating. Maybe it all changed when she said she needed his advice; that always a good conversational starter.

"In town? Aren't you in D.C.?"

"No. No. I'm in New York City. I'm at the Federal Reserve Bank here."

"Oh. I thought you might have been in D.C."

"No. I'm working at the Fed now. If you want to talk, you'll have to come here."

"Sounds good. I'll give you a heads up when I'm going to be there."

"All right. Just give me some notice, OK?"

"Sounds good. Thank you, Mr. Saltzman."

"Have a good day."

Arianne had traveled down a slippery slope, a slope Chandler asked her not to descend. Hopefully, good fortune awaited her at the bottom.

***

The Levi meeting had no sanction. Arianne had to devise an authentic sounding story for her New York fishing expedition. Her travel got thwarted soon after her conversation with Levi due to attacks on U.S. embassies. The attacks were both physical and cyber. The Secretary of State wanted all hands on deck. Chandler accounted for the next obstacle. How could she come into town and not tell him? Fortunately, she caught a break when he had an out-of-town assignment. Her window of opportunity opened.

She boarded the 2158 Acela train arriving at New York's Penn Station before noon. She preferred traveling via train between the two cities. The Acela quiet car made for a great place to get work done or, in her case, catch a couple of winks. She felt fortunate to have an unoccupied seat next to her when her dozing caused her to dive into it. Her slumber turned to hunger when she arrived in the Big Apple. Penn Station proved no destination for gourmet eating. The hallways were full of commuters; the eateries were too narrow, and the tables were not exactly clean. With little time to eat, she grabbed a mozzarella on an herbed focaccia and hurried out of the station, sandwich in hand, laptop bag over her shoulder. Her next destination would be the Red Line train.

The early spring day in New York was dry, albeit a bit chilly. The Red Line train took her to Fulton Street and she walked the rest of the way to the New York Fed. Having been on public transportation many times in Chicago, she was used to this commuting mode. The energy of this city had no match in the United States. The city always seemed alive, yet in a different way than the Windy City. She understood why New York acquired the moniker of the "city that never sleeps." She definitely would not be sleeping in Chandler's apartment tonight.

The New York Fed building exhibited a design in the neo-renaissance style with an appearance not unlike a fortress resembling a Florentine palazzo. Trust and confidence were the architect's goal. Supposedly, this building stored more gold than Fort Knox or West Point, though no military guarded this facility. The owners of most of this gold, not known to most, were foreign central banks. There was a reason to store gold here during World War II, ostensibly to hide it from the Nazis, but that regime had fallen seventy-five years earlier. The gold weighed so much that it sat in a vault below street level, resting directly on Manhattan bedrock.

Levi Saltzman met Arianne at the security desk to sign her in. Levi was a thin, baldish, gaunt looking fellow who appeared to be in his forties. Well dressed in a single-breasted, dark blue suit, white shirt, red tie, and black cap-toe oxfords, he looked every bit the banker.

"Good afternoon, Miss Maxwell." He assumed the appellation of "Miss" from the absence of a wedding ring.

"Hello, Mr. Saltzman, thanks again for meeting with me." Arianne matched his formality and extended her hand for a firm shake that he returned with equal firmness. His averted, shifty eyes, distracted her.

As they left the security area, he kept his eyes towards the ceramic floor. She didn't know if his gaze represented shyness or obfuscation. His badge bore a different color than others. She didn't pay attention to what elevator button he depressed. Rather than going up to his presumed office; they headed down below street level.

"I guess you're taking me to the vault? I can tell my friends I saw all the gold, huh?"

"Hmmm." Levi displayed no amusement and barely looked up.

She surmised they landed above the vault when they exited the elevator - no gold in sight. Saltzman led her to a small office, maybe 10 x 10 that housed a nondescript table, could have been 1940s issue, and a couple of old metal chairs, also likely from the Truman administration. There was no phone in the room or communication jacks. The sole wood door gave no view to the hallway or anything else. Nothing hung on the walls. It would have made a fine solitary confinement cell. The room's temperature forced her to keep on her jacket. She sat on the old chair and deployed her laptop. Her laptop traveled everywhere with her on business and she preferred it to a small tablet without a keyboard. With her next generation cellular access, she could always have a connection, except in this room with an absence of signal.

"Oh. It appears I can't get any connection here."

"Yeah, forget about that. It won't happen down here," Levi explained.

"Let me open my note application and we can start," she indicated. A minute later, she was ready and signaled Levi.

"The Fed really takes their direction now from the FSB. I'm helping the Fed with this transition." At least now, Arianne knew what he did here. "I found information for you Miss Maxwell that discusses expected reporting requirements. I'm sure the Swiss or anyone else will have heartburn, but this is the world in which we live." Levi produced a very shiny silver flash drive from his suit pocket. "There is a file here that I can share with you."

She looked at his shiny, vacuous eyes, considering whether she should plug this drive in her State Department-owned laptop. She couldn't come this far and refuse him either.

"Oh, don't worry, we have anti-virus software out the wazoo around here. The IT department is strict," Levi assured.

She took it from him and inserted it into her USB port. The drive revealed a copy of a document with Malcolm Holloway's signature that outlined anticipated regulation for foreign banks and new compliance mandates around FBAR or the Report of Foreign Bank and Financial Accounts. FBAR became incorporated into the Bank Secrecy Act of 1970, requiring individuals to report foreign accounts to U.S. authorities. The new FSB regs mandated quarterly reporting instead of yearly.

"I'll let you take notes, but that's all. It won't be official until next month, though if you're having diplomatic meetings with the Swiss, it's better to be informed."

She took notes, presuming value for Chandler. "Is there anything else you can think of that the FSB might have up its sleeve?" It turned out to be a poor choice of words.

"Listen, you just asked me about a very specific thing with bank reporting. Now you are asking me for something else." His formerly pallid complexion gained a pinkish tone.

"I just thought you might have something more, you know."

He loosened his red tie as he craned his neck and then spun and looked her straight in the eye. "No, I don't know, and frankly I think we're done here. I gave you what you asked for. I have my own job to consider."

"And what exactly is your job? You said something about helping them with transition," she retorted with a defiant note.

"It's not important. Pack up and let me walk you out." Levi abruptly ended the conversation. He yanked his flash drive out of the USB port and watched her with vulpine sharpness as she shut down her machine and returned it to her bag.

As they retraced their steps to the building's entrance, she noticed once again that no one had the same colored badge as Levi. He gave her a very curt "thank you" at the security desk and left. She by no means hit the mother lode, but she had something. She would have plenty of time to think about how she'd tell Chandler on the return Acela ride.

Back inside the Fed, Levi returned to a regular office, an office with glass panels above street level. He spoke on the phone. "Yes, everything went as planned." He listened for a few seconds. "I understand. Will do, sir. Good night."

***

On her return ride to D.C., Arianne thought about how everything materialized with Alyce Hampton and then Levi. She retrieved useful information from Levi, and evidently pushed the wrong button when she extended conversation to the FSB. *Why did he get so sensitive?* His badge stood out, given that she didn't see anyone else with the same color. *Is he the only consultant working at the New York Fed?* She didn't want to be rude and stare at his badge, so she never saw his title, only his picture and what appeared to be his name. The meeting in the bowels of the building also proved odd. Perhaps he wanted his encounter kept away from curious eyes. *If this was such a secret, why would he share it with her?* Also, Alyce never told her how she got linked up with Levi. Maybe that wasn't important.

There were many questions in her head and no one to talk to. Chandler was gone, she didn't know Axel well enough to call him and even if she did, he'd probably be mad that she took this solo action. She couldn't expose Larry Maxwell, her father, to this. She'd have to reveal too much. There would also be no way she'd talk about this on the phone. Arianne thus turned to an old friend for advice.

Senator Thomas Shaw ranked as senior senator, Democrat from the state of Maine. He also chaired the Foreign Relations Subcommittee on global terrorism. A few years ago the subcommittee needed to consult with the State Department regarding the kidnapping of cyber terror suspects and holding them without specific charges for an undetermined amount of time. The Justice Department gave the nod to these abductions, though foreign countries, especially U.S. allies, balked. Arianne provided legal support for her boss, who testified in closed-door sessions.

After being in D.C. a few years, Arianne drifted from one short-term relationship to another. Men were very attracted to her but she also wanted to be taken seriously as an attorney, not just be the object of lust. Some of this she brought on herself with her coquette manner, a behavior she continued with Chandler. Being self-deprecating, she fell right into a mold of what men eventually thought of her. Shaw didn't treat her that way. They formed a mental connection first. The physical attraction came later.

The attraction breached an important covenant for Shaw, a married family man. The two grew closer mentally and eventually physically. They only saw each other sporadically and frankly she wasn't ready for an intense relationship. She never really had one. Shaw did not impose demands of a conventional relationship. She enjoyed spending time with him while being free to lead her life otherwise. The persistent guilt also haunted her.

For him, however, the relationship had significant depth. He loved her. Unfortunately for Shaw, his wife harbored her own suspicions. She related that to an aunt who was the sister of Emmet Callaghan, a lethal combination for Shaw. It took little time for Emmet to confirm the liaison and confront Shaw. He instructed Shaw to step away from Arianne or risk political damage. This was no idle threat. Shaw took it seriously. Shaw spent his entire career as a professional politician who'd held an elected or appointed office. The risks were too great.

In return, Emmet gained a useful pawn since he never told his sister that he'd discovered anything. To the contrary, he described Shaw as an upstanding character whose wife probably felt neglected. Emmet and the senator reached a mutual understanding. Emmet saw no evil and Shaw saw no Arianne. Shaw knew that if he breached that understanding, he'd lose his career and his family. To date, Callaghan had not asked for anything, though Shaw always feared the inevitable call.

Shaw agreed to meet Arianne for a post-business hours drink shortly after her return from meeting Saltzman. He graded the risk of angering Emmet as minor, especially in a public setting like the Colonist Pub, a D.C. establishment popular with Capitol Hill types. The Colonist served primarily as a drinking establishment with only appetizers on the menu. Barrel aged spirits were their specialty. Replica barrels lined the perimeter of the establishment, where standing patrons used them as tables. An impressive assortment of bottles and mini-barrels lined the main bar area. The place had a private room that sat behind large glass doors. The ceiling sported an industrial look, partially concealed through the use of white paint. The walls were a combination of both painted and unpainted brick. It was a loud and boisterous crowd.

Senator Shaw, who had not seen the object of his affection in some time, waited in a booth, slowly sipping a scotch. He sported his normal congressional attire of a dark suit, yellow tie, and a white shirt. His heart skipped a beat when she approached.

"Tom, it's so good to see you." She embraced him after he sprang from the booth — she did not reciprocate his tenderness. She took off her light coat and placed it on her side of the booth.

"Arianne, you look beautiful as always." Shaw smiled and eyed her from head to toe.

"Thanks, Tom." She looked down after the compliment.

"You and Chandler, I guess you've been seeing him for a while, huh?" It didn't take long for Shaw to inquire about her social life. He knew of their relationship primarily through others. As per his mutual understanding with Mr. Callaghan, he limited his contact with her.

"Yes, he's out of town now in Panama covering something there. It has something to do with the Chinese and the Canal."

The waitress approached. "Hello Senator Shaw. Nice to see you again. What can I get you two?"

"I'm fine with my scotch. Arianne?"

"Oh, just bring me whatever your house white wine is."

"I'll have it out in just a minute."

Shaw returned to his earlier line of questions. "Chandler's a good journalist even if he makes my party look bad occasionally. Are you happy with him?"

"Yes. Yes. I don't think I've dated anyone this long since, maybe, ever. We just don't see each other enough, with him traveling and living in New York, you know."

"Hopefully, you two can at least be in the same city."

"Yeah, me too! Let me tell you in more detail why I wanted to talk to you." She changed the subject, feeling uncomfortable discussing her current love interest. Though they broke off their affair easily and quietly, she wondered if he was just being polite by asking or exhibiting jealousy.

After the waitress returned with wine, Arianne delved into the details of her adventure by discussing Alyce Hampton, Levi, and her trip to the Fed. She couldn't tell him the real reason she started the investigation, so she stuck with her story about the Swiss diplomats.

"I think there's more to this guy, yeah. I do find it strange that this Levi character sent you to the bowels of the New York Fed. It's like he was trying to hide it from everyone else or something." Shaw looked at an incoming text on his phone, temporarily distracted. "I'm sorry, let me-"

"It's OK." Arianne paused, giving him time to reengage.

He typed a few characters. "Go ahead, sorry about that."

"No problem. Well, I thought the meeting setup was weird too. But I couldn't really challenge him on that, so I played along."

"And what he gave you was useful?"

"Yeah, it should help us in our meeting with the Swiss. But I would appreciate it if you could find out anything else about Levi. I don't want to give my boss something that's not accurate. Levi appeared to be a consultant. But I got burned once by a consultant so I am on guard."

"Let me check it out and I'll get back to you. Ahh, let me

make a note to myself." Shaw typed into his phone and put it away in his suit pocket. He reflected on the past. "You know, I still think about our time together. I know it meant more to me than it did to you."

"Tom, that was a while ago. You said it was for the best and you know it really was. It could only get more complicated from there." She looked down at her glass, swirling it a few times. She had no interest in revisiting old feelings.

"I know. I just wanted to share with you that I still think about that time and will always cherish it. I still think about you, and I'm sincere when I say this. I'm happy that you found someone. You deserve it. I hope he realizes what he has."

She did too.

CHAPTER SIXTEEN
TRIDENT

Trips, particularly overseas ones, were great sources of excitement for Chandler. There were new people, new adventures, and with as many frequent flier miles as he'd accumulated, upgraded travel. There were harrowing moments that built his journalistic experience. On a trip to Kandahar, an IED exploded one hundred feet in front of his taxi. During a return flight from Buenos Aires, a passenger became unruly and the flight had to make an emergency landing in Caracas. For a young journalist, these experiences added to the excitement despite their element of danger.

Trips were harder now for one reason and one reason only, Arianne. His most recent trip took him to Panama to investigate a terror plot to disable the Canal. Three years earlier, there had been an attempt to detonate explosives in the new locks, which fortunately a canal worker foiled while performing maintenance. Panama completed the new locks in 2016 to allow transit of Post-Panamax ships that required wider, longer, and deeper lock channels. After the United States' official departure on December 31, 1999, Taiwan became more involved through agricultural partnerships and real estate development in former areas of the Canal Zone.

Panama always had diplomatic relations with Taiwan but not Mainland China. This didn't stop the Communist Chinese from showering investment dollars on the isthmus, so much so that Panama wanted to switch its diplomatic relations to the Communist regime in hope of garnering more investment from the financial powerhouse. A WikiLeaks missive detailed a 2009 attempt by Panama to switch allegiance that the Chinese rebuffed for fear of alienating Taiwan. The Chinese nevertheless continued to invest heavily in the country. They also transited much of their country's shipping traffic through the Canal. Given this transit volume, the Chinese were unnerved by the attempt on the Canal. Though China had no defense treaty with Panama, Chinese warships traversed the canal with frequency, much to the chagrin of the U.S. Department of Defense. Chinese and U.S. warships often passed each other in Gatún Lake.

The Chinese, ever mindful of protecting their interests, had their intelligence services working with Panamanian military to snuff out potential terror acts. Chandler secured interviews with Panamanian military officials, the Chinese trade representative, and Li Zhang, he of the IRC board. During the interview with the trade representative and Mr. Zhang, Chandler asked if recent intelligence collaboration was a sign of further diplomatic, economic and security cooperation between the countries. Mr. Zhang pointed out that the current relationship between the two countries had reached a new zenith, though formal diplomatic relations were not in the cards.

Zhang suggested Chandler broaden his perspective and look towards more global economic and financial cooperation and not just fixate on what's happening between two countries. He emphasized that tighter international cooperation would be instrumental in combating terror and keeping the world out of an economic abyss. Chandler wondered if that made an oblique reference to what he learned from Phish three months earlier on that cold February morning.

Back in Washington now, Chandler got reacquainted with

his girlfriend. After catching up conversationally and physically, they moved from her bedroom to the living room, sitting side-by-side watching TV and sipping cold beer. Arianne prepared to deliver her confession by clutching his hand and turning towards him.

"Remember when you asked me not to snoop around at work?" Arianne started this conversation sheepishly, her gaze directed towards her lap.

"Yeah. I said stay out of it. I had it under control."

"Well, Chan, let's just say that ah, um, I deviated from that a bit." She broke the hand hold and took a sip from her beer, looking straight ahead.

"Define a bit." He perked up, rotating his body towards her.

Arianne still looking straight in front of her, detailed her ruse and conversation with Alyce Hampton, who gave her Levi Saltzman's name.

"OK, but you took it no further than that I hope." He already had a problem with what she did but figured he could contain the damage.

Now she turned towards him. "Not exactly. I thought since I got that far, I could, ahh, that I could continue with Levi."

"I really don't like where this is headed." He'd like it even less when she told him about her trip to New York and the meeting in the Fed building. He looked towards the heavens and threw his arms in the air. "I told you to stay out of this Ari. Why in the world would you-"

"I just want to help you. I know this is so important to you and that's what people do who care for each other." Her eyes welled with tears.

"I know, honey, but Ari. I don't know where all this is going to lead. Have you told anyone about this? Tell me what happened when you met Levi."

She skipped his question to address the Levi encounter. She knew answering the question would bring more worry. She recounted her meeting with Levi and described the interaction in the nondescript room in the bowels of the Fed.

"So he gave you a flash drive and you plugged it in?"

She took another sip of beer, rolling suds in her mouth before swallowing. "Yes, that's how we looked at the document."

"Hmm. Wonder why he didn't just bring a paper doc? Maybe that was more suspicious. Or he could have brought his own laptop and pulled something from the network, but then it would have flagged his access of the file. Did he ask you to bring your laptop?" His mind circled around concern.

"Honestly, I don't recall. You know I take it everywhere." She nervously tucked her hair behind her ears.

Chandler grew suspicious of the interaction but couldn't figure out exactly why. He thought it too convenient that she could link up with someone at State who knew Levi, who gave her information. Granted, her request seemed legitimate.

"And after you saw this document, you said you took notes cuz he wouldn't let you have the file?"

"Yeah, that's right. Then I asked him if he knew if the FSB had anything new planned that he could tell me and that's when he clammed up, got very disturbed honestly and just ripped the flash out of my USB port." She retracted her hand quickly towards her torso, demonstrating Levi's removal of the flash drive.

It was dawning on Chandler. Getting intelligence required

time. You had to develop contacts, gain trust, and above all, be patient. Then you had to interpret the information. It was all about collection and analysis. Her encounter proved too easy. He knew the difficulty Axel had getting investment intelligence. That's why his readers paid so much for his letter. His work took time. The local El Mundo bureaus worked long and hard to develop contacts. No, something did not make sense here.

"Ari, I hate to tell you this but this looks as crooked as a dog's hind leg." He rubbed his chin, trying to unravel the mystery of her adventure.

"I know. Now, after talking to you, it seems that way." Arianne accepted his dog metaphor. "I was thinking about it on my trip back on the train." She had been harboring this worry and now seemed relieved that Chandler reached a similar conclusion.

"So why would Levi give you anything? No offense, but you're not somebody real important over at State. He could have called your boss and checked your story. Why would he give you anything?" Chandler hoped his reflection didn't insult his girlfriend.

"Chan, maybe he did give me something." She took one final swig of beer and put the unfinished bottle on the coffee table.

"Like what?"

"Before he gave me the flash drive, I remembered training on cyber security and I hesitated to plug it in. Then he told me not to worry because of all the anti-virus software they have at the Fed."

"So you think his flash drive had some sort of program that read your hard drive? Or infected your machine?" Chandler read an article about nefarious types grabbing information from unsuspecting people's hard drives. Thieves could also steal data from cell phones using USB thumb drives secretly housed in cell phone charging adapters.

"Maybe he infected my laptop, but I haven't had any problems with it. I've never heard of people stealing stuff from people's hard drives with flash drives." The increased usage of flash drives and other portable storage made them an easy vehicle to conduct digital mayhem.

Chandler had an idea, but he needed someone with IT knowledge. He had befriended the network engineer at the local El Mundo bureau and before he met Arianne, he and Jason Hardin caught a few Nats ball games whenever Chandler was in town. He called Jason.

"Yo, hello."

"Jason, what's up? It's Chandler."

"Hey, Chandler, what's going on dude?"

"My girlfriend. She thinks she has a virus or something on her laptop. For some reason she disabled the AV software and she'll get screamed at if they find out."

"Whoa, dude! Why'd she do that?"

"Not sure. Maybe a few too many the other night. No clue. I was in Panama so I couldn't check on her." Chandler hoped Jason asked no more questions. Since she was due back in the office on Monday, Chandler asked Jason to come by Arianne's the next morning, a Saturday, to look at her machine and clean it up. Jason agreed as long as Chandler got him Nats tickets promised for the upcoming Yankees series. They sealed the deal.

"Jason's coming over tomorrow morning. Glad we can put this out of our minds for now. Hopefully, he just finds something harmless and you can stop your snooping before you get yourself and me in trouble." He still had to figure out how he would explain this to Geringer. "I'm still pissed that you did that!" He raised his voice for the first time in the discussion.

Arianne, whose eyes already held an unusual amount of moisture, finished the confession, lest they get into an argument in front of Jason Hardin. "Chan remember when you asked me if I told anyone about my meeting with Levi?"

"Yeah. Oh no! No, you didn't! Who?" He stood up and glared at her.

She proceeded through the long and difficult conversation about her revelation to Senator Shaw and, more painfully, her relationship with him. To her surprise, he focused more on the revelation to Shaw than her affair.

He paced nervously around the couch attempting to quell the wrath of anger that welled up inside. She assumed a fetal position.

"I gotta think this through now. Now a senator knows what you were doing. I have to think about Geringer and how this gets back to him. Ax sure as hell won't be happy. Oh, man. Damn it!" Chandler felt as if he'd violated the circle of trust between the three men.

A long pause in conversation followed, though his pacing continued. The look of disappointment on Chandler's face angered her. Now she stood up and followed his pacing. "Chandler, I didn't tell him anything, really. The biggest thing he knows is the name Levi Saltzman. I just asked Tom to have him checked out. That's all."

He spun, finding himself within a whisper of angry her face. "Damn it! Geringer's gonna be real mad."

"Will you listen to yourself? I just opened my heart to you about something painful from my past and you're worried about

Geringer and Axel? Are you fuckin kiddin me?" She flailed her arms. Her emotions were no longer contained.

He backed away. "Honey, I'm sorry but I gotta think about Geringer. Damn it!"

That proved the wrong thing to say since she launched herself into the sofa, assumed a fetal position, and let tears flow. She might as well have thrown kryptonite at Superman. Chandler's rant was abrupted, as if his tongue froze. His thoughts pivoted from Levi, Alyce, and Senator Shaw. He turned his attention to her emotional pain, joining her, wrapping himself around her from behind, his chin on her shoulder.

"I'm so sorry, honey. I just got carried away thinking out loud. Sorry. I really am. I love you so much, I don't want to hurt you." He didn't immediately realize he used the "L" word for the first time, but she did. She stopped crying, turned around and looked intently into his eyes and said, "I really love you too, Chandler Scott." Then he realized what he'd said and smiled. The embrace lasted some time.

***

A beautiful Saturday morning in May in the nation's capital was punctuated with cherry blossoms in full bloom, albeit a little late this year. Jason arrived at Arianne's condo around 9:30am. Fashion never came to Jason's attention. Chandler always saw him dressed the same way. He layered his upper half with a tee shirt, a collared long sleeve shirt, and a sweater with a pattern akin to a Mandelbrot set. Except in the summer, he donned a vintage Member's Only nylon jacket, circa 1985. His lower half usually had oversized jeans hanging low on his waist. He covered his feet in classic Converse Chuck Taylors, the black high tops. The paunchy Jason sported a considerable mane of brown hair that had no discernible arrangement. His face had a perpetual five o'clock shadow.

"Jason, this is my girlfriend Arianne."

"It's nice to meet you, Jason. Thanks for coming over on a Saturday. I feel so embarrassed. Can I get you coffee?" Arianne asked, shaking his parched hand.

"Nice to meet you too. Don't worry, your boyfriend is compensating me well for my visit. And yeah, I'd love some coffee," Jason answered. If possible, he'd have a coffee IV dripping into his vein all day.

She headed towards the kitchen while Chandler hung the vintage jacket in the hall closet.

"Dude, she looks this good in the morning?" Jason asked. Chandler winked.

The three gathered at the dining room table. Jason, sitting closely between them, enjoyed his fresh cup of java while she fired up her laptop. After boot up, she slid the device in front of him. She gave a cursory explanation that someone, unnamed, introduced a flash drive on her device. Jason related programs that ran in stealth on flash drives that could copy files from protected partitions or perform a file dump from things like email or other important documents. He also shared concerns about viruses. He knew organizations that were disabling USB drives altogether, which angered users.

"So you think this dude copied files to his flash when he put it in your USB drive?" Jason asked.

"Not sure," Arianne replied, shrugging her shoulders. Chandler coached her on what they would and would not say to Jason.

Jason looked around her laptop file system, his eyes darting quickly around the screen. Arianne and Chandler looked at the screen and occasionally stole glances in his direction.

"I don't see anything unusual so far. Let me look at the system files real quick." Nothing seemed to get Jason's attention here either. "You guys know that I'm no security expert. I'm more of a pure network guy and I know servers and data center stuff. This is a bit outside my realm so I don't want you to think I'm an authority here." Jason maintained his attention on the screen.

"No worries, dude. Just do what you can," Chandler replied. Jason was all they had at this point.

Jason couldn't identify anything that looked untoward. If there were files copied to or from Arianne's device, he couldn't tell.

"Sometimes those copy programs leave signatures. I was on a web forum last month and a bunch of security guys were talking about it. These guys get into some hairy stuff, man." Jason was a single guy who spent much of his free time poking around the Internet.

After a few more minutes of surveying, Jason suggested inserting his own thumb drive to run a couple of programs. Arianne had reservations given the Levi episode.

"You know, I understand if you don't want to run this app," Jason conceded.

"What exactly is this app?" Chandler asked.

The app came from the "Dark" side of the Internet and could sniff out viruses that commercially available products could not. The Dark Internet teemed with products that produced viruses, others that identified them, and some that fixed them. For all anyone knew, it could be the same person or organization developing all three.

"I was surfing one day on the Dark Web and ran across this

guy selling this anti-virus app who said he used to work in government cyber security." Jason explained what he meant by "Dark".

The majority of people transited the "Surface Web" when browsing the Internet. These were the typical searches on web browsers where a user typed a World Wide Web address, if known, or terms where a search engine produced a "www" address. The "Deep Web" comprised abandoned sites and things not meant for the public. Deep web sites were those not indexed by search engines. Site administrators controlled how bots or spiders indexed their web content. A perfectly legitimate site might exist on the Deep Web but could be kept hidden. Visitors to Deep Web sites had to know how to get to them directly. The Deep Web was also reputed to be larger than the Surface Web.

The "Dark Web" hosted sites where illegal transactions occurred, including drugs, guns, and stolen credit cards. This web included encrypted traffic running through a volunteer network comprised of thousands of relays facilitating anonymous communication through software by the name of Tor, an acronym for The Onion Router. The idea was to keep Internet communication anonymous and free from network surveillance and traffic analysis. Terror networks operated freely in this realm of cyberspace, motivating worldwide governments to develop tools to break the anonymity.

In 2018, governments successfully broke Tor. Not to be outdone, private developers created the successor to Tor, Rot, less than a year later to remain a step ahead of the authorities. Freedom loving users of the Internet drew no distinction between Deep and Dark sections of the web. For them, it came down to privacy. Victims of cyber or kinetic terror did not share similar views. This was an ongoing battle.

"Jason, I think you know a lot more about this security stuff than you said," Chandler observed.

"I don't know man, maybe. But seriously though, there's bad shit out on the Dark Web too, like child porn and torture sites," Jason revealed with a devilish smile.

The Dark Web had a little something for everyone. While it was chock full of illicit sites, there were also whistleblowing sites, political forums, blogs, mail and DigiNote sites. DigiNote reigned as the preferred currency on the Dark Web. The site selling Jason's app claimed the developer created it after super viruses intended for U.S. enemies were being unleashed domestically in the name of counterterrorism. The app detected super viruses but did not eradicate them.

"So this app is not a complete fix, just so you both understand. But at least it tells you if you're infected. If you are infected with these superviruses, then you pretty much want to trash the laptop," Jason added with doomed indifference.

"You're kidding, right? Trash the laptop?" Arianne asked.

"Pardon my Greek, but yeah the machine would pretty much be, wait for it, fucked," Jason replied, curling the corner of his mouth and snapping his fingers.

"What do you think?" Arianne needed a lifeline from Chandler.

"Let's run it and see. We really have little to lose at this point, especially if your machine is f'd up like he said."

"I guess we have nothing to lose other than my laptop. Go for it," Arianne replied.

Jason inserted his thumb drive and ran the app. He indicated it could take a little while. Arianne refreshed everyone's coffee in the interim. Jason downed his refill and asked for another.

"Jason, you've got to be wired by the end of the day," Chandler remarked.

"Dude, it's any wonder I get sleep." The caffeine induced insomnia no doubt contributed to his hours on the Internet.

During the next half hour, while they waited for the app to finish, they moved to the living area. Arianne and Chandler watched TV while Jason played a game on his phone. The application beeped, signaling completion. The three raced to the dining table where the laptop remained, assuming their previous positions, Arianne and Chandler flanking Jason.

Jason's face contorted, his eyebrows moved individually and he slurped his coffee, with small droplets trailing off his lip. He wiped with his shirtsleeve. "You guys ever heard of Trident?" Neither had so Jason began the lengthy explanation.

The U.S. government, likely the NSA, developed the supervirus, Trident, to infiltrate military installations, nuclear power plants, or factories. Trident embedded itself in the intended target and destroyed it from the inside out. It could cause a variety of internal failures on PLCs, computers, networking gear, production facilities or military hardware. Successful deployment meant the target would have no idea what hit them.

In this case, the original target was a suspected nuclear missile complex near Pyongyang. After the North Koreans detonated a small hydrogen bomb in 2016, they turned their attention to the delivery mechanism, ballistic missiles reportedly capable of striking targets all over eastern Asia and beyond. The North Koreans, had mastered the art of being irrational. This created uncertainty whether they'd ever use these weapons. A long period of saber rattling by the North Koreans convinced the Defense Department that they were serious this time. The domestic situation in North Korea deteriorated so much that the regime concocted a story about their enemies being poised for an attack. A U.S. air strike did not prove to be an option since it would agitate the North Koreans even more. It would also be difficult to justify this sort of direct military action with the Chinese.

Instead, a U.S. operative placed a thumb drive in the hands of a hotel IT employee who plugged it into the laptop of a North Korean diplomat attending a conference in Shanghai. U.S. intelligence identified the diplomat as a high-ranking military officer with access to the missile complex. Two weeks after the conference, satellite images captured the missile complex explosion. The North Koreans never admitted to the event since the world would interpret it as their own incompetence. Not long after, the regime publicly executed a general responsible for the missile complex. Reportedly, the U.S. informed the Chinese ambassador of their involvement, who summarily protested. The protest waned when the U.S. showed the ambassador evidence of missiles targeting Beijing.

"The report says your laptop was infected with a variant of Trident. This variant looks for its final target and deploys itself there. It is very discriminate but travels easily," Jason explained.

"Oh, my God! What does that mean?" Arianne circled her hands around her head. Chandler walked around Jason and put his arm around her.

"It means that if you were the target, you'd already know. If the target was the State Department, then maybe you would have heard something by now, maybe not. These superviruses destroy shit. I guess we'd have to think about what someone would want to destroy at State. I gotta think State would have some inkling that they'd been hit. But this is military grade shit here, guys. Doesn't seem like State would be a target. You just have people pushing paper there. Like I said, you'd probably already know if they got hit."

"You sound like you know something about this," Chandler remarked.

"The guy had a PDF where he explained how it was used and why it was really more to destroy things than anything else. I mean, that's why I knew all about the North Korea thing. The person who developed this must have been in the NSA or something. He knew shit that a run-of-the-mill developer wouldn't have. He even gave a site where he thought you could buy it if you had a need. It was definitely on the Darknet and could only be purchased with DigiNote." Jason bared his teeth at the thought of an ultimate dirty trick.

The three of them talked for a few more minutes, wondering what there could be at State that someone would want physically destroyed. Chandler realized that any further discussion with Jason would bring in topics that he would rather not make public. Chandler thanked Jason for coming on a Saturday and told him the Nats tickets would be in his office next week. Jason offered them a link where they could research Trident. Arianne gave him a coffee to go as his parting gift.

For the next couple of hours Chandler and Arianne talked in the living room and reviewed what interest Levi would have with her or the State Department. He would not have this conversation over the phone with Axel. They'd have to figure this out themselves. They also had another concern in trusting Jason's application from the Darknet.

"You know you can't say anything about this at work and we're gonna have to trash your laptop," Chandler remarked.

"I know. I thought you'd say that. I guess I'll have to come up with a story."

"Yeah, but I mean we'll literally have to destroy it, like run over it with your car or drop it off a building, something like that," Chandler clarified.

Arianne freaked out thinking about the story she needed to concoct and the discipline that awaited her, especially if State was the intended target. What if it already infected something and it got traced back to her? She'd have to explain the Levi incident and why she met with him, meaning it would come back to Chandler, Axel, and Geringer. Amid this stress, the proverbial light bulb illuminated.

"The virus is not for State. It's for Maxwell Technologies!" Her Eureka moment caused her to thrust her hands in the air, then coming to grips with her Pyrrhic victory.

She realized the implications. Maxwell Tech hired Tyler Sawyer, the developer of DigiNote, to create encryption software for the Tobor operating system used in cell phones.

While some people used phone encryption, no widely available commercial product proved reliable or inexpensive. Government compromised previously developed iterations via disgruntled employees of software companies later hired by U.S. intelligence agencies. Law enforcement proved to be another lever against encryption.

Small developers created various flavors of phone encryption software, but communications were slow and clipped due to the additional computational requirements. End-to-end encryption on millions of phones would severely curtail government efforts to monitor voice and text communication.

The Maxwell encryption technology would not require any changes to the cell phone's hardware - at least that was the intent. As with other development efforts, prevailing wisdom assumed the U.S. government would ask Maxwell for a back door into the software. CEO Larry Maxwell, Arianne's father, publicly stated he would go to court to fight that order.

"What you're saying makes sense. Your father's company had to be the target. Levi then must be more than just some Fed consultant," Chandler opined. "Besides, I think Tyler Sawyer still contributes to the open source DigiNote project so maybe it's not just Maxwell but Tyler who's a target also?"

The two connected the dots, or at least they thought they did. Now came the difficult conversation with her father. Chandler suggested she call him right away. She dreaded this call more than any she'd ever had with him. Chandler would sit close to her on the couch.

"Hi, Dad."

"Sweetheart, how are you? You doing OK?" Larry asked. Arianne had always been daddy's little girl and could do no wrong in his eyes, often to the chagrin of her older brother. She would test that attitude with this revelation.

"Dad, I need to talk to you. In person. I'm going to catch a flight tomorrow morning."

"On a Sunday? You must really miss me and your mom, or is it something else? You sure you're OK?"

"Dad, I'd rather not talk over the phone. I'm fine really. Can we meet in your office? Oh, and Chandler will be with me."

Chandler tapped her on the shoulder and whispered in her ear. "Ask him if Axel can come too." Since Axel lived in Chicago and could speak to other events, he could prove valuable in explaining the tale to Larry Maxwell.

"Dad, I would like to bring Axel Schultz as well. I think

I've mentioned him a few times."

"Yes, the letter writer. Maybe he can give me a good investment tip. My office, huh? That's fine."

"We can probably be there by 11am. Sorry for all the mystery, Dad."

"Don't worry about it. See you tomorrow, sweetheart."

Chandler called Axel, who agreed to meet up with them in Chicago the next day. Axel would be in for his own surprise with this revelation.

***

Maxwell Technologies maintained its headquarters in Evanston, Illinois, just south of Northwestern University. A decade ago, Larry Maxwell merged several facilities in the Chicagoland area into a single fifteen-story building. The centrally located building in Evanston made for easy walking to the Purple Line. The Evanston location also encouraged computer science and computer engineering students at Northwestern to participate in internships and eventually work at Maxwell. Maxwell was prominent in application development and most recently delved into encryption technology for cell phones.

Arianne and Chandler took American Airlines flight 4362 from Reagan to O'Hare. O'Hare had a history of being unkind to Mr. Scott since he spent the night there on several occasions due to weather or mechanical issues. Axel got them from the airport so they could debrief about Arianne's adventure and Trident. The Schultz SUV proceeded leisurely out of O'Hare on I-294 and US-14 to Evanston, allowing sufficient time for Axel to understand the situation and to plan how to address the matter with Larry. Sunday made for a skeleton crew at Maxwell and Larry prearranged for their arrival, simplifying screening.

Given the sensitive nature of their work, Maxwell Tech required a thorough check-in process. The security officer gave each a temporary badge and they took the elevator to the 15th floor where they would meet Larry in his spacious office.

Larry Maxwell's physique belied his age. He had a sinewy but lean look no doubt due to his many hours of running and light weight training. A man of average height, he possessed a full head of gray hair and no facial hair. For their meeting he donned a blue oxford button down cotton shirt without a tie and dress slacks. The shoes were black tassel loafers. He usually dressed this way for the office. He projected a confident demeanor, but not an overbearing one.

Arianne led the group into his office. "Hi Dad!"

"Sweetheart, so good to see you. I've missed you." Larry embraced Arianne warmly and then extended his hand to Chandler. "Chandler good to see you again." Chandler had only met Larry on a couple of other occasions in D.C.

"Thank you, sir. I want to introduce you to my friend and mentor, Mr. Axel Schultz." Chandler always referenced him as a mentor.

"Mr. Schultz, glad to make your acquaintance." Larry shook his hand.

"The pleasure is mine, sir," Axel replied.

"Ari, I guess you didn't coach these two to drop the 'sir' when they talk to me, huh? I haven't been knighted yet." Larry teased. They all shared a quick laugh. "Just call me Larry, but not you Chandler." Larry grinned. "Please let's sit down over here." Larry gestured towards a sitting area with two large leather sofas, a couple of high back leather wing chairs, and a tri-level black coffee table. "Would anyone like something to drink?" They all declined and sat. Arianne sat next to her dad on a sofa while the other two assumed their positions in the wing chairs.

"Now what would bring my beautiful daughter and her entourage to see me on a Sunday?" Larry could not expect the upcoming revelation.

"Dad, I have something I need to share with you," she began. She'd had "serious" discussions before with her dad, although those dealt with teenage indiscretions.

"Sounds serious. But I guess it would be or you wouldn't have come this far," Larry remarked.

To set the stage, Chandler related stories he'd been covering and their integration on Centinela. These segments focused on recent financial turmoil and cyber terror. The stories guided him towards independent research, both for edification and story content. This approach provided Larry the "why" behind his daughter's action.

"And so I wanted to help Chandler with his research. You know, I wanted to surprise him with my own work when he returned from his trip," she explained.

"What sort of research were you doing then?" Larry inquired.

"It was about the Fed and the fake SuperNotes floating around. You know those $100 bills." She responded with this cover story, developed on the flight to Chicago, to shield her father from the actual detail of her encounter with Levi and the larger developing story revealed on that cold February somewhere in New York. "So I had this meeting at the Fed with this consultant and he shared some documents with me via a flash drive. Anyway, when I got back to Washington-"

"When you got back? Where were you?" Larry asked, gesturing with his hands, palms turned up.

"Oh, sorry I was at the New York Fed. So when I came back home, my laptop started acting funny. Luckily one of Chandler's buddies came by and looked at it and said it had some sort of virus. He said the virus looked serious and probably attached itself to an email I sent you. That means your laptop and others at Maxwell may be infected. I think the Fed guy had an infected drive and who knows what else and just passed it along." She hoped this was a sufficient explanation.

"And you had to fly to Chicago to tell me all this? Don't get me wrong. I'm happy to see you, but I'm surprised you didn't tell me over the phone. I think the phone snoops wouldn't get bent out of shape on this one." Larry asked a question she hoped he'd omit.

She had to think quickly or risk blowing her cover story. Placing her hand on his arm she said, "You know, Dad, I could get in trouble at work if they knew my machine got infected."

He caressed her hand. "Sweetheart, that happens all the time. Surely they'd understand."

"Yeah, except I disabled my antivirus by mistake and they told us never to do that. I just want to avoid problems. I also thought that if I told you on the phone and someone heard it, one of your competitors might take advantage of the situation." She hoped this more complete explanation sufficed.

Larry broke contact with her, reclined into the sofa and rubbed his forehead. The other three waited with bated breath for his next words. His delusion of an innocent mistake vanished, making room for sober reason and reflection. A few agonizing seconds passed until he leaned forward.

"This explains a few things. A week ago, Tyler told me about some client development machines that started acting funny. They kept crashing and a couple had their processors overheat and die. Tyler suspected their fans stopped spinning. Never seen anything like it. Our network management team told me they were getting all these SNMP alerts on network switches, fibre channel switches, file servers and mail servers. The other strange thing was that the alerts were only for a couple of networks in this building. We had switches in the development area literally overheat and burn so we had to take them out of service. I've got one of them over here."

Larry walked to a shelf and brought back one of the smoked devices. He placed it on the coffee table and pointed to burn marks that made it to the back panel. "One of my network operators thought it real strange that all this weird activity was only happening here and only in two out of the many subnets that we have. The switch manufacturers had no answers, and neither did the server hardware company. For being this savvy tech company, we were at a loss too. I know I'm getting esoteric here. Sorry, guys."

"No worries. So how did you deal with this?" Chandler inquired.

"Funny you ask. Tyler had the foresight to keep, and this really cannot leave the room, had the foresight to keep a copy of source code offline insulating from any cyber-attack. He said he'd learned his lesson once. Then he and a couple of his guys took infected client machines and servers out of service. Whatever this virus was, it seemed to be really specific, discriminating if you know what I mean. Then they created a new development network with all new hardware and physically isolated it from the rest of Maxwell. We lost about a week's worth of work and thousands of dollars in hardware, but truth be told, we recovered. If it wasn't for Tyler moving code offline, we would've been in a world of hurt."

"Good thinking on Tyler's part," Axel said.

"After we isolated everything, Tyler used some supposedly secret virus checker. He didn't tell me where he got it, and frankly I didn't pursue it. When he ran the program on computers that didn't fry, it came up with some wicked supervirus called Neptune. Tyler said it was probably developed by some government, he wasn't sure. We couldn't get rid of the virus, just identify it. Tyler said that despite our best efforts, these government or military grade infections are just going to get through the best antivirus software. That's why we instituted new security policies in the last few days."

"Mr. Maxwell, ahh Larry, I am going to suggest that everything we have discussed and what I'm about to say not leave this room." Axel set the table to reveal his plan. "There is another reason Ari wanted to deliver this news in person. I've been doing research for my letter and can tell you that the government and now this FSB are not too keen about people using DigiNote. Everyone knows why Tyler Sawyer is over here and his contribution on the Tobor phone encryption software. When you guys develop this encryption for the masses, government will have millions of phones they can't surveil. In this day and age of counterterrorism, it will go over like a lead balloon."

"Tell me about it. I had to convince my board this was a good idea," Larry added.

"Somebody doesn't like this idea. I don't know who and nobody else in this room does either. But Maxwell Technologies was the target. I don't believe this Fed consultant acted on his own and there's no sense in pursuing him. You won't be able to prove anything. You'll get stonewalled and you'll waste a bunch of time. So here's what I propose." Axel made the shape of a steeple with his hands, placing them under his chin, and stared directly at Larry. "Issue a press release saying that Maxwell got hit by an unknown virus that caused extensive hardware and software damage and that it crippled development efforts on your encryption product. This way your enemies think they won and might not strike again, at least for a while. It buys you time. You continue your work with encryption and hopefully have a good product for release before anything happens again." Axel's plan was convincing.

"Candidly, there is some question if ordinary cell phones will have enough processing power to handle our advanced encryption without some modification. That's our goal to just make it a simple app download. But that's another issue. Axel, that sounds like a good plan. I'll get my people to draft something. Only Tyler and the immediate development team will know it's a false release. Somehow I'll have to keep my board in the dark too," Larry explained.

"And since you're not a publicly traded company, you don't have to worry about some stock price volatility," Axel suggested.

"Yes, that's true. Thank you all for coming to me so quickly and for your honesty. Sweetheart, we'll get through this, but you have to be much, much more careful. This could have been a real disaster for us." Larry pointed at Chandler. "You must care a great deal about this guy to help him like this."

"Yeah, you could say that." Arianne looked at Chandler and smiled.

"You know, I'm gonna have to make up a story for your mother about why I had to meet you at the office first. I told her we'd come home for a late lunch after our meeting. Axel, you're more than welcome to come."

"I'll take a rain check on that Larry, but thanks."

This meeting could have gone poorly. Fortunately, the damage at Maxwell was contained due to the sage efforts of Tyler Sawyer. It was always difficult for Larry to stay angry at his daughter, whom he cherished. She felt horribly not telling her father the whole story, but she had little choice. For at least the next few hours, she could just be Larry's daughter and not have to worry about what she inadvertently did trying to impress the love of her life and the collateral damage to her father's company.

CHAPTER SEVENTEEN
PLANNING

Senator Matt Geringer occupied a 2,000 square foot townhome in Falls Church, Virginia with his wife, Louise, whom he met in law school. The two extra bedrooms were for visits from their children and grandchildren. The Geringers spent most of their time here especially since the senator assumed more responsibility in the IAP. It was a contemporary three story structure in a row with seven other townhomes. Geringer asked Chandler and Axel to come over and catch up, though he was unaware of the incident with Levi.

Axel continued to gather intelligence, assessing the veracity of details he got from Phish a few months back. The Trident incident made him wonder what other forces were operating in the background.

"Gentlemen, getting a bit toasty outside, come on in," Geringer opened. The temperature in Falls Church on this July day reached 90 degrees. "How about some ice tea?"

"Ice tea is fine, senator," Axel responded.

"Ditto for me," Chandler said.

"I'm glad you guys were able to come over especially with my wife being out of town. I don't want to draw too much attention to our meetings. Definitely want to have you guys avoid coming to my Senate office. Please, have a seat." Geringer gestured towards the sofa in the living room.

Geringer ventured to the kitchen, poured three glasses of unsweetened tea and returned to the living room. "Here you go, guys." He placed their glasses on coasters on the coffee table.

He then sprawled his large frame on a cushioned leather chair and accompanying ottoman.

"Matt, let me bring you up to speed on something that transpired a couple of months back. I want to preface this with an apology." Chandler explained what had happened with Arianne and her encounter with Levi Saltzman.

Before completing the tale, Geringer interrupted Chandler. "Levi Saltzman? Huh. Interesting. I was just told this week that he'll be named as Under Secretary of the FSB reporting directly to Holloway. When I asked my staff if they'd ever heard of this guy, nobody had."

"Arianne said the person who referred her to Levi mentioned that he was doing work for them so that can't be a coincidence." Chandler continued with the rest of the Levi encounter and suspicion of a virus on her laptop. "A techie friend of mine came over and found this supervirus on her machine."

"I remember some intelligence I read talking about superviruses going all the way back to something called Stuxnet, gosh, like 10 years ago," Geringer added.

"It gets more interesting than that. My friend's special app indicated this supervirus was called Trident or some variant of it," Chandler said.

"Yes. Yes. There was a rumor, just a rumor though, that it was some virus that brought down that missile site near Pyongyang. I got an intelligence briefing that had before and after satellite photos of this North Korean missile installation. It got wiped out, like it had been bombed except no one bombed them. Our operatives said the North Koreans had no clue what hit 'em. I always got the impression the leaders there acted crazy as a matter of strategy, just to get the world's attention. And the, sorry guys, just a second." Geringer looked at an incoming text and smiled.

"I apologize for the interruption. I wanted my daughter to send a picture of my grandson playing ball. Cute kid, looks just like his mother. Anyway, the North Koreans blamed a South Korean spy who conveniently died in the explosion, so they never produced a body. Then to play along with their fabrication, the North Koreans started all these troop movements around the DMZ. South Korea started mobilizing too, and the Chinese got involved to quiet everything down. The Chinese asked through diplomatic channels if we had some involvement and I don't recall if we admitted to it or not. Intelligence didn't say we were responsible. We in the Senate hear about these things, but if we ask questions, the spy agencies clam up real quick. They claim national security, and we're stonewalled."

"Interesting." Chandler compared Geringer's intelligence brief to Jason Hardin's explanation. Jason's had slightly more detail particularly when it came to claiming responsibility for the virus attack.

"What about Freedom of Information Act requests?" Axel inquired.

"They'll just redact a bunch of stuff in a document making it unreadable. We've played that game before," Geringer answered, shaking his head.

Chandler explained that their initial suspicion centered on Arianne's laptop and then moved to the State Department. Arianne then determined the supervirus' target was Maxwell Technologies.

"Did Maxwell confirm the attack?" Geringer asked.

"Yes, they did, but it apparently didn't hurt them too

much," Chandler replied.

"And what about the State Department, any damage there? I didn't hear of anything." Geringer continued with questions.

"Not that Ari knows of. She kept the whole incident quiet other than to say her laptop was destroyed when she left it on the trunk of her car and then ran over it. According to information we read, the virus moves and does not stay resident unless the device is an intended target. It's likely Ari's machine was clean, but we didn't take any chances."

"She covered her ass then. Probably a good idea. She needs to keep a real low profile over there," Geringer demanded in a voice that gradually approached the low end of the hearing range.

"Senator, I suggested to Larry Maxwell that he issue a fake press release confirming serious damage to his software development," Axel added.

"They're the ones working on that phone encryption. Honestly, guys, I'm not real crazy about that. It's gonna make it really, really hard to catch bad guys if that product gets off the ground. But I would never get in the way of free enterprise either," Geringer added.

"Senator, if I may be so bold. The government skims so much data now and listens in on so much that inevitably you guys end up with a bunch of false positives, so you end up wasting time and miss some bad guys," Axel challenged.

"You're right but it's not as if anyone has given us any other option either. Everyone wants to be safe, but when it comes time to implement the measures that will make everyone feel safe, people balk. We could balance safety and liberty if we just did a few things, but I know I'm gettin on my soapbox here. Sorry." Geringer had his own ideas about the reason for the attacks, though this wasn't the right time or place to air them.

"No worries, Matt. You're now up to speed on my girlfriend's little adventure," Chandler summarized, though it was hardly a "little" adventure.

"I hope you see now Chandler why we can't afford any leaks. This thing could get out of control quickly. And it's no coincidence that Maxwell Tech ended up as a target. Somebody caught her snooping and you see what happened." Geringer wagged his finger and scowled. "Don't let something like this happen again or I'll stop working with you! Understand?" Those words served as Geringer's castigation of Chandler. The senator wasn't one to yell and scream, though his dissatisfaction was clear. He wanted to move on since there were other fish to fry.

Chandler deserved the scolding, however mild. The reasons for Arianne's actions were irrelevant. "Yes sir. Understood. You have every reason to be upset. I've already talked to her." Chandler paused the confession and did not discuss her meeting with Senator Shaw. He feared exposing her personal relationship.

Geringer turned his attention to Axel. "I know I don't need to say anything to you Axel." Since they were closer in age, Geringer had an inherent confidence in Axel, though he also gained admiration as he delved into Axel's research. "Now let's get caught up on everything else."

They had plenty of ground to cover. Neither Axel nor Chandler had revealed what they learned from Phish in that cold garage back in February. They both feared Geringer would not accept the information at face value since it came from Omni. Axel, over the course of the last few months, gathered details from other sources trying to validate his hypothesis. His contact at the People's Bank of China confirmed most of Phish's revelations. Axel now felt comfortable telling the senator of the GSB's role and details regarding money, gold, and central banks.

The revelations hit Geringer hard. The color left his face. Geringer stood and paced around the living room, pausing briefly at the sliding glass door leading to the patio. Chandler and Axel remained silent. Even though much of this information came from Omni, Geringer took it seriously.

"This loss of monetary sovereignty won't go over well with Americans." Geringer envisioned a populist revolt.

"Senator, I respectfully disagree. Homo Americanus is so oblivious to everything. They won't care. They just want the economy to work the way it used to. You don't see that much complaining about surveillance. The only ones who will probably give a damn will be Theocracy Party voters, maybe some preppers. Oh, and your party, senator!" Axel exclaimed.

"But people do want some sense of order. You have all these terror scares and now cyber worries and financial markets as they are," Chandler said.

"I've done research showing financial market activity can foreshadow terror events. I haven't published it yet, but it's interesting. The government would do well to conduct this research themselves. They'd catch more bad guys," Axel said.

Geringer took his seat once again. "I'll let you two debate that stuff. I don't know that as an American citizen and custodian of the Constitution that I can stand by and just watch all this unfold. I reluctantly let go of my presidential bid when things weren't even to the extent of what you guys just revealed. We have to fight this."

"Senator, ultimately it's an issue of who will stand with you. Will anyone have the courage to step up? Even if I wrote about it, there would be maybe one thousand worldwide that would know and if any of them spoke of this, they would be discredited and then by extension, me," Axel explained.

"There's an election coming up in a few months and no one will even want to talk about this. I bet it will be about the economy and safety from whatever sort of terrorism makes the headlines," Chandler added.

"All true guys. Nevertheless, I know that some members of Congress won't go for this. I can't believe the Justice Department would let this fly either. There is more work to do here," Geringer concluded.

In an election year, how might people react to these revelations? Maybe they'd be sheep like Axel suggested. Maybe there would be a popular revolt like Geringer feared. Chandler couldn't do anything with this because Rafael would never let him run such a story, not the way he reacted to the DigiNote piece. What would the Jefferson administration do to counter strong opposition? Who would be the credible mouthpiece broadcasting this to the American public?

***

To this point in the middle of 2020, Emmet had enjoyed great success. His investments blossomed with the market's rally, the IRC received more international recognition, and Holloway executed his vision in Washington. He realized the announcement of the IRC's blueprint, through the FSB, would bring significant headwinds. He wanted to devise contingencies to deal with expected challenges. From his office at the Presidio, he gathered Jean-Claude, Nial, and Fran on a conference call. After hearing incoming beeps, Emmet couldn't wait to get started.

"Thank you all for joining me today. Jean, sorry, I know it's late for you."

"I was just about to join my wife for a late dinner. I'll tell her it's you, Emmet, so she'll understand," Jean replied.

They all laughed.

"Jean, just tell her Emmet's talking to you about her birthday gift," Nial joked.

"*Oui*, her birthday is coming up. Emmet, I trust you will have a satisfactory gift?" Jean asked.

"Ahh, well," Emmet murmured.

"Diamonds are a girl's best friend," Fran said.

"If we had this little gathering as a VR meeting, you could show her some fine samples," Nial offered, knowing Emmet was no fan of the new technology.

"I don't want to act like the maggot here, but can we get down to business?" Emmet commanded.

"You Americans are always so driven. You don't know how to relax," Nial chastised.

"That's why we're the only remaining empire!" Emmet retorted.

"I'm sure our Chinese friends might differ on that. And what the hell, you know the American empire will change shortly anyway," Nial added.

They all laughed again. It would be a more integrated world with no empire to speak of. It wouldn't be world government that conspiracy theorists always discussed. Governments would retain political independence, though there would be a new level of centralized control around monetary and financial matters.

"All right, with everything the FSB wants to do, and Jefferson has done more than even we thought possible with Executive Orders, there is concern that members of Congress will question the constitutionality of rules and regulations set forth by the FSB. There could be a popular uprising. There is a bill circulating in the House, with multi-party sponsorship, that won't do us any favors. That bill doesn't even consider what we expect will be the FSB's ultimate scope." Emmet's tone expressed great concern.

"And don't forget ongoing constitutional challenges of the surveillance campaign," Fran added.

The courts wrestled with numerous cases at all levels of the judicial system regarding surveillance by state and federal agencies. The Supreme Court had not gotten involved yet and would rather see a resolution in the lower courts. Even if it reached the highest court in the land, plaintiffs feared that a bench with two Jefferson appointees and two appointees from the previous Democratic president would rubber stamp current surveillance tactics.

"Yes, of course. I think we'll win those cases if they get to the Supreme Court," Emmet said, tapping his fingers on his desk.

"How inconvenient your Constitution is? We just need Americans to get a bit more bladdered so they don't pay attention," Nial joked.

"Alcohol is not gonna solve this problem!" Emmet replied, angrily craning his neck towards the phone. Normally Emmet tolerated Nial's jokes, but he wanted to get down to business.

"It might in sufficient quantities," Nial answered.

"So is there a way around this? The administration will spend a bunch of time in court, otherwise." Fran ignored Nial's second attempt at humor.

"Holloway is investigating if it's possible to 'temporarily' suspend the Constitution due to a national emergency declared by the president. He asked the Justice Department to keep it quiet for now, don't want to scare the natives. But we have another issue that could fold into this. A well-known senator has been snooping around and asking about our consultant. You know the one working at the Fed," Emmet revealed.

"Mr. Saltzman?" Fran asked.

"Yes. Holloway wanted him to grease the skids over at the New York Fed." Emmet knew there was more than skid greasing going on but felt no obligation to reveal that during this call.

"So, is Geringer the one asking questions about our consultant?" Fran asked.

"That's a good guess, but wrong. It's Senator Shaw," Emmet replied.

"The one married to your sister's niece?" Fran asked.

"That one. Candidly though, I'm not worried about him," Emmet declared, his gaze now directed at San Francisco Bay.

"Emmet, such a projection of confidence. How can you be certain?" Jean inquired.

"Let's just say Shaw and I reached a mutual understanding a few years ago on an important matter, but I still need to keep an eye on him," Emmet said angrily.

"I have a feeling the matter was not political. Your tone makes this seem more personal," Nial said.

"Let it rest, Nial. I don't want to talk about that pile of shite now," Emmet replied.

"Guess I was right," Nial concluded.

"I would like for us and the rest of the board to provide ideas for Holloway over what might constitute a national emergency. This assumes the Justice Department will even stand with the president. If they don't, then there will be a fight in front of us. We just need to plan and not get caught with our pants down, understand? I am going to call other board members later today and tomorrow to get their ideas. We need to tighten this thing up. Nial, you ran a country once. What would your emergency be?" Emmet asked.

"A shortage of Guinness or my favorite Glenlivet scotch," Nial joked. Raucous laughter, even from Emmet, followed his comment. "But seriously, a domestic terror threat is always good. You know what an American politician once said about not letting a good crisis go to waste."

"As scary as that sounds, there is truth to that," Emmet added.

Nial continued. "No one is going take seriously some rumored military attack against the U.S. But talk about a terror cell inflicting damage on an airplane or a sports stadium, or releasing a virus, and you will get everyone's attention real fast. Americans did not experience World War I or II like Europe. I believe that makes for more sensitivity when there is a domestic attack. Look at how the country reacted after 9/11 or even after the terror attack in California in 2015, which was really an inside job. One was large in scale and the other was small. But it got everyone's attention for the same reason."

"You speak truth Nial," Fran conceded. "I remember some presidential candidates in 2015 suggested using religion as an evaluation for admission to the country. People forget that our own president wanted to keep Iranians out during the hostage crisis and even ordered Iranians in the country to report to immigration. It doesn't take much to get people worried."

"This country is all about freedom but when people are threatened, they forget about freedom *of* and want freedom *from*. We can use that to our advantage," Emmet commented.

"We have cameras trained on something as small as a rat in

London and life goes on," Nial said.

"We've had this war on terror for almost twenty years so I think people will accept more and more restriction on their liberty if it's a trade-off for safety," Emmet added.

"I suggest a terror scare with some financial event. Create the thought that some terror cell is going to explode a bomb on a commodity or stock exchange and that there are others that will use cyber warfare, or talk about threats to companies with ransomware. That should create enough fear by combining a physical safety scare and something financial that will affect the economy. Suggest that intelligence chatter is picking up terror threats from Omni or some Islamic group. Both have had their hands in several catastrophes," Jean noted.

"But I thought Omni's M.O. was different?" Fran inquired.

"It is Fran but we could create a story that they have gone out of control and are attacking exchanges, banks, brokerages and governments. We can feed this into the Internet and social media with the goal that these stories become conventional wisdom. The Internet is nothing more than an echo chamber and our goal is to offer the right message and drown everything else out. You know when things get serious, you have to, well, bend the truth a bit," Jean suggested.

"I like that idea, Jean. If Americans think that something else will disrupt the economy with as bad as things have been for a few years, they'll want something done. We just need to be prepared. Think of other things that we could use. Maybe a false flag event. Remember, we have an election soon. Let's get together tomorrow at the same time to see if anyone has come up with other ideas. Have a good day, Nial and Fran, and have a good evening Jean-Claude." Emmet closed the call pondering his next move.

A staffer for Senator Geringer, Emily Channing, learned that the Justice Department was investigating the legality of suspending the Constitution for a national emergency declared by the president. Her boyfriend worked as an attorney at the Justice Department's National Security Division (NSD) and saw a document written for the Attorney General. The NSD materialized in 2006 as a result of the Patriot Act.

Their charter was simple - combat terrorism and other threats to national security. Emily's boyfriend couldn't see the document's author but saw the routing to the NSD's Assistant Attorney General for review. The document, clearly for limited distribution, related to domestic terrorism and the upcoming elections. Given the senator's misgivings about portions of the Patriot Act, she knew he'd have a keen interest in the document.

Emily waited for a slot to clear on the Senator's calendar and closed the door of his office to make the revelation.

"Emily, I guess you must want a raise since you closed the door."

"No senator, we can talk about my salary later." She smiled, appreciating his humor. "This is probably something you're more interested in than my paycheck." Emily explained what her boyfriend saw.

"Who else knows about this?" These days, every time Geringer learned details of something related to his discussions with Axel and Chandler, it was just as important to him who knew.

"My boyfriend said there's been some chatter around the NSD."

"How did your boyfriend even come across this? You know what? I don't even want to know. At this point, I'm going to treat this as credible. I appreciate you telling me. I'll need to look more into this." Geringer moved from behind his desk to walk her out of the office. "You definitely merit a raise after this!" He patted her on the shoulder. "Thanks again." He closed his office door and returned to his desk.

Geringer thought about the implications and recent conversation about the GSB plan. If terror would be used to conceive this plan, Senator Thomas Shaw, a chair on a terror subcommittee, might know something. Shaw had worked with the NSD before and the two well-acquainted men served on other committees. Despite strong ideological differences, they had mutual respect for each other. Shaw would be a good source to confirm Emily's boyfriend's discovery. Geringer called him.

"This is Senator Shaw."

"Tom, how are you? It's Matt."

"Matt, how's the former presidential candidate doing these days?" Geringer's abrupt exit from the campaign surprised the Democrats as much as any party.

"Wow, Tom, you had to go there. You still can't get over the Broncos beating the Patriots last year, can you?" Geringer answered questions for months about his decision to drop out of the race. Referencing professional football was one way to deflect the topic.

"That ref blew the call. You know it, I know it and the world knows it!"

"Hey, our celebration was short-lived anyway after we got slaughtered by the Rams in the Super Bowl."

"Yeah, I didn't see that coming. What can I do for you today?"

"Tom, I feel strange asking this question but this just came across my desk and it's troubling."

"When the great Matt Geringer calls me, it must be important. What is it?" Tom laid it on thick.

"One of my staff said that a friend of hers saw something being routed to the Assistant AG over at NSD about the legality of suspending the Constitution if there was a suspected terror plot around election time. The document was eventually to make its way to the AG himself. Do you know anything about this?"

"Holy shit! Suspending the Constitution? I know Jefferson has really pushed the envelope the last few months, but this sounds like the king taking charge of his subjects. And around the election? Wait a second. How did your staffer's friend find out about this?"

"I didn't ask. I have to presume this is legit, that she's not making this up and neither is her friend. With all the Exec Orders flying around, it sounds plausible. I also have concerns since the election is in three months."

"True. I may have jumped the gun here with Jefferson. I shouldn't say it came from him or was even ordered by him," Tom offered apologetically. "I've read some NSD reports about recent terror activity and the country's ability to respond. That said, we don't have any new intelligence that says we're any more at risk, cyber or kinetic. Nothing came up in the last GEOINT report I saw. The threat level assigned by DHS is still the same. I know there was a lot of chatter about the stock market collapse and terror involvement there, but I thought that got cleared up."

"Tom. It was more than just chatter. About the stock market."

"I read a MARKINT brief about the Chinese and Russians,

but hey nothing unusual there. I heard that Jefferson called Chinese and Russian leaders about it but nothing much more came of it. It didn't get the attention I thought it would."

"What about hacking from places other than China and Russia? Did your brief talk about that?" Geringer planted a seed.

"Like where? Do you know something?"

"Not really but, and this is just speculation by some in the media, there seemed to be a thought that it was more widespread than China and Russia." Geringer could not reveal that the source of "media" speculation was Omni.

"Hmmm. I don't know about that Matt. I do have a question for you on an unrelated matter. Who is this Saltzman who just got named Under Secretary at FSB?"

The former Fed consultant, IRC contact, and alleged virus implanter got appointed Under Secretary at the Financial Stability Board reporting directly to Malcolm Holloway. A two line press release devoid of any biography announced the appointment. With the flurry of activity at the FSB, the announcement went down like a mere footnote in a long story.

"I'd heard that he was considered for the position. I asked around my office and nobody seemed to know who he was." Geringer knew about Saltzman through Arianne's little adventure, but he was not at liberty to reveal how he knew. He remained largely in the dark about the guy though.

"I did some digging myself. A friend of mine had some dealings with him and thought the guy was odd." Tom would not reveal any more details about his "friend", Arianne, lest it bring up more questions. Chandler and now Senator Shaw, two men in love with Arianne, both did their best to shield her from unnecessary scrutiny. Even among two Senate colleagues, there was a web of deception. The deception centered on the fact that both Geringer and Shaw spoke of the same person connected to Levi and neither revealed her name.

"Oh. In what way?" Geringer asked, oblivious to who the friend was even though there was a direct connection.

"He just acted all cloak and dagger."

"I guess Levi wanted to waste your friend's time then."

"Who knows? But since now he's with the FSB, that just made me more suspicious." Shaw had every reason to be suspicious.

"Do you think the FSB is behind this talk about the Constitution suspension?" Geringer asked.

"Like I said, there are no new terror threats that I've been briefed on. Unless the FSB has some other fears they aren't divulging. Do you think there is something else? This seems even extreme for Jefferson," Shaw suggested.

"I really don't know, Tom."

"Tell you what, Mr. Geringer. Let me dig around more and see what I can find out. I think I can confidently say that you and I are on the same side of this issue."

"Thanks, Tom. Looking forward to what you discover. Take care."

"Talk to you soon, Matt."

CHAPTER EIGHTEEN
TERRORISM

We have just received breaking news from our sister station in Chicago. Tyler Sawyer, known for his work on the open source DigiNote project, was gunned down late last night in Chicago's Loop District by an unknown assailant. Police have no witnesses or leads at this time. Sawyer worked for Maxwell Technologies of Evanston, Illinois, in software development. Maxwell CEO, Larry Maxwell, is expected to make a statement later today.

This was not the news Chandler or Arianne expected to hear first thing in the morning. The incident hit close to home for both. It was but three months ago they sat across from Larry Maxwell, who spoke in glowing tones about Tyler. The news stopped them cold as they readied for work.

"You know, it was exciting trying to help you out but then the whole incident with Saltzman, the damn virus I infected my dad's company with, and now Tyler. Maybe we're into something that we should stay out of?" Arianne, who was fixing breakfast, yearned for peace and tranquility. "This sort of drama, I mean this isn't my life."

"I know honey, but that's the reason I can't stay out of it. There's too much here to ignore. Look at what I do as a journalist. How can I not pursue this?"

An argument ensued. Each understood the other's position, but now the matter of their relationship needed consideration. She was concerned for his safety. This was perhaps the most important story he'd ever investigated, though he worried about how the pursuit of truth affected her. He needed to prepare for an important interview in the D.C. bureau with Malcolm Holloway and National Security Advisor, Trent Carter. Arianne would stay home to speak with her father about his loss. They resolved nothing that morning and considered their argument part of a healthy relationship.

Chandler drove her car to the bureau and tuned an all-news station. The station's morning host was a Millennial who admired Tyler's work. He discussed how the open source community and others in the tech world viewed Tyler as a hero. The host's social media streams spewed endless eulogies from all parts of the world. He shared his thoughts with the audience.

"Tyler, he was our generation's hero. For all of us kids who weren't the best athletes or maybe we didn't fit in with a certain crowd, he showed us what an impact someone could make. DigiNote freed people from the shackles of government-issued money and he was probably working on the next big thing over at Maxwell. Now he's gone. I only hope the police figure out who did this and why. I can tell our listeners that today is a dark day for me."

Chandler didn't immediately link his death with the Trident incident. After meeting with Larry, the fake press release appeared to convince the tech community that Maxwell's efforts were derailed. If foul play occurred, maybe someone discovered the issuance of a fraudulent press release. Then again, it may have been a violent, senseless act by a lunatic. Still, the thought of foul play lingered and the potential impact on the release of the encryption application.

After arriving at the bureau, sentiment among his colleagues wavered. Some viewed it as a random shooting. Others saw

Russian or Chinese involvement. Some were convinced a radical Muslim cell in Chicago had responsibility. There were many opinions but no answers. Chandler needed to finish putting together a terror segment for Centinela. The segment had content from his trip to Panama and the threat against the new canal locks. Rafael wanted Chandler to emphasize the need for a global counterterror organization staffed by the world's major powers. Rafael asked him to interview two key players in domestic counterterror efforts with the goal of showing how inter-agency cooperation in the United States could serve as a model for other nations.

Malcolm Holloway and National Security Advisor Trent Carter joined Chandler in the studio. Holloway enjoyed significant air time lately. As much as any of his responsibilities, public relations came near the top. Holloway understood that expanding the FSB's role meant appearances on morning news shows, press conferences, and meetings with national business organizations and unions. More than ever, people wanted to know how this new government agency helped them in matters of the economy and to some extent, security. Holloway and Carter were building a tighter relationship and it made sense to interview them together. A couple of hours before taping, Chandler realized he never had that conversation with Axel about terrorism and the financial markets. He thought a quick session would give him something useful for the interview. He holed himself up in a small conference area and called his mentor.

"Ax, did I catch you at a bad time?"

"No, I'm just reading. Trying to get my September issue ready. How can I help you?" Axel sounded perturbed that Chandler interrupted him. He released his letter the first week of every month, which meant he needed to get it to his publisher a couple of weeks prior.

"When we were in Geringer's house you said we needed to talk about terrorism and the markets."

"OK"

"Well, now is the time. I know you might not want to do this over the phone, but I have to interview Holloway and Trent Carter in a couple of hours."

"Oh, the big boys. Must be a PR tour for them. When is your interview?"

"I just said in a couple of hours." Chandler fidgeted in his chair, annoyed at Axel's apparent lack of attention.

"Oh, so I guess I can't make it to your studio in time unless I get beamed there by the Enterprise," Axel made an oblique Star Trek reference.

"Funny. That show's before my time. Can we just go ahead and do this?"

"This can't wait until we meet in person?"

"Not really, I mean I guess it could but maybe a question comes out of our discussion I can ask them."

"Sure." Axel cleared his throat and took a swig of water.

"You said that sometimes terror activity can be foreshadowed by what happens in the markets," Chandler began.

"Yes. Let me give you an example but please don't ask how I know this, although if someone is listening to our conversation, ahh screw it. I am not revealing anything here other than just tying together two facts. You remember what happened on 9/11 and the two airline companies involved in the jet crashes?"

"Ahh, wasn't it United and American?"

"Yes, that's right. Well, right before the 9/11 attacks, there was unusual activity in both American and United Airlines stocks."

"Such as?"

"Such as those stocks were being shorted, being sold by traders that didn't own them."

"Really?"

"Yes, but here's the thing. The other airline stocks didn't show the same amount of trading activity. Just those two."

"Holy crap! Is this considered insider trading? Although who would the insiders be?" Chandler never covered a story about insider trading.

"My source thinks that it wasn't the terrorists themselves shorting the stocks since, of course, they were gonna die anyway. More likely it was people, maybe their social network, that had knowledge that something was going to go down so they took preemptive action."

"Needless to say they made a profit on that transaction."

"Are you kidding me? Yes, they did. But I don't want you to think this was some huge intelligence failure by the U.S. I mean the intelligence analysis I mention here was developed well after 9/11."

"And I guess they've refined it since?"

"Yes, in 2006, British intelligence foiled a plot to blow up several American Airlines jets flying between the UK and the US. Now, nobody is saying how they figured it out, but my source suggested that activity in AA stock probably aided the intelligence."

"Ahh, I see." Chandler's mind worked to figure out what he might ask Carter and Holloway. He swiveled nervously in his chair.

"Remember, terror cells are smaller now and they encrypt their communication. It's not as if you need some big ass organization any more. You just have an ideology and spread it through the media or Internet. Encryption is important in this age of constant surveillance. This is why you have to look for other ways of gathering intelligence." Axel knew as well as anyone how intelligence gathering had changed.

"Yeah, encryption, no doubt. I still can't get over how Tyler Sawyer died."

"I know. I can't believe he just was gunned down randomly like that. It seems like there is more to his death. We can't prove anything, of course. No doubt his work on DigiNote and at Maxwell rankled people in high places. That's the Achilles heel of intelligence gathering now, encryption. If you ask me, I would say...OK I think I don't want to comment any further on that over the phone so let's call it a day."

"Ax, thanks. Talk to you later."

"Hope your interview with the big boys goes well. Bye."

Chandler bolted out of the conference room and had just enough time to get a quick snack and read over notes before Holloway and Carter arrived. He greeted both guests warmly when they arrived in the studio, meeting them both for the first time.

Holloway described himself as a policy wonk and he looked the part - late 40s, tall and slim, light brown skin, afro-textured hair and no facial growth. He dressed well but not especially flashy. He wore a white shirt, heavily starched, a red tie and a blue suit. The shoes were classic loafers, expensive, like you'd see on a Wall Street banker, maybe because he had been a Wall Street banker.

Malcolm Holloway defined the American success story.

Class valedictorian in high school, he graduated summa cum laude from Harvard with a degree in finance and punctuated that with an MBA from the Wharton School of Business. A successful career in banking culminated in his appointment as Treasury Secretary in 2014 and later a transition to the Global Settlement Bank. In most instances, Holloway was the smartest person in the room.

The military formed the backbone of Trent Carter's career. After obtaining a degree in International Relations from Georgetown University, he received his appointment as a second lieutenant in the Marine Corps, eventually rising to the rank of General. He served many tours overseas, including the first Gulf War and the Iraq occupation. After retiring from the military, he served as a State Department liaison in the Middle East and also on various corporate boards. President Jefferson appointed him National Security Advisor upon taking office in 2017.

Carter dressed in a black pinstripe suit, white shirt, and blue tie. His shoes were plainly styled lace-up oxfords. Carter's military background conveyed a strictness of thought with a calm demeanor and a methodical approach to solving problems.

Chandler had interviewed many people in his career though this combination would be as formidable as any. The three sat in identical straight-back, slightly padded pine chairs with low arm rests, making small talk as a technician made final lighting adjustments. Chandler received a signal that taping could begin.

"Today, I'm speaking with Financial Stability Board Secretary Malcolm Holloway and National Security Advisor Trent Carter. Welcome, gentlemen."

"Thank you." Both men replied in unison.

"Mr. Carter, the public has been under progressive layers of surveillance for some time now. There was suspicion of cyber terror during the stock market crash last year. I covered a story in Madrid where terrorists took down one of their exchanges. Ransomware attacks are on the increase. Hacktivists have taken to state and federal government websites. There have been reports about cyber-attacks on the Northeast power grid. I was delayed for several hours last year trying to leave DFW when reservations systems apparently got hacked. Is our biggest security concern cyber terror?"

"I talk to the president about this all the time. People worry about someone detonating a bomb in a crowded sports venue or within our transportation system, or biological and chemical attacks. We have gotten much better at detecting terrorist threats of this nature since 9/11. Our overall level of surveillance, as you indicated, is unmatched in history. While those types of threats are important, and we are still vigilant about such threats, I can tell you categorically we are dedicating more resources to cyber crimes. This goes beyond things like child pornography, human slave trafficking, or say banking and financial fraud. Now we have concerns in areas of critical infrastructure and, as you mentioned in your opening, financial trading centers. We also have to filter out fake terror scares where we close airports or other public transportation systems. The modern day terrorist can inflict considerable damage whether an attack actually occurs or not. They can operate from anywhere in the world so it's not just a matter of physical surveillance."

"I think Americans are well aware of how much surveillance is going on, which is one reason so many people are reluctant to say much on the phone. What are we really getting from all this data collection and mining?"

"I would suggest to you that we are a safer society. We have refined our data mining over the last decade and are applying it towards the combat of cyber terror."

"Mr. Carter, isn't it true that data mining is not well suited to catching terrorists? It's been successful in catching credit card fraud, tax evasion, or loan defaults. But when it comes to terrorism, some would say it falls short."

"I disagree with that conclusion, Mr. Scott. Perhaps you can cite an example." Carter turned his head, perturbed by the challenge.

"Sure. I read that after 9/11, the NSA passed thousands of tips to the FBI and almost all of them proved to be false. That is one problem with collecting so much data, there are a bunch of false positives."

"That example seems quite generalized. I can tell you we have foiled many cyber and kinetic terror plots. Candidly, we don't advertise our successes. Without extensive data scrapes and mining, we would not have been successful. That's not just Trent Carter's opinion, but that of experts in the field. Understand that US soil is what military professionals call an unprepared battlefield. We don't want the battle to come here." Carter exhibited a brief micro expression by pursing his lips, annoyed at Chandler's inference.

"OK, it's also known that one of the Boston Marathon bombers was on the terrorist watch list and left plenty of crumbs in his social media activity. So you guys mined the data and didn't attach importance to this particular case. And this was a dozen years after 9/11."

"I can tell you that our techniques are more refined since the Boston Bombing seven years ago." Carter did not mention that one refinement was the large data center south of Salt Lake City housing untold volumes of surveillance data.

"All right, let's go with the premise that we're more refined in our collection and analysis of data. If we return to your big concern about cyber terror, do you think that occurred last fall during the stock market's decline?"

"We don't divulge any details of our collection or analysis nor do we discuss specific events. You can understand the sensitivity there. I would like to note, however, our concern about financial terror cells in the US or overseas communicating in a manner which does not allow our intelligence agencies to gather the information to thwart cyber-attacks." Carter, whose head recessed into his shoulders, wanted no part of discussing cyber-attacks on U.S. stock exchanges. Confidence in financial markets needed to be maintained.

"You mean encryption technology?"

"Yes, that would be one method. I can also tell you the use of SuperNotes is very disruptive not just here but overseas as well. Terrorists have taken advantage of the economic situation by injecting this fake currency into the world economy. People are so desperate that they're accepting these notes without regard to their authenticity." This was another area Carter did not want to bring much attention to, encryption, thus, the deflection to SuperNotes.

"There are people who would rather have cash these days than deal in credit. Credit card companies have put on the clamps and credit for new, small businesses has just about evaporated. It was predictable, don't you think, that our economy would see a movement to cash and other forms of exchange."

"The administration of President Jefferson showed great leadership in implementing some of these measures to stabilize the financial markets, some of which are painful. Mr.

Holloway, who can expound on that more, is a close partner of mine in combating financial terror."

"DigiNote usage apparently has increased. I say apparently because the exchange of the electronic currency is a private transaction. We are all saddened to learn of Tyler Sawyer's murder and our prayers go out to his family. Do you see DigiNote as a vehicle used by financial terrorists?"

"Certainly it is less than ideal that there are financial transactions operating outside the sphere of the FSB and our other financial authorities. The public needs to understand that terror groups will use any means at their disposal to evade the authorities. DigiNote, I think everyone knows, hampers our ability to track financial transactions. We're also trying to monitor and disrupt illicit transactions occurring on the Internet. This dark side of the Internet is a haven for terror transactions."

"The dark side of the Internet being that which cannot be casually browsed. Can you tell us if or how the government is disrupting this dark side of the Internet?"

Carter squared his shoulders towards his interviewer. "No, I cannot."

"Let me ask one final question Mr. Carter. Do you think our intelligence agencies can identify terror activity, either cyber or kinetic by observing financial markets? In other words, let's say there appears to be unusual activity in a particular stock or market segment. Might that foreshadow terror events?"

"We have a variety of techniques at our disposal, Mr. Scott." A long pause followed Carter's response, during which he stared stone faced at Chandler. "I'm sure Secretary Holloway can speak more to financial markets."

"Thank you for that segue, Mr. Carter. Secretary Holloway,

do you feel the FSB's regulation of financial transactions has somehow led to a reduction in cyber terror?"

"Our charter established by the president last year gives us broad authority to manage and control financial transactions. We see what is going on. So, yes, I believe our partnership with various counterterrorism agencies has thwarted financially motivated cyber-attacks on our institutions."

"I guess the big complaint business has is how everything has slowed to a crawl due to the number of electronic forms required for the simplest business transactions. And we have limits on cash usage." Chandler heard this from several businesses he talked to in New York and D.C.

"We feel that is a necessary step in allowing us to not only monitor financial transactions but it also gives us a dashboard to particular areas of the economy that need to be cooled or stimulated. Consider that a two-pronged approach. One is for counterterrorism and the other for economic smoothing. Our processes will improve so that we are not a burden to businesses." Holloway had fielded this complaint many times over the last few months and delivered the response smoothly and effortlessly.

"You mention areas of the economy that need to be cooled or stimulated. Is that not a form of economic planning?"

"Are you using that term in the pejorative sense?" Holloway thrust his head towards Chandler and furrowed his brow, taking offense to the challenge. He didn't like where this line of questioning was headed.

"I think any objective person would say that. The capitalists in the U.S. used to mock the Soviets about their economic planning. The FSB is looking at so many transactions and you have these temperature gauges that tell you whether to throw hot or cold water on the economy or economic smoothing as you suggested."

"I hope you are not in any way comparing us to a regime that fell to its death over thirty years ago. We are dealing with unprecedented financial circumstances coupled with ongoing terror threats. I don't think the Soviets dealt with that." The normally unflappable Holloway, whose neck tightened, disliked the implications of Chandler's questions. The last thing the Jefferson administration needed was a comparison to a failed regime.

"Mr. Secretary we have this big massive bureaucracy called the FSB and they seem to be like the air; they are everywhere. What-"

"Mr. Scott, was that a question? If you have no more questions, I am concluding this interview." Holloway swiveled towards Carter to signal his intentions.

"Mr. Secretary I-"

Holloway rose from his chair so quickly he nudged it sideways. Carter followed moments later. As Holloway walked out of the studio staffers heard him say, "That's the last time I talk to that network."

While the interview ended awkwardly, Chandler planned on leaving the abrupt termination in the piece. He returned to his desk to catch up on email and after thirty minutes received a call from an obviously angry Rafael.

"Chandler. What the hell are you doing?"

"What Rafa?"

"I heard about Carter and Holloway walking out. This is bad. We need these guys to be friendly with us. They're so important now, they could be a source of good interviews for a long time. Now they'll never talk to us again. That was a hatchet job."

"Holloway just didn't like the comparison to a Soviet planned economy and then he got up and left. How unprofessional was that?" Chandler retorted.

"Yes, on your part. *¡Me estas cagando!*"

"I am not fucking you over, Rafa. That's unfair!"

"*¡Carajo, anda a cagar!*" Rafa hung up on him once again. Rafael left Chandler thinking about another incident where he acted more emotionally in situations where previously there would have been no issue.

Back in his office in Buenos Aires, Rafael spoke on the phone. "We need to keep a closer eye on Chandler. He's becoming a liability." After listening to the unknown person on the other end he replied, "Yes, sir, I will."

CHAPTER NINETEEN
A WALK

The argument with Rafael earlier in the day remained fresh in his mind. He could handle cursing but not Rafael questioning how he did his job. Rafael trained him this way - ask incisive questions and let viewers make their own determinations. *What's happened to Rafa?* Their friendship had also been severely damaged. Needing to reflect on his time at El Mundo and the other things in his life, Chandler took a stroll on a warm August evening in the National Mall. After a considerable amount of walking, he arrived at the west end of the Reflecting Pool in front of the Lincoln Memorial.

This wasn't the first time he'd walked around the Mall to balance his thoughts. He thought about Arianne. They finally admitted their feelings and he was excited about his future with her. He knew she was the *one,* though he had no timetable. Forced to be independent from a young age with no father and a mother who often left before he went to school and got home when it was time to eat, made him think about himself first. His independence manifested as both a strength and a weakness. Taking the next step in their relationship would be difficult for him. It would require thinking about someone other than himself.

The crusade with Geringer and Axel energized him, but he was at a different point in his life. Arianne told him to quit tilting at windmills. *Maybe she was right.* A Texan, however, had a sense of "can do." No task proved too big and no challenge too great. Texans had big ideas and got things done.

Chandler never doubted himself, so why start now?

His feet were tired, no doubt from having the wrong shoes for this length of walk, so he sat on a bench. Engrossed in his thoughts, he failed to notice an approaching stranger. Habakk sat next to him, dressed much as he was as on Christmas Day, a black shirt, khaki pants, and athletic shoes.

"Chandler, so good to see you again." Even in the warm temperature, Habakk appeared cool and placid.

"Why is it that you just seem to appear all of a sudden? Is someone beaming you down from the Enterprise?" He found a great moment to use the same reference Axel had used on him.

"Enterprise?" Habakk lifted a quizzical eyebrow.

"You must not be from the States. An old TV show."

"It is true that I was not born here, but I watch little television. Though I do occasionally watch Chandler Scott on the El Mundo channel." Habakk's comment elicited the first smile since early in the day.

"I haven't seen you since Christmas Day," Chandler observed.

"It was a warm day for December at The Battery much like it is tonight for late August." Habakk fanned himself though he didn't need to.

"Tell me something. After you said goodbye, in Spanish, I waited a few seconds and then chased after you, but you were gone. I looked around and you vanished." Chandler recalled struggling to explain that to Arianne and still couldn't figure it out.

"Are you saying an old man outran you?" Habakk said with a smile.

Chandler shrugged his shoulders and shook his head. "Seriously, I don't know how you did it."

"Must be the shoes!" Habakk pointed at his footwear, proper ones for the walk upon which Chandler embarked.

"Oh, and you speak Spanish?"

"I speak the language in which people can understand me."

"So mysterious, Mr. Habakk. Are you here to shower me with wisdom?"

"I don't know that I bring wisdom. I just tell you what I know. You look tired, my friend." Habakk nailed that assessment.

"Yeah, I've got one wheel down with an axle dragging," Chandler said, reflecting the forlorn hollows under his eyes.

"You definitely have colorful metaphors. May I ask what troubles you?"

"The relationship with my boss has really deteriorated. I mean, he's changed. Heck, maybe I've changed. You know, we just seem to be at odds all the time now."

"Perhaps your boss is under some pressure of which you are not aware?"

"I've worked with him for a few years. I've seen him under pressure before. We've traveled together, laughed, gotten drunk. I feel like I know the guy. He's from the same country as my own father too."

"Sounds like you've had some great times together."

"We really have and I owe him a lot professionally too."

"Is he close to his family? Is he married? Children?"

"No, no, and no. He's a lone operator with lots of acquaintances and contacts all over the place. But I can't say he has like a real close friend, you know."

"What does he want in life?"

"We never really talked about that. I do know the guy is ambitious. Very high energy. Since he lives by himself, he can pretty much be the ultimate company man. He'll fly across the world at a moment's notice. I thought I had a bunch of frequent flier miles. He won't fly coach the rest of his life."

"So what could stress him that has to do with his ambition?"

"I think this is one of those moments that it is better to keep my mouth shut and seem a fool than to open it and remove all doubt." Chandler questioned how well he knew his boss.

"Consider events in this country. The economy, the things happening in government. It has to be an exciting time for him at El Mundo. Lots of material with which to work. Maybe he sees El Mundo taking the next big leap as a network?"

"Our sponsors still like us, so our ratings must still be good."

"What troubles him lately?"

"This is where I think we're at odds. The chaos for him means government needs to step in and take control. He grew up without a pot to pee in or a window to throw it out of. Growing up in that Argentine shanty town, he lacked order and safety. He wanted out, for sure, but his family didn't have the means. Now he sees disorder on a much bigger stage. For him, a strong central plan makes all the sense in the world. I can't believe I'm telling you all this about my boss. We really don't know each other." Chandler violated his momentary vow of silence.

"Chandler, man organized the forces of nature through engineering and science to improve the human condition. But man has been seduced into thinking that human action could also be organized with a central plan. A central plan that tells people how much their money is worth, what to buy, how much to save, what and how much to produce, and how to be satisfied economically, is a fool's errand."

"Mr. Habakk, you are as smart as a whip. I love the way

you explained that. I have a friend that thinks like you do. Are you gonna ask what else troubles me?"

"Is there more?"

"I don't even know why I suggested that. Hell, I haven't had anything to drink so I can't blame that. Mr. Habakk, you just have a way of making me talk."

"Is it helpful?"

"I hear the things you tell me and fundamentally understand them. I then have more thoughts about the things you say, and then you aren't around."

"I may be around more than you think. I just am not around you. So is there something else troubling you?"

"Man! Back to me again. Well, I'm sure if you ask any man about what might trouble him, inevitably a woman's name pops up."

"There is a woman in your life?"

"Yes, she's special. I get that certain feeling when I see her. My search is over."

"Wonderful, so this is a problem?

"No sir. Our thing now is that she thinks I'm fighting battles that I can't win."

"And you feel the same way?"

"You must be a psychologist. All these questions. She has a point. But I didn't grow up walking away from challenges and that's what she's asking me to do, or at least not pursue them as much. To her credit, she's tried to help me."

"What happens if you walk away from these challenges?"

"I suppose nothing. It's not as if the earth will stop rotating. I'm working with two good people. One is a good friend who is someone of great conviction. The other is a man of great character. You have to be true to yourself. I like to think I'm a person of conviction and character and it would haunt me if I walked away."

"You love her?"

"Yes!"

"And she loves you?"

"Yes!"

"Then she will understand. The road will be rife with obstacles but as long as she is traveling with you, you will arrive at your destination together, which is really what you want."

"Why are you so confident?"

"Let's just say I believe in love. And I believe in conviction and principles. Those things are not mutually exclusive. Let's take a walk, my old legs are getting stiff."

They rose from the bench and walked north, neither saying a word. After a couple of minutes they passed the Vietnam Veterans Memorial and emerged on Constitution Avenue in front of the Eccles Building, home of the Federal Reserve.

"Chandler, do you know what organization is housed in that building?"

"This one I do know since I taped a segment for my show in front of it. That is none other than the Fed."

"After the Fed came into existence in 1913, they did not have their own building. It seemed logical to put them in the Treasury building, but they were not really a department like Treasury, and yet that's where they stayed for twenty years. Later, Congress passed the Banking Act of 1935 and gave them their own building."

"Now you're just showing off, Mr. Habakk."

Habakk turned towards Chandler with a look of satisfaction and continued. "Since it was the Great Depression, government wanted to keep with the times by making the building less ornamental and free of imposing columns. They did not want it to look like a monument. The style is called Stripped Classicism, or a simplified classical style."

"Now you're giving me an architectural lesson?"

"Please be patient, Mr. Scott. Consider the great irony that a building created under austere times in a stripped down architecture would eventually house an organization like what the Fed grew to become - they imposed their will on the economy. Now with the FSB taking temporary residence at the Fed you have another organization wielding financial power the likes the world has never seen. I bet they will get their own building, probably in a simple classical style, but rest assured, they will impose their own will."

"What do you know about the FSB?" Chandler took a chance on Habakk having some unique insight.

"The FSB is powerful and will become more so. It was Baron Rothschild who said that he did not care who was in power. He was more concerned about who controls the money. That's who has the real power. I would say the FSB and any other organization like it internationally will have the real power. Don't just follow the money, pay attention to who controls it."

"You don't like international organizations?"

"There are great international organizations. The world is infinitely more connected. Just be mindful of the stated intention of these international arrangements. And be mindful if these arrangements deal with control and issuance of money."

"I don't know who you are. But there's something about you and your voice and your manner. The rational part of my brain tells me you wouldn't just show up at opportune moments for the hell of it. But then again, I don't know why you show up or where you come from. So I should question that too. My gut tells me that I should trust you."

"Mr. Scott, decide if what I am saying has any merit. I cannot decide that for you. I must bid you farewell now. *Hasta la proxima.*" Habakk walked away in those half-moon steps Chandler saw at Christmas.

"Why do you say farewell to me in Spanish?

Habakk turned his head as he walked. "It just seems like the right thing to do."

Chandler focused on watching Habakk's departure this time to gauge his speed, or if by chance, he might vanish into the late summer air. He had a clear view. Habakk didn't outrun him or vanish into the warm air, but disappeared into a small car, a black Mini Cooper that pulled over on Constitution Avenue. When Chandler looked for the license plate, he realized there was none. He fumbled to get his phone for a picture, and by the time he did, the small car sped away into the night.

While focused on Habakk's departure, a stranger stood close by, maybe fifty feet or so. Had this occurred during the day, he might not have paid any attention. This stranger just stood there, took no action, and just stared, making him uncomfortable. He didn't want to stare back, but it appeared the stranger had on long shorts, a tee shirt, and a ball cap turned sideways. In the dark of night, the stranger appeared young, probably in his twenties of average height and build.

Chandler walked and the stranger followed. When he stopped, the stranger stopped, maintaining fifty or so feet of separation. He picked up his pace on Constitution Avenue towards 17th St. He didn't want to run but his pursuer closed the gap, now closer to forty feet. His heart beat at a brisk exercise pace. *Maybe this is what an Olympic walker feels like?*

He thought about turning the chase towards the Constitution Gardens Pond to lose the stranger, but he'd rather be on a main street where he could see more. *What if there is another pursuer?* He'd never been in this situation before, at least not on foot.

There was the time in Buenos Aires, but someone else was driving and robbery was the motive. This hardly seemed like a robbery attempt. If the stranger watched him with Habakk, he could have easily approached, flashed a gun and gotten his loot. *But why did he wait for Habakk to leave? Did Habakk set him up? No way.* He trusted Habakk, or at least he thought he did even though he hardly knew him. He'd only mentioned him to Arianne and not Axel. Maybe he should just turn around and confront the person. *But what if he has a gun? What do they want?*

He turned south on 17th Street and kicked it into gear. *Screw it.* If the stranger wished to chase him at a fast jogging pace, then so be it. Chandler's aerobic conditioning would not permit a lengthy run, though maybe his adrenaline could fuel him. After running the length of two football fields he saw the WWII Memorial on his right. The adrenaline didn't provide the expected fuel. His lungs burned, probably as much for panic as exertion. He didn't look behind to see if he was still being followed.

The stranger's footsteps weren't audible and he only heard his own plus the ambient noise of an evening in the Mall. *Can I dial 911 while running? Should I stop? Why aren't there more people out tonight? Oh wait, there are a few people walking about 200 yards ahead. But what if when I get to them, there is no stranger following?* They may have thought he was drunk or worse, they might recognize him from TV - the embarrassment. There were cameras in the Mall and drones overhead so all this would be captured on video, but what difference would it make if he was dead? *Where are the cops?*

A small, black Fiat pulled up and a door flung open. The driver said, "Get in, I'm a friend of Habakk's." The thought of the cyborg yelling, "Come with me if you want to live," at Sarah Connor popped into his head. Much like Ms. Connor evading the Terminator, Chandler hesitated since he didn't know the driver. The cluster of people stood far ahead. He had another fleeting thought about blaming Habakk for this chase. A test, perhaps? He could hear a drone hovering above, but still no cops. He got in the Fiat reasoning it the best alternative.

The driver looked like a younger version of Habakk, cinnamon skin, clean shaven with jet black hair, slightly curly. He'd estimate him to be about thirty. He also dressed like Habakk, dark shirt and khaki pants with athletic shoes. No telling his height, though he had a strong physique with soft looking hands. This man did not labor with his hands. The car had a fresh, sweet smell. *Was it the man or an air freshener? Why did he even notice how the car smelled?* There were more important things at hand.

They headed east on Independence Ave. The whole time, Chandler asked questions and received no answers. The car moved quickly but not enough to scare him, like a cabbie in Manhattan. They turned north on 2nd Street with the eventual destination at Union Station. The driver finally spoke and told him to get a cab and head to his girlfriend's condo. *How did he know about a girlfriend?* The stranger turned to shake his hand and wished him good luck, *"Buena suerte amigo."* Then he placed a thumb drive in Chandler's hand during the handshake and motioned him out of the vehicle. Chandler complied and the vehicle sped away. Curiously, this time he saw a license plate, one which appeared to be for a diplomat, but he couldn't determine the country.

As he stood in front of Union Station, he had no idea what just happened. Still out of breath, and profusely sweating, he appreciated his relative safety though he now questioned his perception of danger in the Mall. And what should he make of the thumb drive given by the stranger? He hailed a cab and made the short trip to Arianne's.

CHAPTER TWENTY
VIDEOS

The cabbie dropped Chandler at Arianne's condo. He barely noticed the ride. Shaken, he burst through the door and scared her. He told her the improbable tale of the evening's events.

"Chan, this is getting to be too much now. You could've been hurt. You're not making any of this up, are you? Maybe the person you thought was following really wasn't, or they were just playing with you? Maybe someone recognized you and wanted to mess with you, sort of like a weird stalking. People are crazy these days."

"No. I mean first Habakk, you know the man from The Battery on Christmas Day, then the person chasing me, then the other car. I can't make all this up!"

She believed him, though found it odd that the stranger from months before had suddenly appeared again. More than ever, she worried that her man was tilting at windmills. The adventure that was his journalistic investigation had tangible elements of danger now.

She'd invested too much of herself in this relationship to have harm come to him. She ordered him to the shower even though his sweat made him appear like he'd taken one already. Her nose, however, couldn't be fooled. Before showering, he hid the thumb drive in a fake book that rested on the bottom shelf of a storage credenza bookcase. He bought the book, with an old world cover, for her a couple of months ago, not satisfied with her general awareness of security.

The shower did not calm him. Dressed with only a towel around his waist, his hair still damp, he peeked out the window and drew all curtains shut. Paranoia set in.

"Chan, really. Will you get dressed? Let me get you a beer. You're totally nervous right now."

He remained agitated. "You didn't just get chased, honey." Water from his hair slid down his back.

Noticing water accumulating on her tile floor, she gave him a gentle nudge back towards the bedroom. "Get some clothes on and then sit down and watch TV. I'll bring the beer. Sheesh."

A dressed Chandler with mostly dry hair, made it to the sofa and poured the IPA in a frosted pint glass. She kept cold glasses in the freezer for him. He grabbed the remote and tuned a local channel, the NBC affiliate. The personal digital assistant, her Christmas gift, sat boxed in her bedroom, relegating him to pushing buttons on a plastic device. He didn't realize it was so late, the ten o'clock news was on.

We have breaking news tonight at the top of the hour. NBC4 has just learned about the arrest of Senator Thomas Shaw, Democrat from Maine, by the FBI reportedly for an illegal transfer of funds to an account presumed to be owned by the terrorist group Al Amouk. This investigation was supported by both the FBI and Financial Stability Board whose scope extends to monitoring financial transactions and national security. Senator Shaw has been taken into custody by special agents who raided his home in the Arlington Heights area. When asked if Al Amouk had any active cells in the US, the FBI declined comment. In other news, the president authorized....

Arianne cried, first a little and then a lot. Then she shrieked imprecations at the TV. Her melancholy returned, unleashing kryptonite on her boyfriend. "Oh, my God, Chandler. How? He didn't do this!" She slumped on the couch next to him. "He'd never get involved with terrorists. He's been fighting them."

"Could money have been involved?" Chandler didn't know what to say. He'd just finished a nerve-wracking evening and was winding down. He didn't know the senator nor did he have emotional ties, so he thought like a journalist.

"No way. He had plenty of money. He wasn't the richest guy in the Senate, you know, but money didn't drive him. He was comfortable."

For the next hour, she recalled her time working with Shaw and experiences they shared. Chandler listened patiently and let her do all the talking. Emotional support proved the best prescription for her and him.

He'd almost forgotten everything he went through just a couple of hours earlier. Still, the stress of the earlier part of the evening, her emotions, and a couple of beers affected him.

"I'm wiped out. Let's go to bed. We can figure this out in the morning and look at that thumb drive." It took a great deal of Zen mastery to put that drive away and not look at it. He very well might have, had the Shaw story not broken and her need for comfort.

"I need a thumb drive like I need a-" She had no interest in that topic.

"I get it. Let's go to bed."

***

The next morning, in a reversal of roles, Arianne woke before Chandler. She made a light breakfast with toast and juice and awakened her man by straddling him as he lay on his back. Ordinarily this action might have led to something else, not today though. She wanted affection after a difficult night of fitful sleep. Chandler, however, grumbled. He grabbed a pillow and put it over his face.

"Did you have to turn on the light?" he protested.

"Come on, get something to eat and we can look at the drive. I don't want to think about Shaw." She grabbed the pillow and moved it aside. A quick peck on his lips followed.

"OK, give me a minute."

He plodded his way into the dining area, unsure why he felt so groggy. He'd slept well, so it had to be her early call. After breakfast, he retrieved the drive from inside the fake book. Now came the quandary about inserting an unknown flash drive once again.

"I'll just use my work laptop. I seriously doubt someone is gonna want to hack us. We're no more secure than any other business so they could've hacked us any time," he reasoned.

"Good choice cuz you weren't touching my laptop."

They set up in the living area, seated on the couch, laptop on the coffee table. Nothing unusual happened when he introduced the drive into his laptop. The drive contained but a single folder called "Videos." Within the folder, there were several MP4 clips.

The first clip showed Rafael and Emmet sitting in the outdoor patio of a mansion. The clip appeared to come from a high-powered lens. It began with a very wide pan showing the entirety of, presumably, the Callaghan grounds and then zoomed tightly on the patio scene. The videographer filmed from a perch higher than the mansion.

The men relaxed while enjoying wine. Malcolm Holloway

sat with them. They were looking at a document and smiling. At the end of the video, they shook hands and man-hugged. Chandler had no idea that Rafael knew Emmet. In fact, he denied meeting Emmet. *Why would he lie?*

The next clip had Emmet and Senator Shaw meeting in a coffee house. He could not discern the location. This encounter suggested an opposite mood of the first clip. Shaw wagged his finger at Emmet. Other patrons in the coffee house gave furtive glances at the men.

If this was D.C., surely someone in the shop would have recognized Shaw. Emmet was a public figure, though he could easily walk in the nation's capital without many people knowing him. A large, imposing man, perhaps security, hooked the senator's arm and escorted him from the table. Shaw and Emmet glared at each other as the former was led out the door. Considering what happened with Shaw and his arrest, this encounter raised suspicion.

The last clip had Emmet emerging from a small building, small by U.S. standards. But this appeared to be a European city. Chandler recognized the GSB building in Geneva from a picture Axel shared with him. Emmet walked with the managing member of the GSB, Jean-Claude Bienfait and another unrecognized person.

"I wish I knew who that other person was," Chandler commented.

Arianne pointed at the screen. "If you mean this baldish, gaunt looking man, I can tell you exactly who that is." She figured he knew what Jean-Claude looked like from his appointment to the presidential commission.

"No way. How would you know?"

"Because that is Saltzman!" She tapped the screen over his

image.

"Whoa. Are you sure? I need to call Ax."

They replayed the video clips a few times to gather more detail. Satisfied that nothing else emerged, he called Axel and Geringer and suggested they meet soon.

***

Molly Sanders, Geringer's chief of staff, wondered why Chandler Scott and this gentleman named Mr. Schultz were meeting with her boss in the Hart Building office. The senator offered little detail surrounding the meeting, atypical since she knew details about her boss' schedule.

As far as she knew, Mr. Scott was there for an interview and Mr. Schultz was consulting on a banking matter. She knew Mr. Scott from his interview last year, but took it upon herself to find out more about this Mr. Schultz.

Due to Geringer's campaigning on behalf of IAP presidential candidate, Alfonso Chancellor, it took a couple of weeks to set up the meeting. With the election just two months away, Chancellor and his VP nominee needed to press the flesh with potential voters. Geringer made campaign stops as well. After his abrupt decision to abandon the race, Geringer felt he owed it to the party to campaign on Chancellor's behalf.

Chandler and Axel sat across from Geringer, his massive desk between them. The three men opened their discussion with the Shaw arrest. Geringer doubted the legitimacy of the charges.

"I've known Tom for years. I've served with the man. That's not him. I don't know what they got on the guy, but it smells fishy to me," Geringer declared.

"My girlfriend Arianne said the same thing." To date, neither Axel nor Geringer knew of her connection to Shaw, making Chandler cringe after he made the comment.

"If they set him up, who the hell would have done it and why?" Geringer asked.

"Senator, I might have that answer for you. This is one reason I wanted to meet," Chandler replied. He took the laptop out of his bag and placed it on the senator's desk so all three could see it. After powering up, he plugged in the thumb drive provided by the mystery driver from the Mall.

The three watched the first clip with Rafael, Emmet and Holloway looking relaxed having a drink.

"Freeze that. Who's this guy?" Geringer asked, leaning in and pointing at Rafael.

"Oh him? That's my boss, Rafael Mendoza." Chandler thought Geringer already knew what he looked like.

"And where was this video shot?" Geringer asked and then peeked at an incoming text on his phone.

"I think it must be at the Callaghan Mansion. I remember asking Rafael specifically about Emmet and he denied he even knew him," Chandler added while restarting the video.

"That should tell you something, Chandler," Axel said.

The action moved to the second clip with Emmet and Senator Shaw in a heated argument and the large man grabbing the senator's arm. Chandler didn't know about Emmet's "mutual understanding" with Shaw, and he would not bring up Arianne's relationship with Shaw in this conversation. He wanted to protect her from any ill opinion.

"Clearly, there is some riff between these two but it's hard to know what it is," Chandler said.

"Enough I guess to have Emmet's bodyguard grab a senator's arm forcefully. Hmm, Emmet has a bodyguard?" Geringer asked.

"So you think Emmet had something to do with Shaw's arrest?" Axel connected dots.

"Can't say for sure but two people that know Shaw think this was way out of character," Chandler said. He did it again and slipped about Arianne.

"Two people?" Axel turned up his right eyebrow. A curious wash covered his face as he gazed at Chandler.

"Oh sorry. You were gonna say something, Matt." Chandler quickly deflected, noticing the senator appeared ready to speak.

"About a month ago, I was alerted that the National Security Division at the Justice Department was looking into the legality of suspending the Constitution in a national emergency. I called Tom. We talked. I asked him if, because he's on the terror committee, if there was some threat out there and that was the reason Justice was even looking into this. He claimed he hadn't heard anything but would investigate," Geringer explained.

The door to Geringer's office cracked open. His chief poked her head in and withdrew quickly, diverting the attention of the three men.

"Sorry guys. She's been texting me. Continue," Geringer asked.

"I guess him, Shaw, looking into it caused a problem then," Axel opined. "If he was set up, this could be a reason. I get the sense there was something else too."

During the third and final clip, Geringer appeared puzzled. He knew it wasn't a U.S. city and he saw people he didn't recognize.

"I recognize Callaghan and Bienfait, but who is the other man?" Geringer pointed at all three, stopping on the last. "And where is this?"

"First of all, this I believe is in Geneva at the office of the Global Settlement Bank. The man is none other than Levi Saltzman," Chandler revealed.

"That's Saltzman?" Geringer asked rhetorically, pointing at the screen. After the FSB named Saltzman Under Secretary, there was little detail on his background or even a picture. Only those that worked directly with him knew what he looked like.

"Yes, sir. Arianne confirmed it," Chandler replied.

"One question I have not asked so far and I guess I should have right from the beginning is where the hell you got this video?" Stern displeasure was visible in Geringer's countenance.

"Senator, Matt, that is kind of a long story-" Chandler began with a sheepish grin.

"Oh, God, this isn't some Omni thing again is it?" Geringer had a hard enough time swallowing the first intelligence stream from Omni, though after Axel's confirmation with his contact at the People's Bank of China, he presumed them to be more reliable.

"No. No. Nothing like that. Last night I was followed in the National Mall. I was legitimately concerned for my safety. There was hardly anyone around. I went into a full run and couldn't shake the person. This car pulled up, I guess a good Samaritan, and told me to get in. I guess the driver saw what was happening. He gave me a lift towards Union Station and then I caught a cab. Well, when he said goodbye, he shook my hand and placed a flash drive in it and sped off," Chandler explained.

He intentionally omitted Habakk. He'd never told Axel about Habakk and it made no sense to introduce that now. They probably wouldn't believe him and think he was drunk or high. As far as Chandler knew, Habakk had no part in any of this.

"You got in a car with a perfect stranger and he gave you this? I'm struggling with your story." Geringer wrestled with Chandler's unbelievable truth. He spied an incoming text.

"Matt, that's what happened. I have no reason to make that up and the video seems legitimate," Chandler retorted. He thought he'd earned enough capital with Geringer to avoid questions about his story's veracity.

"Well, then someone must know what you've been looking into. They had to know you're a journalist to feed this to you. The person following you I guess was trying to scare you more than anything, but why?" Geringer speculated.

"There are a lot of doctored videos out there. Technology has come a long way. You almost need to do forensics on video to see if it was altered, but I'm inclined to think this is valid. It puts some pieces together. Rafael and his conflict with Chandler. Rafael's journalistic shift. The trumped-up charges with Shaw. More detail about this Saltzman character and his elevation to Under Secretary. It is possible to connect these dots." Axel always had a way of bringing clarity to a discussion.

"Don't be angry at me for being skeptical. Ever since I joined up with you two, there's always this mystery about how all this info comes to light. Guys, I'm a senator and not long ago a candidate for president. Both of you understand I can't just throw bullshit out there."

"Senator, all I can tell you is that gathering intelligence can be very messy, disorganized, and unpredictable. Then it's up to the analyst to connect the dots. Sometimes connecting the dots produces an unintelligible picture. I would say this picture is not crystal clear, but we can at least see the outline of something.

I've had contact with Omni for many years. I have contacts in other parts of the world that have taken me many years to cultivate. I trust them. We also have the serendipity factor where some information conveniently comes our way. Maybe there is someone out there who wants us to have it. Maybe they feel we are in the best position to do something with it. If it had not been for Gustavo Sáenz testifying in front of your committee, we might have never met. Think about that. I think if you reason through what I say, you will agree." One of Axel's many strengths was patiently listening and analyzing and delivering a powerful conclusion.

"All right. You make solid points. Yes, we have an outline. I would just like to add the right colors to the rest of the picture," Geringer said.

"These videos are just strengthening my hypothesis about what is going on. We have a great deal of information here and I believe there is more than even meets our eyes," Axel added.

"Yeah, and I don't like any of it. If there is more than what we already think we know, this is gonna get real serious guys. I haven't shared anything with Senator Chancellor since I don't want to distract him from his campaign. Ahh, let's wrap this up. I've got to catch a flight back home to Colorado. And Molly's been texting me and you guys saw her peek in. Look, we should meet again soon and hopefully we'll have more." Geringer unfurled his 6'4" frame from his chair and shook hands with Axel and Chandler. This meeting was officially over.

Chandler headed to the El Mundo bureau, and Axel made a couple of stops before returning to his hotel.

CHAPTER TWENTY-ONE
GLOBAL FINANCIAL UNION

On his drive to his hotel in Arlington, near Reagan National, Axel received a text from the concierge indicating a package awaited him, unusual since he wasn't expecting anything. The desk attendant handed him a white box about five inches each side with a picture of a dark chocolate bar wrapped in gold on the lid. Axel thought the hotel had a strict policy to only accept flat envelopes, so this delivery proved most unusual. Two Iranian diplomats also had a "gift" box delivered to their D.C. hotel a couple of years earlier. The detonation killed both men and injured hotel patrons in adjacent rooms.

They never found the perpetrators and the Iranians claimed Mossad agents were involved. The Jefferson administration suffered a great diplomatic embarrassment with that incident and since then, Homeland Security strongly recommended that hotels not accept such packages. His curiosity tugging at him, Axel took the box and headed to his room. Surely he was no target of the Mossad.

Axel didn't need much from a hotel room. As long as it had a queen-sized bed, a work desk, free Internet, and no smoke odor, he managed just fine. He sat at the work desk, placed the box on the flat surface and opened the lid. Inside, a small card from the hotel manager thanked him for his stay. Beneath the card lay tissue paper, the kind one might see when wrapping a gift. After giving a cursory glance at the presumed box of chocolates, he replaced the lid, put the box on the desk and called the hotel manager to thank him. The room phone provided single button access.

"Hello, this is Axel Schultz."

"Good afternoon, Mr. Schultz. How can I help you?" the manager responded.

"I wanted to thank you for the gift. The chocolates."

"The gift, sir? I'm sorry we do not provide gifts for our guests. Where did you get this gift?"

"From your desk attendant."

"Sir, for liability reasons we do not send these things. The desk attendant should know better. Let me send someone to your room to retrieve it."

"No, that won't be necessary."

"Actually sir, it is. When you made the reservation, the agent, or if you did it online, should have noted that we cannot accept packages. The Department of Homeland Security advised us against this practice."

"Yes, I do recall but you're saying I can't keep it?"

"No, you cannot, sir. We will come get it and call the police so they may inspect it."

"I can't believe this! Are you kidding me? I'll take the responsibility."

"I'm sorry, sir. I'm just following policy. We'll have someone up shortly. Please take no further action with the box. Good bye, sir."

A frustrated Axel knew he probably had a couple of minutes before they arrived. He could give them the box and be done with it. If he refused, no doubt he'd have the police banging on his door not long after - no need to attract unnecessary attention. Something told him this could be part of the serendipity he talked about earlier.

If the hotel didn't accept boxes and he wasn't expecting

anything, this must be something valuable. Or it could be something that would kill him. He didn't have any enemies that he knew of. This would be extreme for a disgruntled subscriber. He'd only had three refunds in all his years as a publisher, so that couldn't be it. A bomb? Poison? A deadly gas? He figured if someone wanted him dead, all this trouble would be unnecessary. A simple bullet would do the trick. These were the thoughts of someone with no family responsibilities. Nevertheless, he proceeded cautiously, considering the manager's warning.

Examining the box, his olfactory sense told him there was something sweet inside. He shook it and heard a rattling, suggesting too few for a box this size. He brought it to his ear. No ticking. He opened the lid once again, disposed of the tissue paper and noticed two rows of four very dark chocolates, probably 90% pure. He took each and placed them on a napkin. Next was a cardboard divider concealing the bottom layer. A little over one minute remained before hotel management arrived.

The bottom layer contained more tissue paper and no chocolates, explaining all the rattling. He took out his pocket knife and sliced through each chocolate. Eight cuts later, nothing emerged. He reexamined the tissue paper and divider. Nothing caught his attention. He looked carefully inside the box. Imprinted inside the lid, emanating from a corner in a nine or ten point old style courier font, were a string of characters, too small for him to read. His glasses were thankfully nearby. The string of characters read, "*Divider.*" Thirty seconds. Time ran short. Attention returned to the box's divider discarded earlier. It proved unusually thick, given the rest of the box's dimensions. A quick squeeze with his thumb and forefinger revealed something embedded with a square to rectangular shape. He cut around the shape, placed the fragment on the desk, and reassembled the box. A knock on the door followed.

Axel displayed an exterior calm, though excited beneath the surface, as he answered, "Yes?"

"Hello Mr. Schultz. I'm with hotel security. You have an unauthorized package, I believe. May I please have it?" The large male security officer showed no emotion.

"Yes, of course." Axel handed the box over, giving one last glance at his reassembly.

"Thank you, sir. Have a nice day."

After closing the door, he returned to the desk and peeled back the cardboard layers of the cut out shape to reveal digital media. He plugged the media into his multi card reader that connected to a port on his digital tablet. A single file existed on the media, which appeared to be a decryption key necessary for an asymmetric cryptographic scheme. The key by itself meant nothing. He knew something else would be forthcoming, though he had no idea from whom or when.

Several hours later, an encrypted file arrived via email from an unknown domain. Now the key gained significance, especially when it successfully decrypted the file. This file's content provided the color the senator needed to make the picture clear.

***

After Axel made his discovery, he asked for a meeting with the senator and Chandler. Geringer, who had departed for Colorado, did not receive Axel's text until landing in Denver. The senator suggested a Sunday morning meeting the following week in his D.C. office. Sunday morning time was typically unscheduled. Molly, his chief, would grow more suspicious of yet another meeting with the two, so it was best to keep her in the dark. In the ensuing week, Axel camped out in D.C. and did not share the news with Chandler. He wanted everyone to hear the news simultaneously. He wasn't trying to hide anything but thought it prudent to confirm the intelligence revealed in his hotel room.

The senator flew back to D.C. late Saturday and got to his office early the next day. Without the Senate in session on Monday, quiet prevailed in the Hart Building on this September morning.

Geringer looked like someone who'd had little sleep, thus the need for the large tumbler of coffee on his desk. Chandler and Axel assumed their positions in the leather club chairs opposite of the senator who leaned his head back, prepared for Axel's tale.

Axel recounted his hotel adventure with the unwanted box of chocolates. "After the hotel manager told me I couldn't keep the box, I wasn't happy. But I understood the policy after those Iranian diplomats bit the dust."

"That was a big deal around here. The Iranian ambassador chewed out Jefferson I heard," Geringer related.

As Axel continued with his story, Geringer and Chandler commented on how much the tale sounded like a spy thriller. Axel argued that he had to be the intended recipient of the secret key and, by extension, the encrypted file. The other two offered no rebuttal.

"So you think the file came from Omni?" Geringer asked.

"When I get stuff from them or when I have in the past, there are these weird domain names in the addresses and sometimes they use proxy email servers so truthfully, it's hard to tell where they come from. The way this transaction went though, this method was not like them. This isn't the way I've worked with them in the past. I know if something is coming and usually because I've asked for it. This came out of nowhere. I'm struggling though to figure out who sent it. If it wasn't Omni, then this brings someone else into this equation," Axel concluded.

This new equation variable piqued a great deal of interest, though the main event lay in the decrypted file. He detailed the existence of two documents, a PDF called "Global Financial Union" aka GFU and another PDF called "Notes." He didn't print the electronic file since he'd have to use a shared printer at the hotel and instead made hand notes with details for Chandler and Geringer. The GSB authored the document with collaboration by the FSB. Axel summarized the staggering details.

"Senator, I suggest you take good notes," Axel said.

Emmet and a group of private investors were finalizing the purchase of El Mundo. They planned to turn the TV network into a mouthpiece for the IRC and the GFU. Rafael Mendoza would be named CEO.

All details from the garage chat session with Phish earlier in the year were confirmed.

The FSB had hackers on their payroll that were disrupting domestic electronic financial transactions deemed illegal. Hacking occurred on the Surface Web and Darknet. The FSB was working with domestic intelligence agencies to crack DigiNote.

Other hacker groups orchestrated the stock market's fall last year and were secretly paid by members of the IRC, including several prominent board members like Vasily Mozgov, Li

Zhang, and Leopoldo Sabatini. IRC-funded hackers were also culpable in other attacks on financial institutions and infrastructure. Ironically, payments to the hackers were with DigiNote.

The GSB would maintain personnel at Internet network access points and hosting centers to monitor specific financial activity.

Banks and credit unions would be subject to new regulatory control imposed by the FSB. Since compliance costs and legal liability were expected to be high, a massive consolidation would leave very few institutions. This made financial management and monitoring easier.

Alternate lending vehicles, such as online platforms, would be illegal.

All currencies were to exist in digital form only.

The GSB would hold gold reserves. Private gold ownership would be allowed, but would no longer trade on public exchanges, or used for payments or collateral. Measures would be implemented to take it out of public hands through favorable exchanges when paying taxes or other government fees, the only gold payments allowed.

The new world currency would be the Mundi. Mundis would only be used for international exchange. Domestic currencies were to remain in digital form only.

The GSB had the authority to direct central banks to credit private bank accounts and set interest rates.

Bank deposits above a fixed amount would be taxed.

Any rule proposed by the FSB running afoul of the Constitution would be validated through Executive Order.

A separate notation suggested the president freeze election results in the event no candidate received the required number of Electoral College votes. The election would not proceed to the House and Senate. The freeze would be in the name of national security and economic stability.

Geringer stopped writing and looked up towards the ceiling. "Good Lord! What have they done?"

"Senator, I hope this makes the picture clear for you. We now have verification of the Global Financial Union as described earlier this year to Chandler and me. We have connected the association between the GSB and the FSB and in particular Malcolm Holloway. We can tie hacking in financial markets last year to specific IRC members as part of a false flag attack. I believe the IRC, operating through proxies, has been responsible for other cyber-attacks, again as part of a false flag effort. It's clear now why Rafael Mendoza has been spraying the editorial can of whoop ass on Chandler. Regarding the rest, it fits within the scope of ultimate financial control some have always wanted, especially the FSB. Oh, and I'll let you and Congress debate the whole election freeze thing. I can see a big Constitutional fight there. That will rock the country." Axel summed up the entire document nicely. His earlier hypothesis was now confirmed.

"Axel, my God, I can't find argument in anything you said. There is so much for me to think about now." Geringer paused and swiveled his chair. He looked up at the eagle in the IAP logo above his credenza. "I have a man, a good man, running for president. Should I lay this on him? What would we as a party do with it? I could see the press just saying that it is some late stage stunt by a desperate political party. There won't be any way to prove any of this until maybe after the election, and by then it will be too late." Geringer swung around to face the men. "Mr. Schultz I will ask once again that you keep this out of your letter. Chandler, I will ask the same of you at least until I decide what I'm gonna do. Besides, you probably couldn't tape this story anyway, not with your boss apparently being someone who's collaborating here."

After making those requests, Geringer received a text from Molly. She was coming over. "Guys, you need to leave. My chief is heading over here. She didn't know about this meeting and I would rather have you guys gone before she gets here. Sorry for the rush."

Chandler and Axel stood and shook hands with Geringer.

"Senator, we'll talk again soon. I trust you will make the right decision for your party with this information," Axel said.

***

After a few days of thoughtful, prayerful consideration, Geringer shared information with Chancellor. He knew all along it was the right thing to do and felt awful placing this burden on Alfonso so close to the election. Geringer traveled to the party office in New York where Chancellor camped with his team.

They met in the same conference room where late last year he met Axel Schultz for the first time, the man who inundated him with information from a mysterious hacker group.

Now he laid his political reputation on the line by revealing the Global Financial Union to what undoubtedly would be a skeptical audience that included IAP chair Alex Carpenter, Chancellor, campaign manager Loretta King and her assistant, Tammy Blakely. The group sat around a conference table, Chancellor and Geringer on one side, the rest on the other.

"Matt, we didn't expect you to come all the way to New York. We were gonna be in Washington the day after tomorrow," Alex said.

"I know. This is important. I'll need all of you to keep an open mind to what I'm about to reveal," Geringer said.

He pulled out his notes and painfully detailed the entire GFU plan, noting that the information was a culmination of intelligence gathering spanning many months. Nobody interrupted him. The mouths in the room were agape initially, then the faces turned to skepticism.

"Come on. Where did you get all this?" Alex asked. Despite Geringer's heartiness and sincerity, he remained dubious. It took him many weeks to accept his withdrawal from the presidential campaign. This was another bombshell.

"Yeah, seriously," Loretta added.

"If I told you, you might not believe me. I've been working with a publisher of a financial and economic newsletter and a journalist some of you know, Chandler Scott of El Mundo." They all knew Chandler, but not Axel.

"Who's the publisher?" Alex inquired.

"Axel Schultz," Geringer answered.

"Never heard of him," Loretta countered. "Could you search on this guy?" She turned to her assistant, Tammy Blakely, to fulfill the request. Tammy typed quickly on her phone.

"Matt, it's one thing to use El Mundo, but a newsletter publisher? Are you fucking kidding me?" A flushed and agitated Alex could not digest what he heard.

"Is El Mundo going to run this story? Hell, they're in the middle of it." Alex's resentment towards Geringer for dropping out of the race was surfacing, inflaming the pores in his body.

The transition to Chancellor had been smooth, but it took a lot of work on Alex's part. Though Chancellor was a worthy candidate, he lacked the political stature of Matt Geringer and

Alex worried about the IAP's election chances.

Chancellor cast a look of scornful indignation at Alex, withholding his verbal disapproval for the manner in which Alex addressed Geringer. Geringer, the father of the IAP, deserved respect.

"I don't know the answer to that. Chandler's had recent battles with his boss, the man I mentioned who might be taking over, so I don't know. I told Chandler not to cover this on his show," Geringer answered.

"So you think just because you 'told' a journalist not to do something that he'll listen to you?" Alex's effort to restrain his anger was slipping.

His abrasiveness also wore on Loretta, who felt Geringer deserved more deference. "Alex, please!"

"Yes, he will," Geringer said in his deepest bass as he sat up in his chair and squared his shoulders to Alex.

"And you got Emmet Callaghan in the middle of all this too. I know he's a big contributor and supporter of Jefferson and he's big in the IRC but this other shit you told us, it seems like he's pulling these strings behind the scenes and you can't prove any of that," Alex said. An indignant crimson washed over his face.

"He's right, Matt," Loretta contributed.

"Hey, everyone, I got something on Schultz," Tammy interrupted. "His website gives his bio. Seems pretty straightforward. Nice early career. Savvy investor. Self-made man. He's somebody that could write a book on success. Says he has an international following of about one thousand subscribers who pay him $2,700 per year for his research. He has some free stuff on here. Mostly about economic theory and investments."

"Nice. And this is your source?" Alex pursed his lips in defiance.

"Look, damn it!" Geringer could no longer repress his temper, raising his voice and slamming his fist on the table. "I didn't arrive at this decision lightly or quickly. You understand? This is a process that developed over several months. And my God, think about what this will mean."

Alex was unperturbed by the outburst. "So you've been sitting on this?" His gaze revealed a conflict of emotions.

"The reason I didn't talk about this before is because a) I knew you would react like this and b) I had to be sure," Geringer countered.

"Let's just pretend for a minute all this is true. And we're really suspending disbelief here. What are we gonna do with it? Huh?" Alex spread his arms, palms pointed towards Geringer.

"That's something I've been wrestling with for some time," Geringer replied. He turned towards Chancellor. "Alfonso, you've been reticent. What say you?"

The time arrived for the presidential candidate to say something before the other two came to blows. The chasm between the hot shot young party chairman and the party's father quickly evolved into a canyon.

"This reminds me of the time I was playing in the Fiesta Bowl and we were an extra point away from tying the game and forcing overtime. That was the safe route. I wanted to go for two. We called time out and I told coach that when we ran the option, the defensive end would come in hard towards our tailback. I'd only kept the ball maybe once on that play all game. The tailback probably kept it twenty times. I thought I could just walk into the end zone. I talked coach into it." Alfonso set the stage for one of the most dramatic endings in

Fiesta Bowl history.

"It was a great moment for the Longhorns for sure," Alex added, temporarily distracted by the sports memory.

"Matt, this is no game. I'm not going to fool anyone this time. If I go out there with this and it's wrong, I'm finished. The other possibility is that it's true, but the voters don't care. They want leadership and solutions. We can't refute how good a job Jefferson's done in taking the leadership with all this. He's popular right now and the country has rallied around him, or at least there hasn't been any criticism. The country's worn out."

Chancellor paused to gather his thoughts, looking out the window. The others remained quiet until he returned his attention to them.

"Now this other stuff about freezing the election results, again if true, will be a fight that could really divide the country, maybe not. Electing a president, man, that will make the 2000 election results seem like a high school debate. Our party will not accept the freeze, and I sure as hell know the TP won't go for it. There are probably a bunch of GOP leaders that will fight it too. That will get ugly. For now, let's proceed as if the information is true, but we will keep it in this room. No leaks. We should prepare challenges, legislative and legal, to the GFU proposals as well as the election freeze. If and when these things come to fruition, we will unleash our challenges."

Chancellor demonstrated the leadership required in times such as these. The assembled group understood he'd be a great Constitutional steward.

"Alfonso, you sound like a president. The country would be lucky to have you serve," Geringer said.

"Thanks, Matt. Coming from you, that means a lot," Chancellor answered.

"Yeah, let's plan on unleashing president Chancellor," Alex urged.

"True, we need to get going with our debate preparation. Matt, you're more than welcome to stay. I definitely could use your help," Chancellor added.

Part III

2020

CHAPTER TWENTY-TWO
THE DEBATE

The Washington University Field House in St. Louis hosted the third and final presidential debate on October 14th. The 2020 debates were unique given the appearance of two third-party candidates. No such format existed in 2016. The nonpartisan nonprofit Commission on Presidential Debates or CPD awarded the event to the university after a successful history of hosting debates. The candidates were on an elevated stage adorned in patriotic red, white, and blue colors. A red carpet draped the stage with blue vertical paneling behind four podiums. A glass cutout, home for a TV camera and photographer, emerged from one panel. The moderator faced the candidates with his back to the audience in a U-shaped wooden desk. Another camera, some twenty feet behind the moderator, rested on an elevated platform. There were two other elevated cameras at forty-five degree angles to the moderator embedded in the audience. The stage lighting appeared bright. The audience sat in rows of metal chairs at ground level behind the moderator. Remaining audience members filled bleachers on a mezzanine level to the moderator's right.

The debate began at 8pm local time and ran for ninety minutes with five minute breaks at the thirty and sixty minute mark. The moderator would be Antonio Mujica of PBS with video feeds provided by CNN.

"Good evening from the campus of Washington University in St. Louis, Missouri. This is the third and final debate of the

2020 campaign, brought to you by the Commission on Presidential Debates. The Commission would like to apologize to the City of St. Louis for scheduling this debate in the middle of October baseball fever, which is almost like a seasonal affliction in this town."

Laughter and cheers erupted for the local team, perennially in the playoff hunt.

"My name is Antonio Mujica of PBS. The questions I will ask tonight are mine and from the Commission. I have not shared them with the candidates or their staff. As a reminder to our audience, please place any electronic communication device in vibrate mode. Now, please welcome the candidates for tonight's debate. Representing the Democratic Party is President Benjamin Jefferson." Jefferson received vigorous applause and whistles as he walked to his podium. Mujica waited a few seconds for the applause to wane.

"Representing the GOP is Kansas Governor Alicia Scarborough." Scarborough walked to her podium to warm applause with no whistling. Once again, Mujica waited for the noise to settle.

"Representing the Independent American Party is Texas Senator Alfonso Chancellor." Chancellor walked to his podium and received applause in equal intensity and duration as Governor Scarborough. A few in the audience flashed "Hook 'em Horns" hand signals.

"And finally, representing the Theocracy Party is Mr. John King." King approached his podium to polite applause like you might hear when someone sinks a putt for par.

"Your campaigns have agreed to a specific set of rules. I will ask each candidate the same question and you will have two minutes to respond. I may ask follow-up questions based on your response, at which point you will have one minute to respond. At the end of the debate, we will allow each candidate to close with three minutes of their own content. Each candidate's microphone will be muted except during their response time and immediately after their time allotment." Microphone muting became necessary after the contentious presidential debates in 2016.

"Governor Scarborough, tell us why the country should elect you?"

"I served two terms as governor of the great State of Kansas returning to private life in 2018. My state weathered the economic crisis much better than most. We did not see bank runs in our state as in others. Our state's unemployment rate was well below the national average and because of guidance given by my administration to our state pension fund managers about how to structure their investments, our public pensions are in the best shape of any in the country. I've never been in Washington and special interests have no control over me. I am guided by a great Republican president who was governor of the great state of California, responsible for bringing the country out of the doldrums of the 1970s. Some in the audience remember those times. Our national prestige was damaged and he brought us back. We're in similar straits today. I promise to bring the same level of executive competence to the Office of the President. If you want someone that will make your life better and restore our national prestige, elect me." Applause followed.

"Mr. King, the same question."

"This once great nation has taken a direction our forefathers surely would never have envisioned. There is not just economic decay, but moral decay. There is little respect for the law. Gangsters operate freely in our most populated cities. Police are afraid to confront them. This was a predictable outcome given the legal action that emerged after the public began filming every interaction with police. Our public servants were under assault in this very city where our debate's being held tonight. Mob rule emerged when a minority took exception to the outcome of a grand jury decision. I will restore the honor and pride of our law enforcement. I will not let our public institutions of higher learning be held hostage by a minority incapable of hearing dissenting opinion. God is no longer in our schools and our children are not learning. Personal privacy is a thing of the past. Big Brother watches everything we do. The War on Terror has produced more terrorists eager to harm us. Ladies and gentlemen, there is a reason for all this. We have strayed from God's law. What does our Pledge of Allegiance say? It says we are one nation under God. Well ladies and gentlemen, we are no longer a nation under God. My presidency will return us to this place." Applause followed and King beamed with pride.

"Senator Chancellor, why should you occupy the White House?"

"Ever since 2008, the nation has teetered economically. We have been told that government and the Fed can fix all of our economic ills. We've been fighting a war on poverty for 50 years and yet so many remain poor. The War on Drugs has been very expensive, produced untold violence, and swelled the ranks of our prisons. The very institutions that we were led to believe would solve these problems, have not. During my time in the Senate, I have fought tirelessly to curb the ever expanding reach of these institutions and empower individuals and businesses. Critics will say that I have been unsuccessful and to that I say, guilty as charged. But that does not diminish my resolve to continue the fight. The Wizards in government, the Fed and now the FSB are taking us down another very slippery slope where we will no longer recognize our economy or for that matter, our way of life. The external, international influences on this administration are producing policy that might be right for other countries, but not right for us. The IAP provides an alternative to what you have seen. If you value personal and economic freedom and less government intervention, I would be proud to serve as your president." Chancellor glanced at his notes during the applause that followed.

"President Jefferson, why should the people of the USA reelect you?"

"My party has been in office since the great crisis of 2008. My predecessor faced a unique challenge upon arriving in office and stabilized both our economy and financial markets. When I was elected in 2016, we faced similar challenges. Like in 2008, our country weathered the storm and stabilized. Internationally, we were seen as the paragon of financial crisis management. My administration has instituted a series of reforms that were recommended by the best and the brightest in business, government and academia. There is more work to be done, of course. Now, however, is not the time to change direction. Changing direction will bring the nation to the brink of economic collapse, which is something no one wants. I cannot stress how important it is for this nation to stay the course." Strong applause followed. President Jefferson looked like a candidate certain of his reelection prospects.

The next set of questions centered on drug legalization, military incursions in the Middle East, domestic terror and a reinstitution of the draft. The applause was polite after all candidate responses, as if watching a golf tournament. Mujica handled the questions flawlessly and asked follow-up questions deftly. The candidates respected their time allotments and did not abuse the five minute breaks. After breaking at the sixty minute mark, the audience was quiet with anticipation of the most important set of questions.

"I would like to thank the candidates for their courteous responses and adherence to the time limits. I would also like to thank the audience for their very polite applause. This feels like the PGA championship I attended here in 1992." The audience enjoyed the comment.

"The final set of questions relates to the financial and economic challenges facing the country. I will ask each candidate for their vision on the economy and how to get the country healthy again. We'll begin the questions with Governor Scarborough. Governor, what would the GOP propose to get the country going again?"

"The GOP advocates a slimmed down government. We cannot continue funding the trillion plus dollar deficits of the last few years. For instance, since 2008 the number of people receiving benefits from government is roughly 62% of the entire population. This means that you have a bunch of money going into Washington, or borrowed into existence, and it just goes out the door to be distributed. To distribute that money, you have a massive bureaucracy. If you look at where employment growth has been the last few years, it's been at the Federal government level. We would order each agency in the Federal government to cut its workforce by 15%. We would immediately institute a tax decrease across the board for individuals along with a maximum 15% corporate tax rate. Profits acquired overseas by US companies can return to the US with a tax holiday for a three-year period. We would also encourage companies that have recently domiciled in overseas jurisdictions to return to the US via favorable tax treatment. In my first one hundred days in office, I will appoint a commission to overhaul our tax code. These steps would immediately revitalize the economy and put Americans back to work again." Strong applause followed the governor's comments.

"Thank you Governor. Senator Chancellor, what can the IAP offer Americans?"

"Americans need to ask themselves if they are satisfied with how this administration has handled the economy. For years we have been told that government is the solution or a central bank is the solution. Are we better off today with all this intervention? The IAP believes in letting individuals decide what is best for them economically. We still need strong government, but that government should be there to ensure economies can operate without interference. We believe that government should focus strongly on criminal law and contract law - the creation, enforcement and interpretation of those laws. Anything else is above and beyond what our Founding Fathers intended. The two main political parties have deviated from these intentions, but we allowed that to happen. Capitalism has survived for so long because of its ability to adapt. It doesn't need government telling it how. The people or the market, the basis of capitalism, will make adjustments on their own. Our form of capitalism, now, is state sponsored. Businesses seek favors in return for contributions. Government imposes regulations. Businesses send armies of lobbyists to D.C. to influence legislation and those regulations. The small business finds it difficult to compete in this environment since they have neither wealth nor lobbyists. America, the IAP and my candidacy represent a new path, a path we once traveled but long ago forgot. Thank you!" Strong applause and mild cheering followed his comments. The Longhorn fans raised their horns in approval. Chancellor surveyed the audience, relishing the adulation.

"Senator, judging from the response, you struck a chord. Mr. King, how would you and the Theocracy Party revive the country?"

"First, I will establish a council that would have oversight with respect to legislative bodies like Congress and judicial bodies like the Supreme Court. Their objective would be to weigh in on laws or legal decisions not deemed compliant with Biblical teaching. I will propose an immediate Jubilee or forgiveness of debts. The American people are tired of debt slavery imposed by bankers and government officials. Immediately upon taking office, I will dismantle our domestic surveillance apparatus. All of this spying is not defeating the terrorists, we need a new approach. I will reintroduce God into our schools. I will impose restrictions on minors' usage of certain websites, particularly social media. Social media is ruining our youth who are inundated with immoral messages. Once we have a society and government built on God's law, we will naturally find solutions to our economic woes. Our party rejects the recent Executive Orders issued by President Jefferson, putting man in a very subservient position to his master, the government. We believe those orders will harm the economy further. We would also stop the immoral wars in which our country is involved overseas where untold numbers of innocents have been harmed by our superior technology. Nothing has been gained by our foreign incursions other than death, destruction, refugees and terror on our soil. Thank you."

King's comments elicited firm applause and a mixture of mostly cheers and some booing. The crowd had gotten more demonstrative now.

"Thank you, Mr. King. Mr. President, bring us home."

"I would like to thank my opponents tonight for what has been a very civil and constructive debate. I know the American people appreciate the flow of ideas. My fellow Americans, the last few years have been difficult. I know there are elements in this country, and on this very stage, that believe that government and central banks caused these problems. I submit to you how fortunate we are to have such a close partnership between the two. I would also posit that our close relationship with business provides us with a conduit of ideas as to how best manage our crisis. It's not as if we consciously sit around and work to make government bigger and more powerful. Rather, necessity dictates our actions. Senator Chancellor is correct when he says that capitalism's strength is its ability to adapt. Part of that adaptation is government involvement, which then reforms the capitalist structure. If we dismantle everything my administration has done to this point to create stability, we will suffer grave consequences. That is not my opinion but the judgment of those appointed to the special commission and other experts from around the globe. My message is to stay the course, vote for Jefferson." Strong applause followed the president's comments. Jefferson smiled, projecting supreme confidence.

"Thank you, Mr. President. Now I would like to ask each candidate for a concluding-" Mujica could not finish because of an interruption.

King, whose eyes had been downcast, lifted them and glared at his target. "Mr. President, you talk about your special commission and experts from around the globe. Are these so-called experts from the Global Settlement Bank?" He turned to the audience, seeking approbation.

Mujica wondered why King's microphone was not muted. He was so dumbfounded for an instant that words failed him.

"Ah, um, Mr. King, I'm not sure what's going on here but-"

"Mr. President, why don't you share with the American people your plan to outsource our banking and economic policy to a foreign entity like the GSB?" King did not look at the president and but rather straight ahead, sensing the cameras were on him now.

"Mr. King, please we had-" Mujica was summarily rebuffed again. His confused eyes searched the audience. He shrugged his shoulders with doomed pessimism. Mujica's earpiece had an issue as well. The SS Mujica was sinking and he was going down with the ship.

"Mr. President, are you going to talk about how your GSB-influenced policy abolishes cash and coins? Are you taking our gold? Are you coming after our guns too? These are violations of our Constitution! Remember that document, Mr. President." This time, King turned towards the president, who was on the opposite side of the stage, repeatedly jabbing his finger at him.

A loud gasp came from the crowd and chatter started. Governor Scarborough was in shock. Her face grew pale. Chancellor feigned surprise, though he was intrigued by how King knew all this. Jefferson remained silent, though his face tightened. Mujica desperately tried to regain control of his sinking vessel. The cameras rolled.

"I suggest Mr. King that you-" Mujica got interrupted by King yet again.

"What about our gold, Mr. President? What are you doing with it? Are you going to take it away and make it illegal again?

Tell the American people about how the Dollar is going to be kicked aside for some new international money. Were you planning on suspending the Constitution if you don't get your way?" King preened towards the audience with a smile of undaunted self-confidence.

Mujica's jaw dropped. Some in the crowd echoed Mr. King's questions to the president while others were telling them to shut up. A couple of men in the first row stood and jawed at each other. The formerly quiet audience began talking amongst each other, ignoring what was going on in front of them. The cameras were still rolling. TV ratings were on the increase. Social media caught fire and those who weren't watching the debate found it on the Internet or TV.

"Mr. President, in light of these provocative-" Mujica's voice was drowned out by someone yelling from the second row. A man in the back of the room grabbed a microphone and bellowed such that his voice did not modulate well. Another person wrested the microphone from his hand and a scuffle ensued. Police came to restore order. There weren't supposed to be microphones embedded in the audience.

Two Secret Service agents, considering the action behind Mujica and the elevated tension, whisked a stupefied Jefferson off the stage. One of them spoke into a mic in his lapel and said, "Get Air Force One ready. Bear headed to Lambert."

The Secret Service agent used the president's codename, Bear, to signal his departure for the airport. Another agent stood near King and watched him like a hawk.

Mujica, who had gotten up moments earlier from his desk, shuffled towards the president offering a pitiful, apologetic expression. A Secret Service agent on the president's left arm shoved the hapless Mujica, who stumbled before regaining his balance.

Governor Scarborough scampered to Senator Chancellor and sought comfort on his arm, as if she just witnessed a crime. Chancellor maintained his composure and put his arm around the governor. King stood triumphantly on stage, chest pressed outward as if parading in front of the Roman Emperor. Mujica headed back to his chair, realizing he failed in his main role, maintaining order. By now there were more arguments in the crowd and at least a couple of scuffles. Police had their hands full. Those sitting in the bleacher section cleared out. Those not scuffling were tapping furiously on their phones.

The cameras were still rolling, though some networks quit showing the live feed to return to their studios for commentary. Viewers were told that this was an ill-conceived ploy by a candidate with little chance to win and that King behaved in a very un-presidential manner. There was also speculation about the microphone control and audience scuffle. Some suggested the presence of professional agitators. The Internet lit up with commentary on various news sites. Social media continued to explode.

***

At the IRC office at the Presidio, Emmet had gathered to watch the debate with Fran and other IRC staff in the media room. Emmet saw this as a final check box for President Jefferson, who led in the polls. In Emmet's mind, Jefferson just needed to steer the ship clear of any icebergs. The election would be a clear mandate supporting Jefferson, and by proxy, the IRC's policies. Everyone was smiling until Jefferson ran into the iceberg named John King.

"What the!" Emmet yelled and spit up his drink.

"Oh, my!" Fran yelled also, being dually shocked by King's

words and Emmet's water spray.

"What is that motherfucking maggot doing?" Emmet's seethe of rage almost choked him. He watered his shirt. The rest of the IRC staff went silent.

"This is most unusual," Fran added. She grabbed a couple of napkins to wipe Emmet's irrigation from the table.

"Most unusual? It's a fucking disaster! I'm gonna-" Emmet halted his commentary as King continued with his harangue of the president. "What is that fuck, Mujica doing? He needs to shut King down!" Emmet looked ready to throw his drink at the wall.

"Mr. President, are you going to talk about how your GSB influenced policy abolishes cash and coins? Are you taking our gold? Are you coming after our guns? These are violations of our Constitution! Remember that document, Mr. President."

After those questions by King, Emmet fired a fastball at the media room wall, scattering everyone but Fran. Fortunately, the glass projectile did not break. Emmet's arm was not what it used to be.

"Mujica looks just as shocked as everyone else. He's apoplectic at this point, Emmet," Fran explained in a calm, controlled voice, attempting to influence his agitated state. She retrieved the glass and placed it close to her on the table. "And how is it that he's even able to speak? I thought the microphones were muted at certain times?"

"More importantly, how the shit does King know all this? There is no way that got leaked to him." Emmet gnarled his teeth as his anger grew.

"I agree, I can't see how that lout or his organization could put those thoughts together. They're too worried about God."

"All he does is talk about God this and God that, like God was going to come down and save us all. Maybe he thinks he's the Second Coming. I hope God can save him when we're through with him." Emmet made such tight fists that walnuts surely would have crumbled in his hands.

Fran grabbed the remote near Emmet and lowered the volume. "What do you think we should do?"

"How could anyone vote for that shit head? Who wants to run a country like that? I suppose the Holy Spirit will be his Secretary of State. Fuck! Tell me, Fran, who would vote for that maggot?" Emmet readied his arm to throw whatever else was within reach. Fortunately for the room, Fran had just moved a couple of nearby glasses away from him, including hers.

"Emmet. Focus. We need to come up with a plan." She needed to remain calm, lest she agitate him further.

"I need to call Holloway. Can you just turn that off?" Fran clicked the remote. Emmet pulled out his cell and dialed Holloway. He became impatient when the phone wasn't answered on the first ring. "Come on, pick up. Hey, Malcolm! Did you see this shit unfold?"

"Yes, Mr. Callaghan, I did. I don't know what to say, sir," said a stunned Holloway. Even the smartest guy in any room had little to say.

"Well, find the source of that goddamn leak and silence them. You better talk to Jefferson too. I can only imagine he's back on Air Force One, headed home. Are you in D.C.?"

"Yes, sir, I am."

"Good. You better head to the White House and meet with the president. I've got to huddle with some people to figure out damage control."

"Will do, sir. Have a good evening."

"Yeah whatever."

Emmet clicked off with Holloway and called Jean-Claude, who answered groggily. "Emmet do you have any idea-"

"Jean. I need for you to listen carefully." Emmet summoned enough calm to give Jean the summary version of campaign Jefferson's collision with the King iceberg.

"*Sacré bleu. Mon dieu.*" Emmet understood Jean-Claude's reaction.

"We need to have an emergency call with the rest of the board to come up with ideas for damage control," Emmet demanded.

"Agreed. I will make calls, and you do the same. *Bonne soirée* Emmet." Jean-Claude terminated the call.

Emmet next called Rafael. He was in Buenos Aires and turned off the debate early to meet with a lady friend. "Hello, Mr. Callaghan."

"Listen carefully to what I'm about to tell you." Emmet repeated what he just told Jean-Claude.

"*¡Esto es un quilombo!*" Rafael acknowledged the freaking mess.

"Please speak fucking English. You better make sure your network puts the right spin on this, or we will have a big problem when people vote next month." Emmet had no problem with Jean-Claude's French, yet he didn't tolerate Rafael's Spanish outburst.

"Yes, sir. I will get to work on this right away. If-" Emmet abruptly ended his call with Rafael and turned towards Fran who remained in the room during his lightning round of calls.

"If I ever see that maggot King, I'm gonna-," Emmet snarled.

"You better compose yourself before you head home to Brenda. She'll have no idea why you are so upset."

"Fuck it. I need a cigarette."

"But you gave that up a few years ago. No need to do that to your health."

"My health is the last thing I'm worried about right now. Fran, drive home safely. I'm outta here." He stormed out of the media room, leaving Fran alone.

The IRC, who enjoyed the protective comfort of the former citadel at the Presidio, demonstrated their vulnerability with John King's asymmetric political assault.

Some staff that had been in the conference room with Emmet watching the debate congregated in the building's lobby after he hurled the glass. As he stomped by them, they parted like the Red Sea not wanting to incur his wrath. Emmet squealed his BMW 760's tires as he left the parking lot and drove to the nearest convenience store for a pack of smokes. It had been five years since his last puff.

***

Arianne and Chandler were enjoying a quiet evening at her condo watching the presidential debate in the living room. He leaned towards one end of the couch and she leaned against him. Then things got interesting.

"Where in the cotton pickin hell did King get that from?" Chandler blurted. He popped up and moved her off him. He placed his elbows on his thighs, leaned forward and stared at the TV.

"Oh, my God, Chandler!" She covered her mouth after saying this and looked at him.

They both continued to listen to King's harangue.

"What about our gold, Mr. President? What are you doing with it? Are you going to take it away and make it illegal again? Tell the American people about how the Dollar is going to be kicked aside for some new international money. Were you planning on suspending the Constitution if you don't get your way?"

"That man has more guts than you can hang on a fence. He just stirred up the ultimate hornet's nest."

"When you interviewed him, I mean I know you didn't ask him anything like that but did you get the sense he knew?"

"No way. When I did the interview, it was like two months before that whole thing with Phish and the warehouse, so I didn't even know. He kept talking about the State and Leviticus and a Jubilee. There is no way that he would even have the contacts like Ax to sniff out something like this. He could never even get close to Omni. Omni probably thinks he's wacky, anyway. But I'll tell you this - his supporters are gonna go hog wild with this information. He did say he and his party were gonna be heard. They were heard loud and clear tonight!"

"It looks like a couple of people are going at it," she said pointing at the screen. "Oh, wow!"

"Mujica's lost total control of this thing."

"What do you think this means for Chancellor?"

"I really don't know. Geringer told him about what we found and I guess Chancellor kept it under wraps. He must have feared the fallout it would have, and there you saw it in living color. Chancellor kept his cool. Did you see the look on Scarborough's face?"

"Yeah, she looked like she had seen the devil. And you're right, Chancellor was one cool customer."

"And what the hell is Jefferson going to say to respond to

King? He had to keep his mouth shut."

"Do you think there's a chance everyone will think that he's just trying to stir things up to bring more attention to his party?"

"I suppose. There are people who think he's one bubble off plumb."

"I can tell you're worked up now. You're reverting to your Texas metaphors. Let's just turn this off." By now, El Mundo had cut back to the studio hosts. She grabbed the remote and clicked to a sports channel.

"Sorry, honey. I'm not sure what to do right now." Jimi Hendrix alerted him to a call. It was Axel.

"Hi Ax. I bet I know why you're calling."

"Are you kidding me? Where did King get all that? Phish may never talk to us again. Or who knows, maybe Omni doesn't care? I don't know what to think." Axel let his guard down, talking about this on the phone. The event's significance dampened his inhibition and Chandler's.

"Well, there's obviously a leak somewhere."

"We should call Geringer soon. He's got to be floored."

"The leak, this leak, the more I think about it - let's think about who knew this. There was me, you, Ari, Geringer and whoever else was with him the day he told Chancellor." He looked at Arianne who nodded in agreement.

"That's right!" Axel concurred.

"So eliminating the obvious ones and figuring that Chancellor wouldn't do this, we need to find out who else was around."

"Yes. Yes. You could be on to something. But what if someone bugged the senator's office? Did he tell Chancellor in the senator's office?"

"That's a good question. We should call the senator. Let me add Geringer." Chandler conferenced in Geringer.

"Hello, senator. I've got Ax on the line too. I bet you saw this coming about as much as you saw the Cubs winning the Series, huh?" Amid chaos, Chandler found the opportunity to remind the senator about the Cubbies beating the Rockies for the NL pennant.

"Gentlemen, I don't even know what to say. First, there was the shock of all this coming out of King's mouth and then the realization of how the hell he knew it," Geringer said.

"Ax has a thought on that senator. Ax?"

"Senator, where did you share the information with Chancellor?"

"At the IAP office in New York. The same one where we met for the first time. Are you sure you want to continue this on the phone?"

"Senator, at least the thought about all of this is out there. We need to identify the leak."

"OK, proceed," Geringer responded.

"Is there any chance that office is bugged?" Axel inquired.

"It might be. It's not like we sweep for that kind of stuff. I would say if it were, it would be the administration's doing and they sure as hell would not want this released. But honestly, I don't think that's the case. That seems extreme if you ask me. After Watergate? Maybe I am being naïve here, guys," Geringer said. "But I don't think so."

"Let's put that thought aside for the moment. Who else was with you the day you talked to Chancellor?" Axel continued.

"Alex Carpenter, Loretta King and her assistant Tammy Blakely. What are you suggesting here, Mr. Schultz?"

"Bear with me, senator. Carpenter wouldn't leak this, right?

He's gotta be loyal to his party."

"Oh, yeah. No chance. In fact, he was surprised that I would believe what was in the document given that it came indirectly from you. They thought I was nuts for trusting you." Geringer's remark did not derail Axel's thought process.

"Tell me about Loretta."

"Alfonso goes way back with her. They knew each other when he played ball in college. I think she ran track or something like that. She ran his first campaign and is real active in Texas politics. She helped him start the first IAP chapter in Austin. Oh, and she *also* challenged the authenticity of the information. And besides Axel, what would she have to gain by feeding this to John King. You're telling me that she would double cross her friend of so many years? It doesn't make sense!"

"Sounds fair, senator. And her assistant?"

"I don't know her real well. I believe she's from Texas also, but not sure where."

"What about her background?"

"Hmm. I know she was married to that football coach, what's his name? You know the one that got caught with the young coed on a road trip." Geringer referenced a scandal a few years back.

"I don't watch sports. Especially those where adults run into each other with helmets on," Axel said disdainfully, despite his participation in the game as a high schooler.

"It made the news a few years back. And poor lady, she had to find out about it on the evening news. Chandler, do you know who I'm talking about?" Geringer asked.

"Yeah, and I'm surprised she still uses Coach Blakely's last name. He was always rumored to be looser than ashes in the wind. But that coed he hooked up with was smokin hot." Arianne still sitting next to Chandler, furrowed her brow at his comment. He covered the phone's mic and whispered to her, "Well she was."

"So I take it they divorced. Was it a bad one?" Axel inquired.

"Once you're a public figure like Coach Blakely, your dirty laundry gets out there. I think it was ugly. But just because her ex hooked up with a hot coed, what does this have to do with the leak?" Geringer asked.

"Do you know anything about Mrs. Blakely's family?" Axel continued his methodical questioning.

"No, but I seem to recall-" Geringer said before being interrupted by Chandler.

"Sorry to cut you off but I might shed some light here. I remember reading something about her father being a minister or he had some affiliation with a church in Texas. Don't quote me on that, but that is what I recall. Let me see if I can do a quick search online." Chandler walked with his phone towards the kitchen where he had his laptop on the counter and brought it back to the living room.

"Ax, this was all a few years ago and I'm going on memory. I know Chancellor never mentioned it. The times I've been around her, she seems to keep to herself, just takes a bunch of notes. She spoke up in our meeting when Loretta asked her to look you up," Geringer added.

"Interesting. Very interesting. I never thought I'd be talking about some coach and a damned divorce the day of the last presidential debate. Sorry guys, but usually I'm into more weighty matters. This sounds like a soap opera." Axel fretted at the necessity of this line of questions.

"Well Ax, that is life in these-" Geringer said before being interrupted again by Chandler.

"Sorry, but I found that her father was a minister, and she was at least partially home schooled."

"That's fine, but what does that prove?" Geringer asked.

"Hmmm. Based on what you said, Mrs. Blakely at least seems to be a person of interest," Axel concluded.

"Let's think about this for a minute, guys. Why would she do this? The woman she works for was skeptical about the document. Hell, everyone in that room was skeptical about the document. I can't believe Tammy thought she was helping Chancellor by leaking this," Geringer commented.

"This could go many ways. I can tell you there are voters out there who don't trust either the GOP or Jefferson and his party. This sort of thing would make them trust the two main parties even less. The fact King made this public and not Chancellor, who is, like it or not, seen as being part of D.C. politics, might make people think he knew something and sat on it. And that is, in fact, true. So if I had to guess, King did this with the hope of not only stirring the hornet's nest but also showing everyone how they can't trust anyone but himself. He who is a God-fearing man that would not lie to them." Axel once again summarized everything well.

"Brilliant as usual, Ax," Chandler added.

"Fine, Mr. Schultz. That still doesn't prove she leaked it."

"No, it doesn't. But wasn't it Sherlock Holmes who said that when you have eliminated all which is impossible, then whatever remains, however improbable, must be the truth?"

"Mr. Schultz, please! You're invoking Sir Arthur Conan Doyle at a time like this?"

"There is nothing else left, sir. Holmes also said that little

346

things are infinitely the most important. These small details about her ex, the acrimony of the divorce, and her father might tie together to be the answer. And another thing. How do you explain King's microphone being turned on when supposedly it was to be turned off? Then you have those people in the audience stirring things up."

"Let's just say you're right. You want me to call Chancellor and tell him he has a mole in his campaign with just your theory?" Despite their association for a few months and the intelligence Axel had amassed, Geringer still harbored doubts.

"Since you ruled out a bug who else comes to mind?" Axel persisted with his analytical approach to uncovering this mystery, an approach that served him well and stood the test of time.

"Yeah, I suppose we can't rule out a bug. Even though Watergate was a long time ago, it seems far-fetched. My instincts tell me this wouldn't be something the GOP would do. Hell, there are some in that party that know about the GFU. And frankly, I can't see the TP pulling off something like that. And wouldn't that be considered immoral for them to steal this information somehow?"

"You would think, but these are unusual times," Axel replied.

"Senator, now that this is out in the open, I feel an obligation to tape a segment for my show. I won't reveal how I received the information or who else may have known. I will definitely not mention your name or your party's." Chandler felt trepidation about making this declaration, anticipating the deep voice to come barreling back at him.

"Chandler, I can't stop you and it would be against my nature to even contemplate it. The press serves an important role and one of those roles is to check government. I do appreciate your sensitivity towards my party though. The reality is, until recently I was not 100% convinced this Global Financial Union or something like it was real. Play your journalist role." Geringer's deep voice provided more validation than threat.

"Thank you, Matt." Though he did not require his approval, Chandler appreciated the objectivity towards journalism.

"I will have to meet with Chancellor in private. Thanks for calling Chandler. Nice speaking with you, Mr. Schultz. Have a good evening. Sorry for the abrupt ending, but this has been quite a day."

"Take care, senator. Good night."

"Ax, I have a beautiful woman leaning against me. I don't think there is more to do this evening. Let's talk later."

"OK. I'm headed to D.C. soon. There is too much action going on there to miss it. I might be able to get something for my letter. Good night."

"Good night."

CHAPTER TWENTY-THREE
ROGUE JOURNALIST

The El Mundo D.C. studio buzzed with chatter about the presidential debate. Chandler met producer Jared Clarke to discuss taping a segment around the debate and aftermath. Chandler revealed he had material confirming King's allegations. A naturally skeptical Jared imposed upon Chandler to produce sources. Chandler would not oblige.

"Did you clear this with Rafael?" Jared asked.

"No."

"Let me call him." Jared dialed Rafael in Buenos Aires and explained Chandler's proposed segment. Rafael requested to speak to Chandler.

"Chan, Jared told me what you want to do and I want you to hold off on that right now."

"Rafa, I have good material here." Chandler's material included Rafael's elevation to CEO, a portion of the story he would omit for obvious reasons.

"I don't know anything about your sources. I don't want to give that crazy candidate more air time. Who knows where he got all that. Just give this some time."

"How long?"

"At least until after the election. I need to look at your material. Let's plan this out better. If we don't do this right, we will look silly."

"But Rafa. Come on, man!"

"*Me chupas un huevo!*" Rafael had little use for Chandler's pleas.

"What's happened to you? You've gone all chicken shit on me." Chandler reached his breaking point after months of journalistic struggles with his boss.

"Chandler, go home. Take the day off. I'm tired of arguing. Do what you are told!" Rafael hung up. Chandler, dejected, gave the phone back to Jared.

Jared surmised the conversation did not go Chandler's way. On the other hand, Jared thought it could be a good segment if properly vetted. They could tape the segment and save it for later editing and review by Rafael. If he didn't like it, he could trash it. Besides, Jared had some discretion in this process since he was one of two producers assigned to Centinela.

"Chandler, I'm going to leave the studio to attend to an urgent matter." Jared winked at him. "If you want to tape something, use the studio. I don't think it will hurt just to tape it. But that's all I'll let you do. We won't do any editing or final production work. Rafael can look at it later and decide if he wants to air it."

"Sounds good. See you when you come back from your urgent matter." He followed that with a wink. This seemed a good compromise.

Jared left the building. Chandler entered the studio to tape the segment. He finished the segment as quickly as he could figuring, significant editing to follow. There were other matters to attend to while at the D.C. bureau. After being ensconced at his own desk for some time, a security officer approached and hovered over him.

"Mr. Scott, please give me your badge," he said in a cold, leveled tone.

"I'm at a loss here. What's going on?" Chandler shrugged while lifting his eyes from the monitor.

The officer replied, stone-faced, "Mr. Mendoza asked me to remove you from the premises. I need your badge and credit card. Leave your laptop plugged in. We'll send your personal belongings to the address on record."

"Am I being fired?" With eyes still lifted, Chandler felt a shock and flounder.

"I don't have that information. You can speak to Mr. Mendoza. Let's go." The security officer motioned his arm to expedite Chandler's departure.

Chandler took no immediate action, remaining seated. He'd never been fired, suspended or even disciplined. His job reviews were stellar. The show maintained high ratings and sponsorship remained solid. Employees around the bureau stopped their work and spied on the officer and Chandler. He realized there was nothing else to say and no reason to cause a scene. After a few seconds of thinking it over, he complied with the officer's request. He gathered his cell phone and jacket draped over his chair. After checking for keys in the jacket's pocket, he rose slowly. He didn't see this coming.

Many long faces watched as they headed towards the lobby. As the security officer walked him out the front door, Chandler passed a bewildered Jared Clarke headed in the opposite direction. Chandler twisted his lips, shook his head and continued the troubled procession towards his vehicle.

He had Arianne's car and surveyed the lot, trying to remember where he parked. His mind bounced. As he unlocked the door, someone charged up behind him yelling in a breathless voice.

"Chandler! Wait! I have something for you." Jason Hardin had probably not run that far or fast since junior high gym class.

"What is it?" Chandler asked. Jason handed him an

envelope. "What's this, my severance package?"

Jason, panting, bent at the waist and supported his hand on the car. "The segment you just shot. The video. Sorry, I overheard your conversation with Jared and figured you were talking with Rafael."

Jason forced air into his burning lungs. "When you went into the studio and started taping, I had a feeling shit was gonna hit the fan. Anyway, take this file and do something with it. Rafael is never gonna do anything with it. When your girlfriend got hit with that Trident supervirus, I figured you must be into some wicked shit. I don't know what you're into but it looks complicated, man. When you told Jared you could support what King said in the debate, I figured this must be for real. I mean if El Mundo's not gonna give a story like this its due, you know, who will? So take this as my parting gift to you, dude." Jason's reflated lungs allowed him to stand.

"Parting? Are you leaving?"

"Maybe, but it sure seems like you are! They may find out what I did and then I'm toast. I don't care. I have skills that other employers value, so I'm not worried. You might make me famous."

"Dude, this is not something you want on your resume, trust me. But hey, thanks. I owe you one. Maybe more Nats tickets."

"At least that, with some Skins tickets too!" Jason high-fived Chandler and walked back to the building, hands on hips. Chandler grinned as he watched Jason. The security officer was still within sight, glaring at him.

Chandler drove back to Arianne's, wondering about his future at El Mundo. He called her. "Hey,"

"Hi, where are you?"

"Headed to your place. I think I just got fired." Chandler detailed the filming and argument with Rafael.

"Oh honey, I'm so sorry. Maybe it's not as bad as it seems. Rafa will calm down and you'll be back. Listen, I can't get away yet but I'll be home as soon as I can OK? Love you!"

"Love you too!" Chandler disconnected and called Axel. He told Axel to come by Arianne's in the morning because he had a surprise for him. Axel had already been in town to be part of the "action" in the nation's capital.

Chandler's next call was to Geringer. "Hello senator, it's Chandler."

"Hi. What can I do for you?"

"Senator, I wanted to let you know that I taped that segment disclosing what I know about allegations made by King. My boss wanted to stop it, but I did it anyway. I think I may have been fired today, or at least suspended. So, it probably won't go on the air. But someone gave me the unedited video. I'm going to give it to Axel tomorrow."

"And what will he do with it?"

"I'm going to ask him to release it through his contacts so they can leak it out on the Net." The phone snoops would be left to wonder about Axel's contact or contacts.

"Well, you know what I'm gonna say about that especially given who I think you mean. I'd rather it come out through someone else, but at this point it's all out there now with what King did. I talked to Chancellor about the mole in his campaign. He thinks it's the same person we discussed but wants to try something to confirm it. I don't want to say any more. Do what you think is right. Be careful, Chandler."

"I will, Matt. Goodbye."

***

Axel had been in D.C. the last week to be around, as he put it, "action" in the presidential debate aftermath. Chandler called the previous day so that he could come by Arianne's for a surprise. The surprise was the unedited video recorded in the El Mundo studio the day before. It was difficult for Chandler to sit on this story for so long. His interest was less about giving credibility to King's allegations than it was about his role as a journalist. He lay awake most of the night thinking about the impact of his video's release.

"Ax, good to see you, come on in!" Chandler extended his hand for a vigorous exchange with his mentor. The burst of adrenaline came from the expectation of the video being released soon. He needed the burst given how drained he was from the events of the last twenty-four hours.

"Thanks, this town is definitely hopping now. I've just been hanging around places and the chatter is intense." The normally reserved Axel had a little bounce in his step.

The two made their way to the living room. The smell of Arabica filled the air.

"You need any coffee? Ari brewed a pot before she left for work."

"Oh, so you're a house sitter, huh? I'll pass on the java." Axel derived enough energy from the city's chatter.

"That may be my role until I figure out if I have a job."

"So you still haven't called Rafael?"

"No, it's too soon. He might not talk to me. Better let things cool off. But after what I'm about to share with you, he'll probably heat up quickly." He related taping the segment and Jason's stealth video delivery. "I want you to give this to Phish. It's the only way this will get out now. Rafa will kill it. He may have deleted the original already, who knows."

354

"You know what this means if I give this to Phish, right?" Axel wanted him to understand that there would be no control over how or when the video might become public.

"I know I'm charging hell with a bucket of ice water, but at this point King's already put this out there so people are talking about it. All I'm doing is putting whatever is left of my journalistic integrity by validating it. Omni can do a much better job of releasing it than I ever could and really I won't look like a rogue journalist since everyone will assume Omni hacked into El Mundo. The video doesn't mention sources so that protects everyone. And truth be told, we don't know where some of this came from either, like what you got at your hotel. Did Phish ever confirm they sent you that?"

"No, but I haven't asked. Like I said before, I have a feeling it wasn't Omni. Not really their style. Not with a box of chocolates. If I ask Phish and it wasn't Omni, I'm not sure how he'll, or should I say they'll react. That information was consistent with Omni's and added more. It was a good validation of my hypothesis. But there were other hands at work with this source. There's someone, or who knows more than one person, working in shadows that wanted us to know this."

"Interesting. So someone else knows about all this and it doesn't appear to be a hacker group. Who woulda thunk that, huh? I suppose I can say that some of our sources were unknown. At the end of the day I'm just telling the world that I worked on this story for months and believe what I'm saying. You yourself said it might make no difference to the voters."

"I still believe that. The voters won't understand or care about the implications. Some will, but most won't. They just want the economy fixed and terror quelled. The best thing that can happen in this election is for Geringer's party to win more seats in Congress or state races. Even if the TP wins more seats, it at least dilutes power of the other two parties. My big concern is the whole idea of freezing an election. That's gonna be trouble."

"It is. Let me get you the video. I already made a copy." Chandler retrieved it from the fake old world book on the shelf. That book had seen its share of secrets.

"I don't know how soon I'll get a hold of Phish and I have no idea if they'll even do anything with it. I've never had an exchange like this before either, a large video file. I get stuff from him, not the other way around. I'm not sure how it's going to happen, but you know I'll try."

Chandler gave the digital media to a still seated Axel and placed both of his hands around his extended hand. They'd never man-hugged. The exchange became emotional for Chandler, who thought about hugging him, but didn't. He felt grateful to have him as a friend and mentor. In some ways, Axel filled a fatherly void.

Axel stood up quickly, bereft of emotion. "I know what I have to do. Let me get to work and I'll keep you posted." He made his way to the door while Chandler followed. "By the way, you look tired. Perhaps you should take a nap?"

"Yeah, you could say that."

***

Getting the video to Omni would be a new endeavor. Axel frequently traveled the Internet's dark side. That's how he cultivated the relationship with Omni and other contacts who wished to remain anonymous. For the last couple of years, he used Rot, successor to a popular software application for anonymous web communication, for his Darknet interactions. Axel used Rot to communicate with a Darknet server where

Omni monitored user posts. He left posts for Phish using a pseudonym furnished by the Omni hacker. The posts notified Phish that Axel wanted to talk or that he needed a particular piece of intelligence. They developed their own language for Darknet interactions and communicated via chat or instant message sessions. Phish could also send Axel encrypted messages directly to his regular email to be subsequently read with keys given separately, though never delivered in a box of chocolates.

The Darknet was under constant assault by the U.S. Department of Defense and specifically DARPA; the agency credited with building the Internet's precursor. DARPA developed a set of tools under the name Memex to assist law enforcement in finding websites, especially those on the Darknet. Memex made the Darknet less dark, leading to obstacles for Axel in his communication with Omni and other sources. A full-scale war erupted between those who wanted to preserve the Darknet and the authorities who wanted to shed light on it in the name of terrorism and other crimes.

Per his standard operating procedure, Axel visited websites he thought Phish might monitor. After three days, Axel received an encrypted email that he read using a key Phish sent him. He got this key last year in a most unusual manner.

Axel's publisher forwarded a postal letter from a supposedly disgruntled subscriber, one that did not use email and had their newsletter delivered via snail mail. The letter repeated a number identifying how much the subscriber lost due to Axel's poor investment advice. The figure was $2,483,115.27. After seeing the figure several times and picking up on other clues, he figured the letter had to be from Phish. He deduced that Phish wanted him to go to a locker at Union Station, number 248, whose combination was 31-15-27. The locker contained digital media with a decryption key.

The email from Phish contained instructions to visit the same warehouse he and Chandler traveled to on that cold winter day several months back. His stay in D.C. meant taking a little road trip to the Big Apple. Fortunately, Phish scheduled the meeting time at noon, which allowed him to leave early for a day trip.

When he arrived at the warehouse, it looked just as abandoned as it did before, the only difference being warmer temperatures of late October. He didn't have trouble getting in via the door where they entered previously. It remained stuck in the partially open position after he kicked it. No burly man emerged from the shadows.

Instead, a young twenty-something materialized out of the warehouse's hollows. The dark-skinned man wore a Rastacap over long dreads. A myriad of indiscernible tattoos covered his neck. His jeans looked like they'd been drug behind a car. The multi-pattern flannel shirt covered a black t-shirt. The man smelled of ganja. Phish never identified the person at the drop site, so Axel had to be sure before he gave up the flash drive.

"Yo man, whatchu want?" Rastaman asked.

"Who's asking?" Axel replied with grim, defiant eyes.

"I ain't got time for yo bullshit, old man," Rastaman said in a confident tone, taking a step toward Axel.

For a fleeting moment, Axel questioned why he was in this warehouse again and had concerns for his safety. He glanced back at the door from which he entered.

"Bitch, I ain't playing wit' you no mo." Rastaman tilted his head to the right and took another step forward.

If a physical assault was in the offing, Axel felt he could handle him, but what lurked in the shadows was more troubling, especially if there were others.

"I have something but I need to hear specific words from you," Axel said.

With that, Rastaman started laughing. "Yo, I'm just playing wit you dog." He closed the distance between them and gave him the characteristic hip-hop greeting - Rastaman wrapped his hand around Axel's thumb and executed a quick chest bump.

"I was beginning to think I was in the wrong place," Axel replied in a relieved tone.

"No, you cool dog. Holy Mount Zion. Holy Mount Zion," Rastaman cheered.

Those were the code words provided by Phish confirming Axel had the right person. The video media left Axel's hand and a still laughing Rastaman disappeared into the dark. After about sixty seconds, he saw a door open well in the distance at the far end of the warehouse. Rastaman exited.

Axel drove back to D.C. and arrived in time for dinner at his hotel. For the next couple of days, nothing happened. No communication came from Phish, and his posts on the Darknet went unanswered. For all Axel knew, Rastaman drove off to his purple haze and had not delivered the information to Phish. On the third day, Axel received his confirmation.

***

On this Halloween morning, Chandler read email and browsed on his tablet during breakfast at Arianne's. He had plenty of time these days to have a casual breakfast. Attempts to reach his boss proved futile. No one else from El Mundo contacted him either. His journalistic career rested in limbo. While browsing a sports site, his mail program notified him of a message from Axel. A link took him to an unfamiliar site, though he quickly recognized the video running - his last segment at El Mundo. He called Arianne from the bedroom. An hour after viewing the video, emails and text poured in from friends and former colleagues. He spent the next couple of hours replying and acknowledging the video's authenticity. Arianne turned on the TV.

NBC4 has breaking news about a video just released on the Internet by the hacker group Omni. In the video, El Mundo TV journalist Chandler Scott reveals a major economic and financial reorganization under the banner of the Global Financial Union. The video implies a significant loss of financial and monetary sovereignty for the United States. The video appears to substantiate the allegations made by candidate John King during the explosive third Presidential debate. We will post a link to this video on our website. Calls to El Mundo were not returned though we have also learned that Mr. Scott is no longer employed by the network. We suspect that Omni hacked into El Mundo's network to obtain the Scott video. More details as they become available.

The news confirmed what he suspected. He no longer had a job and would not be seen as a rogue journalist operating outside of his network's direction. Omni would take the blame for hacking El Mundo and releasing the video. There would also be questions for El Mundo. Chandler understood that he was part of the story and the questions would arrive soon, questions he was not ready to face. His girlfriend's cell phone buzzed incessantly with calls and texts.

"Chandler, this is getting out of control." Her fears about the outcome of his idealistic pursuits were coming home to roost.

"I know. I'm afraid it won't be long before the press finds

out where you live." Chandler of all people knew that.

"I need to call my boss. No way I can go in today. I need some time off." Arianne could only imagine the distraction she would be at State.

She called her boss, who understood his employee's predicament and granted her an indefinite leave of absence. Chandler contemplated their next move. Her condo would be under siege and for the peripatetic Chandler, he could not fathom living under house arrest. He could not lay this stress on Renee's doorstep and Gustavo seemed an unlikely candidate for him to seek refuge. They couldn't stay in Washington or New York.

"What should we do now?" She asked with a look of concern and anger.

"We need to make ourselves as scarce as a hen's teeth."

"I'm amazed at how funny you can be during stressful times, honey." Her reply concealed legitimate fear that her routine was about to experience major disruption. She waffled between feeling angry at him for the disruption and yet proud for what he was able to accomplish. The Trident incident convinced her that Chandler, Axel, and Geringer were into something much deeper than she ever imagined.

Aware that he needed to take quick action, Chandler called the one person who'd provide a solution.

"Ax, hi. I guess you got the video to Phish, huh?" Chandler opened the conversation with the understatement of the year.

"Yeah, sorry I didn't call you. I wanted it to be a surprise. Honestly, I wasn't sure if Phish was going to do anything with it. I'll tell you sometime how I got it to him."

"Well, it was a surprise all right. One thing I didn't think through real well was the aftermath of the video's release. El

Mundo's not saying anything and they claim I'm no longer employed there, so the press will look to me for comment. The other thing to consider is government's reaction. Someone may want to question me."

"All good points. There will be a siege on your apartment in New York and your shared place in D.C., probably Arianne's place at some point too. I'm not sure what the government can say or do at this point. This has already been out there and debated for a few weeks now. The video stamps credibility on the whole story and vindicates John King. That story's been dying down, though. People are focused on the election. So at this point I think it will be more about the press hounding you."

"Agreed. I don't want to go to my mom's. She'll freak out. My dad, I don't want to lay this on him. He's got his own family."

"Look, just come stay with me. Have Ari come too. We can drive to Chicago, and she can stay with her parents, or hell she could stay with me too if she wanted, but I'm guessing being that close to home, she'll want to stay at chateau Maxwell."

The more Chandler thought about it, the more it made sense. Planes and trains would attract too much attention, so the automobile won. Axel agreed to come over and rescue them in a couple of hours. Chandler hadn't been on a road trip of this length since college.

"Ari, start packing some clothes. Ax is coming over in a couple of hours. Hopefully, there won't be any press by then."

"Where are we going?"

"Chicago. Ax has a plan. If you need someone to check on your condo, make arrangements, fast."

The two spent the next hour getting things together. She had no idea how much to pack. Chandler couldn't tell her.

362

Most of Chandler's stuff had a home in New York, so he had less to think about. The Schultz rescue brigade arrived a couple of hours after their conversation. Axel found parking in front of her residence and surveyed the street before exiting. He scampered to her front door and took charge.

"I want both of you to put on hats and sunglasses, or hoodies if you have them. I haven't seen any press, but there was a lot of talk at my hotel about you before I left. I have a large SUV so I should have a decent amount of room. But let's move!" Axel snapped his fingers.

They moved rapidly to gather their belongings and headed to Axel's SUV. Just as Axel whisked them to safety, they spied a news van.

"This is kind of exciting. A road trip," Chandler remarked, concealing his trepidation about what lay ahead.

"A seven hundred mile road trip to be exact. Buckle up folks, it's going to be a long ride. Ari, the offer still stands about taking you to Winnetka," Axel said.

"Thank you Axel. I really need to call my mom and dad. They've been trying to reach me all morning." After the Trident incident, Larry Maxwell would be unhappy about his daughter having to hightail it out of the nation's capital due to her boyfriend's journalistic adventures.

"Same here. My mom and dad have been calling and I haven't gotten back to them," Chandler added. He didn't have the same concerns as Arianne since his parents were at least somewhat used to his adventures.

"You'll have plenty of time for that. Hey guys, I forgot today's Halloween. I should have brought costumes for both of you. We didn't need the glasses and hats after all!" Axel teased.

***

He sat quietly contemplating his upcoming call. As he looked out his home office on this Halloween day, he saw the hills of Las Trampas Regional Wilderness area. The long, slow drag on his cigarette pushed warm smoke into his lungs. He exhaled slowly; the smoke escaping his mouth and nose. It had been five long years since he enjoyed such a simple pleasure. His wife didn't know he started again so he kept the exterior doors to his office open. She would find out soon.

The RMS Carpathia did not come around to rescue the Jefferson campaign after colliding with the iceberg named King. That said, a good PR campaign could come to the rescue. Now a faceless hacker organization diluted the PR effort. Emmet knew that rogue organizations like Omni would be impossible to control. He waited on a conference bridge for Rafael and Holloway, two people who hopefully had some answers.

He heard a beep on the bridge. "Rafael's on the call."

"Hello, Rafael, we're waiting on Malcolm," Emmet said. "This is not what we needed so close to the election and you have to fix this."

"Yes, that video. I don't know how Omni did it. I'm having my IT people look into it."

"Your IT people. Fuck. We have more to worry about than a goddamn IT problem!" Emmet yelled. "You can figure out your security problems later! I need some goddamn solutions!"

"Yes, sir."

Another beep followed. "Hello, Malcolm's on."

"Good, we're all here now. I don't need to remind you how damaging King's outburst was and this damn video could be to the campaign. The president has dropped several points in the polls and it's not all going to the GOP. Other parties are going to pick up votes too. Rafael, what is your plan for damage control?"

"Sir, we're still trying to investigate this matter."

"Mr. Mendoza, did you hear anything that I was fucking saying to you earlier? Fuck the investigation! We need spin control here. You're in the goddamn media. Tell me something!" Emmet boiled. He extinguished his cigarette, dropping it in a soft drink can.

"I understand, sir."

Emmet lit another and drew on it, caving in his cheeks.

"Mr. Callaghan if I can offer a suggestion?" Holloway interjected. "Why don't we say that Chandler Scott was working with Omni? We can frame a story around the fact he is an only child who grew up without a father and never accepted authority. Pick someone in the IT department to take the fall for assisting Chandler. Show someone with technical knowledge helping him. It would be a stretch that some reporter could have pulled this off by himself. Better to say he had tech help. Make sense so far?"

"Yes, please keep going," Emmet implored.

"Rafael, you can say that Chandler had problems with colleagues. Make up a bogus discipline report or whatever you have at your network. Emphasize that no credible sources were used and that he took advantage of King's rant to create a sensation for himself and his show. Tie some unfulfilled ambition for Chandler to his motive, like a big splash in the ratings for Centinela. You can further affirm that his sources were not vetted and the clip was not edited. With this story, El Mundo appears no more vulnerable to hackers than anyone else and you can blame it on an inside job. More importantly, it brings into question Chandler's sources and discredits his video, at least until the election is over."

"Yes I see," Rafael answered.

"I would even throw Omni under the bus too. Say that they fed this false information to King. You can also claim that Omni and King had people in the audience during the last debate to stir things up. I would avoid details about how Chandler and the tech passed the video to Omni, just say they were working together. It all wraps up with him being a disgruntled employee with an ax to grind who worked with a vile hacker group. Other major networks will pick up on your story and get it out to a broader audience. Use the power of the press here." As was typically the case, Holloway had a solution to a problem. The goal was to keep the Jefferson campaign healthy until Election Day.

"I like it, Malcolm. I like it," Emmet declared, taking another drag. "Will that work Rafael?"

"Yes. Yes, it will," Rafael answered. Despite the conflict he'd had with Chandler the last few months, he never envisioned that he would have to destroy him professionally.

"Malcolm, keep doing what you're doing. We need to make sure your plans continue. The election is too close now. Should we worry about how the IAP might use this story?" Emmet inquired.

"I don't think they're going to do much with it. They're still a new party so if they come out in support of King's allegations and now this video, the press will ask them a bunch of questions. There may be questions for which they don't have an answer or maybe others they don't want to answer. Don't get me wrong, these allegations will help the IAP in the long run, but their play will be to just stay quiet. This is a party to watch out for." Malcolm understood that he'd have to work with both third parties whom he anticipated would mount a challenge to the FSB's expanding authority.

"Agreed. Rafael, you need to move on this today. Get something out there today. Put it on a news hour today! Use the story Malcolm concocted."

"Yes, sir."

"Let's wrap this up. I have another call. Have a good day, gentlemen." Emmet examined his cigarette and noticed it had burned to the filter. He must have smoked it exceptionally fast during the call - time for another.

He scheduled his next call with the investor group purchasing El Mundo. They planned to transform the network to champion the GSB's international goals and the FSB's domestic goals. Emmet envisioned the IRC feeding a stream of stories to them. The IRC could have their own show.

He understood the importance of media shaping or at least guiding public opinion. El Mundo would cover news stories as they always did, although there would be more interpretation of their investigations, to the benefit of the Global Financial Union. The network would not tolerate rogue correspondents and ineffective management. During the call, the investor group decided Rafael did not represent an asset to the network's future.

Emmet knew what he had to do. He lit another cigarette. It had been so long since he smoked; he forgot how light-headed he could get after sucking hard on those sticks. He called Rafael in Buenos Aires at El Mundo's headquarters.

"Hello Rafael, it's Emmet again."

"Sir, I am already working on it. It will get done," Rafael said, anticipating questions about Operation Discredit Chandler.

"Mr. Mendoza, I'm afraid the investor group thinks we need to head in a different direction. A change of leadership. The events of the last couple of weeks have made them very reluctant to install you as CEO. The position's profile will be much higher. There is more at stake to support our objectives. I hope you understand."

"But sir, I-"

"Just make sure you get that news brief out. You know how important it is. Oh, and we will put together an exit package for you."

"Maybe there is something I can do to prove myself. Just tell me what." Rafael's voice, quivering with anxiety, conveyed great desperation.

"We've made our decision." Emmet hung up. He was callous to the ignominy and pain he'd just inflicted on a loyal soldier.

Rafael worked with his local bureau chief to develop a news brief to be aired on the 6pm EDT news hour from Buenos Aires. The network executed Operation Discredit Chandler.

Rafael Mendoza's life would end ignominiously during Halloween's full moon in the year 2020. A janitor found his body in the bathroom collapsed in a stall, an empty prescription bottle on the floor.

CHAPTER TWENTY-FOUR
ELECTION DAY

Chandler camped at Axel's condo after his D.C. escape with little contact with anyone from El Mundo save for Jared Clarke and Michelle Reyes. She regretted contributing to Operation Discredit Chandler. She supplemented the news brief with an in-studio piece suggesting he had an ax to grind with his former employer. Fearing for her job, with a disabled husband and three kids at home, she couldn't disobey orders. Chandler understood. Despite her misgivings, she had a hard time believing the video clip. As a lifelong resident of D.C., she had faith in government.

After El Mundo put her on the air, major networks requested a series of interviews with their employees in D.C. and New York, anyone who knew Chandler. El Mundo received so many inquiries that it became difficult for Michelle and others to do their normal jobs. Quickly, El Mundo's new executive management put a stop to it and all El Mundo's employees were under gag orders.

El Mundo not only had the distraction of Chandler's video but also the death of one of its top leaders. Chandler took Rafael's passing hard, never having dealt with suicide on a personal level. Rafael yearned to be king of the hill so it was difficult imagining a scenario where the high energy Argentinian would kill himself. The Buenos Aires police confirmed the death a suicide. The medical examiner assigned the cause of death as to overdose of oxycodone that caused him to stop breathing. Chandler knew he had recurring back problems, but was unaware of its severity. There was no reason to doubt the ME's findings, though the suicide's motive proved elusive. This was a man of many acquaintances, no close friends, and no steady girlfriend. El Mundo was his life. He rarely mentioned family, so who really knew him? They never found a suicide note.

November 3, 2020 marked Election Day in the United States. The parties imposed an abbreviated campaign season that began at the start of the year, and the fruits of their efforts would be reflected in voting booths. Chandler and Axel would spend a leisurely day in the condo after a brisk morning walk along Lake Michigan. Axel had his own virtual reality headset that Chandler made use of to finally take that tour of St. Peter's Basilica.

Arianne would arrive by dinner time from her folk's place in Winnetka. It took a couple of days for her to soften her father's attitude towards Chandler. He bristled at the fact his daughter escaped Washington like a fugitive to avoid unnecessary publicity. He blamed Chandler. Arianne convinced her father that over the course of the next few weeks, Chandler's revelations would be validated. King's presidential debate rant had elements of truth, truth that would rattle the nation. In his pre-frontal cortex, Larry reasoned that what his daughter told him was true. His fatherly devotion, however, told him his little girl needed protection.

The day before, Geringer called to check on Chandler and confirmed Tammy Blakely as the mole. He had Chancellor tell Loretta and Tammy about intelligence he'd uncovered about a U.S. missile strike against a North Korean reactor. A day later, King told a reporter about the alleged strike. The hoax fit well within the Theocracy Party's misgivings about U.S. military incursions overseas. When the reporter asked him to confirm the reactor site, King took a major misstep. Unfortunately, for King, he named a reactor site where there were American scientists helping with a contamination leak, something a candidate should have known. King had difficulty recovering from this gaffe.

It turned out Blakely's father supported the Theocracy Party and her ex-husband, the coach, supported President Jefferson. In a two for the price of one, she pleased her father by getting back at her ex. Loretta fired Tammy the day after King's interview.

Chandler, ensconced in Axel's living room looking out towards Lake Michigan, called Renee to find out about her vote in Texas. "Hi Mom. Did you get out and vote?"

"Yes, I went early this morning before work. I don't think I've ever seen this many people at my precinct. They're saying we could have a record turnout."

"Good. Oh, and I won't ask you how you voted. Ari is going to come by a little later, and we're going to watch the returns with Ax."

"How are you? It's been a few days now for you in Chicago. What are you thinking about?" Renee had a lengthy conversation with her son on his journey out of the nation's capital, but he never mentioned his immediate future.

"I'm doing well, honestly. Ax has been real good with me too. I've even helped him with one of his letters. He said I should come work with him. At some point I'll have to return to New York just to check on my apartment. I can pay bills remotely so I'm not worried about that. The stuff in my frig, that's a different story. And Ari. She's got to return to Washington at some point. We've got a few things to figure out as a couple."

"Hang on to that girl, Chan. She's a keeper. I wanted to tell you that I've had a few reporters call me for interviews, but I've declined them all. Thankfully, I've been able to lead my life. I guess the election has everyone distracted."

"Definitely. It's a big day for sure. Mom, I hope we can see each other soon. Maybe I'll come down to Dallas before I head back to New York."

"That would be great. Talk to you later. Bye."

"Bye Mom."

Axel came in from the kitchen and asked Chandler to turn on the flat screen. "TV on. Tune…What the heck am I doing?" Chandler found it difficult operating in a world without his Venus. He grabbed the remote.

Exit polling shows that former El Mundo news personality Chandler Scott's video has had but a minor effect on President Jefferson's reelection chances. Political analysts speculated that the video could hurt Jefferson and throw votes to the other campaigns. The focus of voters appears to be solely on the economy, an economy mired with high unemployment, little credit activity and ever-present concerns about cyber terror. In response, the country has turned to hoarding goods and cash, using DigiNote and bartering. Theocracy Party candidate John King continues to form an apocalyptic vision around the Global Financial Union mentioned in the debate. His recent misstep accusing the government of launching a missile strike against a North Korean reactor has apparently not damaged him much. Mr. King blamed his gaffe on false information leaked by the Jefferson administration.

Arianne arrived and settled in for a light dinner with the

men. The three spent the rest of the evening talking and watching returns. Early projections showed Jefferson winning New York and California, his home state. The pundits declared GOP candidate Scarborough the winner in Florida, Pennsylvania, and her home state of Kansas. Chancellor did what few felt possible just a few months ago and stole Texas from the GOP. It was a great moment for the party, though they had an uphill battle to win the presidency.

Axel and Chandler were still up at midnight. Arianne had fallen asleep in the office that doubled as Chandler's sleeping quarters for the last few nights. By the end of a long night, the networks acknowledged that the country faced something it had not encountered in over two hundred years. The final Electoral College projection estimated President Jefferson with 239 votes, Governor Scarborough with 198 votes, Senator Chancellor with 80, and Mr. King with 21. No candidate had the required 270 votes.

Axel overcame a nervous contraction of his breath and exclaimed, "Holy shit!"

"I guess we'll find out now about the election freeze," Chandler said.

There was always consideration that having multiple parties run for the highest office in the land could produce this outcome. Chandler and Axel had spent over a year uncovering the machinations of organizations impacting the economy and structure and scope of government. One hundred years after women were granted the right to vote, something unique in American electoral history lay ahead.

There would be no short road to President Jefferson's fulfillment of his reelection aspirations.

***

November 4, 2020 would be unlike any other Wednesday in Emmet Callaghan's life. Rather than celebrating, uncertainty filled the day. His supported candidate received the most popular and electoral votes, but an insufficient number to be declared victor. The Constitution had a process for dealing with such a contingency. Emmet wanted to know if there were alternatives. There was something about a man who had the gall to seek alternatives to the Constitution.

The IRC office in the Presidio was a tobacco-free facility. When you're the big cheese, you bend the rules. Emmet smoked in his office, though he justified it with the use of vapor cigarettes. He sucked hard on his recently acquired vape pen, awaiting his assembled group to join a conference call. Today this group included Jean-Claude, Nial, and Holloway.

A few months ago, Emmet discussed events that might prompt a suspension of the Constitution under the guise of a national emergency. Most of the discussion centered on kinetic or cyber terror events. They didn't envision an Electoral College problem, even though that was outlined in the master GFU plan. Evidently, they overestimated Jefferson's popularity.

After hearing three beeps and having attendees announce their arrival on the bridge, Emmet began. "I think everyone is here now. Malcolm help me with Civics 101 and tell me what happens when a candidate doesn't get the required number of Electoral College votes?"

"I think everyone on the call understands that Jefferson will have more votes than the others but not a majority. The Electoral College is a strange beast too. In most cases, the winner of the state's popular vote should receive all the electoral votes. Some states have no obligation to cast a vote for the candidate who wins the popular vote," Holloway explained.

"That could cause all hell to break loose. Could you imagine if the electors in Texas threw their votes to Jefferson even though Chancellor won," Emmet added. Though that would make the IRC power structure happy, even they did not relish civil disturbances.

"Yeah, I wouldn't count on anything like that. For now, let's figure on electoral votes going like they always have, to the winner of the popular vote. The Electoral College vote this year will be on December 14th. But this won't be like 2000, where the candidate that won the popular vote lost the electoral vote. That can happen if you don't win the right mix of states. This is a different dynamic," Holloway said.

"Fucking third parties did it this time," Emmet added.

"The next thing that would happen would be for the vote to move to the House of Representatives. It would be up to them to pick a winner. Each state casts one vote for one of the top three contenders. That has every opportunity to be real messy. It's only happened twice in history and that was two hundred years ago. If you think the 2016 GOP convention was messy, wait until you see this. There is uncertainty around this outcome. The only thing we can conclude is that TP candidate King is out since he polled the fewest votes," Holloway continued.

"You Yanks have a messy system," Nial muttered.

"And yours is better?" Holloway retorted.

"Gentlemen!" Emmet had no time for debate. "Malcolm, I presume that if this thing got locked up in the House, it would pretty much bring the implementation of our plans to a halt?"

"It very well could. Everyone would be distracted with it. I could see Congress balking about the FSB implementation without any elected leadership in place. It could get ugly."

"Malcolm, why don't you lay this out for Jefferson and maybe some key Congressional leaders. Just like you are telling us now. Say that we have this crisis and so forth and we can't delay implementation of the existing or proposed plan while a bickering Congress tries to figure out who our next president is. Something like that," Emmet suggested.

"*Très bien,* Emmet," Jean-Claude said, approvingly.

"It might take an audience with the Speaker, the Senate Majority Leader and some representation from the third parties with the president," Holloway suggested.

"And you, Mr. Holloway. You have to be part of this," Emmet insisted.

"That might work. No promises here, gentlemen. You're asking some of these guys to take a leap and just trust what I'm saying," Holloway said.

"Malcolm, you have a great way of explaining things and you're very calm in your delivery. You will appeal to their sensibilities," Emmet opined.

"All right, I'll call the president and make the suggestion. He should be able to coax the right Congressional leaders to attend. This will be a fight, gentlemen. Be assured of that. What happens beyond that is anyone's guess." Holloway concluded.

CHAPTER TWENTY-FIVE
EXECUTIVE ORDER

Maybe the recent Thanksgiving holiday or the full moon on November 30th made for strange bedfellows. The president asked key leaders to come to the Oval Office on the Monday after the holiday for what he termed a "historic meeting." Who could turn down an opportunity to participate in such an event? Not Alfonso Chancellor, the IAP candidate. Definitely not the Speaker of the House, Republican Janice Rossi, or Senate Majority leader, Democrat Michael Dean. The Theocracy Party merited inclusion too, hence Milton Wise, Congressman from Mississippi. All dressed in their best clothes, fitting the occasion. Though the meeting was advertised, no press were allowed.

The president and Holloway sat in the two end chairs and guests were on the sofas. On one couch were Chancellor and Rossi and on the other were Dean and Wise.

"Thank you all so much for agreeing to be here today so soon after the holiday. I mentioned that I thought this was a historic meeting and that is no hyperbole. I trust everyone's cell is off?" Everyone checked their devices to ensure compliance. These leaders felt range of emotions, from Chancellor's trepidation to Wise's anger. Chancellor, of course, knew of the GFU plan and feared what came next. Wise felt nothing but contempt for the president, particularly after the press' smear campaign against his party's candidate, John King. President Jefferson exhibited a calm demeanor and Holloway mirrored this emotion.

"People have been critical of the Electoral College process for a long time. I suppose this election gives them another opportunity for criticism. We have a document, the Constitution, which directs us in matters of governance. When faced with an Electoral College impasse, which is what we expect, the Constitution tells us how to proceed. However, I don't think the framers of this important document could foresee an economic crisis of this magnitude or duration. The Founding Fathers could not anticipate cyber and kinetic terror threats we face, nor could they foresee a country on the verge of economic calamity. My administration, with the leadership of Secretary Holloway, has crafted a plan to cure our economic malaise. I will now turn it over to the secretary."

Though Holloway was an appointee, many influential members of Congress viewed him as an economic genius and a policy wonk whose objectivity seldom came under question. Holloway had spent a great deal of time with Congressional leaders as part of his constant PR campaign. Jefferson hoped Holloway could appeal to this group's sensibilities.

"Thank you, Mr. President. I'm aware how controversial the FSB's policies have been. When the president appointed me, I told him how difficult the task at hand was. Well, difficult tasks require creative, out of the box solutions. After leaving government in 2015, I spent years at the GSB studying the exact problems we face. We gathered voluminous amounts of data and worked with the brightest minds around the world in government, central banking, and business. FSB policy is the product of those studies. What Mr. King said during the presidential debate that the journalist confirmed in the Internet video is substantially accurate."

This was the first time the Jefferson administration validated

King's rant and Chandler's reporting. Jefferson wanted the pragmatic Holloway to deliver the message in a factual, unemotional manner. The revelation produced a scowl on Congressman Wise's face. There was little or no reaction from the Democratic and GOP contingency, as if they knew. Chancellor knew the truth and kept a poker face.

Holloway paused, expecting an immediate challenge from Wise or Chancellor, and appeared surprised when none occurred. "Ahh. There are, there are sweeping reforms we'd like to, we'd like to announce. Ahh."

Holloway's lamentable confession created his stammer, causing Jefferson to interject, "Yes, we wanted to wait until after the election to announce this."

Holloway regained his composure, thankful for the interruption. "Yes. That's right. If you want to say postponing the announcement was political, well that is not for me to answer. I am a policy wonk, researcher and hopefully a good administrator. The administration felt an announcement of that magnitude would be a distraction for the election. I guess it was anyway, thanks to Mr. King. We have great momentum now. The stock market's recovered, the government bond market has at least stabilized. The unemployment rate and the credit markets are improving."

Chancellor interrupted him. "Mr. Secretary, you make it all sound so rosy. It's not that way at all. And getting rid of cash is a drastic step that will be difficult for Americans to accept."

"Senator, a benefit of our plan is that once all money is electronic and trapped inside the banking system, we can more easily tax. Every financial transaction will be on record and we can assess a tax accordingly and more quickly. I envision that filing a tax return will be a thing of the past, and what person wouldn't like that? I will also say that we can't have a US-based recovery only. It has to be worldwide. Economies are just too interconnected now. If we grind our plan to a halt or if we're unable to implement new policies, we risk grave, grave damage to the economy, not to mention the fabric of the country. I would be happy to meet with your party's leadership to discuss the merits of the plan in more detail. Unless anyone has questions, the president has more."

Nobody raised questions. Wise was still fuming and like Chancellor, he presumed King's allegations and Chandler's video contained fact - Holloway provided no new information. The other two remained silent. In Jefferson's mind, it was mission accomplished for his lieutenant, Malcolm Holloway, who was relieved that his work in this meeting was done.

It was now Jefferson's turn to make this meeting historic. "What I'm asking each of you to envision is Congress, or rather the House, coming to agreement on electing a president. Look at the last few years and now we have, no offense Alfonso or Milton, third parties that while good for discourse create more opportunity for disagreement. We don't have a parliamentary democracy here. I would like for each of you to consider my proposal."

Jefferson paused, surveying his audience, save for Holloway. He stood to deliver the historic proposal, sensing it would convey greater authority. "The proposal is for suspension of election results until the FSB has implemented a new round of policies in concert with the rest of the world economies. The period of suspension could be anywhere from six months to a year. That should afford sufficient time to bring additional stability to the United States and other economies. At that time, the election of 2020 can proceed to the House and Senate for resolution. The new president can serve out the remainder of the term and a new election would occur in 2024."

Nobody responded. They cast their eyes, avid with curiosity, on each other. The Speaker of the House and the Senate Majority Leader then focused on the president. Wise turned to Chancellor, waiting for the IAP leader to speak. Chancellor did not oblige.

After what seemed like an eternity, Wise could no longer hold it. "Mr. President, are you suggesting that you'd remain in power?"

The president, still standing, answered without hesitation, "That is correct. I feel that I at least have a mandate to continue based on the election results. I won the popular vote."

Chancellor took his turn. "Mr. President, I'm no Constitutional scholar but it seems you are asking for a suspension of the Constitution. There's no precedent for this. You have no authority, sir."

"True, but there's no precedent for the economic or terror mess either. My administration inherited this and we're just trying to fix it. If I had to wait for Congress to pass laws to help me fight cyber terror or take the emergency measures I took last year after the stock market crash, everything would have gone in the toilet."

Wise and Chancellor were no fans of endless surveillance and the FSB's appropriation of the economy. Democrats were content to go along with their president. The GOP was ambivalent. They wanted to challenge Jefferson while realizing they would have taken the same action.

"So that means you get to change the rules of the game, Mr. President?" Wise yelled, meeting Jefferson's declaration with resolve and strength.

"As the secretary told you, the risks of a distraction by an election in Congress' hands are significant. I want to make sure we have a United States of America by the time the next president takes office," Jefferson countered as he took his seat.

Wise cursed under his breath, cast an impudent gaze, and rotated away from the president and Holloway. The Speaker and Senate Majority leader remained silent with their heads down. Holloway anticipated further reaction, not aware that the GOP and Democratic representatives likely knew the meeting's content beforehand.

Chancellor used the silence to stand and walk towards the president's desk. All eyes followed the unexpected action. He then turned to face the group. "Mr. President, there will be legal and legislative challenges to this action. This is highly irregular. If we discard the Constitution when it's convenient, we will go down a slippery slope, one that may be difficult to recover from." He pointed to the US flag behind the president's desk. "I'm talking about the very essence of these United States of America. You may find some states that no longer want to be united."

Jefferson's proposal would test the nation's courage, their resolve, and wisdom — democracy itself. Yet he did not expect secession. Such things were for other countries like Spain or buried deep in U.S. history.

"Senator, we can't stop you or anyone else from mounting a legal or legislative challenge. I can tell you those types of challenges will be just as counterproductive as Congress, ah the House, electing a president. That will be another test for the unity of the nation for sure. Now is not the time for this, Alfonso," Jefferson argued.

"I'm inclined to agree with Senator Chancellor, Mr.

President." Wise looked at Chancellor instead. His contempt for the president was obvious. He barely wanted to address him by his formal title. Turning his attention to the other two, he offered, "I don't know why the Speaker or Majority Leader are so reticent. Surely, both of you see what's going on here. Don't you?" His question elicited no reaction from the Speaker or Majority Leader.

If the Speaker or Majority Leader would answer, the president gave them no chance. "I didn't expect full agreement today. It's only November 30th. It'll be a couple of weeks until the Electoral College meets. Then three weeks after that, Congress does the official vote tally. So you have time to decide what's best for the country. I will tell you that sometime immediately after the Electoral College meets, I will address the nation via a press conference on the proposal I outlined today regarding a suspension of election results. It would be great if I had your support prior to then. If not, then I'll assume you're going to mount a challenge. That is your prerogative. But I'm going forward with this plan, with or without your support. Thank you for meeting today. I will make Secretary Holloway available to you or your staff for more detailed policy questions."

The president stood, signaling the meeting's conclusion. Holloway, the Speaker and Majority Leader quickly followed. Chancellor remained standing from earlier and Wise, arms folded, remained seated, unsatisfied with the president's message. Chancellor walked over to Wise and placed his hand on his shoulder.

"Congressman Wise, is there anything else?" The president asked.

"Come on Milton, we can chat." Chancellor wanted to coax him out of the Oval Office. The president said his peace and there was nothing else to be gained. Wise reluctantly stood and marched out of the room. Chancellor acknowledged the president and Holloway with a nod of his head, though he recognized neither the Speaker or Majority Leader. He then followed Wise out of the Oval Office.

History would mark November 30, 2020, as the beginning of a tortuous journey for the United States of America.

***

As expected, on December 14, 2020 the Electoral College failed to elect the next president. As promised, the president on December 16th delivered a historic address in the White House Briefing Room. His closest advisors urged him to make this address from the Oval Office, free of immediate journalistic inquiry. Jefferson thought it important not to hide behind the safety of his office.

It was high noon in the nation's capital. There had been considerable speculation that Jefferson would address the nation after the Electoral College vote, but few knew what he would say. The White House kept the outcome of the historic November 30th meeting under wraps. Chancellor convinced TP Congressman Wise to maintain his silence while they developed legal challenges. The Speaker and Senate Majority Leader only told a few key leaders in each party and swore them to secrecy. The press corps could only imagine what the president was about to say.

Jefferson approached the podium like he had many times before. His entry silenced the previously boisterous assembled press corps. Camera clicks were the only remaining sound. Jefferson waited for that noise to abate.

"My fellow Americans. To suggest the last couple of years have been tumultuous would be a severe understatement. Our economy has struggled for many years. Our financial markets have been rocked. Terrorists are attacking us physically and in cyberspace. Our citizens are suffering. I know you look to your elected leaders for guidance during these times and I feel a great responsibility to provide this leadership. My life as a public servant reflects this desire.

"Last month's elections proved that freedom is alive and well in this great nation. Four presidential candidates fought long and hard to give you the best that America has to offer. While the candidates differed in their philosophy, all had the best of intentions for you and your families. Those differences of opinion are not a weakness but a strength of our political system. These differing philosophies inject new ideas and fresh perspectives.

"The election also proved that you, the American people, embrace various political philosophies. The two main parties continue to garner the majority of the vote, though others are strengthening their numbers. Third-party candidates won eleven states. Their voices must be heard and understood. Such diversity in voting, however, presents challenges that the framers of the Constitution duly considered.

"Since the Electoral College gave no candidate the required 270 votes, they elected no president through the process with which many are familiar. The Constitutional framers considered this possibility and directed the next step to the Congress via a contingent election. The House will elect the president and the Senate will elect the vice-president. It has been nearly two hundred years since we had to exercise that step. There have been overtures threatening filibusters and other legal challenges. There is also concern that a Congressional vote will not reflect the will of the people.

"My fellow citizens, I relate this not to bore you with a civics lesson but to present what will be a significant undertaking for our nation. An undertaking layered on the crushing economic, financial and terror threats we face. My administration has taken unprecedented steps to deal with these woes. To this end, the Financial Stability Board, led by Secretary Holloway, has brought trust and confidence to our financial markets. Make no mistake, we still have much work to do but we have established the foundation necessary for this work to continue to its ultimate conclusion, which is to make America great again. In short, having Congress elect the next president and vice-president will compromise our ability to focus on getting the nation on solid footing at a very critical time. This is not just an economic concern but one of national security.

"After consultation with the Justice Department, Secretary Holloway, Congressional leaders, the Secretary of the Treasury, the chairman of the Federal Reserve, and our overseas partners, effective immediately I am invoking Presidential Order 14666. This Order will temporarily freeze the results of the 2020 election until such time the country finds itself on better economic footing. I will subsequently issue another Order lifting the suspension so that the election may proceed in Congress. I make this decision after careful, thoughtful, and prayerful consideration. Suspending the Constitution is not something I take lightly.

"We are at a unique moment in history. The financial crisis affords us a rare opportunity to forge a new era of cooperation. This era will bring global economic stability and political tranquility. Ours will be an example for the rest of the world. The United States is a shining city upon a hill whose beacon guides freedom-loving people everywhere. Help me shine that light. Thank you and God bless the United States of America!"

"At this time, I will entertain a few questions."

Every reporter in the Briefing Room called on the president. Jefferson, above the din of their voices, calmly picked someone in the first row.

"Mr. President, you mention the suspension is temporary. Could you give the American people a sense of temporary?"

"I would like to give you a precise answer but that is not possible. The FSB needs to have the flexibility to make policy decisions that stabilize markets. If we fix a date, it will hamper their efforts."

The cacophony beckoning the president began in earnest. "Yes, all the way in the back row." He pointed to the selected reporter.

After some initial confusion, the female reporter proceeded with her question. "Mr. President, you mention that an election decided by Congress has not occurred in two hundred years. This clearly is a rare event, albeit one considered by the Constitution. Do you expect any legal or legislative challenges to the issuance of this Executive Order?"

"We have had numerous conversations with the Attorney General who assures me that the Office of the President is within its right to issue such an order if there is a threat to national security. I would also add that a legal challenge will have an adverse impact on our economy's stability and the FSB's implementation, so such action would be ill-advised."

Reporters achieved an ear piercing level, as if expecting the end of allowed questions.

"Yes." He took the next question from the front row. "No, him."

"Mr. President, could you address the allegations made by Mr. King in the last debate that were then corroborated by El Mundo correspondent Chandler Scott via the hacked video released on the Internet by Omni?"

"I hope to address those statements sooner rather than later. And provide you more rather than less. It's fair to say we are working with our overseas partners to develop a mechanism to ensure greater financial and monetary cooperation. I expect Secretary Holloway will have an announcement soon."

"Mr. President, if I may follow up. So you do not deny the scope and breadth of what King and Scott alleged?"

"As I mentioned, Secretary Holloway will have an announcement. Thank you, everyone." He scurried out of the Briefing Room.

"Mr. President! Mr. President! Mr. President!"

He ignored their pleas.

***

Emmet Callaghan sat alone in his IRC office watching the president deliver his historic address. He ditched the vape pen for the real thing.

"Mr. President, if I may follow up. So you are not denying the scope and breadth of what King and Scott alleged?"

"As I mentioned, Secretary Holloway will have an

announcement. Thank you, everyone."

"Mr. President! Mr. President! Mr. President!"

Feeling entirely satisfied, he called Jean-Claude. The phone rang many times before Jean-Claude answered.

"*Oui.*"

"Jean, Jean!"

"Emmet *sacrè bleu!* You interrupt my dinner. What is it?"

"Jean, we did it! When you wake up tomorrow morning, our dreams will be one step closer to reality!"

"Don't be so overconfident. This is round one of this boxing match. *Bonne soirée Monsieur Callaghan.*"

***

In the Hart Building, where Geringer and Chancellor met to discuss challenges to the president's Executive Order, they watched Jefferson deliver his historic address.

"After consultation with Secretary Holloway, Congressional leaders, the Secretary of the Treasury, the Chairman of the Federal Reserve, and our overseas partners, effective immediately I am invoking Presidential Order 14666. This Order will temporarily freeze the results of the 2020 election until such time the country finds itself on better economic footing. I will subsequently issue another Order lifting the suspension so that the election may proceed in the Electoral College or Congress as required. I make this decision after careful, thoughtful, and prayerful consideration. Suspending the Constitution is not something I take lightly. "

Geringer got up from his chair and turned off the TV.

"Matt, he did it. He said he would, and he did. Man! I guess in the back of my mind I was hoping. Just hoping,"

Chancellor's strong constitution withered under the shock of Jefferson's announcement. He shook his head in utter disbelief.

"What a day for this country. Who'd have thought this just a few months ago?" Geringer remarked while contemplating the IAP logo behind his desk.

"What now, Matt? How's the country going to react to this?" This was largely a rhetorical question — Chancellor feared the outcome.

"I'm afraid of what will happen, frankly. I know many will agree with Jefferson but just as many will be provoked to unrest. We've been on the verge of a civil fracturing for years now. Political differences and racial tensions have been boiling for some time."

"Yes, they have. We'll need great leadership in Congress and at other levels to keep everything together."

"No doubt Alfonso. For us, this is going to be the Constitutional equivalent of playing for the national championship. We need to practice our game plan like we were earlier today. I'm afraid we're gonna have to cut holiday time short this year. I'm gonna suggest we caucus with other Congressional leaders, and not just in our party either, to review Article II Section 4. I wanted to give him a chance, but he's gone too far." That article of the Constitution dealt with impeachment.

"I agree. This is presidential misconduct. If we can't rally around the Constitution, then what do we have?"

"Yeah. Let's get the hell outta here," Geringer said in voice charged with disgust.

Alfonso walked out first. Geringer followed, first looking into his office, staring at the American flag and the IAP logo, and then smiling while looking at a picture of his family. He turned off the light. He hoped the president's action didn't turn off the light on the United States of America.

***

After a few weeks at Axel's condo, Chandler returned to his Manhattan apartment. Axel kept him busy collaborating on his letter and even made Chandler the subject of his December 2020 issue. He never visited Renee, though he and Arianne planned on heading to Dallas in the next couple of months. A couple of weeks after the election, Arianne returned to her D.C. job at State, though people that previously were friendly kept their distance. Despite the bumps of the last few weeks, their relationship remained strong. Her father came full circle with Chandler and now envisioned him as his future son-in-law. At this point, they didn't announce nuptials.

As expected, members of the IAP and TP held a joint press conference denouncing the president's election freeze. A few members of the GOP spoke out as well in network interviews. There were protests in the capitals of several states and Washington D.C. Previously dormant militias in western states raised the issue of secession. The National Guard quelled social unrest in some of the nation's largest cities, and a couple of governors asked for federal help. Washington responded by dispatching armed members of Homeland Security and military. Government's most vocal critics, particularly those speaking of secession, were rounded up and taken to special camps run by Homeland Security where it was rumored they would be reeducated by psychological operations officers.

Social media and blogosphere critics quickly went silent for fear of attracting unwanted attention from Homeland Security. Main Street yearned for economic peace and tranquility, though they wondered if there was another way, something that maintained the fabric of the nation's most sacred document. The rest of the world watched and waited.

Chandler didn't know what the future held for him or the country. El Mundo fired him, and he'd received no offers from other networks. He had a non-compete clause in his employment contract prohibiting him from working for a national or international network for six months. Freelance work, however, was permitted. Geringer confided that an impeachment proceeding could come at any time.

Arianne spent the holidays with Chandler in New York. They were unable to enjoy the New Year's Eve celebration in Times Square since NYPD determined they could not guarantee security. Instead, they had a quiet dinner at a local restaurant and turned in early. On New Year's Day, a still sleeping Arianne gave Chandler an opportunity for a morning walk in The Battery. There were many competing thoughts percolating in his brain. He stood by the park's fencing, drawing inspiration again from Lady Liberty, and wondered about hauling her to D.C. to remind the country's leaders of what she represented. Like that day almost a year ago, a stranger appeared to him except this one looked familiar - Habakk. Habakk squeezed his shoulder, gave him a warm smile and stood in contemplation of the Lady.

"Another coincidence? You always seem to just show up." Chandler was surprised and gratified.

"What are your thoughts on the election and the aftermath?" Habakk asked. He didn't need to be a mind reader to know that this consumed his thoughts.

Chandler felt defeated in battle, especially given the election's impact on the country. "I don't know what else I could've done. And look at what's happened."

"Yes, it was Cicero who said that laws fall silent during times of war. How would you get the law to speak again?"

Chandler pivoted in haste towards Habakk. "War? You think we're in a war? Wait a second! You always seem to ask me a bunch of questions. I feel like I should be the one asking. I get the sense that I'm like the only person who can see you. Where do you live? What do you do for a living?"

Habakk maintained his view towards the Hudson. "I live in many places and consider myself a trusted advisor. I'm just here to help."

"OK then riddle me this. What do you think is gonna happen with this mess of a country that you think is at war?"

"Chandler, this is nothing new. The country has faced many transitions in its history. America would not be what it is without the successful negotiation of these transitions. First, there were the Articles of Confederation. Do you think it was easy to get thirteen colonies to create this document and then agree to it? This was the birth of a country in the middle of a war with its parent. Then that document was replaced by the Constitution, a brilliant document in its own right. There were many compromises in drafting it and it's been amended twenty-seven times. Remember the Civil War? That ripped the country apart. Friend became foe. We had World War I and II and the UN to bring the world together. Korea still has a tenuous armistice. What about Bretton Woods and Nixon's violation of that agreement? Vietnam was as divisive as any conflict the nation ever had. Consider the effects of the first Gulf War, then 9/11 and the Patriot Act. We have had many acts of terror on US soil and surveillance and monitoring."

"Are you trying to cheer me up?" Chandler stared into eyes that helped, yet frustrated.

"Think also about the economic challenges. There were several panics in the nineteenth and twentieth century. Just when they told everyone not to worry, there were more financial panics in the twenty-first century. Recent panics gave government an opportunity to expand its power by making laws go silent in a manner of speaking."

"So where is this headed?"

"America has a unique culture, one that has put men on the moon, become the breadbasket to the world, and orchestrated a revolution in civil rights. It has been the champion of the innate rights of men and women everywhere. America can overcome challenges because it believes in liberty. That liberty allows for the vision and creation of better outcomes. If you don't have liberty, it's difficult for that vision to materialize. Trust me, the country needs vision." Habakk shifted his gaze towards Lady Liberty, the sun casting light on her.

Chandler mimicked his action and looked at her too. "So you think our liberty's been throttled and that will not allow us to compromise cuz we won't have the proper vision?"

"Perhaps. Liberty has been slowly eroded. Do you think the vision should come from individuals or government?"

"But individuals make up the government."

Habakk turned towards Chandler, who did the same. "It is, but think about this Global Financial Union. Some will embrace it because it provides freedom *from* something. But government has also eroded the freedom *of* something. How does freedom of speech feel when you can't speak freely on the phone or while sending text messages? How does freedom feel when government tells you what money you can and can't use? How does freedom feel when the nation's most important document, the essence of its government is cast aside when inconvenient?"

"So what's the answer?" Chandler grew exasperated with questions answered with more questions.

Habakk, sensing frustration, smiled warmly again. "There is no single answer. Keep fighting for freedom *of.* That way the pressing matters of the day can be addressed thoughtfully and intelligently. Ironically, when people fight for freedom *from,* they restrict everyone's freedom."

Habakk, for the first time in this conversation, acquired a serious, yet placid countenance. "The most important thing, the most important thing to remember is to keep the mind open. Avoid intellectual laziness and make sure everyone is free to express and critique. People should be free from retribution when they express and critique. The loss of these two will signal the end of the social order as we understand it. Something else, something unknown and probably undesirable will then emerge. I think there are plenty of historical examples to support my point. In fact, some of these things are emerging now."

"You sound a lot like my friend Axel."

"Do you know Edmund Burke?"

"Nope," Chandler said, shaking his head.

"He was a statesman and philosopher from the eighteenth century who said, 'No one could make a greater mistake than he who did nothing because he could do only a little'. Keep doing a little Chandler. Keep doing a little."

Chandler contemplated Habakk's words. His journalistic course and the nation's crucible lay ahead. It became clear to him. "I see what you mean."

Regardless of political or economic outcomes, he needed to continue to be an agent of discovery and information. Chandler's job was to create discourse, encourage expression and critique, and fight intellectual laziness. He bore no responsibility, nor did society, of protecting its citizens from ideas or opinions that might be contentious or offensive. If anything, he should be an agent of promoting spirited debate and supporting elected officials who protected freedom when others attempted to suppress it. Only in this environment could the nation emerge successfully from crisis. There would be others who would not share this view, others who were equally committed to navigating the crisis but in their own way.

"It's time for me to go." Habakk extended his right hand and enveloped Chandler's right while shaking it. "I'm proud of you."

He turned, first perusing at Lady Liberty with quiet satisfaction, and walked away. Unlike other times, Chandler didn't try to catch him - he just watched his image fade away in The Battery.

The sun shone a little brighter on Lady Liberty, and hopefully on the future of the United States, his career as a journalist, and his life with Arianne. He walked back to his apartment contemplating all of the little things he needed to do.

The story continues in Rebellium, the second book in
the Chandler Scott series. What will Chandler
discover? What dangers will he face? Will the nation
face an existential crisis?

ABOUT THE AUTHOR

Jim Mosquera has an academic background in Industrial Engineering and held management positions in the telecommunications industry. Developing expertise in financial markets and economics through his own study, he produced a column in a national publication and edited a financial newsletter.

That work led to a series of books on the economy and financial crises known as the **Escaping Oz** series (Protecting your wealth during the financial crisis, Navigating the crisis, An Observer's Reflections). He is also the author of the **Chandler Scott** series (2020, Rebellium, Division, Hope).

Sentinel Consulting, a firm he founded in 2014, assists businesses with financing and debt restructuring. Mr. Mosquera is a frequent contributor to numerous financial news outlets.

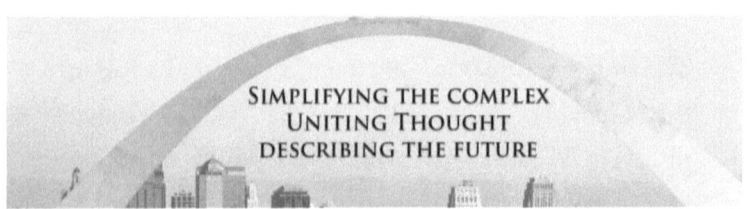

SIMPLIFYING THE COMPLEX
UNITING THOUGHT
DESCRIBING THE FUTURE

His non-fiction work will make you question proposed solutions to financial and economic problems. His novels are so realistic, the stories will hit close to home.

Follow the author at https://JimMosquera.com

www.ingramcontent.com/pod-product-compliance
Lightning Source LLC
Chambersburg PA
CBHW030627020726
47493CB00006B/1607